PRAISE F

"*The Moorwitch* weaves a spell as vivid as the magic within its pages. Prepare for a sweeping fantasy that rings of classic tales, mystical realms, and sweet romance, all threaded into one enchanting tapestry."

—Sara Raasch, *New York Times* bestselling author of *Night of the Witch*

"Breathtaking in both romance and magic, this is a must-read!"

—Beth Revis, *New York Times* bestselling author of *Night of the Witch*

ALSO BY
JESSICA KHOURY

For Young Adults

Origin
Vitro
Kalahari
The Forbidden Wish
Last of Her Name

For Middle Grade Readers

The Mystwick School of Musicraft Series

Mystwick School of Musicraft
The Midnight Orchestra
The Dark Refrain

The Skyborn Series

Sparrow Rising
Call of the Crow
Phoenix Flight

Stand-alones

The Ruby Code

THE
MOOR
WITCH

THE MOOR WITCH

JESSICA KHOURY

Published by 47North, Seattle

www.apub.com

Amazon, the Amazon logo, and 47North are trademarks of Amazon.com, Inc., or its affiliates.

EU product safety contact:
Amazon Media EU S. à r.l.
38, avenue John F. Kennedy, L-1855 Luxembourg
amazonpublishing-gpsr@amazon.com

ISBN-13: 9781662532245 (paperback)
ISBN-13: 9781662532252 (digital)

Cover design by Logan Matthews
Cover illustration by Elena Masci

Printed in the United States of America

For Traceen,
who channels love into every stitch

For your own ladies and pale-visaged maids,
Like Amazons come tripping after drums,
Their thimbles into armed gauntlets change,
Their needles to lances, and their gentle hearts
To fierce and bloody inclination.

—William Shakespeare, *King John*

PROLOGUE

All it takes to change your fate is a bit of thread, the book begins. I whisper the next sentence aloud. *"But Weaving magic is not for the faint of heart."*

This isn't helpful. I already know this bit. I don't need vague warnings. I need a spell, and I need it *fast*.

I turn the pages frantically with my left hand, my heart splintering with terror. With my right, I unwind a length of thread from its wooden spool. Sunlight pours through the library window, glinting off the broken bits of porcelain strewed on the carpet. The pieces had been my aunt's favorite vase just minutes ago. Once milky white with pretty blue flowers painted on it, now it's just heaps of sharp, jagged edges. All it had taken was a slip of my elbow and—

Focus, Rose, I order myself. *What's done is done . . . unless you can find a way to undo it.*

I glance at the ticking pendulum clock on the mantel.

Aunt Lenore will be home any second.

"Fates, help me," I whisper, my eyes stinging with tears. Do the goddesses care about one frightened eight-year-old? Will they spare even a moment at their celestial loom to help me?

I doubt it. I'm alone, as I have been since poor Uncle Artie died. That was two years ago, and if I've learned anything since then, it is that prayers can't save me from my aunt's temper.

My only hope is magic.

Thread pinched between my fingers, I choke down a sob of panic and smooth the page of the book lying on the carpet beside me. My shaking finger follows the line of printed text as if it were the dotted line on a map, leading me to safety.

My ears snatch at every little sound, fearing the thump of Aunt Lenore's cane in the hallway. For now, all I hear is the usual noise of Wimpole Street outside the window: fancy ladies chatting; horses pulling carriages over the cobblestones, their hooves clopping almost as loudly as my heart; newsboys shouting headlines; the small white dog next door yapping at everyone who goes by . . .

I turn pages with sweaty hands, skimming diagrams and lists of instructions: threads crisscrossing, embroidery taking shape, strange geometry promising terrible and wonderful power. Every page shows a new spell, and in the margins, Uncle Artie's neat handwriting adds notes and warnings.

There! I smack the page with a triumphant shout.

A Spell to Mend Broken Pottery. Perfect. And it's a cat's cradle, the quickest sort of spell to Weave. No needles or hoops or cloth needed. Just clever, quick fingers, and I have ten.

A creak sounds in the hallway.

I freeze, heart skipping a beat. My stomach hardens into a tight, cold knot, and fear pulses in my eardrums. My fingers move to the bruises still green and ugly on my arms.

I watch the door and the thin crack I accidentally left open when I slipped inside an hour ago. I should have shut it. I can't believe I made such a big mistake.

But the door stays cracked, and no further sounds come creeping in. Still cold with fear, I turn back to my book, thread, and broken porcelain.

My hands shake as I bite off the length of thread with my teeth, tie it in a loop, and stretch it taut between my fingers.

"Crisscross, loop and toss," I whisper as I begin to Weave the thread into a cat's cradle, eyes flickering between my fingers and the instructions in the spellbook. "Hurry, hurry . . ."

Tick, tick, tick. Is the clock speeding up? On my wrist, the circular white scars of past burns prickle painfully in warning. Is that the scent of Aunt Lenore's pipe smoke on the air?

I have to fix this. I will. Magic can fix anything.

Magic is what I think about when I'm daydreaming over scrubbing potatoes. Enchanted cat's cradles and embroidered hexes are what I sketch when I ought to be helping Cook tally the larder. Ever since I found that first spellbook in Uncle Artie's library, in those short, happy months before he died, I haven't been able to stop thinking about it.

Aunt Lenore boarded up Uncle Artie's study after the fever took him, but being naughty and quick, I managed to raid a few of his shelves before then. There are books of magic hidden all over the house, where only I know to look. This one—*The Westminster Weaving Primer*—I hid right here in the library, beneath Aunt Lenore's nose. It felt proper, since this is the only spot in the house where you can hear the great bells of the Westminster School of Weaving ringing at noontide. Most days, I sit in this very spot and close my eyes and imagine I am one of the students inside, learning to stitch enchanted tapestries at the great looms.

But daydreaming is exactly what got me into this mess. I should have been minding my elbows, not chasing my wandering imagination.

The Weave is soon complete, suspended like a spiderweb between my hands. The white threads turn to gold in the sunlight. But the Weaving is only the first part of the spell. Making shapes out of thread is one thing—anybody can work a needle or tie a knot. It's channeling living energy into the threads which makes them come alive with magic, filling wool and linen and cotton with power. And it's the patterns you Weave, stitch, knit, or tat which turn that power into spells. At least, that's how Uncle Artie used to describe it to me.

Letting out a slow breath, I close my eyes and shut off all my senses but one: the strange, hidden sense that lets me connect with the living energy around me. After a moment of silent searching, I feel it: humming in the fuchsia blooms and aspidistra leaves in Aunt Lenore's sitting room; throbbing in the ivy clinging to the outer wall of the house; pooling in the veins of the spinach and cabbage leaves bundled in the kitchen two floors below.

At my touch, the energy responds, reaching back to me in bright tendrils, like a curious kitten being teased out from beneath a cabinet. Carefully, I pull it in, twining it up and around my racing heart like wool about a spindle. *The heart is key*, it says in the *Book of the Moirai*, which I keep hidden under a floorboard in the larder. *It is this organ which lets the Weaver draw the energy in, convert it to magic, and thread it out of her fingertips.*

My entire body tingles, the hairs on my arms standing on end. Magic crackles around my bones; it sparks on my tongue. It tastes like ice: sharp and brisk, awakening every corner of my mind. It feels a little bit like the time I stole a sip of Cook's brandy: shot through with lightning.

Never do I feel more alive, more bright, more powerful than when I channel magic. I wish I could feel like this always. Aunt Lenore wouldn't dare lay a finger or anything else on me then. I wouldn't let her.

But I can't keep it all inside me, or I'll burst apart like an ember cracking from heat.

I let the magic flow out of my fingertips and into the Weave stretched between them. The thread glows gold until it brightens the whole library. Frightening shadows leap up from the chairs and sofa and the wooden globe on its stand. My spell is almost too bright to look at.

Maybe the Fates *are* listening, because it works. Before me, the broken shards skitter over the carpet, piecing their jagged edges together like a puzzle cleverly assembling itself.

I give a long sigh of relief as the threads I wove with turn to ash. This I carefully brush into a cigar box I brought just for this purpose; I'll be sure to empty the ashes into the hearth.

But at the sudden *slam* of the library door, the box drops from my startled hands and bowls through the pile of still-shifting porcelain shards. The spell collapses, and broken pieces fall apart onto the carpet, atop a layer of ash.

"Aunt!" I cry.

Aunt Lenore stands in the doorway, a long-stemmed pipe between her fingers, her purse dangling from her wrist and her eyes flinty. Her gown is black, as all her clothes have been since Uncle Artie's death two years ago.

Our gazes connect, and my bones turn to ice. She towers over me like a nightmare come to life. Even for a grown-up, she's very tall.

"You rat," Aunt Lenore snarls.

I jump to my feet and dart behind the sofa, terror pressing against my lungs and making it difficult to breathe.

"Is that my mother's vase?" Aunt Lenore says, advancing slowly. There's nowhere for me to run, not with her blocking the way to the door. "And is that one of my poor dead husband's spellbooks? Which I *explicitly* forbid you from touching?"

"I—I can explain! It was an accident!"

"Didn't learn your lesson the last time, did you?" Aunt Lenore brandishes her pipe. She picked up the habit after Uncle Artie's death, and now I rarely see her without one of the vile things lit between her lips. The smoke stings my eyes and makes me cough. "You don't deserve magic, girl. Your soul is too corrupt. Your heart is too vile."

"It is not!" I shout. "I want magic, Aunt. I have a right to it, same as anyone!"

The spool of thread is still clutched in my hand. Hurriedly I pull off a length.

Aunt Lenore hisses, "No, you don't!"

She stabs her pipe at me, the hot bowl burning into the soft skin of my throat. Pain explodes up my neck, and I choke on the bitter scent of tobacco and burned flesh. With a scream, I throw myself sideways, into a bookshelf. Books crash to the floor, and I stumble, trying to see the door through the jagged lights bursting in my vision.

"Murdering little brat!" Aunt Lenore kicks at me, and I drop and curl up with a cry. The whole house must hear us by now, the staff stiffening over their chores, eyes wide and lips tight. But none will come to help me. They've seen what happens when they try.

"You deserve worse than this," Aunt Lenore says, pausing to catch her breath. "You took the love of my life from me!"

"I loved Uncle Artie too," I sob.

"Hussy! How dare you say his name?"

She raises the pipe again, this time to drive it into my cheek, but I'm too quick. I scrabble upright and make for the door, and in my hands is the Weave I finally managed to tie.

I channel into the thread as I run out of the library, then turn and kick the door shut. The spellknot in my hands flares white hot, and then the door vanishes entirely.

It's only an illusion spell. In minutes Aunt Lenore will find the doorknob and escape; I have to make use of what little time I have.

Fighting back always makes Aunt Lenore twice as angry, and I've never dared use magic against her before. I don't want to find out what the consequences of such naughtiness would be.

I limp down the dark hallway, gasping for breath. Aunt Lenore's sharp kicks found too many bruises from my last punishment, and now they throb anew. I have to stop every few steps to let out a sob and work up the strength to go on. The burn on my neck screams.

The beating on the library walls sounds like the knock of a corpse come back to life, trying to escape its coffin. How long until Aunt Lenore finds the knob?

In my panic, I turn left at the end of the hallway instead of right toward the stairs and find myself trapped at a dead end. There's nothing here but wood-paneled walls.

Then comes a crash down the corridor and Aunt Lenore's voice calling out, "You'll pay for that trick dearly, little witch!"

"I'm not a witch," I murmur, looking around desperately. "I'm a Weaver."

I press myself against the wall, hoping Aunt Lenore might overlook my small form in the darkness. My fingers find fine cracks in the wainscoting.

Cracks that are too evenly spaced to be an accident. There is a pattern carved into the wood, and it seems to whisper *This way, this way!*

I try to shut out the sound of Aunt Lenore's footsteps as she stalks down the hallway, the stench of tobacco smoke searching me out. I cover my mouth and nose, afraid it will make me cough and give myself away. For a moment, terror blackens my thoughts, but I squeeze my eyes shut and force it back.

My fingers follow the cracks, which are arranged in the pattern of a simple concealing Weave. When I find the center of the pattern and press it, I hear a soft click. The wooden panel in front of me shifts inward quietly; my breath catches in my throat.

I carefully slide the panel aside to reveal a narrow tunnel. Without a second thought I dive inside, taking care to replace the panel behind me.

I crawl along until I feel the ceiling of the passage rise and find I can now stand. The space is narrow and colder than Aunt Lenore's heart. I must be inside the very walls of the house. I swallow a sob, feeling as if they are closing in to crush me.

My progress takes me past the room where my aunt's two ladies' maids are ironing sheets. I hear their soft whispers through the wall and slow my pace. Would they help me or just give me away? As I raise my hand to beat on the wall and call for aid, they speak.

"Should we do something?" says the younger maid, Mary, who's new to the house.

"Try," replies the older one, Lillian. "You'll only end up like your predecessor. She was blacklisted by the mistress for stepping in to protect the girl. She had to sail for the continent because no one in England would hire her."

Tears burn in my eyes at the memory of poor Bess. She bravely stood up for me the day I got the scars on my wrist. It did neither me nor Bess any good.

With a shudder, I move on past the maids' room, trying to remember what room comes next. No one will help me here. They're afraid too. This whole house is soaked in fear, like water dripping down the walls. I'm *drowning* in it.

Gasping for air that suddenly seems gone, I beat a hand against the wall—only to feel another panel depress beneath my palm. It opens a hidden door. I fall through with a shout, into a dark, musty space, and land on a thick carpet smelling of cedar and thread and paper.

My heart misses a beat. I know that splendid smell, even years later. I'm in Uncle Artie's study.

It's been two years since I was in here. He'd been alive then and had often shared his spellbooks and thread with me in hopes I might one day channel magic too. He spoke of sending me to a Moirene school to properly learn how to Weave and to make something of myself.

Scrubbing away a tear with the heel of my hand, I turn slowly, taking in the room with all its bittersweet memories.

Nothing has changed in that time. One shuttered window looks out to the street, letting in enough light to reveal the crimson walls, bookcases, and great desk. A portrait of Uncle Artie hangs on the far wall, over a hearth. He looks kindly in it. In one hand he holds a spool of thread, and on his chest shines the medal King George gave him for distinguished service in the Telarii Guild, Weaving defensive wards against the French in the Battle of Alexandria. He used to love to tell me the story. How a person so good could end up married to someone like Aunt Lenore, I have no idea.

Moving slowly, I find the desk piled with all the spellbooks I've been forbidden to touch. Even knowing the trouble I'll be in if Aunt Lenore finds me here, I can't help but feel a rush of excitement as I place my hands on those marvelous tomes. How many wondrous spells lie within, spells that can protect me, make me stronger, set me free?

I realize then that I can no longer hear my aunt's footsteps.

But beneath the barred door, in a sliver of sunlight, a shadow moves. My heart stops.

"Oh, Rose. You have gone too far this time."

I hear the sound of splintering wood as Aunt Lenore tears one of the bars off the door.

No point in caution anymore. I fling open the shutters, flooding the room with light. Aunt Lenore shrieks in response.

"Go on!" she cries. "Touch one thing, and I'll have you hanged for thieving!"

I flip through the books desperately, eyes racing over the pages, looking for something—*anything*. There are books of healing magic, books of war magic, books of dangerous illegal magic, even. Some are so heavy it takes me both hands to even lift them.

When I reach for an old, battered book bound in soft leather, it flashes and stings my finger, and I pull away with a yelp. Popping my finger in my mouth, I squint at the faded title.

The Book of the Moorwitches.

I've heard that word before, *moorwitch*. They were the first Weavers in England, wild women who learned magic, some said, from the faeries. They were terribly powerful, and fought the invading Romans with spells few today could wield. Some stories even told tales of how they moved from one place to another in an instant—how useful a spell that would be!

Someone—Uncle Artie?—sealed the book with a complex ward knot, threads bound neatly around the cover. The pattern is mesmerizing, an intricate design that draws my mind in and turns it inside out. It's the sort of knot that seems to have no beginning or end.

9

But for as long as I can remember, patterns have whispered to me. Whether it's a spellknot illustrated on a page, or the veins on the back of a leaf, or the way the flour dances in the sieve when Cook tosses it, patterns *make sense*. They tell me their secrets as if they *want* to be understood.

This one is no different. I stare hard at the knot on the forbidden spellbook, mapping the lines, tracing them with invisible fingers, spiraling round and round until . . .

There!

I find the secret string tucked beneath the pattern which unravels the Weave all at once. The protective shielding vanishes.

I heave open the book as Aunt Lenore rips another bar from the door.

The pages are yellow and the script so faded I can barely make it out. The book has to be hundreds of years old. Uncle Artie left no notes in these margins; I guess he never had need for such forbidden magic.

Despite Aunt Lenore's attempts to wall me off from all knowledge of magic, I know a little about the laws governing Weavers. Some spells can get you thrown in jail. Others can get your hands crushed beneath rocks.

But many of the spells in *this* book would result in a swift execution.

I hesitate, shivering at the gruesome images on the pages. I should not be holding this. I shouldn't even know this sort of magic exists. Guilt twists like a snake in my belly.

But then another crash in the hallway startles me. How many bars are left over the door? Four? Five? I have only minutes to find a way to save myself. There's no time to search the other books. Fear overcomes guilt. I continue turning pages.

I find no secret to transporting myself to some far-off haven. Instead, there are spells to stop the heart, to choke the lungs, to turn intestines into snakes. The images make me shudder, and my courage slips. I can't do any of these, not even to my aunt. No wonder my uncle warded this book shut.

But then I find one that isn't quite so gruesome: *A Spell to Summon Immortal Protection*.

That sounds promising.

I look up as the door begins to shudder. Aunt Lenore's almost got it open.

Heart jumping, I scan the instructions for the spell, skipping the prologue about *the price of certain magicks*, searching instead for the important parts about which threads should go where.

It's a complicated Weave, no simple cat's cradle. I glance around and spot Uncle Artie's pegboard hanging on the wall. Wooden, round, with two dozen pegs set around its perimeter, it is meant for Weaving more complex spells.

I take it down and set to work.

The thread slips in my clammy hands, a short piece breaking off. I use it to tie back my brown waves of hair, which are now damp with sweat. Across the room, the door shudders as the boards nailed over it rip with splinters and cracks.

I Weave as quickly as my fingers can move. Will this spell even work? Am I strong enough to channel the magic to fill it? What sort of immortal protection will it summon?

Despite my many unanswered prayers in the past, I hope for the Fates, the blessed Moirai: Clotho, Lachesis, Atropos. Spinners of life and determiners of death, who watch all humanity through their great looms.

"Help me," I whisper. "Please, send an angel, send a demon, I don't care. Please just save me!"

In moments, the Weave is done. The pattern looks like a winding spiral, an illusion that seems to stretch infinitely inward. I stare at it until the sound of a key in the door shakes me into motion. She must have torn down all the boards.

My time is up.

Planting my hand on the threads, I let out a long breath and then channel.

This time, I am not cautious.

I drain energy from the plants in the sitting room, sensing them wither and brown. I wrench it from the ivy, from the vegetables in the larder, from the moss growing in the cracks of the walls. In my desperation, I nearly pull it from Leo, Aunt Lenore's grumpy old cat, but with a shiver I pass him over. That is dark magic I will not draw upon, not even to save my own life.

Please be enough, please be enough, please—!

I gasp as the pattern of threads flares white, so bright I am forced to look away. The room fills with a howling wind that pushes books off the walls and sends Uncle Artie's portrait crashing to the floor. I cry out and duck behind the desk, tasting ashes on my lips as the thread crumbles and is swept away by the unearthly gale.

Then, suddenly, all falls still.

The wind dies; the pages stop rustling. I'm trembling and dizzy, my eyes wet with tears. My neck still pulses with pain from the pipe burn. I can't hear Aunt Lenore. Did she open the door? Was I too late? I can only wait and quiver in a silence so deep I wonder if I've gone deaf. Shadows thicken around me as if night has fallen all at once, snuffing out the sunlight.

Finally, after a long moment, I lift my head, letting out a long, shaky breath.

And feel a cold hand close on my shoulder.

CHAPTER ONE

Twelve years later

"All it takes to change your fate is a bit of thread," I say quietly.

I draw a spool from my pocket and slowly unwind it, spun wool the color of goldenrod coiling around my finger, rough and frayed from use.

"Magic," I continue, as the twenty small girls and four boys before me watch raptly, "is the great equalizer. We may only be a small charity school, but the magic we can spin is as true and strong as that of the greatest Weavers in England, or indeed—the *world*. And as Weavers, magic is our right. It is a power no one may take from us."

My fingers dip and curl, twisting the thread in patterns as familiar to me as the beating of my own heart. Around and over, through and beneath, the threads tighten into place, and as I Weave, I channel magic into my hands through the tips of my fingers.

For a moment, my heart seizes.

A spasm of pain radiates through my chest, and I think, *No. Not again.*

I push through the pain, my head spinning, and channel into the cat's cradle. The thread begins to glow.

The students lean forward on their desks, hands clutching their spools, eyes wide. This is a young class, most of them new to Weaving. But they'll learn quickly. My students always do; they are survivors all, the outcasts and rejects, who must scrap and fight for every day, every crust of bread, every warm ember in the cold winter winds. It seems so short a time ago that I sat among them, in my brown, shapeless frock with my hair unspooling from its braids, desperate for the magic my own teacher, stern old Sister Elizabeth, wove for us.

Most of these children will go on to be teachers as well, the girls governesses to luckier children, the few boys to military appointments. They'll pass on everything I teach them, all the embroiders and weaves, knots and patterns. They'll live modest lives, but at least they'll have a chance with the magic at their fingertips. Without it, they—I—would be nothing. Strays in a loveless world, kicked to the gutter. Magic is their only hope, just as it is mine.

When the spellknot is complete, a symmetrical net spread between my hands, the magic releases and snow begins to drift down from the ceiling. The children cry out in joy, rising to their feet and lifting their hands. Snowflakes melt on their palms, and they lick the cool water delightedly.

To hide my shaking hands and weak knees, I quietly lean against the wall. In my chest, my heart squeezes in reproach, and I wait for my pulse to settle before I dare lift my head.

"Sister Rose?"

I look down at the small curly head in front of me. Carolina. One of our newest. She reaches out and grips the edge of my pinafore. Snowflakes rim her face, clinging to the delicate wisps of strawberry hair curling at her temples.

"Are you all right?" she asks.

"Of course," I lie.

"Is it your heart again?"

"I'll be fine. Go back to your desk, dear."

She turns away with a little skip. I straighten and put on a smile, but then hear a step behind me. I turn to see Sister Agatha in the doorway. She stares at me, her gray eyes accusing.

"Sister Agatha!" I call out, hating the stitch of desperation in my voice. "A moment!"

But she is already gone, a harsh smirk on her lips.

I cannot abandon my class to pursue her, despite the knife of dread twisting in my gut. How much did she see? What does she think she knows?

"I'm fine," I whisper. "I'm *fine*."

Turning back to the class, I calm the children and send them back to their desks. They are flushed and bright-eyed, taking out their embroidery hoops and polishing their needles. They follow my instruction dutifully, little fingers stabbing their needles in and out of the muslin stretched over their hoops. Not spells, these, just basic stitches they'll later combine into true Weaves. I walk between the rows of desks, critiquing their work. Their small fingers fly with the dexterity of youth and keen minds. The room fills with the gentle, soothing sound of needles clicking against thimbles.

The door to the classroom opens, and a round, apple-cheeked woman walks in, her skirts and tight-fitting veil stiff with embroidery. I straighten as the children all jump to their feet, bodies rigid with respect for their headmistress.

"Good morning, Mother Bridgid," the children intone, and I mumble with them, out of habit, as if I were nine years old again and crammed into one of those tiny chairs.

"Sister Rose Pryor," she says, smiling rosily. "Would you join me in my office? Sister Agatha can take over your class for the remainder of the afternoon."

My heart falls as Sister Agatha creeps into the room, giving me a quick, sly smile. I do not look at her as I exit, my hand pressed to my pattering heart.

I walk as one already condemned, trailing after Mother Bridgid to her office. The left wall of the hallway is lined with small, foggy windows, looking out onto the chaotic jumble of Pye Street. It is filled with beggars, thieves, and desperate souls, some come to beg for a drop of magic, some for bread, some for more nefarious purposes. The Perkins Charity School sits in the shadow of her older, more prestigious

15

sister, the Westminster School of Weaving, with its famous abbey and all the dour sisters inside at their looms, Weaving prayers to the Fates. Those who cannot find charity there often wash up on our doorstep. And as sworn adherents to the Order of the Moirai, my sisters and I are duty bound to help them as best we can.

For a moment, my eye snags on a tall man leaning against the public house across the way. His gaze traces the outline of the school with eyes pale as the snow.

My chest pinches. I let out a gasp and grip the edge of the window.

"Sister Rose," the headmistress calls from her office doorway. "If you please."

I glance her way but can form no reply. The blood has drained from my body, leaving my heart clenching behind my ribs.

He can't be here. It's impossible.

I look out the window again to see that the man is no longer there. Or never was there, more like.

It's been twelve years, I remind myself. *He's not coming back.*

But as I step into Mother Bridgid's office, I have to work to find my breath. The room feels cool despite the low fire in its blackened stone hearth. That cold is nothing to the chill that seized me when I thought I'd glimpsed that face. That beautiful, cruel, impossible face.

He's not coming back.

The stone walls of the headmistress's office seem to lean in on me, the ancient, rugged beams holding up the low ceiling in dire need of varnish. Though tidy, the room is packed with crates of thread and muslin, embroidery hoops and broken looms. All donated, all worn and in need of repair. As far as Moirene schools go, this is one of the smaller establishments, and a poorer one reliant on charity.

Mother Bridgid sits on her hard wooden chair by the fire. On her breast, the glint of silver thread draws attention to the trefoil knot embroidered on her collar, the sign of our order and the color of her station. The three loops are symbolic of the three Fates, watching us dispassionately from their celestial looms.

My own such knot is plain blue wool stitched neatly on my collar, but as precious to me as if it were spun gold.

"Remind me how old you were, Sister Rose," she begins, "when you came to the Order of the Moirai?"

"I was eight," I say softly. "It was after my aunt was institutionalized."

"Ah. And the sisters delivered you here, to the Perkins School. A charity case, like our own humble students."

I nod, my cheeks warm. Above her chair spreads a faded tapestry of the Fates at their looms. I try to distract myself by tracing their familiar forms. Fair Clotho turns out threads from her spindle, which dark Lachesis measures out. And withered Atropos, in her black gown and veil, looms with her shears, ready to snip short some unsuspecting life, her expression calm but resolute.

Of the three Fates, it is Atropos whose face always fascinated me most. Today I can nearly feel her breath on the back of my neck, my body tense as I wait to find out whether those shears will end me or not.

"You have been a great boon to this institution," Mother Bridgid continues. "Which is why it grieves me to hear your troubles persist."

My eyes return to the headmistress's face. "I thank you for your concern, Mother, but I assure you that I am well."

"Sister Agatha testifies otherwise, I fear. This is the third time I've had to speak with you about these chest pains." She studies me beneath a furrowed brow. "They happen only when you channel?"

I press my lips together, swallowing the protest I know is futile. "Yes."

"And they began . . . ?"

"A year ago, Mother." As I have told her before, and as I am sure she recalls. In truth, I felt them longer ago than that, but I was able to ignore the pain for a while. I feel a sudden need to prove myself, to assure her my situation is not so dire as she may think. "My magic was never the strongest. But I more than made up for it with study. I was the first of my class to memorize all five hundred and eighty knots in the Newtonian Canon. I was the only one to complete the Gordian Knot."

"And yet," Mother Bridgid says, tapping her chin, "your magic wanes."

I flush, looking down at my hands. "I can still Weave almost anything you like."

"Then do."

"I beg your pardon?"

"Weave for me. Now. It seems you know all five hundred and eighty of Newton's knots." Mother Bridgid smiles. "Suppose you try number two hundred and four."

"I can do that." I nod, my confidence rising. Newton 204 is a cat's cradle, my specialty. I place a log from the firewood basket on the hearth, meaning to split it in two, for Newton 204 is a sundering spell.

Mustard yellow thread unspools with a whisper. I clip off a length with my teeth and tie it into a wide loop, then wind my fingers through it. The fibers settle into the spaces between my fingers, taut and vibrating, as if eager to begin.

One breath to still my nerves.

Another to still my fingers.

Then I begin.

My Weaving is effortless and swift. Newton 204 is an advanced knot, but that doesn't daunt me. There are forty-one steps, and within seconds, I'm halfway done. A web is forming between my hands, slackening and tightening as I Weave, faster and faster. Mother Bridgid is nodding to herself, her eyes tracking my every move. But as skillful as my work is, I know it's not truly what she is judging. This is the easy part, for me.

There are two steps to executing a spell—first the Weave, then the magic. Lay out the boundaries of the spell, the pattern it will take, and then flood it with the energy to make it come alive. The thread *wants* to be woven, it urges me on, and my fingers move almost faster than my thoughts can follow, driven by a deep instinct I've always had inside me. Ever since I was a little girl, I could see a Weave once and replicate it perfectly the next day. I have an instinct for patterns, and thank the

Fates for that, else I'd never have been able to keep up in my classes. I may have been putting it mildly when I said my magic has always been weak.

But I learned years ago how to stretch a teaspoon of magic further than most girls could a pint.

When the knot is complete, I go still; sunlight lancing through the leaded windows illuminates the spellknot and turns the yellow fibers into gold. Motes of dust sink through the geometric gaps in the Weave, bright sparks in the sun.

"Neatly done," Mother Bridgid says. "But then, there was never any doubt as to your skill. Please continue."

I hesitate, drawing a few deep breaths before beginning the second stage of the Weave. But with every rise and fall of my lungs, my heart beats faster, fluttering like a trapped moth.

Don't ruin this, Rose.

Don't sabotage yourself.

You didn't survive two years of your aunt's torments or twelve years of grueling lessons and endless practice only to falter now.

I recall the beloved opening line of *The Westminster Weaving Primer*. *All it takes to change your fate is a bit of thread.*

I close my eyes and let out a final breath, then open the channels and doors and conduits inside me, and I *reach*.

Living energy pulses in the ferns arranged behind the headmistress's desk. It courses through the ivy clinging to the outside wall. It bubbles in the moss between the paving stones lining the yard. Even here in the heart of London, where all is stone and brick, there is living energy. And at my touch, it responds, reaching back to me, curious. I pull it in, twining it up and around my mind like wool around a spindle, harvesting it in strands and strings. I gather it all up inside me, living threads bundled together in my heart, where it is spun into magic.

But it's not enough.

My heart is already squeezing with pain. It's like gasping for air while a hand is tightening on my throat—I reach, and I sense the energy around me, but I can't pull enough in. My skin turns clammy; if I'm going to fail, this is where it happens. This is where it always happens.

Not this time.

Not this time, *please*, Fates above!

Opening my eyes, I let out a breath and attempt to channel what meager energy I've gathered into the thread stretched between my hands. The magic rushes from my clenching heart, scouring me from the inside out.

For a moment, light begins to glow at my fingertips and wicks into the thread.

Then it goes out.

Panic spikes in my gut. No, no, *no*!

I grasp desperately at the uncoiling strands of energy, but it's too late. They're torn apart like a spiderweb in a gale, and the magic releases from me in an untidy wind that gusts around the office. Papers on the desk flutter high; ash in the hearth clouds the air and sets Mother Bridgid to coughing.

She pulls out her thread and Weaves a fast settling spell that returns the ashes back to the fireplace, seeming to make time run in reverse. In the chaos I sink, trembling, to my knees.

"I can try again," I whisper. "If I wait a moment, it will work."

I look up at Mother Bridgid. She must see the naked desperation in my eyes, because she sighs and shakes her head, even as she coughs into her kerchief.

"Sister Rose, I am sorry."

My lungs squeeze, depriving me of breath. "Sorry for what?"

"For you. For our school, in what it loses in you. It's undeniable that you are uncommonly skilled in your technique. It's been many years since we had a teacher as clever. But the neatest Weaves in the world are useless if you cannot fill them with magic."

"But I *can*," I whisper. This will pass. Surely it must pass. I am not a woman of high ambition. I don't wish to embroider for the queen or Weave in battle with the Telarii. I don't wish to sit at a loom in

20

Westminster Abbey. I want only to teach. To help other girls like me find their way in the world. That's all I've ever wanted.

"I'm sorry, dear." Mother Bridgid rises to her feet. Her tone is firm, but the pity in her eyes is worse than any pain in my chest. It is the expression of a doctor informing his patient that her illness is much worse than she'd feared. "I am afraid I have no choice but to—"

"I just need time!" I say, before she can go further and speak the words I fear most. "To rest, to recover. Please, Mother."

Her lips press together, as if she is warring against her own conscience. I hang upon her expression, breathless with dread, waiting to see which way she will go. Her eyes, though sunken into her lined face, are bright and calculating as she studies me. I keep my shoulders straight and try not to look *too* desperate, but I fear I am not accomplished enough a liar to be convincing.

"This school is my home. My entire life." I rest my hands on my knees, palms up and pleading. One small white scar shines on my wrist where the sleeve pulls up.

"Time, then," she says at last, and my eyelids flutter with relief. "A year's leave. If your pains persist after that, however, I am afraid I will have no choice but to dismiss you from the Order."

I swallow a knot of sudden dismay. A *year*. I'd hoped for a week, a month at most, but a *year* . . . ! Still, better this than the alternative— being dismissed entirely. Which I am sure she was about to do.

She gives my hand a soft pat. "This is for your own good, my dear. You are playing a dangerous game. My uncle had a bad heart, you know, and he was a Weaver. We told him to give it up, or he'd kill himself."

I wait, my voice frozen in my throat.

"He didn't listen, and he's dead now," she adds, her words slow with emphasis. She gives me a hard look. "Magic, my dear, is not for the faint of heart."

CHAPTER TWO

That evening, after packing up my threads and hoops, I leave my classroom and make my way down Pye Street, heading for the boarding house where I and the other teachers have rooms. The towers of Westminster Abbey are at my back, their needlelike points piercing a low skein of grim cloud. An early spring chill coils about my throat, leaching the warmth from my skin. Despair sweeps over me in a black fog.

A *year*. I've been put on leave for an entire *year*. And Mother Bridgid made it clear I would not be given accommodations in that time, suggesting I seek lodging in some country village for the benefit of my health.

I wonder, now, if she expects I will not return. Perhaps she hopes I will settle down into some other life, or perhaps she suspects my condition will worsen.

Clenching my teeth, I press on. I *will* return, whatever her suspicions. This is where I belong. It is the only place I have *ever* belonged.

Dirty slush, deposited by winter's last feeble cough, piles along the wall, heaping in the gutters. Boys with brooms race each other to push aside more of the stuff, clearing the way for the carriages and carts clotting the road. A Weaver moves from streetlamp to streetlamp, Weaving quick fire spells with scarlet string to light the wicks above. He nods to me when he passes by, his gaze flicking to the battered threadkit hanging over my shoulder; it is a nod between colleagues, a wish of good fortune. Frost clings to the edges of his beard, despite the warming knots embroidered on his collar and hat. The street is busy, mostly with beggars stumbling back to their corners and bridges, or with furtive men seeking the warm beds of the comfort houses. Everyone I pass is locked inside their own world of trouble, with little thought or compassion to spare for mine. We all scuttle on our individual ways, heads down and arms folded, skittish as ghosts.

I have not been so alone since losing my aunt. For twelve years, the Perkins School has been my home, my sanctuary, an island of surety and hope amid the tossing chaos of London's unforgiving streets. It gave me the magic I had always craved, the thread and needles with which I wove my own path through the world, and then purpose when I was brought on to teach after my graduation. The Order of the Moirai even delighted in me once, the sisters intrigued by my aptitude for patterns and the deftness of my hands. There was talk of promoting me to some higher rank, moving me to teach at the more prestigious Westminster School.

But then my magic turned against me, fickle as a gambler's luck.

I try not to think of my students. Of sweet little Carolina, of clever Edwina, of the timid but gifted Anne. They are Sister Agatha's responsibility now. I can only hope they will still be here if—*when*—I return.

I sag against the cold wall of an inn, the strength draining from my knees, staring at a patch of flickering light cast by the lamp around the corner. An illusion of warmth, of sunlight, just enough to make the cold all the more bitter and cast light over a scrap of discarded newspaper under my shoe. Advertisements shout at me from the page. A threadshop boasts the strongest silk in England. A theater invites one and all to an Illusion Spectacle, the likes of which has never been beheld. The Order of St. Edgitha of the Needle is ordaining a new bishop, a Weaver renowned on the continent for his prayer knots.

"Sister Rose?" says a small, whispery voice.

I turn and see a shivering girl, her ragged shawl clutched around her.

"Carolina? What are you doing out here?"

She sniffs. "Is it true you're leaving?"

I sigh and take her hand. "Come with me. You're freezing."

Her lips are blue. I guide her out of the alley and up the rickety steps to my tiny rented room. It's scarcely larger than my narrow bed, and frigid. Shutting the door against the cold, I pull out the thread and needle I keep in the brim of my bonnet. It takes three attempts to thread the needle with my cold fingers.

Carolina perches on the edge of the bed while I stab the needle through the hem of her dirty dress, but her shivering makes the job difficult. The light is weak and my fingers are stiff, but I know these knots too well to make a mistake. I've been stitching them all winter, for my students, for myself, for any shivering soul who came begging at the school doors.

While I sew, Carolina runs her hand over my thin coverlet and sings under her breath, an old song every child knows.

In the shadows 'neath your bed,
She spins her spells with spider's thread,
Her hair is black, her eyes are red,
And if she sees you, you are dead.

Her song makes me shiver.

"One day," says Carolina, "I'll Weave a spell to catch a faerie and wish for it to take me to faerie land, and I'll learn to fly and never be cold again. Do you believe in faeries, Sister Rose?"

My lips thin; that icy fear returns, crackling over my heart like frost. Like a cold hand on my shoulder. I recall the glimpse I had through the school's window, of the silver-eyed man, but push it away. "I believe we must make our own magic."

The spellknot is done. When I channel into it, it glows like an ember on the fabric of Carolina's thin wool skirt. This time, the magic doesn't fail me. The light fades after a moment, sinking into the thread and binding to its fibers.

"Better?" I ask.

She nods miserably. "Don't leave us. You can't. Sister Agatha's not nearly so nice as you!"

"You just keep your mind on your work," I tell her, trying to hide how her words tug at my weary heart. I wrap her hand in mine. "Be patient with your thread and keep your needles sharp. You'll be a fine Weaver one day, Carolina."

"But I'll miss you!" Carolina complains. "Are you leaving because of your gentleman friend? Is he come to take you away and marry you?"

"My—what?"

"Your gentleman friend. The tall one with the white hair. He told me to tell you he'd be along shortly to—ouch!"

I realize I've been squeezing her hand tighter and tighter. Releasing it with a wince, I murmur an apology that I cannot hear for the blood roaring in my ears.

"Tall, with white hair?" I ask her. "Are you sure? Was he elderly?"

"No," she says with a frown, rubbing her hand. "He looked about the same age as you."

Dread sinks through me like an anchor in deep water.

"What did he say, Carolina? When did he—?"

A knock sounds at the door.

I jolt to my feet, forcing my clammy hands to Weave a quick fireknot for better light. Pulling Carolina close, I watch the door and pray the sound was a trick of my imagination. That there was no knock. That there is no one standing on the other—

Knock. Knock. Knock.

I drag in a ragged breath, the flame dancing over my hand nearly flickering out as my fingers tremble.

"Are you going to answer it?" Carolina whispers.

I glance down at her, then back at the door. I force myself forward, one step at a time, and clear my throat. Pressing my palm to the door, I lean to the crack and speak through it.

"Pardon me?" I say. "Can—can I help you? Are you seeking a spell?"

"I am indeed," the person outside drawls in a cultured accent, and his voice makes the hairs on my arms rise. "A spell, and clever hands to Weave it."

Slowly, I rest my forehead against the door and shut my eyes. This cannot be happening. After all this time . . .

"Open the door, Rose." The command is soft but unyielding, with a faint note of warning hidden between the words. If I do not open it, he will.

I obey, if only to order the person outside to leave at once. As the door swings open on its creaking hinges, I summon my most authoritative schoolteacher's voice.

But my voice tangles into a knot at the sudden sight of that face. It is the summation of all my nightmares for the last twelve years. It is a face I have glimpsed a hundred times in shadowed corners and bustling crowds, only to blink and find my eyes have been tricked again. How cruel a face it is, with its delicate, almost feminine angles and lovely cold eyes, lips bloodless and sly, high cheekbones angled like a cat's, so that his features draw to a narrow point at his chin. He is carved out of winter itself, a creature of snow and ice.

It *was* him I glimpsed through the school window.

My body goes rigid. The world shrinks away. The pain in my heart suddenly stabs like a knife, piercing my lungs through.

"Hello, Rose Pryor," says the faerie. A slow, thin smile spreads his pale lips. "How I have missed you."

CHAPTER THREE

I step between Carolina and my surprise visitor, shielding the child from his roving silver gaze. He looks about my room with an air of bemusement, as if he has never seen a place so shoddy and humble and cannot fathom why anyone would endure it.

"*You,*" I choke out.

His gaze drifts back to my face, and he spreads his hands elegantly, as if to say, *Me, obviously.*

I stare at him as my heart flutters in panic, feeling all of eight years old again.

He is real.

He is *here.*

"Carolina," I say softly, and though I do not turn my gaze from the faerie, I feel her big brown eyes on me, "go back to the school."

"Sister Rose?"

"I will be all right. Go, and say nothing of this to Sister Agatha or anyone else." I give her shoulder a weak squeeze, and into her hand I press one of my embroidered kerchiefs. The spellknots on it ward against minor injury, discourage ill intentions toward the bearer, and distract watchful eyes. It should help her sneak into the school unnoticed. "We wouldn't want them to know you were sneaking out, would we?"

She nods, frowning slightly at the kerchief but gripping it tight, and slips by me. She doesn't argue, thank the Fates. The faerie's hand flicks as she slides past him, his fingers tracing her unruly red braid. I choke on a breath until the end of her braid slips free of his touch, and she vanishes down the stairs.

"She reminds me of another little Weaver," he says. "One of surpassing cleverness, who summoned me to her side with an ancient moorwitch spell."

"Why are you here?" I ask.

He smiles. "Come. Let us take this conversation somewhere warmer. We have much to discuss, my clever little witch."

We go to the Red Finch, a public house across the road. There I sit in rigid trepidation, in a hard wooden chair near the fire. Half the tables are full, with patrons brooding over empty tankards or halfheartedly gambling over dice. A tired musician fiddles for his supper in the corner, receiving more curses than coin for his trouble. The place stinks of smoke, burnt bread, and spilled beer.

The faerie sits across from me, his spine straight as a poker, his hands folded one atop the other on the table, his black gloves beneath them. His fingers are bony and very pale, his nails long. I stare at them so I do not have to look at his face, frozen to my chair like a block of ice. My skin feels too tight, and I fidget with my sleeve, where I keep a skein of thread always hidden for emergencies. The fiddler switches to a new ballad, his tune as sharp and callous as the winter wind, and every scrape of his bow sends a chill rippling over my skin.

"You have grown up," the faerie says, eyeing me brazenly. "And grown lovely. But I cannot help but wonder if the young woman is as clever and bold as the little girl?"

The faerie appears to be not a day older than when last I saw him. A stranger might guess him to be twenty or even younger, but I know he is a good deal older than that, perhaps far older than I can imagine. He seems at ease in this humble environment, despite his expensive black tailcoat and blue silk cravat, which would be more suited to some high-society dinner than a saloon barely outside the Devil's Acre. His hair—frosty blond—is shorter than it was twelve years ago, but still long enough for him to tie at his nape with a black silk ribbon. His eyes are the chilled, light blue of aquamarine, with darker cracks running outward from his irises, so they seem faceted like diamonds; when he turns his head, the light plays over those hard angles, making his gaze glint. Against the alabaster paleness of him, the black of his lashes is almost startling, their long fringe luring attention to the ageless jewels of his eyes. The more I stare, the less he fits here, in this human place.

I gaze around to see what the others make of him, but curiously, no one else gives him a second look. Then I notice the glamour knots embroidered on his collar and sleeves, which must make him appear more human to them than he does to me. Glamour knots are like that—they cease working on someone who has seen one's true appearance already, as I saw him twelve years ago—but even so, when I glance away, he shifts in my periphery. Lines appear in his face. Golden highlights soften the shocking white of his hair. He remains handsome, beautiful even, but not unnaturally so.

The effect makes me shudder.

Emma, a serving girl who has waited on me here before, brings us hot tea. She gives me a little frown, her lips pursed in judgment, as she glances from me to the wealthy stranger I'm with. She, at least, seems to recognize he is not her ordinary sort of patron. I read her suspicions easily enough, and blush even though nothing could be further from the truth.

"Dinner?" she asks, the word sounding like an accusation on her lips.

"Bring my companion a plate of your best," says the faerie, looking at me while he says it. "And for me, fresh strawberries dusted with sugar."

"Fresh—" Emma's eyes bulge. "It is *March*, sir."

"Check your stores, my dear," he returns coolly, and he dismisses her with a flick of his hand.

Emma, looking scandalized, starts back to the kitchen. I feel a sudden urge to grab her apron and pull her back, to beg her not to leave me alone with him. It feels jarring to see him here, in so common and familiar a place, as though he shouldn't be capable of existing outside shadowy corners or snowy forests or the pages of a faerie tale book. Some foolish part of me had thought I would be forever safe from him, if I only kept to the light and the densely packed streets of London. There is no place less like a faerie tale than this, and yet there he sits, his slender dark eyebrows drawn together as he studies me.

"You have hardly blinked for the last ten minutes," murmurs the faerie, his head tilting to the side. The motion causes his fine white hairs to shift, revealing the pointed tip of his ear and the blue gemstone dangling from his lobe like an icicle. "Are you feverish? You do seem alarmingly pale, but I'm no great judge of these things. You mortals are such fragile creatures. And how *thin* you are. You ought to eat better."

I cannot quite convince myself he is there. I am still holding out hope that he is a trick of my frostbitten imagination.

"Why do you look at me that way?" He waves a hand; on every finger glints a band of silver. "Did you think I would not return? Did you think I had forgotten our bargain?"

"Twelve years," I murmur.

Twelve years of jumping at shadows and hearing his whispers in the back of my mind. Twelve years of wondering if I'd dreamed the entire thing and if perhaps I was mad. Twelve years . . . and yes, I had begun to hope he might have forgotten. After all, what is one petrified eight-year-old girl to an immortal faerie?

More than I had wanted to believe, apparently.

"My aunt cannot speak," I say. "She cannot even feed herself. They keep her in an institution, caged like an animal."

He rubs his forefinger over his bottom lip as he considers me. "And does that not bring you comfort? She will never hurt you again. Is that not what you asked of me?"

"I never asked you to . . ." I swallow hard. "I was eight years old. I didn't understand—"

"You understood how to Weave the summoning spell." His voice loses a bit of its polished ease, deepening and betraying his age. "You knew the powers you called upon. I saw into your heart when you made your bargain with me, and I knew what you *really* wanted. You wanted her to suffer as she had made you suffer."

"I was a *child*, and I felt as children feel, in untempered extremes. I was hurt and terrified, and I wanted to be free of her. I couldn't think beyond that!"

"Indeed, but do not parade *ignorance* before me as if it could cleanse your conscience. You called for me, and I came. I offered you a bargain, and you accepted. You tied the vowknot yourself, and I gave you what you wanted." He leans forward, hands splayed on the table. Whether it is a slip of his glamour or a trick of my eyes, it seems for a moment that each of his fingers has one too many knuckles. "And now there is something that *I* want, and you will help me get it."

I open my mouth to reply, then shut it as Emma returns, setting before me a plate heaped with steaming pork, roasted potatoes, and soft bread. Before the faerie she places, with an expression of bewilderment, a plate of fresh strawberries dusted with sugar.

"I . . ." She stares at the plate, then gives her head a shake, as if it were filled with fog. "Can I get you anything else?"

"This will do," the faerie says. "Away now, my flower, and don't bother us again."

She floats off, still with that dazed look in her eyes, and vanishes into the kitchen.

The sight of the food only turns my stomach. I sit back in my chair and summon the courage to look him in the eyes as he delicately cuts a strawberry and slides it into his mouth on the flat of his knife.

"Why now?" I ask. "Why did you wait all these years to demand your payment?"

"I have many other *investments* to keep track of, not just you. Though, dear Rose," he sighs, as he cuts another strawberry, "you've always held a special place in my thoughts. The little girl with the

31

cleverness to Weave a spell few masters would dare. Oh, yes." He pauses to point his knife at me. "You hold a special place indeed."

A flush creeps up my neck, a mingling of pleasure and shame. If he knew how I struggle to complete even a basic summoning charm these days, I doubt he would speak so flatteringly. I doubt he would be here at all. I look down at the table and say nothing.

"I confess," he adds, "I'd thought to find you in some place of high esteem. Weaving in your little queen's court. Why are you not in some rich appointment, crafting glamours for the aristocracy with silken threads? When I discovered you had spent these years in a slum school, teaching unwanted waifs how to sew paltry healing spells, I thought perhaps my investment had been ill made."

I sit up straighter, my hands curling into fists on my lap. What pleasure I'd felt at his earlier flattery now turns cold.

"I am not eight years old anymore, Sir *Faerie*. Perhaps my work is low, but my skill is not. Perhaps I prefer the company of the desperate children you'd call *unwanted*, to all the high courts of Europe." I can practically hear my old schoolteacher's rasping voice in my ear: *Pride, Rose Pryor. That's your first fault.*

"Or perhaps," he says slyly, "you have a certain reputation, a souvenir of that night to go along with that scar."

My stomach turns over as I put my fingers to my neck and the burn scar left by my aunt's pipe. Of course the faerie knows all about me. He probably had ways of spying on me for the last twelve years, keeping watch over his little *investment*.

Mad, they call me. I know it well enough. More than a few have said it to my face. *Mad and fae touched.* It's astonishing how close people can get to the truth without ever knowing the details.

My aunt was well known in certain circles, or at least her fortune was. So her sudden mental break twelve years ago was inevitably noted. The famously sharp-tongued Dame Lenore's mind snapped in the course of a night? Suspicion had bred in the papers, theories coupling with theories, spiraling around me wherever I went. They said that

I, her only relation, had to be involved. That wretched niece of poor Arthur, whom Dame Lenore kindly took in though they were no blood kin. The niece without a penny to her name, but with a flair for magic.

But I did not hurt my aunt. At least, not directly. I didn't Weave the spells to steal her mind and turn her wits, leaving her unable to even feed herself.

He did.

It had all happened so quickly, a blur in my memory: the faerie's appearance, silver and shining and terrible against the crimson walls of my uncle's study; my garbled plea for aid; the threads of the vowknot winding around my fingers as I accepted his terms. He had freed me at a cost: *a favor to be performed by my twenty-first birthday,* I had vowed in my child's voice, thinking such a day an eternity away, while my aunt's torments were daily. I would have sold my *soul* to be free of her.

Perhaps that's exactly what I did.

"What do you want?" I whisper.

The corner of his cruel mouth quirks. "I want to go home."

It was not the answer I had expected. Ten virgins sacrificed by a full moon, maybe, or some equally horrible thing. But to go . . . *home?* It sounds so ordinary.

"You want to go to . . . faerie land?"

Amusement arches in his brows. "Faerie land? A child may call it that, I suppose. To my folk, it is the World Below, or Elfhame."

"Why can't you just *go*? Isn't that where you belong?"

"It isn't as simple as snapping my fingers, child. I have not been there for many centuries. Most of the doors to Elfhame were shut long ago, when it was made apparent that my people and yours could not dwell together in peace. Time among your mortals has taken its toll on me. You forge so much iron these days . . ." His eyes slip away, his voice fading, and for a moment he seems a thousand leagues distant. "There are those Below who may . . . challenge my return. So I must return at full power or not at all, and to do that, I need your assistance."

His expression is serious as it shifts to me, his age apparent in his eyes. It is like being held in the gaze of a mountain or a ruin or some other ancient, unknowable thing.

I lean back, wishing Emma would reappear, but she—and every other serving girl and boy—seems to have vanished entirely.

"In Elfhame," the faerie says slowly, "there is a tree. I require but a piece of it. You, little bird, will flit into the realm of the fae, pluck a branch from this tree, and bring it to me."

I stare at him, feeling the strangest urge to laugh.

Slip into Elfhame? A world *full* of monsters like him? Steal a piece of some sacred faerie tree and sneak out again?

I want to tell him how impossible it is. That I won't be beholden to the oath of a child, however skilled a Weaver I might have been. I want to tell him to go *stuff* himself with iron.

But then he says, "Do this for me, and your heart will be whole again."

I inhale sharply. "I have no idea what you—"

"Do not act the witless fool with me. We know one another better than that." He leans toward me, tapping one long nail on the tabletop. "I can guess at the pain you've been feeling when you channel. We draw near your twenty-first birthday, do we not? And still your vow is unfulfilled. Or did you think the vowknot you tied was merely ceremonial?"

I press a shaking hand to my chest. Of course I knew. I'd known from the moment the pain had begun what the true cause of it was, though I'd never let myself fully believe it.

"You can deny me this favor," he adds. "I cannot compel you. But it *will* cost you your magic. For it was your heart you swore upon when you tied the vowknot to seal our bargain."

Yes, I remember.

Vowknots are specific things, requiring clear collateral. And I had made my vow with the one thing I held dear, the only thing in my life that had ever—and still only—brought me joy.

34

"*I swear on my heart,*" my eight-year-old voice echoes back to me. The heart. The precious catalyst wherein a Weaver spins energy into magic. I offered up as collateral the very crux of my fledgling power.

The idea of refusing him is alluring. I could walk away right now. I could prove I am beholden to no one. I could hold my chin high.

And I would lose my magic entirely.

My lungs tighten, my skin going clammy, the way it does when I realize a spell is going to fail. In that moment, I feel the crushing sum of all that panic and fear and, most of all, overwhelming *helplessness.* I'd become less than nothing. A ghost in my own skin. A quivering mouse. Dependent on others, forever crushed in a world that despises poor, plain women with murky reputations. I simply cannot survive without it.

Picturing life without magic is like falling, plunging from heights unfathomable through dark and empty air. It is a feeling worse than death, to have all control and strength wrenched from my hands.

It is the same feeling I found at the end of my aunt's pipe, when she pressed it into my skin.

But beyond fearing life without it, the deeper truth is that I *love* magic. Everything about it—the thread forming arcane patterns between my hands, the immediate connection I have to the things living and growing around me, the rush of energy through my body, and the smoky burn of magic at my fingertips. All those hours as a child, lit by sterling beams of moonlight, buried in stolen spellbooks and spools of thread. Even knowing my aunt would beat me when she caught me at it, I could not resist magic's lure, my need overpowering my fear.

And even more precious to me now are my students and my classroom. I treasure our quiet lessons bent over embroidery hoops, as I teach them how to Weave their way free of an uncaring world. To claim *their* freedom as I'd claimed my own. Without my magic, I can never return to my classroom.

Long before I wove the spell to summon the faerie, magic was my freedom. Magic was my hope. Magic told me that if I studied hard and practiced often, one day I might Weave for myself whatever life I wished.

And I would sacrifice all that for . . . what? Pride? Stubbornness? A life of destitution on the streets, now that even a desperate charity school will not employ me?

For magic, I would sacrifice anything.

I lift my teacup and drain the lukewarm contents and wish it were something more bracing.

Then, setting down the cup, I meet the faerie's eyes and say, "You want me to break into the world of the fae, steal a magic branch from a sacred tree, and get away whole again? And in return, my debt to you will be paid in full?"

His eyes spark like blue fire. "When you have delivered to me a branch from the Dwirra Tree, Rose Pryor, your debt to me will be paid in full."

"Will you tell me nothing more? How dangerous is this? How do I enter Elfhame? How do I escape again?"

"We've a journey ahead of us. There will be time for all that."

"Well," I cast about, feeling as if I've stepped into a rushing current and lost my footing. "Can I know your name?"

The faerie draws his hand to his chin, his lips curling into a dangerous smile. "My name?"

"If I am to undertake this impossible and deadly favor, I'd like, at the very least, to know the name of the creature pulling my strings."

He laughs, and every head in the room turns his way as that rolling, lovely laughter shatters his glamour spells and reveals his true form, from his too-long fingers to his pointed ears to the unnatural sharpness of his teeth. I look around in alarm, expecting someone to cry out "Demon!"

Instead I find myself staring at *dozens* of pointed ears and sharpened teeth, as the creatures I'd been fooled into taking for other patrons now shed their glamours as well. Even the fiddler leers at me, his face gleaming with scales. I am surrounded by a host of fae, and their laughter is like the chittering of beetles, their eyes bulbous and black. There is no sign of Emma or any other human.

Chills crawl over my scalp. I half rise from my chair, breathless and shocked, as they cackle at my expression. The entire inn is populated with their kind, a veritable hive of immortals, all elongated limbs and silken, ageless skin. And the one seated before me, I sense with sudden certainty, is their leader.

"Very well," says the faerie, his cool eyes never leaving my face. "You may call me Lachlan."

CHAPTER FOUR

I wake the next morning in a high bed, burrowed beneath three blankets and wrapped in delicious warmth provided by the still-glowing coals in the little hearth. Lachlan had purchased me a room at the Red Finch, one of their finest, at a price I couldn't have afforded with even a month's wages from my teaching salary. But despite the soft bed, it had taken me hours to fall asleep, worrying whether I was a fool to agree to this mad mission. It didn't help that Lachlan had rented every other room in the inn for his faerie cohorts, and they carried their reveling on through the night, drinking and banging about and singing strange, lilting songs in a whispery tongue I did not recognize. How a community of the creatures could cavort so openly in the heart of London while avoiding notice, Fates only know. It makes me wonder how long they have been here, and if there are far more than I ever knew.

Not that I know much about faeries. They fit into the same category as ghosts, demons, and selkies; that is, most folk prefer to not believe in them at all, except perhaps on the darkest and most storm-ridden of nights, when even the wildest stories feel possible. If it were not for that fateful summoning spell I found in my uncle's study, perhaps I, too, would be a skeptic. The most commonly accepted explanation for them is that it was the fae who taught magic to humans, long ago, before vanishing from the world forever.

Clearly, at least half that story is false.

When I push myself out of bed at last, I find a new dress laid out on a wing-backed chair by the hearth, blue linen, plain but tasteful, with a new corset and petticoat. I put them on queasily, wondering who left them, and who chose them for me. They fit perfectly.

"Miss Pryor."

I turn and see Emma standing in the doorway. "Yes?"

"Mr. Murdoch says to tell you he's waiting below."

It takes me a moment to remember Mr. Murdoch is my faerie. Lachlan Murdoch. A common name for an uncommon creature, and I have no doubt it is not his true name. Not that I'd prefer any other—the less I know of him, the sooner I can put him and all this behind me. If I can just keep my head down and fetch him this branch, I'll owe him nothing more and never have to see him again.

"Where is my other dress?" I ask.

"Mr. Murdoch had us burn it."

My face heats. Perhaps my things were threadbare and unfashionable, but they were *mine*.

In the dim saloon, my faerie escort waits, with several of his followers hovering about. Their guises don't fool me now that I've already seen through them. But in my periphery, I see glimmers of their magic, beards and bellies and liver spots that humanize them to all other eyes.

Lachlan, however, would be resplendent in any form. Today he wears all black, even his cravat spilling from his collar like silken ebony. His hair is loose but neatly combed, tucked behind his pointed ears. He stands in the parlor as if he owns it, cocky as a king.

"Well," he says, looking me up and down. "You are a bluebird in midwinter, Rose Pryor. I knew that gown would suit you."

"You had my things burned!"

He rolls one shoulder in a lazy shrug. "I can't have my new *assistant* dressing like an urchin."

I open my mouth to echo *assistant?* But the way he emphasized the word stops me; I realize there are some folk across the room taking their

39

tea and watching us with interest—not faeries, but honest, blessedly ordinary folk one might find in any ordinary saloon.

I catch his meaning and curtsy, playing into the role.

"Let's go then," he says, with a brisk nod. "We've shopping to do."

◆ ◆ ◆

He whisks me all over London in his personal coach, a black, satiny affair drawn by matching dark horses. It is driven by one faerie, while another plays footman. People who watch us go by look for a half moment as if they are caught in a dream, and then when we've passed, they shake their heads and move on.

I sit on a bench upholstered in dark-blue fabric and watch the shops and houses through a window curtained by red velvet. The faerie sits across from me, one long leg thrown over the other, his chin resting on his hand, his eyes half shuttered.

In the corners and shadows, his fae lurk. They seem to be guards of some sort, the way they hover about. Silent and unobtrusive they may be, but they stick at the corners of my eyes, their glamours flickering so that at times they seem completely human, and at others, they are all beetle eyes and moth wings and clicking teeth.

"Who are the others?" I ask. "Your family?"

"They are my companions. We all left Elfhame together, long ago. Though we are not so many in number as we were then." A shadow passes over his face.

At the first stop, a dressmaker's establishment, he descends and offers his hand, gloved in dark leather. I take it hesitantly and am surprised by how gently he helps me out.

In the shop, Lachlan is greeted with a flurry of delighted exclamations. The owner, a Madame Alexandra, knows him by name, and sends her girls fluttering to me. It's like being set upon by a flock of excitable parrots. They pull me away and begin pinning and measuring about my person, exclaiming things like "this will bring out the green in her eyes" or "a good figure, if too thin. We'll add more to the bustle."

"How do you know Mr. Murdoch?" I ask them.

"Oh," one says. "He brings us the most excellent cloth. No one in London supplies such rare silks and cashmeres."

"He is a cloth merchant?"

"The finest." She giggles. "And the *handsomest*. How fortunate you are to assist him."

When they've finished with me, they return me to Lachlan's side, dizzied and blinking.

"The gowns will be ready this evening," says Madame Alexandra. "And you're *certain* we cannot do any spellwork for you? I employ some of the best Weavers in London." She casts a critical eye over me. "We have charms to inspire industriousness in your assistant, or to alert you of any little thefts . . ."

My face heats, and I start to cut in, but the faerie's soft touch on my arm stops my tongue.

"It will not be necessary," Lachlan says.

They discuss business then, talking cloth and shipments, and I walk away so as not to lose my temper at having my integrity impugned. In one back room I spy several Weavers bent over gowns, carefully stitching spells into hems and cuffs and bodices. The walls around them are filled with potted plants, ivy curling over the ceiling and ferns springing up in the corners, to provide a ready source of energy for them to channel, even in winter. I gasp a little, recognizing Maeve Reilly, an old classmate from my school days. She always did have the quickest hand at embroidery. I pull back before she can recognize me.

I'd always imagined working at a dress shop would be glamorous, embroidering and tatting and knitting spells for ladies and duchesses. But those girls looked exhausted, their eyes red and their hands cramped.

Finally Lachlan calls me over, extends an arm, and sweeps me out and onto the street in a whirl; my head is still spinning from the hasty fitting session.

"Sir, why are you—?"

"Because I need you to succeed," he interrupts. "And to do that, you must look as well as play your part to perfection. It is a narrow rope we must walk together, and I will not let shoddy hems be my undoing."

"I think I'd like no more debts to you, Sir Faerie," I say wryly.

He tosses a spool of black silk thread into my hands. "Then pay your way. Embroider my coach with your clever little warming spells, and consider yourself my assistant in truth."

At a loss, I relent and let him shuffle me back into his black coach. What on earth tidy hems have to do with sneaking into Elfhame is beyond me. I should think this task would depend more on subterfuge than manners.

But he is relentless in his transformation of me from charity-school teacher to respectable merchant's assistant. We flit from shop to shop. He buys me three pairs of shoes, two bonnets, a coat fringed in dark fur, lace handkerchiefs, and a dozen other odds and ends to fill up the two valises he also purchases. At every shop, the owners bob and bow and flatter him, all of which he accepts with cool indifference, as if it is perfectly natural for the world to turn on the tip of his pale finger. They attempt to conjure more coin from his purse with the promise of spells worked into each piece, even the shoes. He turns them all down.

At one shop he tells me to wait in the coach. It's a tall, solemn establishment in a good part of town; the doors and windows are all trimmed in black, and its stone walls look thick enough to keep out an invading horde. With a little start, I notice the small plaque depicting crossed bobbins engraved in bronze.

"The Telarii Guild," I whisper. My poor dead uncle was a Telari, one of the royal battle Weavers who served in the army. They are known for their powerful martial tapestries designed to alter the course of battles or even entire wars. It is said a single tapestry woven by rebel Telarii was responsible for the successful revolution of the American colonists; woven with stripes and stars, it warded the rebels in many battles.

Lachlan returns a half hour later, carrying a large parcel wrapped in oilcloth under his arm. I've been working on the warming spells, my needle drawing Lachlan's black thread through the thick velvet curtains, and already the coach is feeling like a summer afternoon. I stop when he opens the door. He ignores my curious stare and barks at the driver to continue. The parcel sits beside him, and he keeps a protective hand on it, his mouth set in a grim line.

"What is it?" I burst out, unable to stop myself.

He gives me a sidelong look. "A king's ransom is what it is, Rose Pryor."

He will say no more of it.

By the time the lamplighters take to the streets, we arrive at the final stop, and at the sight of it I sit up and let out an awed sigh, even the mysterious package by Lachlan forgotten.

"The King Street Threadshop," I murmur.

Lachlan, across the coach, gives me a satisfied smile. "I thought you might appreciate this one."

I descend from the coach as if caught in a dream.

I've heard stories of the King Street Threadshop all my life; Weavers speak of it the way priests speak of the Basilica of the Fates in the Vatican. There is not a thread in the world which you may not find on these shelves. It supplies Weaving materials to Queen Victoria herself.

The shop is three stories, with glittering marble staircases leading to the upper floors. Rows and rows of shelves display every thread imaginable, from twine to yarn to rope, in every color and material. Various counters are staffed by white-gloved attendants, ready to fetch whatever the heart could desire.

Yesterday, I would not have been allowed through the front doors. But now attendants ask if they can assist me, nodding deferentially. I pass other Weavers shopping and get a thrill when I spy golden embroidery on some of their collars, forming the emblems of their guilds—the Telarii, my own Order of the Moirai, the Spindle Wefen, the Aurobrus, the Order of Edgitha of the Needle. While some, like

43

the Telarii, are more inclined to battle magic, others focus on healing, tapestries, agriculture, or the archiving of spells from across the world.

Finally, I come to a glass case set apart from all the others, surrounded by a velvet rope and lit by an elegant chandelier. A stoic guard stands watch behind it, his gaze following me as I approach.

When I see what rests on the velvet cushion inside the case, I gasp. "Is that . . . ?" I look up at the guard.

He nods curtly.

Sea silk.

Harvested from a special clam by only a handful of people who know the secret of its location, sea silk is the rarest and most expensive thread in existence.

Lachlan catches me staring at the sea silk and issues a flat "*No.*"

I sigh as he pulls me back to the front of the shop.

The attendants have lined up five threadkits, each one made of shining wood and gilded with silver or gold. Ranging in size, each wooden box is fitted with small compartments, pegs, and grooves to store all the Weaving essentials. Their straps come in leather, hemp, or braided wool. They are stunning, each probably costing as much as a horse. I touch them all, exploring their compartments and features, but finally take my own kit into my hands and shake my head.

"I've had this since I was eight," I say. "It's like an old friend."

My threadkit is nothing special. It's sturdy but cheap oak with more scratches and nicks in it than an alley cat. Every girl who ended up at the Perkins Charity School was given one just like it. Those years had been difficult, with too little food shared among too many girls; teachers like Sister Agatha, who corrected mistakes with hickory switches; long, miserable hours spent in solitary confinement for speaking out of turn. But the threadkit was the first thing that had become *mine* after I left my aunt's house, and it has never failed me.

"Oh, come," Lachlan scoffs. "It looks like it was dragged behind a carriage."

I smile and shake my head, unwilling to budge.

He sighs at last. "Very well. But at least make sure you have an ample supply of materials inside."

In that, I have no trouble availing myself of his purse.

I order more thread than I could possibly Weave in five years. Waxed cotton in four different shades and several worsted spools. A skein of twine, a ball of beeswax linen, flourishing thread, ecru twisted silk, coarse Shrewsbury, a range of crewels, and a dozen spools of standard ounce-thread, not far removed from the stuff we wove in school, but of a higher quality. The attendant tells me it was made by nuns in Flanders who pray ceaselessly to the Fates as they spin, and it is the most coveted of its kind in all the world.

To the threads I add bobbins, bodkins, and twenty different types of needles, from darners to long-eyed sharps to Whitechapels, and a cushion of Naxos emery with which to sharpen them. Last to go in is a pretty thimble of shining brass.

I watch with dazed wonder as the attendants pack the whole lot into my battered threadkit. My fingertips prickle with the need to rifle through it all, to run each thread through my fingers and feel the potential magics it could hold. I hover until the clasp is latched, then clutch the kit to my breast as if its contents might suddenly realize how unworthy I am and vanish like melting snow.

In the coach once more, Lachlan sits across from me and shakes his head.

"Mortals," he mutters. "I do believe you just swindled me out of a small fortune. You couldn't possibly need a *tenth* of what you bought to complete my favor."

With him, even string comes with strings attached.

"What now?" I ask.

He stares out the window, his gaze a thousand leagues away.

"Now," he murmurs, "we go to Scotland."

45

CHAPTER FIVE

Three days later, after spending far too much time cramped in a coach with nothing to do but embroider spells, I find myself on the moors of Scotland, a north wind dragging at my hair. Before me slumps the ruined remains of some ancient castle, green with moss. The road ends here, a narrow track overgrown with weeds. Lachlan's procession of coaches, carts, and wagons is still trickling in, and fae emerge from them blinking and stretching and shaking themselves. I am the only mortal in the company, a fact I have felt keenly every moment, like a mouse among wolves.

With the exception of the castle, the landscape is empty to the horizon. A few stalwart copses of yew and ash twist here and there, but by and large, all is dismal gray. Snow spreads in a scant layer, broken by jagged twists of heather and grass that bristle over the hills.

"The last functioning doorway to the world of the fae is . . . *here*, in the middle of all this nothing?" I ask.

Lachlan's whisper in my ear makes me jump; I had not heard him step close. "Only a fool looks at this place and sees nothing. You are no fool. Look again."

I sigh at him, but when he walks away, I squint and study the ruins.

The castle is in dreadful condition, a remnant of the Middle Ages, scored by age and weather. Stone walls sag and crack, and moss has so overgrown it that entire portions have been swallowed entirely, giving the structure the appearance of a ship sinking into the mire. On the northern wall of what must have once been the great main chamber, the outlines of arched windows remain. Everything is soaked through; rain battered our line of coaches the length of the journey from London, and I'd been looking forward to a bit of warmth and dryness. No such luck, me. Even the stones squelch.

"Wait a moment . . ." I go to the nearest wall and trace a pattern carved into the stone, so worn away by time only parts of it are still visible. But I recognize them all the same. "It's knotwork."

"Moorwitch knotwork," says Lachlan. "This castle was built by the very first Weavers in Britain."

"Oh," I breathe, looking around with heightened interest. I think of a leather-bound book musty with age, its yellowed pages crinkling under my hands and whispering ancient, forbidden magic; a spell to summon immortals. The famous moorwitches' power exceeded anything the Order of the Moirai can Weave nowadays, if the old stories are true. It was the moorwitches who repelled the Romans in their first invasion, and after them, the fierce Norsemen. But not long later, they vanished entirely and without explanation, taking with them a wealth of Weaving knowledge and history. The Order rose to power after that, taking over all magical affairs, and the moorwitches faded into myth.

While I explore the place, noting more instances of old carved spells, Lachlan's faerie troupe set about erecting canvas tents in the heart of the ruins. They abandoned their human glamours the second day into our journey, when we'd left behind the Great North Road with all its bustle and turned onto the narrow, overgrown track which had taken us through wilder and wilder countryside and eventually led us here.

Though they dress in human garb, the other fae are somehow less human than Lachlan, their ears more sharply pointed, their limbs longer and gaits more loping. They move as I'd imagine uprooted trees might, swaying a great deal. Their eyes are large and luminous like cats' eyes, but nearly entirely blackened by their pupils. I think Lachlan is something different than they are, some other sort of faerie, but I cannot begin to imagine what. I haven't yet worked up the nerve to ask.

"Where is the doorway to Elfhame?" I ask Lachlan. "I've searched the entire ruins and seen nothing."

"If only it were as simple as that," he says. "No, this is merely to be our camp for the next few weeks. Now come, and I will show you where the doorway stands."

Well, a walk will do me good after three days cramped in a coach, squeezed between two fae who hissed whenever I fidgeted too much. Securing my threadkit over my shoulder and my new bonnet atop my head, I nod.

Lachlan leads me down a stone stair of dubious integrity and then out of the ruins altogether, past the boundary wall that's half sunk into the mud and moss.

Soon I am panting. "Is it far, this thing you want to show me?"

"Why? Are your feeble human legs—?"

"Call me *feeble* one more time, and I will walk back to London myself, vow be damned."

He chuckles, which surprises me. It's a human sound, and I wonder if it's something he picked up in his centuries-long furlough in England. Or, rather, the "World Above," as he calls it, often with a disdainful curl of his lip.

Lachlan wears a tailcoat and breeches still, but every day since London, he's produced a bit more *frill*. Lace at his cuffs and throat. Sapphires in his ears. Gemstones appearing on his silver rings. The others have adopted similar attire, with a particular penchant for the gaudy and bright. They remind me of magpies, hoarding all things sparkly. Only on Lachlan do these accoutrements actually look stylish. He seems like the sort who might walk into a room wearing a ridiculous crystal-beaded cape, and a week later, every highborn young man in London would have one.

As I hasten to keep up with his long strides, I pinch myself to be sure I am here, with the silver faerie I summoned when I was a child, on a quest stolen straight out of a storybook, tramping over frozen heather.

Impulsive, I think. *My second fault.* Agreeing to mad things before I've half thought them through. Old Sister Elizabeth would be shaking her head at me now and saying that's what comes from too many daydreams and not enough prayers.

Finally, pressing a hand to a stitch in my side, I catch up with Lachlan atop another hill. The ruins have grown small enough behind us that I can hide it behind the pad of my thumb.

But it is forward I now look, and I let a long, frosty breath curl from my lips.

There is civilization here, after all: a little village tucked into the moors, quaint as a picture. Whitewashed cob houses with smoking chimneys, a square lined with shops, pens bustling with sheep. I spy a few people moving about, no more than specks at this distance. The land between us and the village sweeps away at a slope; we are quite high above it, with a panoramic view of the moors on either side. North of the village spreads a forest, trees flowing around the bare hilltops and rock crags like a dark river.

"Blackswire," says Lachlan. "A place of no note whatsoever, excepting that somewhere near it, the last door to Elfhame stands."

"It's so *common.*"

"Appearances are deceiving," says Lachlan. "For example, one might look at *you* and see only a poor charity-school teacher."

I glance at him, my lips tightening. "I am not ashamed of my position, Sir Faerie."

"But *I* look at you," he goes on, "and I see a woman who ought to be Weaving charmed lace for queens and battle cloaks for kings. As you shall, once your debt to me has been paid. The world is about to change in mighty ways, and Weavers of great skill will be needed as never before."

Though I can't fathom what he means by that, my cheeks warm a little. I have no desire to Weave royal lace or battle cloaks. I love teaching, and I love my students. Not that I expect him to understand that. And I do not love the way he looks at me down the length of his nose, as if I am a pet whose leash he is proud to hold. To change the subject, I ask, "This is where the moorwitches were from, then?"

"Aye, many were from this region, and many came to it, for this is where they passed in and out of Elfhame to learn their craft. There were once doors to the World Below open all across these moors. Only one now remains functional."

"Were you there then, during the time of the moorwitches?" I stare at him, suddenly wondering how grossly I've underestimated his age. After our travels, I'd begun to almost see him as human, or at least, not very *in*human. But that sense of familiarity evaporates, leaving me feeling small and uncertain beside his vast history and experience.

"I remember them," he says. "Wild, fearless women hungry for magic, leading their tribes like wolves with their pack. They came to us with offerings, with carved stone, with bears' teeth, with bronze amulets and rare jewels, to pay for the knowledge we imparted."

"What went wrong between your people and mine?" I ask. "Why did we stop visiting Elfhame and learning magic from the fae?"

The old stories I grew up hearing never spoke of this. The fae were rumored to have once walked our lands and shared their knowledge of magic with mortals, but the details of their vanishing are vague. The immortal folk seem to have faded like old ink into the pages of history.

He shifts, his gaze wandering. "Your world began to change, and my people would not change with it. The moorwitches faded into history, and a new breed of humans arose—ones who loved order and iron and their foreign gods, and there was not room for us. So we diminished and withdrew into the World Below." His lip curls. "Like rats in a warren."

I wait, but he seems determined to say nothing more on the matter. "So, where is the doorway, then?"

"Alas, I cannot take you any closer than this."

He lifts a hand and prods the air, and a ripple of sparking light spreads at his touch. The glow shimmers across the hilltop into the sky before fading again, with a soft sound like glass wind chimes. Lachlan inhales sharply, withdrawing his hand, his fingertip smoking slightly.

"A ward," I breathe. "I've never seen one so large before. It must be *enormous.*"

"It surrounds the village, the countryside around it, and a few nearby estates. Several hundred thousand acres all told."

My hand goes to my threadkit.

"I could not undo such a ward from the outside," I say slowly. "My skills—"

"You needn't undo it, Rose. At least, not yet. The ward is not for you."

Before I can stop him, he grabs my wrist and lifts my hand toward the ward. I brace myself, stomach clenching as I expect the sharp sting—but it never comes. My hand passes easily through the air which denied his a moment ago.

"It's only for fae," he says.

I snatch my hand from his, rubbing my wrist where I can still feel the icy sting of his fingertips. "I don't understand. If it is meant to guard the doorway, why keep out your own kind?"

His blue eyes glitter coldly at the rooftops of Blackswire. "As I told you before, not everyone in Elfhame would welcome my return." He turns to look at me, his gaze softening. "Truly, I only wish to go home. I am weary and fading in this iron world."

I stare at him as the wind rises over the moors and sweeps at my skirts. "Why did you leave?"

He ignores my query. "I'll tell you where to find the door, but it will likely be hidden behind layers of spellwork. You will also be required to find the spell to *unlock* it. In the meantime, you will report back to me every three days. I want to know who you've spoken to, where you've gone, what you've seen."

"Oh, is that all? You aren't interested in what I had for breakfast or how many times I pricked my thumb with my needle? And how am I to return to you every three days, on foot? Blackswire is at least a two-hour walk from here."

"Ah." He gives me a sly smile. "That is where the Telarii shall aid us, though it cost me your weight in gold. Come, little witch, and I will show you grand magic indeed."

CHAPTER SIX

The road I follow through the wood that afternoon is dark and muddy, enclosed by a tunnel of intertwining branches. I pull my shawl tight and press on, carrying a valise in each hand, with my threadkit slung over my shoulder so that it knocks awkwardly against my thigh with every other step.

At least I am finally alone. No more faeries to hiss at me or pull my hair or look at me as if I might be tasty with a bit of gravy. Lachlan gave me two valises—one with my new clothes inside, the other bearing the precious spell bought at terrible expense from the Telarii—some final instructions and advice, and a manufactured tale to explain my presence. I've been walking for an hour now, approaching the village of Blackswire through its northern wooded border.

I review my predicament as I walk.

My birthday is in a little more than three weeks. In that time, I need to find the doorway to Elfhame, discover the spell to unlock it, sneak in, steal a branch, sneak out, and return to Lachlan. And to do all *that*, I must first find someplace to stay in the village of Blackswire. Perhaps there is an elderly widow who could use a pair of helpful hands in exchange for a bed, or a farmer in need of some tracking spells for his wandering sheep. I have some money from Lachlan to pay for room and board, but my pride smarts at taking further charity from him. Even if I *am* here on his business, I am not without my own resources.

Doubt and dread are twin devils dogging my steps, mocking me from the shadows. I know my task will not be as simple as *find the doorway and steal the branch*, and I suspect there is much Lachlan has not told me. But the occasional twinge of pain in my heart drives me forward like a cattle prod—as does the tantalizing hope of success.

If I can restore my magic fully, I can return home sooner. I won't need an entire year to rest. I could be back in my classroom by the month's end.

Lachlan gave me directions to find the Elfhame doorway, but they had been vague and will no doubt require some exploration. I consider forgoing my cover story and simply making inquiries in Blackswire— *Pardon, but have any of you ever come across a gate to faerie?*—but Lachlan explicitly forbade me from mentioning my quest to anyone. He'd warned that there might well be fae hidden about, ones hostile to him, and that if they knew I was looking for the doorway, I would soon find myself suffering some fatal "accident."

"What did you do," I'd asked, alarmed, "to incite so many enemies among your own kind?"

He'd grinned and replied, "Perhaps I killed and devoured too many snooping mortal maids."

Shuddering, I shake away his words, press on, and think how different this place is than London.

Beyond the clean air and emptiness, there is a deeper, more essential difference that fills me with nervous excitement. In London, nearly all the green things have been tamed and pruned, shrubbery trimmed into hedgerows, gardens walled, trees cut to make way for new buildings. But here, energy flows unbounded, a roar compared to the whisper I grew up hearing. The plants grow wild, a vast tangle of clattering limbs and evergreen needles. And though the wood is dormant for winter, it takes only the slightest nudge of my sixth sense, and life awakens around me like ripples spreading over a still pool.

Old magic shivers beneath the ground. Wild energy, the life of the moors, washes over me like a dash of cold water, tugging at my senses.

Power babbles in the deep roots, in drops from the tangled branches overhead. It curls in the dormant wood, and I feel as if a hundred unseen eyes are watching me from the shadowed depths of the skeletal winter trees.

For a moment, I shut my eyes and let my mind relax, opening the channels through my body so that I might feel this place better. Perhaps I can even sense the doorway to Elfhame itself, if it is close.

The magic rushes in, wild and green and whispering. It fills me up until my fingertips tingle and my hair follicles prickle. It pools on my tongue, a burst of crisp, cool flavor. Down to my very bones it seeps, like my entire body has been frosted over.

I channel too long. My heart squeezes in reproach, a sudden splinter of pain which shocks me back to my senses.

With a little gasp, I pull out a spool and unwind a length of thread, fingers Weaving a quick wind knot to release the magic into. Around me, leaves and branches sway in the release of a controlled gust that pours from me, magic turned to air. Energy returning to the earth. The wind rolls through the trees, clattering branches like a pack of elemental wolves, snarling and quick.

I hear a sudden whinny, as from a frightened horse, and a cry of pain around the bend. A very *human* cry.

Dropping my valise, I hurry ahead, lifting my skirt to free my steps.

Around the curve in the road, I come upon a scene of chaos: a horse on its hind legs, nostrils wide with panic, its saddle askew and reins swinging free. A large black dog is barking and leaping about as if possessed. And in the ditch lies a young man, unmoving.

"Easy!" I shout, running forward and Weaving before I half have a chance to think. I dart between horse and fallen rider, raising a cat's cradle between my hands and channeling fast.

Fates be thanked; the calming knot works at once. The horse drops and snorts, its head lowering. I keep the Weave raised until the thread flakes into ash, and by then, the horse is standing still, breathing easily. The dog whines at me.

I turn to the young man in the ditch and find him limp on his stomach, eyes shut but, thank the Fates, breathing.

To my relief, he is entirely human. He must be in his mid-twenties, olive-skinned, with dark brows and full lips, facial bones rigid over shadowed cheeks. His ancestors might be Italian or Spanish, or hail from even further east—the Ottoman Empire or Persia. Raven-black hair hangs low over his forehead and curls slightly over his ears. His cheeks are rough, not quite bearded but in need of a shave. It is a handsome face, if a little stern and mud spattered; I study it curiously, breath held, moving a hank of hair to inspect a fresh cut on his temple. It doesn't look too deep.

He's dressed in riding clothes—wool tartan scarf, white shirt, and olive vest, with a heavy coat muddy from his fall. There is a short sgian-dubh sheathed in his right boot, its pale staghorn handle carved into the head of a raven.

His dog bounds forward and begins licking his ear, and it's then I see the blood matted in his hair, where he must have struck his head when he pitched off the horse. He is no doubt concussed.

"Oh, fiddle and Fates!" I shoo the dog off him, then rub my temples. "Now what?"

I suspect it was my spell which startled his horse and knocked him from his seat. I cannot leave him lying in the mud with a concussion, especially since it looks as if it'll start raining any moment.

"This is a fine mess, Rose," I mutter, as I unspool more thread.

With grunts of effort, I manage to roll the stranger onto his back. There is mud smeared over the side of his face, and his dark lashes flutter softly on his cheeks. I wait to see if he will wake, but he doesn't. His mouth is parted just enough to show a glint of his teeth, and his breath is a warm cloud over his lips.

I pull the needle from my bonnet and begin to sew lightening spells into his coat and trousers. In the mud and damp and dim light, this is no easy task. His dog hovers at my shoulder, as if suspicious I might be up to no good.

"You're lucky it wasn't my old classmate Margaret Appleby who found you," I mutter to the man. "She was a dreadful sewer. You'd be full of holes by now."

I blush when I begin working on the fabric against his thigh, careful to slide the needle so it doesn't stab his leg. Thank the Fates he's unconscious. I've never put a hand on a man's thigh before, much less had to be so keenly aware of his skin and my fingers. By the time the embroidery is complete, my face is as hot as a London street in summer. I am much relieved when I can move on to his sleeves and lapels. When I am done, he looks rather like a spider has been spinning over his clothes.

My heart aches from the effort of channeling into all the little Weaves. Twice the magic fails, and I have to sit and breathe for several long minutes before I am ready to try again. But when I do reach for it, it comes whispering out of the trees and moss and the dormant ferns nestled under the loam, waiting for spring. Fates, the magic is strong here.

When I finally attempt to lift the man, he is easy enough to carry, no heavier than my valises. Those I tie with hovering charms, then I loop their handles on a string tethered around my wrist, so that they float along behind me.

"I don't suppose you'll be any help?" I say to the horse.

No, the creature has fallen asleep; my calming charm worked *too* well. And frankly, I'm a bit terrified of it. I've seen more than one poor waif trampled beneath the carriage horses before. I eye the sideways saddle, then decide to let the horse find its own way home.

How far am I from Blackswire? I should be able to carry the stranger there myself. But I'd better hurry; the lightening spells will burn through soon.

I hoist the man over my left shoulder like a sack of onions and set off, my valises floating behind me, my threadkit thumping against my hip. The dog trots at my side, tongue lolling.

The wood is getting darker by the minute, and colder too. Mud turns to ice, and my panting breaths coil away in pale wisps. At least the effort of carrying the man is keeping most of me warm, but I'm starting to lose the feeling in my toes.

When the woods break twenty minutes later, I find not Blackswire waiting, but a manor house on a hill. My knees are beginning to shake, and the first of the lightening spells is turning to ash. I pause to hoist the man higher on my shoulder, breathing hard.

Heathered hills undulate beneath the mist, broken by the occasional jut of rock, like the bones of long-fallen giants, drenched in pale moss and snow. A few pools, silver-skinned with ice, twinkle in low pockets of land. The sky here is a vast granite expanse, heavy with dark clouds. I inhale deeply; the air tastes of water and moss and crisp northern wind.

The manor atop the hill cuts a severe silhouette against the pale sky, not quite a house, not quite a castle, but something in between. Peaked roofs are lifted by wrought iron corbels, and snarling gargoyles stand watch at every corner, stone claws curled over the eaves.

The entire structure seems to scowl at me. It looks as if it were abandoned years ago, but then I spy smoke wafting from one chimney. There is no other structure in sight, nor any sign of the village.

"Right," I murmur. "Ominous manor it is, then."

A splash of water lands on my cheek, and I glance up just as the clouds release a steady rain. That decides it, and I start forward. The dog bounds ahead, stopping every now and again to give me a goading bark.

The young man is getting heavier as more of the lightening spells disintegrate. I press on, trying to keep a grip on him, back and shoulders aching.

"This is really," I pant, pausing yet again to adjust for his increasing weight, "*not* where I imagined I would find myself a week ago. Hold on, sir, nearly there."

When I finally reach the main doors, my legs buckle, and I land hard on my knees. The man goes sprawling, so covered with mud now

I doubt his own mother would know him. The dog whines and noses his hand, then gives me a reproachful look.

"What?" I growl. "It's not as though *you* were any help."

I check the back of the stranger's head—not bleeding, thank the Fates. But he is dangerously pale.

Breathing hard, I glance at the relief carved into the doors' wooden faces: a great raven, wings spread, feathers remarkably detailed. I don't have the strength to stand, so I reach out and knock at the mud-splattered lower corner.

At once, as if someone was waiting there all along, one of the doors opens.

Behind it stands a girl of ten or eleven, with large green eyes and a shocking amount of black curls, springing every which way. A black cape billows behind her, knitting needles hang from a string around her neck, and an eye has been drawn with what looks like soot in the center of her forehead. There is a healthy flush in her cheeks and an intelligent spark to her eye that tells of mischief. The dog leaps up, plants his paws on her shoulders, and gives her cheek a great, sloppy lick. The girl laughs, shoving him off, then blinks at me.

"Hello there," I say, feeling lightheaded from the ache of carrying an unconscious Scot for miles through a cold woodland. "Might you have any idea who this fellow is?"

The girl squints at the young man slumped in a mud puddle, the last of my Weaves flaking to ash on his clothes, blood still wet in his hair. He groans, his lashes fluttering slightly as rain runs over his face.

"Oh, aye," the girl says. "That's my brother, Connie. He's the laird of Ravensgate. I'm Sylvie. Would you like a cup of tea?"

CHAPTER SEVEN

I am installed in the kitchen by the housekeeper of the manor, an apple-cheeked and pepper-haired Scotswoman named Mrs. MacDougal. Seated on a hard chair by a roaring fireplace, with a cup of tea and a tartan wool blanket, this is as warm as I've been in months. Even here, in the lowest floor of the house, I can hear the rain and wind battering the walls.

Sylvie and I had managed to drag Conrad North, laird of Ravensgate, through the front door before the housekeeper had found us and let out a shriek. Then an old man with a crinkled face and a beard to rival a goat's—*Mr.* MacDougal, I'd assumed—had come stomping in to scoop the laird up and haul him upstairs. I have not seen him since.

In what I've seen of the house, I've got the impression that it has been largely left to cobwebs, with furniture covered by oilcloth, closed doors, ticking clocks, and a general air of ruin and abandonment. But the kitchen is tidy as a pin and warm. Dried herbs hanging on rafters above my head fill the room with the rich scent of thyme, rosemary, and mint.

Mrs. MacDougal is off tending to the injured laird, which leaves me with the little girl for company. I have seen no sign of any other residents, either family or staff. Mr. MacDougal was sent to gather the horse I left sleeping on the road. I pity the man, out in this storm, and hope the lightning now crashing outside hasn't sent the animal bolting into the wood.

Sylvie North sits on the hearth with her chin resting on her hands and her bright eyes fixed on my face. Her gaze has not left me since she opened the door; her brother's injury hardly seemed of interest to her. It makes me wonder in what sort of condition he often turns up.

"London!" Sylvie exclaims. "I wish *I* were from London. I haven't been anyplace at all. Did you go to school? Are you friends with the queen?"

For the last ten minutes, she has peppered me with an endless stream of questions, moving from place to place like a vibrating hummingbird, chair to table to hearth to floor. The dog, Captain, bounds wherever she goes and lays his shaggy black head on her lap so she can scratch his ears.

"I hope your brother is all right," I say. "Are your parents at home?"

She waves a dismissive hand, making the knitting needles around her neck clatter. "It's just me and Connie. No parents. And he's hit his head harder than that before."

My eyebrows lift. "Has he?"

"Once, he fell off the stable roof. Broke his arm and his nose."

"What on earth was he doing on the roof?"

She grins. "Trying to fetch me down."

I find myself not doubting a word of it. The girl hasn't stopped fidgeting since I met her.

"What's that?" she asks, nodding at my threadkit.

I open it to reveal the gleaming new spools inside. "Well, it's my—"

I'm interrupted by an earsplitting squeal from Sylvie North. "You're a Weaver!"

"Yes, I thought I might craft a pain-relieving spell for your—"

"Show me some magic!" Sylvie claps her hands together. "Make time stand still. Or—I know!—make it snow indoors! Can you turn me into a wee falcon? I've always wished I were a falcon."

"Sylvie North!" The commanding Scottish voice comes from our left, and I turn to see Mrs. MacDougal approaching at a vigorous pace. "Leave our guest be."

"I told you, I'm not Sylvie," Sylvie says. "I am a harpy, Weaving entrails on my loom, with human heads as my weights and their bones as my needles!"

"Miss Pryor," says the harried housekeeper, "you must excuse our resident harpy. Last week she was the Egyptian goddess of death, and the week before that she was Elaine of someplace or other—"

"*Astolat*," Sylvie corrects her. "I was Elaine of Astolat, languishing for love of Lancelot." She spins around, her needle necklace clacking. "I collect frogs. Would you like to see them, Rose Pryor of London? I have twenty-eight. Well, twenty-seven. Dionysus has escaped."

"Not again," groans Mrs. MacDougal. "If I find that beastie in my bed again, he'll be in the pot for supper. Now go and sit with your brother. He is awake, but we must keep watch until we are sure the damage isn't worse than it seems."

Sylvie casts a wistful look at my spools. "But—"

"*Now*, lassie!" Mrs. MacDougal's voice brooks no argument.

With a groan, the girl trudges away, her gaze lingering on my threadkit until she has left the kitchen.

Mrs. MacDougal sighs. "Aye, that's our Sylvie, our wee summer squall. She has a way of getting underfoot."

I smile, thinking of my students back home. "She seems like a bright little thing."

She turns to me, her eyes narrowing, and I instinctively sit up straighter. Mrs. MacDougal reminds me a bit of my old teacher Sister Elizabeth, who also had that way of looking at me as if she suspected I'd spit in her tea.

"So you're a witch, then?" she says.

I stiffen. "*Weaver*, madam, is the correct term. *Witch* is an old word and was not always used kindly."

She flaps her hand. "Aye, I forgot how you modern types are. You are quite young, aren't you? And pretty." She says this the way a cook might call a carrot *scraggly*. "Well, I suppose it's fortunate you found our Mr. North after his horse threw him."

"Oh, he . . . told you what happened, then?"

"He said the storm spooked Bell, though I've never known the horse to jump at the wind before."

I smile weakly. "I do know many pain-relieving charms—"

"I think that as long as you are with us," Mrs. MacDougal replies, "it would be best to keep your spools in their box."

"Oh." I blink. "Well, of course, it is your house."

"It is Mr. North's house," she corrects me. "And he is particular about the . . . activities performed inside it."

Meaning he is no lover of magic. I've known people like that, who saw magic as perverted or wicked, even though the majority of society accepts it as useful. Even Queen Victoria is trained in it and keeps a host of Weavers at her beck and call. I tense, feeling protests rise in my throat, but I swallow them and feel a bit less sorry about knocking the laird of Ravensgate off his horse and onto his arse. So much for asking if I might Weave some household spellknots for them in exchange for room and board. "I suppose once the rain has stopped, I shall be on my way to Blackswire. Is it much further down the road?"

"An hour's walk," she says. Then her expression softens a little. "But I suppose we ought to feed you and set up a room for the night. It's dark now, and rain or no, I cannot send you out in the cold."

The moment I try to fall asleep, Ravensgate seems to awaken, creaking and groaning like an old woman with a secret she is dying to share. A hard rain patters against the windowpanes.

The guest room Mrs. MacDougal arranged for me is very much like the one I had in my aunt's house. The four-poster bed is too large and high, requiring steps to reach its top, and the walls are the same crimson as my uncle's old study. Rolling restlessly, I try to drown out the howl of the moor wind with a cashmere pillow embroidered with little leaping foxes. Its gold fringe tickles my neck.

The rain slows to a gentle patter, then stops altogether. Night deepens until the tall pendulum clock in the corner ticks an hour past midnight with its ornately scrolled hands.

Then something scratches at my door.

I bolt upright and light my bedside candle with a quick fire knot, momentarily forgetting I'd been ordered not to Weave within this house. My hair is down and wild around my shoulders, unruly brown curls relaxing after being bound tightly all day.

"Who's there?" I call softly.

There comes another scratch, followed by a soft whine.

With a sigh of relief, I push out of bed and find a pair of silk slippers in the corner; they're patterned in what must be the North tartan, green stripes on blue with threads of yellow and red. Shuffling across the cold floorboards, I open the door, and there is the black dog, his nose snuffing at the carpet. He bounds up when he sees me and issues a happy bark.

"Hush!" I scold, crouching to tap my finger on his muzzle. "What are you after, then? Shouldn't you be sleeping by your master's bed?"

He slaps his great wet tongue on my hand. Stifling a laugh, I push him away, and he finally goes, padding quietly down the carpeted corridor.

I start to close my door again, then stop.

The hallway bends away to the right and left, draped in soft shadows. The floorboards beneath my feet groan as I lean forward to peer into the gloom, and on the walls, oil paintings gleam with the light of my candle; I glimpse the arch of a horse's neck, a leaping fox, a frowning woman in stiff clothes and a high wig.

"Is that . . . ?" I murmur.

I step across the hallway and take a closer look. The woman in the painting frowns at me, clutching a fan to her breast as if askance at my curiosity. She is draped in a tartan arasaid that matches my slippers, pinned at her breast with a raven brooch. The style of her gown dates her as being perhaps two hundred years old. I press my finger to the painting, feeling the coarse brushstrokes beneath the fading varnish, and, squinting, make out the little box beneath the woman's other hand.

"Is that a threadkit, madam?" I whisper. "Were you a Weaver?"

She glowers reproachfully, and I find the answer hidden in the delicate strokes of red paint around her bodice—unmistakably some sort of embroidered charm.

"How very curious," I murmur, stepping back. "No magic in Ravensgate, indeed."

I glance down the hallway, in the direction the dog had gone, my heart thumping and all hope of sleep banished. More paintings beckon in the darkness, my candle's flame reflecting on their red walnut and silver frames.

It couldn't hurt, perhaps, to have a *bit* of a snoop.

Nosiness is, after all, my third fault.

I snatch the candle from my bedside and slip down the hall. I worked out that Sylvie and Mr. North sleep one floor above, and the MacDougals a floor below, so I don't fear waking them. Even so, I go quietly, feeling like a spirit in a ruin. I creep past austere portraits, the eyes of North ancestors boring into my back, and suits of armor that glint in the light of my candle. None of them hold threadkits or spools, though I find one little portrait of a woman at a spinning wheel. There's no telling whether the thread she spun was meant for spells or for simple cloth.

Most of what I pass is covered, shapes of furniture spectral as they loom up out of the shadows, set in motion by the dancing light of my candle. Ordinary objects become fiendish in that light, as if I have entered the realm of demons. I am Dante descending, thrilled by my own terror. Spiders spin in every corner, their pale webs rippling slightly; a cold draft of air is blowing from somewhere ahead. I have the sense of walking downward, delving deeper into a tomb that's lain untouched for centuries.

At a narrow window, I pause to adjust my slippers, my eyes wandering over the dark moors. Silky clouds flow across the moon, dimming its light and casting strange shadows over the rolling hills. Pale, watery mists creep in the low valleys.

There is someone out there.

I peer harder at a glimmer of movement, a wisp like shifting moonlight. Is it a woman? For a moment, I am sure of it—there is a woman walking on the moor, ghostly white and illuminated by the moon.

But then I blink, and she is gone. Where the "woman" had been, I see only mist breaking around a craggy rock.

Unsettled, I turn, thinking it's high time I went back to my room. But then I see a door hanging open, not three steps ahead.

I chew my lip a moment, then curse under my breath and go in, unable to resist.

The room is vast, six of my bedrooms put together. Large beams lift up a vaulting roof, so high and grand it puts me in mind of the great Westminster Abbey, where shuttles of the looms whir as my Moirene sisters spin their prayers to the Fates. On the far end of the room, a round window looks out to the darkling moors and a pale, round moon floating on fragments of cloud.

Bookcases brace the walls, all of them near to bursting with books upon books upon books, two stories of them, with the upper balcony accessible by a winding iron staircase in the far corner of the room. A thrill runs through me at the sight, and I creep along the carpet, moving through beams of diffused moonlight.

There are other items stored on the shelves—a wooden comb with a wolf carved on the handle, a spyglass, a set of fossils, a heavy bronze fox, a framed map of the estate—but it's the books that command my attention.

Among them I find histories, encyclopedias, poetry, and essays and books of law and agriculture. Whoever stocked this room had an eclectic taste, and an educated one. I see volumes in French and German and Latin, and even a few in some languages I don't recognize at all, in script I cannot read. It reminds me of my uncle's library, though his collection was only a fragment of this one.

I finally stop in front of a shelf lined with leather books, some so faded I can't make out the names printed on the spines, and raise my candle. Those I can read make my skin prickle: Spenser's *The Faerie Queene*, King James I's *Daemonologie*, Sowerby's *A History of Magic*. Beside them is a whole set of Shakespeare in slender leather-bound volumes, jumbled together with loose papers and journals. Seeing an estate map among them, I start to reach for it, but the moment my finger touches the paper, a soft male brogue speaks behind me: "If you mean to thieve, you might start with something a wee bit more valuable than those old things."

I start so violently that the candle falls from my hand. The flame flicks out, throwing the library into darkness. I can hear the hot wax spill across the floor, and the candle clatters as it rolls.

Then another light blossoms not ten paces away—at first I think it's magic, but then I see the match between Mr. North's fingers. He holds it to another candle by the chair he's seated in, and its light flickers over the library.

I stare, my voice frozen in my throat. He's watching me with a bemused expression, his head bandaged and his injured leg propped on a footstool. On the table by him lies his sgian-dubh, beside a pile of wood shavings and a half-carved wolf. The dog, Captain, is lying on the floor at his feet and gives his tail a great thump, as if we'd only just met and he weren't half responsible for luring me down here in the first place.

"M-Mr. North," I stammer. "I apologize, I was just—"

"Snooping?" he offers.

"I . . . well, I suppose so." Intensely conscious of the fact I'm wearing only a thin nightgown and shawl in front of the laird, I nevertheless raise my chin; he *could* have spoken up the moment I entered the room instead of letting me make a fool of myself. "I did not know you were here."

"Clearly. You're Rose Pryor, I take it?" His Scots tongue rolls my name like a peel of oak beneath a whittling knife. "And do you often go about prowling through the personal effects of your hosts, creeping like a wraith in the night?"

My face heats. "I couldn't sleep. Your dog was scratching at my door."

Captain lifts his head and gives me a betrayed look.

"How are you feeling, m'lord?" I ask, to change the subject.

"You needn't call me that. I am no nobleman, just a country landowner. And I am feeling well. In fact, remarkably well. *Unnaturally* well. One might almost imagine it were . . ." He frowns, then fumbles with his clothes until he finds an item in his pocket which he now pulls out and dangles in the air: a lacy handkerchief, embroidered with a healing spell. "Magic," he finishes, the word sounding very much like an accusation.

I take back the kerchief I'd stuffed into his pocket on the road, wadding it into my fist as if it were something shameful, though it was in fact a neat bit of spellwork. "It was the least I could do."

"'Tis my pride that suffered the most, I assure you, despite your best efforts. I know a spell when I see it, and the wind which spooked my horse was no ordinary wind."

"Ah" is all I can manage to say. Plainly he is not the bumpkin I'd half hoped he would be. "All right, it was me. But in truth, I had no idea you were on the road. It was an accident."

"Hm." He looks as if he only half believes me. "Well, I should like to know more about my guest with a knack for magic, and how she came to be traveling alone in my wood, and why she should be nosing about my manor at this Fateless hour. Sit." He nods at an armchair by the hearth, upholstered in a fanciful toile de Jouy of knights and castles.

Once I've perched myself there, he settles back in his chair, taking up the sgian-dubh and the wolf. His thumb guides the blade over the wood, skillfully peeling it away in thin, fine curls. His fingers are as long and graceful as any Weaver's, his nails trimmed and clean. Every subtle movement makes the muscular tendons along the backs of his hands tighten like the warp threads on a loom.

"Mrs. MacDougal told me you're in Blackswire on business," he says, startling me from my thoughts. Heat flushes up my neck as I realize how long I've been staring at his hands.

"I'm awaiting my employer," I recite, falling back on the story Lachlan had concocted for me and hoping he cannot see my blush. "He is a cloth merchant, come to buy wool. But he took ill on the road and is convalescing at an inn some distance from here. He sent me ahead to wait for him, and my hired coach deposited me not far from your estate."

Lachlan will remain "ill" for several days or even weeks, of course, until I've found Elfhame and returned with his prize.

Or until I turn twenty-one and feel the magic dim from my bones for good.

"And how long have you worked for this thread merchant?" asks Mr. North.

"Not long, since I left my teaching position at the Perkins Charity School in Westminster."

"You were a teacher of magic." His eyes lock on mine as he speaks, and he gently blows upon his wolf to clear away the fresh shavings. They glitter in the air, a few specks clinging to his lower lip. He brushes them away with a slow swipe of his thumb, not once taking his eyes from mine. "I'd have thought you of some higher position, judging by those wards. Did you sew them yourself?"

His glance has settled on my sleeves. I pull at them self-consciously, surprised he noticed the embroidery winding up to my elbows. Most people don't; the thread matches the fabric and the stitches are tiny. The patterns are sewn all over my clothes, around the hems and neckline, tucked into the seams, worked into my stockings and petticoat. There is even a little spell woven into the lining of my bonnet, which is still drying by the hearth in the kitchen. I sewed them in the jolting, crowded coach I rode here in, with much silent cursing at the fae who'd been pressed against me, hindering my elbow movement.

The spells are wards, indeed; most of them repel physical attacks, some discourage enmity. There are also some illusion charms to make me appear slightly taller and stronger. The difference is so subtle no one would notice unless they were listening and watching very carefully. But since I've woven the same embroidery into pretty much all my clothing, they'd never have a chance to tell the difference. Even the ragged gown I'd worn before Lachlan replaced my wardrobe had been stiff with protective charms. I began to sew them not long after I left my aunt's home, replacing them every few weeks when they wore away, until the crafting of them became an instinct, something I performed almost without thinking. There has been more than one occasion in which my wards came in handy, stinging a man's wandering hand, discouraging bands of pickpockets who shadowed me down the darker alleys. Teaching in one of London's poorest districts has its perils, and I suppose after all these years, I am still my aunt's niece.

"You have experience with magic, sir?" I ask, my tone as sharp as the needle hidden in the seam of my sleeve. "From what Mrs. MacDougal told me, I'd got the impression you were not keen on the craft."

His face darkens. "Do you think me a simple country laird? And that because I live a remote and solitary life, Miss Pryor, I must be ignorant as well?"

"Forgive me if I implied anything of the sort," I reply, taken aback by the heat in his voice. I'd not meant to offend so deeply, but clearly, I touched some hidden nerve. "I saw you've some Weavers in your family tree. There was a portrait—"

"Ach, if I knew who half the people in those portraits were, or whether they were even related to me, I should count myself the most educated man in Scotland." He waves his hand, dismissing the topic. "So tell me, in what sort of Weaving does a charity school instruct its pupils? No great magic, I should think. Do you specialize in household spells, adept at scouring pots and dusting cobwebs away?"

I flick my hair back, outraged by his patronizing tone. "I taught magic, yes, and arithmetic and reading and history and French, if you must know. Though considering the state of your manor, sir, I think you might benefit from a few *household spells.*"

He scrapes the edge of his knife over the wooden wolf's bristling hackles. "Ach. Magic is just a lazy shortcut out of honest, hard work."

I draw a sharp, angry breath. What would he say, I wonder, if I demonstrated just how much *honest, hard work* it would take me to embroider a hex on his pillowcase? Perhaps something to make him itch all through the night, or to wake with his hair twisted into a thousand impossible knots? *Lazy shortcut,* indeed! I have never been so thoroughly offended in so short a time by so arrogant a man.

"I do not know what sort of Weavers you have out here in your backwater country," I reply, my voice cool and my temper hot, a perilous combination, "but in London, where *I* come from, it is St. Edgitha's healers the folk call for when their children fall ill. It is the Telarii they send to defend our coast against the French. It is the Weavers of the Moirai, my sisters and brothers, to whom they entrust their education. It is magic, woven largely by women's hands, that has knit together the ground beneath your feet, oh country laird. Or are you so ensconced in your remoteness and solitude that you forget there is a world beyond your moors?"

He returns my gaze with a glower of his own. He has a tiger's amber eyes; they remind me of the bright illustrations in a book of poetry I had loved as a girl.

Tyger Tyger, burning bright . . . In what distant
deeps or skies, burnt the fire of thine eyes?

I shake the words away, unsettled and unsure why.

"Tell me, Miss Pryor," he says in a low, almost purring tone, "are all
the charity-school teachers in London as proud as you?"

"If they are not, they should be. It is *honest*, *hard* work, and I
have nothing to be ashamed of. I will not apologize for my position,
my reputation, or my craft, not even to a laird sitting pretty in his
backwater castle."

His lips quirk with wry amusement. The expression erases some
of the sternness from his face and reveals a sly dimple in his left cheek.

For a moment I forget what we are arguing about. That wicked
little smirk puts a hitch in my breath and insensibly recalls an image
to my mind—an illustration from one of my childhood storybooks, of
the Greek hero Jason standing at the prow of the *Argo*, as cocky and
handsome as an artist's pen could summon.

No. Oh, no, no, no. I will *not* overlook his rudeness for the sake of
one Fatesdamned dimple.

"I thank you for your night's hospitality," I add in a strained tone,
"but I plan to move on to other lodging in the morning."

"And I thank you for carrying me home," he returns with a short,
mocking nod. "And I extend to you all the comforts my 'backwater
castle' can offer for the night. But I must request, in the strictest
terms, that you refrain from exercising your *craft* while you are on my
property."

"Of course. I would not dream of burdening you with my gifts.
Shall I give you my threadkit to lock away until morning? Do you
wish me to strip off every becharmed article of clothing I am currently
wearing and toss them in your fireplace?"

He gives me a startled glance, his eyes flicking to the embroidery
on my nightgown's bodice and lingering a fair moment longer than
necessary. My cheeks grow hot as I suddenly recall I am wearing little

else and bringing his attention to that fact was perhaps a foolish thing to do. I do not know this man, nor his notions of honor. Perhaps he has none.

I run my hand over my hip, as if to smooth the gown, but really slipping a finger into a secret pocket where there is a skein of thread. If I need it, I could Weave a stunning spell in a trice, something far more potent than the charms worked into my nightgown. The embroidered wards curl up the seams on my ribs and meet just over my breasts in a complex knot that is meant to discourage unwanted attention and wandering eyes.

Curiously, they seem to have little effect on Mr. North.

Then he curses and looks down at his thumb, where his carving knife has slipped and drawn blood.

"Damn it all," he grumbles, his brogue a layer thicker. "There is nae need for such dramatics. Please stay clothed, Miss Pryor. In fact . . ." He rises and casts about a moment, then takes up a heavy coat from the back of his chair. He extends it to me with his good hand. "Here. Take it. The halls get drafty at night."

Releasing a short breath, I let go of my emergency thread in order to take his coat. He waits until I sweep it around my shoulders like a cape. It smells of horse and the outdoors and some other, distinctly male scent that makes me a little lightheaded. The sleeves hang down to my knees.

Well, fine. He may have some shred of honor, but that does not absolve him of his other bad qualities.

The laird wraps a kerchief around his injured thumb. "Now, is there anything further I can do for you, or are there any other rooms into which you'd like to stick your nose?"

My shoulders stiffen beneath the heavy wool coat. Perhaps I ought not to have been snooping, but his offensive nature makes it very difficult to feel guilty. "I would like a book. Perhaps reading would help me sleep."

His eyes narrow, as if he suspects I might try to set them on fire, but he waves his injured hand at the shelves. "Borrow what you like." Then he turns away, looking out the window at the moors. Taking the chance, I slip the estate map down, then grab a volume from the shelf and hide the map inside.

"*A Midsummer Night's Dream*," I say. "It's my favorite."

Turning, Mr. North scoffs. "Only children put any stock in faerie tales."

Bristling, I grip the book to my chest. What would he say, I wonder, if I told him an entire host of faeries is camped out just beyond the ridge he's gazing toward? Instead, I reply pertly, "Only fools fail to comprehend that in faerie tales often lie the greatest truths of all."

He grunts. "And what truths might these be?"

"Truths of love," I say softly, considering the book in my hands. "Of desperation. And of folly."

"Ach. Well, if that's the case, I have all I need of such truths already."

I lift my head, struck by the melancholy in his voice, as if for a moment his gruffness has cracked to reveal something deep and old and terribly sad in him. He is gazing out the dark window, eyes intent on a distant ridgeline as if searching for something or someone, as if he's already forgotten I am here. If one of my students came into the classroom with such an expression on their face, I would pull them aside and gently ask what was wrong.

But he is not one of my students. I remind myself I am angry at him, and whatever problems he has, they are none of my concern.

"Well, thank you for the book," I say simply.

He does not turn from the window but flicks one hand in dismissal. "You are welcome to it, Miss Pryor. Do keep your threads in their kit. And please, try to refrain from snooping through my house again."

I cannot escape his stifling study quickly enough; the books in it which had whispered to me now seem to sulk, like children forbidden from playing.

And their master, as far as I am concerned, is an arrogant, prejudiced arse. Never mind his dimpled smirk, or the graceful cleverness of his fingers as he'd carved the wolf.

I shall be glad when dawn comes, and I can leave this moldering manor and never be forced to endure another moment of its laird's insufferable company.

CHAPTER EIGHT

At dawn, I'm startled awake by the blast of bagpipes.

The windowpanes seem nearly to rattle at the screeching sound. I dress quickly, every blasting note like a splash of shocking icy water to my nerves. The notes are so violently played that I cannot even tell what song they're supposed to be.

Baffled, I stumble out of my room and down to the kitchen, where Mrs. MacDougal is cooking bacon and Sylvie is sitting by the fire, her legs kicking as she eats an apple. The girl brightens when I enter. The sound is louder down here than it was upstairs. I resist the urge to clap my hands over my ears, as if it would do any good.

"What on earth is that noise?" I ask.

"Mr. North has many hobbies," Mrs. MacDougal says, her voice strained. "Some more regrettable than others."

"Connie only plays his pipes when he's really happy or in a black temper," explains Sylvie.

After my conversation with Mr. North last night, I can easily believe which is the case this morning. Before I can stop myself, I say, "He's not very good, is he?"

Mrs. MacDougal sighs. "He makes up for it with *zeal*. Best to just let him get it over with."

She puts down breakfast, and Sylvie digs in. Grand the house may be, but it seems no one stands upon much ceremony here. I sit and wince at the racket Mr. North is making and wonder why the housekeeper keeps giving me dark looks out of the corners of her eyes.

Then she says, "So you're off to Blackswire, then, Miss Pryor? Or should I say, Sister Rose?" Her eyes flick to the trefoil knot embroidered on my collar.

I touch my fingertips to the symbol. Perhaps I should have removed it, but I haven't had the heart. I am still technically a Moirene sister, and wearing the symbol of my order makes me believe I will one day return to them.

"Miss Pryor is fine. And yes, I suppose I am off to the village."

Sylvie pouts. "But you've only just got here."

"Miss Pryor did not come all this way to see *us*," the housekeeper reminds her.

Her husband comes in from outside, bringing a draft of cold air with him. In heavy work boots he shuffles over and sits, muttering, "No eggs today, Mrs. MacDougal. That damn racket has scared them right back up into the chickens. I've a mind to puncture the bag when the lad's next away."

Just then, the bagpipes cut off, and we all release relieved sighs. Then the kitchen door opens again, and Conrad North limps in, clutching an enormous set of highland pipes, ruddy cheeked from the cold. The laird's sgian-dubh is tucked into his belt, and his black hair is untidily ruffled, making him a human counterpart to the shaggy dog who trots in at his heels. A gust of wind blows in with them, ruffling the plaid kilt tied about Mr. North's waist. I catch a glimpse of muscled bronze thigh and have to fight back the tide of heat that creeps up my neck. There aren't many kilted men running about London, but honestly, I have spent enough time assisting in the healers' ward to have seen my share of male flesh. I should certainly *not* be blushing at the barest flash of a disagreeable Scotsman's thigh.

With a cough, I go back to my breakfast, once again thinking of that wretched storybook illustration of Jason, standing proud on his ship with his short windswept toga and his long muscular legs.

Fates. What is *wrong* with me?

Mr. North stops short when he sees me, as though he'd forgotten I was here. Then he grumbles something unintelligible and throws himself into a chair, his pipes taking up half the table. The petrichor and earth scent of the moors rolls off him, along with the more rustic scents of stable and horse.

"Here, Sylvie," he grunts, taking an object from his pocket and tossing it to her.

She catches it with a shout; it is the wolf I saw him carving last night, finished and really quite lovely, one paw raised and its head low as if it's about to pounce upon a rabbit.

"Oh!" Sylvie kisses its nose. "My little Fenrir! He's beautiful, Connie, just the best!"

"Nothing less for my shield maiden of the north." Conrad's words elicit a pleased flush from his sister.

He falls upon breakfast without ceremony, shoving bacon into his mouth. While he chews, he crosses his eyes at Sylvie, who giggles. If he woke in a black temper, he seems to have exhausted it through his pipes.

"So, Rose Pryor of London," he says, his first verbal acknowledgment of my presence this morning. "You're still here."

I sip my tea and pointedly do not look at him. "How is your thumb, Mr. North?"

He waggles it at me; the cut has been bandaged. "Miraculously, I have survived, even without the aid of magic. How was your book?"

"Riveting. I particularly loved the part where the faerie queen woke to find her lord was actually an ass."

A crash sounds from the washbasin, where Mrs. MacDougal has dropped a pan. She curses under her breath and, for some reason, glares at me as though it were *my* fault. Sylvie is looking back and forth between me and her brother with wide eyes.

The laird leans back in his chair, tumbling his teacup in his palm as if it were red wine. His lips are slanted to one side, hinting at his dimple. Like bronzed mirrors, his eyes seem opaque, reflecting my own face back at me. "What's the plan today, then? More snooping?"

"Well," I begin. "I shall walk to Blackswire this morning and ask after lodging. Perhaps there is an inn . . . ?"

"Nay, there's not an inn. But there are a few families who might put you up for a time. Mr. MacDougal, ready the cart."

"No, please," I quickly insert. "I prefer the walk."

Mr. North shrugs and begins draining his tea. "Suit yourself. But you cannot go hauling your bags all the way to Blackswire. Once you find a berth, send word, and Mr. MacDougal will bring your things to you."

"She can stay here!" Sylvie chirps. "Why not, Connie? We have a million beds and—"

"I don't think that's a good idea," I say gently.

"Nay, 'tis not," her brother growls behind his cup. "Miss Pryor has made up her mind. I do believe we are too *backward* and *simple* for such a highbrow, worldly soul as she."

I give him an icy look, which he returns with equal coolness.

Sylvie pouts. "But—"

"I said *nay*, and I won't tolerate any sass, you wee wench."

"Numpty!"

"Harpy."

Sylvie grins and digs her elbow into her brother's side, and he yelps and falls backward off his chair, as if mortally wounded. Then he lets out a real cry of pain when his injured leg strikes the table.

"Honestly!" Mrs. MacDougal throws up her hands. "Barbarians! The lot of you!"

When I slip out of Mr. North's crumbling manor ten minutes later, the moor is cast in gray fog aglow with the afterlight of dawn. It is cold enough to freeze the blood in my veins. Even though Mrs. MacDougal's hot breakfast and tea warms my belly, for half a moment, I regret leaving the comfortable kitchen for this frigid air. Saying farewell to Sylvie's disappointed face was even more difficult. The girl reminds me painfully of my students.

But thinking of my class reminds me that I have a mission to do, and the sooner it's over and done, the sooner I can go home. Once I'm far enough away from the manor that Mr. North cannot spy upon me, I sew a few warming knots into my shawl. Though as I channel into them, I almost wish he *would* glimpse me through the austere windows of his library lair. It warms me almost as much as my magic, imagining him chafing at this act of defiance.

Over the moors, eerie sounds creep and prowl: low groans that could just as well be waking ogres as wind through trees; sudden, startled crashes in the bracken by small animals; chuffs in the distance that may be cattle or horses or the disapproving grumbles of the Fates themselves for all I can tell. I follow the drive to the road, then cut east, over the moors and out of sight of the manor.

Climb the highest northern hill, were Lachlan's instructions. *Then spy a southern bluff with three rocks like your craggy Fates jutting from its face. The gate lies halfway betwixt these and is like to be guarded, so tread with caution, little witch.*

Toren's Rise is the highest hill in the area, according to the map I stole from Mr. North's study, and it lies north of the manor, a few hours' walk.

Before long, the wildness of this place seeps through my skin and pricks my bones, and I find myself hurrying, breathing faster, as the sun rises and the fog melts, revealing a land far stranger and more beautiful than I could have imagined.

The moors here are jagged and broken by rock, great crags leaning out of the moss and casting long purple shadows over the bristling heather. Winds from every corner meet here to gambol, tussle, and court, so the land seems alive with great invisible beasts. My bonnet is tossed from my head, and my skirts wrap around my legs and flutter behind me. Like a small ship I am driven by those winds, pulled and pushed along until I am breathless.

When I finally reach Toren's Rise—unmistakable for its height, which soon sets my calves to complaining—the sun is three handsbreadths in the sky. My warming knots have turned to ash, but between the sunlight and the exercise, I don't need them anymore.

A steep rise blanketed in heather takes me to the peak, where the land suddenly drops away in a craggy bluff. Looking down into a deep, narrow ravine, I reel a bit at the height. I am breathing hard, my lungs burning and legs aching, but every inch of me is aflame and alert. The wind has awoken something wild in me, and before I can stop myself, I open wide and drink in the energy of this place.

It rushes in, a hungry tide. I let my head fall back and draw it into my core, let it search me out. I hold it as long as I can before my heartbeats begin to strike like a knife driving in and out, in and out. Then, with a sob of pain, I channel the magic into an illusion knot strung between my hands.

A flock of blackbirds burst from the threads, airy and indistinct, ravens of smoke and shadow. They screech silence and beat no wind from their diaphanous wings. Hundreds of them pour from me, a great black cloud, and in moments they dissipate into the wind.

Letting out a long breath, I sink to my knees and press my hands to my chest, ashes trickling through my palms.

That was foolish and purposeless, and now I've weakened myself. It will take longer to trek through the moors, longer to find the gate, longer to—

Shutting my eyes against the panic which threatens to swallow me whole, I try to still my heart.

Chin up, Rose, I tell myself. *No more getting carried away. Remember why you are here. Remember what you stand to lose. Remember what you stand to gain.*

Magic without pain. No one and nothing to fear, ever again. A purposeful place in the world, uncontestable and necessary. I think of my students, with their wide, desperate eyes, and I remember what it felt like to be one of them. Alone, afraid, so very small.

I set my eyes on the distant bluffs. The land to the south is forested, its trees old; I can tell even from this height the trunks there are vast and ancient, the crowns high and proud. Those trees have stood for centuries and no doubt hide centuries of secrets.

But I am here to discover only one.

A scramble down the back of the bluff takes me upon a little southbound path, perhaps no more than a deer trail, but it affords easier passage through the heather and the thicker undergrowth which crops up as I pass into the wood. Among the trees, the wind grows thinner. Where it rioted over the open moors like a herd of wild horses, here it slinks, fox-like, in and out of shadows.

I know better than to strike into unknown forest without some path out again, so I remove a spool of sturdy red wool from my threadkit and tie a length to a branch. I let it unwind as I walk, my finger stuck through the center, taking care not to let it pull taut and snap the line.

Go to the lowest point of land, Lachlan had told me. *You will know the gate when you see it.*

So I follow every downward slope, sliding and slipping over leaves and snow, soon breathing hard, my heart racing now not only with exertion, but with the thrill of closing in on my destination.

The gate is near; I can *feel* it, as the ancient trees bend and bow overhead, their great limbs, even in winter, heavily draped in pale moss. I leap from rock to rock over a half-frozen burn and startle three stags in a wide clearing. Heart skipping a beat, I stumble to a halt and watch them toss their antlers as they bound away, springing over melting snows. In moments they've vanished into the wood. For all the silence of their steps, they may as well have evaporated.

Halfway between Toren's Rise and the Three Fates Bluff, as I've inwardly named the craggy cliffs to the south, I slow and catch my breath, walking measuredly through the silent trees and watching for any sign of the gate to Elfhame.

This part of the forest, I sense in my bones, is older than the rest. Perhaps this is the most remote and untouched strip of land in all of Britain. The trees are giants, grandfathers and grandmothers wizened with moss. As I walk among them, they groan and creak as if fully aware of their age, and my coming here has woken them from centuries of slumber. Beneath the crisp scent of the snow, I breathe in the earthy bouquet of wet soil and rotting oak.

Are they here, the fae of the stories? Lachlan's long-lost kin? Are they watching me circle their doorstep, a foolish girl searching out powers she has no business provoking? Or have they fully withdrawn into their own strange world?

After what seems like hours of wandering, I step between two trees, ducking low beneath a curtain of moss, and feel a tug on my finger.

I've run out of thread. The last length falls away from the spool; I catch it before it is lost.

My search has ended in a nondescript patch of forest. Though the trees are remarkable for their girth, little else about the place is noteworthy, and my shoulders slump with disappointment. I hadn't truly expected to find anything on my first foray, but still, the failure has made it clear this will be no simple task. I am not strolling down to the market to buy blue ribbons; I am seeking entrance into an inhuman world ruled by an immortal race, armed with nothing more than a spool of thread, my wits, and dying magic.

Wrapping the thread around my finger, I begin to make my way back.

But I go not ten steps before I realize the thread has gone slack, and it must have broken somewhere along the way. When I find the frayed end, and no sign of the rest of the trail, I curse under my breath.

"Oh, just a little faerie's favor, Rose," I growl, as I wind up the thread I'd managed to gather and begin to Weave a cat's cradle. "Just a little jaunt to the frozen arse of nowhere to search for an ancient faerie door which may or may not even exist. Fates damn me for a fool!"

Letting out a puff of frosty breath, I shake away my frustration and focus on my threads. I know the manor lies somewhere to the east, but with the sky too clouded to reveal the sun, I have no idea what direction I'm facing. In London, I could have found my way through the streets by smell alone, but out here in the Fatesforsaken wilderness of Fatesforsaken Scotland, I am helpless.

Well. Not *entirely* helpless.

It takes only a thread of magic, pulled from the trees around me like a teaspoon of water ladled from a river, to fuel my wayfinding knot, and from the glowing threads, a small bright bead of silver light rises and hovers in the air, soft as a glowworm. I reach out, and it darts away, blinking faintly, then waits just out of arm's length, indicating *north*.

Dusting the ashes of the burnt threads from my hands, I set off, keeping the bead of light at my left elbow, like a quiet companion.

Before long, I find I'm no longer thrashing through undergrowth, but following a narrow path that gradually widens. Alongside it, little green shoots push up through the soil, promising blossoming snowdrops and unfurling ferns over the days to come. The path is hard dirt, broken by the occasional root, but from the encroaching undergrowth I can tell it hasn't been used in some time.

The path ends at a crumbling cottage set in a small green glen, everything damp and fuzzy with moss, and the slope of the roof skinned over with snow. The stone walls are half collapsed on one side, and a door hangs ajar. Clearly the place is abandoned, and I nearly pass it by and continue on the path, which bends away to the right.

But then I notice the debris scattered around the cottage. It's all old and half covered over in moss and leaves, but there's no mistaking the curved embroidery hoop jutting from the loam. Warily, I circle the cottage before going in and find on the other side a mound of moss with a plain wooden marker driven into the top, its face carved with the trefoil knot of the Fates, a standard grave marker, though there is no name upon it.

Who lived here, I wonder, in the middle of the wood? Judging by the empty, half-burned spools I find in the nearby refuse pit, it was a Weaver. Oddly, there are also a great many crude birdcages piled about, some broken, others holding the grisly remains of the birds which died in them. I don't linger over them; the little piles of bones and feathers make my skin crawl.

I go inside, startling the fox which had taken up residence there. It bounds away with a yelp, scaring my heart into my throat. Pausing a moment to find my breath, I look around.

There is little left that is usable; the narrow bedframe has collapsed, as has the table. A chair still stands in the corner, looking sturdy enough, though I do not give it a try. More Weavers' clutter is strewn across the floor—spools and hoops, bobbins and pegboards. My heart sinks, feeling a strange kinship with the anonymous Weaver who died here, and I begin looking through the cottage, hoping to find a name I can add to the grave. Some small remembrance, a way to honor the soul of a fellow magic user.

At last, I find a small bureau that had been crushed by the collapsed wall. I manage to pull open one drawer, and inside I find a thick pile of folded papers amid loose spools and half-finished embroideries. One of these spells I recognize, with a sudden sickening lurch. I take out the hoop and gaze grimly at the threads worked into it.

"A draining spell," I murmur. Suddenly all the birdcages outside make sense. I've heard of Weavers using such dark magic, pulling energy from living creatures rather than plants, in order to wield twice as much power. But the law strictly forbids it, and transgressors are often punished by the severest of methods: the crushing of one's hands beneath rocks, or even hanging, if one were wicked enough to draw from another human. What kinship and sympathy I'd felt for the occupant of the cottage now evaporates; I better understand why someone might have left them buried without a name. Fates only know what dark purposes they had turned their magic to.

A minute later, I find out, when I open one of the papers and discover the letter written on it in ink so old it's nearly faded away. I read it quickly, my heart beginning to knock and my hands going clammy, then toss it away and read another. Then another and another . . . on every single one, the same exact message is written verbatim.

> My Dearest Philip,
> I have found the faerie Gate, on this, the eve of my deadline. I must open it tonight, even if it means turning to a breed of magic that I swore I'd never use. I will open it, and then, at last, I will finally be free of my debt, free to return to you. We shall be married as we had planned, and I will never depart from your side again.
> With all my love,
> Fiona

The date, penned below the signature on every one of the hundreds of letters, is from forty years ago, though clearly some of the pages are far newer than that.

I drop the pages with a strangled cry and back away, until my head clacks against the doorpost. Looking outside, my eye falls on the nameless grave, only now I *do* know the name of the body below it, and more than that, I know who drove her there.

Lachlan.

CHAPTER NINE

I cannot find the strength to summon another wayfinding spell, so I stumble through the trees in the vague direction of east until I am dizzy with hunger and fatigue and, most of all, anger. One of Fiona's letters is stowed in my pocket, crinkling with every step I take. I'm so rattled I can barely focus on where I'm stepping, and I trip more than once on jutting roots.

I need to speak to Lachlan, and soon. But first, I need to secure lodging in the village.

At last the wood breaks, and the moors roll ahead. Bending between the hills is a dirt road, and I smell the comforting aroma of cookfires. The surrounding land is fenced and lined with bare fields awaiting spring planting or dappled with grazing sheep.

The path to the village follows the line of the tanglewood, twisted trees on one side, the open moor on the other. The trees break like a wave over the heather, gnarled branches snarling, leaves rattling in the wind. Even in early spring, they look bleak. For a while I walk alongside a flat, lazy burn, its surface stippled with undulating ripples left by light-footed insects. Every now and again, a fat fish surfaces with a slurp and sucks down a bite.

Then the path turns and there is Blackswire, a neat arrangement of stone buildings and shops, its outskirts peppered with crofts, whitewashed cob houses, and thatched roofs. The town sits in a low, flat green surrounded on three sides by forest, and on one by moorland.

A sound catches my ear—the voices of children. Perhaps one can point me to a nearby farm, where I might beg for a berth in a hayloft. But when I round the bend and see them, I find a familiar face: Sylvie North.

She's standing in the center of a ring of five other children: three boys and two girls. They are holding hands and blocking her every attempt to escape. Sylvie is wearing one of her costumes, this time a fur cape with a feathered collar, and the black paint she used to paint whiskers on her cheeks has run from the tears streaming from her eyes.

"You smell!" a boy shouts. "Why are you wearing that dirty old rug, Batty Sylvie?"

One of the girls laughs. "My mum says you're a child of *scandal*, and the Fates don't even Weave a thread for you."

"Maybe that's why your parents are both dead," says another boy. "Punishment for their sins!"

"Is that why you wear *bones* and paint your face, Batty Sylvie? Are you evil too?"

I've begun to Weave a hex before I've half had a chance to think. Then I realize inflicting a rash of warts on Sylvie's tormentors will only make her more of a target. They still haven't noticed me standing at the bend in the path.

Looking around, I spot three large bundles of wool tied with rope and guess these were being hauled by the children from their parents' farms when they came across Sylvie and stopped to torment her. Furtively, I go to them and begin tying knots around the ropes, then release just a touch of magic into each one. The wool bundles begin to rise, pulled aloft by my hovering charms.

Then I back away and tuck myself behind a tree and wait.

It takes only a moment before one of the girls spots them and screams. The children gasp and cry out, one boy lunging upward to grab at a bundle, managing to get his fingers around the rope binding it. But my hovering charm pulls him up too. He is forced to let go or be borne into the sky as well. The wool bobs and drifts away, toward the town, like small clouds. They'll drift back to earth harmlessly in a few minutes, but of course, the children don't know that.

"It's her!" cries a girl. "It's Sylvie doing that! Just look at her eyes!"

Sylvie's eyes are wide with shock. But now she blinks and glances quickly around, eyes narrowing with suspicion, and then she spies me behind the tree. I give a small wave and a wink, and her mouth, which had been pressed into a thin line of anger and pain, now parts in a devilish grin.

"Indeed, 'tis I! Sylvie the Terrible!" she roars, and she raises her hands and makes a dramatic show of waving off the bundled wool. "I curse thee, Simon and James and Douglas! I curse thee, Mary and Felicity! May you all grow goat's beards and lizard's tails, and may all your food taste of frogs!"

The boys and girls scream and take off running toward the town, pale with terror, as Sylvie stomps around and howls and waves her hands. By the time they're out of hearing, her horrible groans have turned to peals of laughter. She gives me a triumphant grin.

"Did you see them go?"

"Like sheep from a wolf," I reply, stepping out from behind the tree.

"Aye, sheep! And my mum was a shepherdess, Connie says, so I should know how to handle them." She wipes tears away, and I know behind her laughter, she is still raw from their bullying.

"What are you doing all the way out here? Were you on your way to school?"

"School?" she snorts. "Connie doesn't let me go to *school*. I thought maybe you'd get lost on your way to the village, so I came to help you."

A pang of guilt wrenches at my stomach. "Well, it's lucky for me you did. I admit, I was quite lost."

She smiles, then suddenly grabs my hand and holds it fast. I stare at her small fingers in mine with some surprise, but do not pull away.

"What do you mean," I ask, "when you say your brother won't let you go to school?"

She shrugs. "They use a bit of magic there. Not that the likes of Mary and Felicity McLure can channel, but the teacher can a little, and she does a bit of spellwork. Connie's against *all* magic."

I bite my lip, my own inner voice admonishing me to be quiet and leave well enough alone. I'm not here to pry into the affairs of the Norths, but to save my magic and go back to my own life. Nobody's asked me to care about one country girl's French and arithmetic. The Weaver in me urges me to bid Sylvie farewell and be on my way.

But the teacher in me wins out.

"Where is your governess, then?" I ask. "Who is in charge of your education?"

She gives an exasperated groan. "Connie, I guess. When he has time, once or twice a week. Mrs. MacDougal teaches me a bit of cooking when the mood strikes her."

I lift my eyes to the streaks of cloud above, searching for patience. "Is that so?"

Sylvie frowns, her eyes narrowing at me. "What? I know how to read. I read all the time. I'm not *stupid*."

"That's good." My tone is strained, and I cannot help but hear the echo of her intolerable guardian in her words. She's so quick to take offense, just like Mr. North. "Reading is good."

"I had a governess once. Old Miss Teague. She smelled like beeswax. Connie fired her."

"Why?"

"She taught me history."

"*History?* Is he against history too?"

"Well . . ." Sylvie winces, her fingers worrying at a seam in her sleeve. "History about Weaving, mainly. About how the Telarians—"

"Telarii," I correct without thinking.

"Right. Those ones. Anyway, she taught me how they turned the battle of Waterloo against that wretched wee devil Napoleon." Getting caught up in the glory of it all, Sylvie leaps about, firing an imaginary rifle at the trees. "First, they captured Napoleon's battle standard, weakening the magic barriers around the Imperial Guard! Then—"

"Your brother fired her for teaching you *basic history*?" I ask.

She pauses and looks at me, her rifle-arm lowering. "Ach. Well. I might have bribed her to go into more detail than necessary about the magic behind Napoleon's battle standard."

"It *was* a good piece of spellwork," I admit. "Come on, then. I'll walk you back home."

I hadn't planned to return to Ravensgate, but I can't very well leave Sylvie to be preyed upon, should her tormentors return for vengeance.

She grins, linking arms with me. "Will you show me how you did that thing with the wool bundles just now? What sort of magic was it?"

Her brother's face flashes in my memory, his eyes stern as he commanded me to not practice magic in his house. And despite the fact we're well away from Ravensgate, I still hesitate.

"Please?" Sylvie begs. "I won't tell Connie, I swear it on my—"

"No need for swearing," I cut in. The gesture may be empty without a vowknot to seal them, but still the words make me uneasy. "But all right. I will show you. Just don't mention it to your brother."

As we walk back to the manor, I thread several hovering knots for her, letting her tie them to little branches, then quietly channeling into them. She crows with delight every time one floats away. She's a fast learner, her fingers quick.

"A week after I was sent to school," I say, "the other girls tied my hair to my bedposts and pretended they were going to cut off my ears. I cried all night."

"Children are beasts," she replies. "I should know. I am one."

From what I've seen, though, children are more like mirrors, reflecting the attitudes of the adults around them. Those girls in school would never have singled me out if the teachers had not gossiped about me first. *That one is fae touched; mind her closely. Wicked hands Weave wicked spells.* I had told myself I didn't mind, that I'd rather have focused on learning Weaving over making friends anyway. But I know what it is to be lonely.

I take Sylvie's hand and hold it tight as we walk. The road bends away from the forest and into the moors. In the bushes, a few red highland cattle graze lazily, lowing at us and shaking their great shaggy heads.

"Sylvie," I say, "why does your brother dislike magic so much?"

"I think . . ." Her voice hitches. "I think it has to do with our pa. I think magic might have killed him."

"Was he a Weaver?"

"I don't know. Connie will never tell me anything about him, or my mum neither. He and I had different mums, but his died and mine ran away. I guess she must have died too, because she never came back for me." She lets out a huff of breath, then changes the subject. "Where's *your* mum and dad?"

"They got sick," I reply, lost for a moment in memory so faint it's little more than a scent in my nose—baking bread, a cottage on a hill, strong hands hoisting me into the air. The sadness is a coil of cold wind around my ankles, swirling and then fading again. "And so did my uncle. It was just me and my aunt until . . . she couldn't care for me anymore."

She nods. "Like me and Connie."

"A bit."

"He's not a *bad* brother, you know. Just overprotective. And once he makes his mind up, not the Fates themselves could change it. Or so Mrs. MacDougal says. He never lets me go anywhere or do anything! We used to get invitations from other families, you know, for balls and parties and such. Even some as far as Stirling or Edinburgh! But he declined them all, and the invitations stopped coming."

I press my lips together, pressure building in my temples. So she not only is a pariah in her own village, she has no peers of her own class to confide in and learn from. The poor child's completely isolated.

"Sounds lonely," I say at last.

"Aye," she sighs. "That's why I was so excited when you showed up. We almost never get visitors. Except for the ghost, of course."

I glance down at her. "Er . . . ghost?"

"You'll probably catch a glimpse of her at night, if you keep your eyes sharp. All white and glowy like a . . . well, like a ghost. Conrad thinks I'm mad as a loon, but I've seen her more than once, and I know what I saw."

Once again my thoughts stray to the pale figure from last night. And once again, I remind myself it was only a wisp of fog. "Do you have chats with this ghost?"

"No, I don't think she can speak," says Sylvie. "She just stares at me for a bit, then disappears. I think she might be the ghost of my mum, or Conrad's."

"Perhaps she is." I give her shoulder a consoling squeeze. "At any rate, I'll be sure to keep my eyes sharp."

When we near Ravensgate, Captain bounds up to us, barking, and draws Sylvie into a game of chase. They run in great loops about the drive.

I stand uncertainly, eager to give Mr. Conrad North, laird of Ravensgate, a piece of my mind but unsure where to start looking for him, when I hear a sudden cry of pain from the stable.

CHAPTER TEN

My hand moving to my threadkit, I hurry to the half-open door, the scent of hay and livestock wafting out. Stepping around the door, bracing for anything, I peer into the dimly lit interior. My eyes scan the piled hay and horses in their stalls, seeking the person in pain.

Another cry draws my eye to the corner to my left, where in an open stall, Conrad North is crouched over a prone sheep, his kilt hiked over his knees. His shirtsleeves are rolled to his elbows, revealing muscular forearms, and he's got one hand shoved up the sheep's backside.

For a moment, I am struck dumb. And so, it seems, is the laird. He gapes at me, his dark brows knitted together in surprise.

Then the sheep lying on the straw before him gives another plaintive bleat, and I realize it is the animal, not the man, in distress.

"Easy, Thistle. It's just an uninvited guest." Mr. North withdraws his hand, encased in a leather glove, from the sheep's interior. His eyes remain fixed upon me, narrow with suspicion. "Miss Pryor. You have come back so soon. Did the villagers drive you out, then? Did you knock any locals off their horses, or get caught snooping through their private effects?"

"I found Sylvie on the road," I say, unable to tear my eyes from the grisly scene before me. "She was being taunted by some children."

He inhales, his lips tight. In the dim light of the stable, his eyes are less amber and more obsidian, mirror dark. He turns his eyes back to the sheep, which is writhing its legs in distress, and no wonder. Mr. North has apparently been rummaging about inside it as if searching for loose coins.

"The Cotter and McLure whelps," he growls. "They're wee beasts, but Sylvie knows better than to take stock in the words of bullies."

"Are you sure of that?" I look out at the girl, now rolling in the drive with Captain licking her face, her squeals of laughter piercing the air. "Her tears seemed evidence to the contrary."

Mr. North's ungloved hand tightens at his side. "She shouldn't be going to town at all. Swing that door open, will you? I need more light in here."

I push the stable's second door wide, letting in a broad beam of light. It illuminates the pitiful creature under Mr. North's hand. He's probing at it again, causing the thing to struggle. With his other hand, he tries to hold the ewe still, but is clearly failing.

"What *are* you doing to that poor thing?" I demand.

His reply is strained with both effort and pique. "Well, I'm not torturing it or sacrificing it to my dark gods, or whatever the hell your tone implies you *think* I'm doing."

"Language, sir!" I gasp.

He rolls his eyes. "The sheep's birthing, but the lamb is breech. Come closer—I need your hands."

"My . . ." I look down at my palms, then up at him. "Mr. North, I am not trained to—"

"I dinnae give a damn about your training, Miss Pryor," he retorts irritably. "I need a pair of hands, and Mr. MacDougal's caught up in the south pastures for some time. So yours will have to do, if you can stand to get a wee bit of dirt under your pretty nails. Trust me, you're not my first choice of help either."

Uncertainly, I step nearer. "Does she have no friends her own age?"

Mr. North seems to choke. "What, Thistle?"

"*Sylvie.* Surely she doesn't always stay here, with a housekeeper and a—" I bite my tongue before the words *prejudiced bastard* slips out.

But he gives me a thunderous look that makes me think he knew precisely what I was going to say. "I hardly think we require the input of a stranger in our affairs. Now, roll up your sleeves—if you can, with all that embroidery work—and kneel there by Thistle's head. She won't bite." He pauses, then adds, "Nay, that's a lie. She may bite."

So much for not wanting the input of a stranger in his affairs. I touch my sleeve and grimace. "Don't you have . . . people, for this sort of thing? Aren't you a laird?"

He gives an exasperated growl. "I believe we've been over the part where I explained Mr. MacDougal is occupied. And I'd be a poor sort of laird if I could not tend my own livestock when necessary. Now, will you help me, or will you stand by and let poor Thistle knock herself senseless while I help her deliver her lamb?"

Bracing myself, I roll my sleeves and kneel by the sheep. She bleats pitifully, and my heart beats in sympathy. But my total inexperience with this sort of thing coupled with my lifelong unease around animals leaves me feeling ill.

"Just soothe her," Mr. North says, taking stock of my queasy expression. "And Fates, try not to faint. 'Tis just a lambing. Though admittedly, Thistle, old girl, your bairn's a big, stubborn thing, just like her ma. Ach! I can see a wee hoof, now, there's a smart lass! Hold her still, Miss Pryor."

Wincing, I cling to the ewe's woolly neck while the laird inspects the situation unfolding at Thistle's other end.

"Please don't bite me," I whisper to the creature. "You're, er, doing very well. I assume."

Even in school, healing had never been my preferred area of study, particularly any topic involving as many bodily fluids as childbirth.

After a few minutes, I say, "I do know a spell—"

"Nay," Mr. North grunts. "I've birthed hundreds of lambs with no other help but nature's own. You will not interfere with your tricks."

"My—" I clench my teeth, my neck hot. "I could take away all the poor creature's pain! You'd deny her that relief?"

"This isn't Thistle's first time. The old girl can hold her own. Now hush and pass me that jar of lubricant."

I press my lips together, glaring at him as I pass him the jar. The blasted Scotsman summarily ignores me as he smears the jellylike substance inside the sheep's birth canal. I avert my gaze, the whole sticky process leaving me even more nauseated.

"It's all well, Thistle," Mr. North murmurs. "Ignore the uppity city lass. She does not understand us ignorant country folk."

"Ignorance! That's just my point." I jump on my chance to continue the conversation I'd come for in the first place. "A girl Sylvie's age should at least have a governess. What of her education?"

He scowls. "I cannae see how that's any of your business."

"Has Sylvie been tested for magic?"

"Eh?" he splutters.

"It's the law, you know," I say coolly. In my lap, Thistle gives another soft bleat, and I smooth the wool between her ears while still glowering at the laird. It's not the poor ewe's fault her master is such a beast. "I presume you still fall under the queen's law? All children are to be tested for Weaving abilities by the time they're six."

"Aye." Lowering himself to one bared knee, he gently loops a light rope about the tiny hoof emerging from the sheep's far end. As he works, his dark hair dangles about his face, damp with sweat. "She was tested years ago, by a Weaver in the village. Naught came of it. Not that I find it any of *your* concern. You seem to meddle worse than you snoop. Might you have any more vices a man ought to beware?"

"I have ten."

He blinks. "I beg your pardon?"

Impatiently, I explain, "In school, my third-year teacher listed all our faults for us in order that we might pray the Fates would change them into virtues. Most girls were given four or five, but I was given ten. But that is *not* the topic at hand, sir. About Sylvie—"

"Ten!" He makes a guttural sound in his throat, as if choking down a curse—or perhaps a laugh. Then I'm forced to turn my attention away as Thistle bleats and strains again, and Mr. North gently pulls on the rope about the lamb's little hoof, easing it out another few inches. I hold fast to her neck all the while, trying to calm her panicked thrashing.

When she relaxes again, Mr. North sits back and brushes back his hair with his arm. "One day, Miss Pryor, you shall have to list all ten of your faults for me, so that I might guard myself against your wicked ways."

I give an outraged laugh. "Yes, and afterward we might list *yours*. I have a few ideas where we could start."

"Was *impertinence* on your list, by any chance?"

"As a matter of fact, sir, it was number four."

Is that a hint of mirth in his dark gaze? If so, it only lasts a moment, so brief I might have imagined it. Feeling Thistle shudder, I bend over her and murmur soothing nonsense into her ear, forcing down the nausea in my belly as ropy, wet substances swing from her bucking hindquarters. I thank the Fates I ended up in a Moirene school, and not an Edgithan one. The Order of St. Edgitha of the Needle are almost invariably trained to be healers and midwives. I do not think I would have fared well in such a field.

"Is it because she is a girl?" I ask, once the ewe is calm again.

Mr. North exhales in exasperation. "What are we talking about?"

"Your sister, and the reason you deny her a proper education. Is it because she is a girl?"

The laird's eyes flash. His shoulders snap back, and he finally takes his gaze off the sheep to glare at me. "What do you take me for? A medieval tyrant? I care not if she be lass or lad, she's brighter than any of those ragged wains in Blackswire!"

"And yet you forbid her from going to school!"

"She is better off at home."

"Then at least send for a respectable governess."

"Ach!" He turns his attention back to Thistle, easing the lamb out a bit more while muttering curses under his breath. "Spare me your sanctimonious lectures, Miss Pryor. You're upsetting my sheep."

Thistle's black eyes roll as she strains again. I believe her attention is thoroughly on other matters than our conversation. "I know what it is to be deprived of proper schooling, Mr. North. If you care for your sister's future—"

"*You* could be my governess!" cries Sylvie.

The laird and I both turn to see the girl clinging to the doorway, her cheeks wind chapped and her eyes bright.

Mr. North sighs. "Sylvie . . ."

"I know she's only here for a short time," Sylvie presses. "But I can learn quickly! I'll practice my French *every* day, and I'll even do extra conjugations! Maybe Miss Pryor can help me understand that awful arithmetic you can't seem to explain properly, Connie—"

"Multiplication," he says in a strained voice. "It's called multiplication, and as I told you before, if you just imagine a bunch of wee boxes in your head and fill those boxes with equal amounts of apples—"

"I tried that!" she cries. "But the apples keep spilling out and rolling around in my skull!" She cocks her head to the side, eyeing Thistle. "Maybe if we tried the sheep method instead? Mr. MacDougal says *they* multiply as easy as rabbits. How do sheep and rabbits do it, then? Surely it's not that different for humans?"

I bite back a laugh. "Hm, yes, Mr. North. How *do* the sheep and rabbits multiply?"

Mr. North gives a long, rumbling sigh as he gives another tug on the lambing rope. Thistle strains, and all conversation pauses as I console the ewe and try to hold her head still as Mr. North works on freeing the lamb trapped inside her. Sylvie hovers about with bored impatience, presumably having witnessed this particular miracle of life before.

After a moment, Thistle relaxes again with a weary chuff of air, and I give her a soft pat. The lamb is still not out, despite the poor ewe's heroic efforts. I glance at my threadkit, thinking of at least a half dozen spells that would relieve the creature's suffering if her bloody-minded master would just overcome his bloody-minded prejudice against magic. Honestly!

"Aye," Mr. North says gruffly. "So perhaps not all my teaching methods are successful."

Sylvie squeals, spinning a full circle. "Is that a yes, Connie? Can Miss Pryor stay with us? Can she be my governess? *Please*, Connie—"

"Hush!" he interrupts. "Here it comes!"

The sheep tenses once more, then begins to jerk.

"Hold her!" Mr. North orders. "Miss Pryor, pay attention!"

My heart beating wildly, I wrap my arms around the ewe and bear down on her while Mr. North pulls at the lamb. Sylvie goes still, her hands clasped at her chest and eyes wide.

"C'mon, Thistle," the laird murmurs. "C'mon, lassie . . . *there!*"

All at once, the lamb slides free of its mother with a wet, sickening slurp, then lies in a still heap. I release the ewe with a gasp and stare breathlessly as Mr. North wipes away the sticky substances from the lamb's nose and mouth. He then drags the limp little creature to Thistle's nose, where it lies unmoving. Unbreathing.

"Is it . . . ?" I reach for my threadkit. Damn the man, if I can save the lamb's life with a bit of magic, I *will* do it.

"Let it be," he commands.

"But—"

"I *said*, let it be."

I bite my tongue, fingers twitching.

A moment later, the lamb draws a shuddering breath, and Thistle nuzzles its small head.

"Ah!" Sylvie cries. "You did it, Connie!"

"Aye, with some help." Mr. North glances at me as he pulls off his glove. "Come, Miss Pryor. Let ma and bairn get to know one another. Our job is done."

Sylvie flings her arms wide. "I shall call her—"

"*Him*," corrects her brother.

"I shall call him . . . *Apollo!*"

"A fine name," Mr. North says.

"I . . . I just birthed a lamb," I whisper.

"Well." He raises an eyebrow. "You helped. Sort of. You dinnae pass out, at any rate, and for a moment there I did have my doubts . . ." He tosses a dirty cloth at me. "Now do clean yourself up. You're absolutely filthy."

I look down at my dirty skirts and muddy hands while he chuckles to himself.

Honestly, the *gall* of the man!

Mr. North shuts the stall door, and we lean over it, watching the ewe and lamb grow acquainted. Thistle licks her babe clean, and soon little Apollo is hobbling about on his spindly legs, searching for the teat.

"I am not depriving her of an education," Mr. North says at last. "I have taught her as best I can."

In the heady afterglow of the lamb's birth, it takes me a moment to remember the thread of our conversation. I lift my eyes to his and see him watching the lamb. A thin seam of worry is stitched vertically between his brows, making him seem older and wearier than I'd first taken him for. His sweat-damp hair clings to the back of his neck and temples, but over his forehead, it sticks upward where he'd pushed at it with his forearm. I feel the sudden, irrational urge to smooth it back. I suppress the mad notion with a flex of my hand, turning my eyes back on the lamb.

I think of Mr. North's rigid prejudice and unyielding mistrust of my magic. Of *me*. He would not even let me use my threads to comfort a distressed animal. My pride balks at the thought of taking another moment's hospitality from the likes of such a disagreeable man.

But then I think of Sylvie surrounded by those horrid children.

I think of myself, deprived of magic and education as a girl, desperate to be free of the one person who was supposed to protect and nurture me.

"I would be willing to instruct Sylvie," I say slowly, "in exchange for room and board for the duration of my stay in Blackswire."

Sylvie crows, flinging herself around her brother in a fierce hug, then skipping away out the door. "It's settled then! I must go tell Mrs. MacDougal!"

She's gone in moments, and when I turn back around, Mr. North is facing me squarely, one arm propped on the stall door. He leans very near, so that I can smell the hay stuck to the coarse wool of his jacket. His dark amber eyes bore into mine.

"You can stay," he says softly. "It may be a governess will do Sylvie some good. And you are only temporary, after all, as you await your employer's arrival. But mark me, I am bringing you on as a teacher, *not* a Weaver. If I even suspect that you've channeled in my house or breathed a word of magic instruction to my sister, I will toss you out on your pretty arse."

I suck in a breath of indignation, my cheeks flushing with heat. "*Language*, my lord." If he were one of my pupils, I'd take him by the ear for a scolding.

"As I told you." He pulls back, and the air around me cools. "I'm no noble. Only a country landowner, and a guardian who takes his duties very seriously. My concern has always been, and will always be, that child's safety."

"I assure you," I reply icily, "that her safety, and *any* child's safety, is of paramount importance to me too."

"Then you agree to my terms?" He sticks out his hand. The same one that a short time ago was shoved inside a sheep's innards. Gloved, but still.

After a moment's hesitation, I take it. His grip is warm and firm, engulfing mine against a palm as calloused as any farmhand's. He holds my hand for a few heartbeats, his eyes studying my face, as if searching for any sign of deception. Insensibly, I am put in mind of Lachlan's cold, ageless hands, and the other bargain I struck years ago.

But this does not feel the same. I am not a frightened little girl, but a woman of resolute mind, with magic in my fingertips. I will endure this unsufferable laird for as long as it takes to find the way into

Elfhame. Then I will bring Lachlan his branch and bid Conrad North farewell for all time.

And then, at last, I will finally be free to go home to my classroom, where I belong.

Mrs. MacDougal, her lips pursed in disapproval, helps me settle back into the guest room where I'd spent the previous night. I can feel her suspicion rolling off her like an icy wind and do my best to be cheerful and helpful. It does not thaw her regard of me.

I can only breathe easily again when she leaves, shutting my door behind her. Alone in my room, my hand clutching the letter in my pocket, I make sure my door is locked before taking out one of my valises from the wardrobe. It's two days before I'm supposed to report back to Lachlan, but after what I found in the cottage, I can't wait that long. I need to know what happened to Fiona, and I know Lachlan has the answers. I told Mrs. MacDougal I needed to rest after my walk to town and back this morning, and she seemed relieved to leave me to my room for the afternoon.

Opening the valise, I pull out the large tapestry Lachlan acquired from the Telarii Guild, holding my breath as I do. It unrolls with a rustle, heavy as a carpet, thumping on the floorboards.

The tapestry is magnificent, perhaps the most expensive thing my hands have ever touched. It is one of a matched set, and the twin is with Lachlan in the castle.

Pushing a chair to the window to stand upon, I hang it from the curtain rods and then step back to drink it in. The pattern is elaborate, worked in vibrant crimson, deep cerulean, ocher, ecru, and bursts of yellow gold, all winding in a spiraling starburst that reminds me of the pattern I first wove to summon Lachlan into my uncle's study. The threads are expertly woven, and it must have taken years to complete, which tells me this plan of Lachlan's has been some time in the making.

I pull up the lower corner of the tapestry to inspect the back, where the threads are rough and bundled, showing the depth of the craftsmanship. The ends of the threads are frayed and tangled together like the shaggy hide of one of the highland cattle Sylvie and I passed on the road. I run my hands over it and feel the strength of the weft beneath, and within it, the hum of enormous magic. The tapestry practically simmers with energy. I marvel as long as I can, before remembering I should get this over with before Mrs. MacDougal calls me for dinner.

Reaching out, I put a hand on the tapestry and let out a long, slow breath. Dread and hesitation mix in my belly, but my skin is alive with eager curiosity.

Telepestry is one of the greater arts of Weaving; teleportation through tapestry is extremely expensive and thus quite rare. I cannot think of anyone I know who ever attempted it. And the threads are limited in use, as all threads are. Lachlan told me this tapestry had perhaps a half dozen uses in it before it would turn to ash. Looking at the artistry of the Weave, I feel a wistful pang that it should ever be reduced to such.

Using the tapestry requires no channeling on my part; I wouldn't have the strength to fill it even without my old vowknot strangling my power. No, this tapestry would have called for multiple master Weavers pouring energy into it over the course of many days. Now it is fully charged and humming. When I close my eyes, I can hear it like the muffled sound of a beehive.

Grand magic indeed, Lachlan had called it only yesterday. It feels like a month ago now.

As an afterthought, I cross the room and rummage through the items on the bureau, settling on an iron snuffer. I tie it beneath my overskirt, hiding it in the folds of my dress. It knocks against my thigh as I return to the tapestry, feeling slightly more protected.

There is one long, braided thread hanging from the center of the pattern, and I take firm hold of it. Then, with a little exhalation, I step forward, pushing into the Weave.

The tightly woven threads part between my hands reluctantly, as if reality were pushing back against this intrusion into its laws, insisting such magic should not be possible. But I push through anyway, wrenching threads apart as if they were vines, struggling to pass between them. Then I am through, into what seems like another world—another *reality*—entirely. And the sight that greets me there is dizzying.

CHAPTER ELEVEN

Lachlan had described this place as the *outside* of the world, reality turned inside out, where the very fabric of existence might be seen in its raw form.

To my right and left, and all around, I see nothing but threads: thousands, millions of them, twisting and twining every way, and *pulsing* as if they were alive. It reminds me of the backside of the tapestry itself, and I feel like an ant crawling through them. My steps land on a woven ground which gives way slightly, as if I were walking on damp earth. The threads around me move like rivers, stretching into infinity, no gaps between them that aren't filled with even more threads. In them I see every color of the spectrum, and colors I've never seen before, and some threads glow as if infused with magic.

Lachlan did *not* prepare me for this.

Where the threads rub against me, they feel nothing like wool or silk at all, but the way I'd imagine the sting of a jellyfish might feel— sharp and alive and sizzling. I flinch away from them, mind reeling, remembering Lachlan's pointed warning not to grasp them.

This is not a power given to any, mortal or immortal, he had told me. *It has been tried, and the price is always death.*

My ears fill with the sound of countless rushing and whispering threads, like the roar of a fast and powerful river, and a little like the buzz of a thousand congealing voices on a busy London market day. It's enough to drown me if I am not careful; already I feel the many currents of threads pulling at me, threatening to sweep me away.

Lachlan had warned me to hold fast to the guide, lest I be forever lost on the wrong side of reality, and to keep my eyes shut until I was firmly through. But terrible as this place is, I couldn't possibly block it out; it's the same urge I get to stare straight into the heart of a thunderstorm, even with the lightning splintering the sky around me. I dare not remove either hand from the guiding thread, but I can still look around and boggle at the warp and weft all around. I push through, forcing one step after another.

My mind feels as if it's crumpling, buckling under the impossibility of this place and this magic. Lights spark in my vision, and I hurry forward faster, now watching the thread in my hands as it leads me through.

It takes no more than eight steps before I find myself pushing through the other tapestry, one which materializes before me out of the great teeming, flowing fabric all around. Every portal, Lachlan had explained, has an anchor—a mirror of itself which forms the exit point, like two doors spread far apart. Gasping now for air, my head aching from the effort and my stomach tossing violently, I let out a cry and throw myself through the second tapestry, and land on the dirt floor of the ruined castle, the fae all around me.

After catching my breath, I turn and see the twin to the tapestry in my room hanging behind me, fully intact despite my having just climbed through it. It is hung on a wooden frame like a tanner's skin, the guide thread dangling from its center. Around it rise the stone walls of the castle ruins, and the damp moor air chills my skin.

I step away, still reeling, to search for Lachlan. Fae glance at me as I pass, and whisper to one another in their rustling language. I ignore them and work my way through the ruins, wrapped tightly in my shawl, one hand gripped around Fiona's letter. The wind whistles through the cracks and gaps in the walls.

If Lachlan is surprised to see me two days early, he does not show it. He stands in front of the ruins, more wild and fae than I've seen him yet, with a silver brooch binding the lace at his throat. His hair is unbound, pale strands loose on his shoulders and fine as silk threads. He wears no coat, despite the cold, only an old-fashioned doublet of royal blue, shot through with silver threads, over tight breeches and knee-high black boots. He looks like a dandy lordling out of a bygone century, and on any other person the outfit would be ridiculous. Instead, he makes me feel underdressed and at odds with the setting, as if I am the one out of time, not he.

Lachlan spreads his hands. "Rose Pryor, did you miss me—?"

"What happened to her?" I demand, stopping short and clenching my fists. I am still trembling from my strange passage here; when I shut my eyes, I see the great forest of threads pulsing on the back of my eyelids, whispering and coiling and twisting like snakes.

Lachlan frowns. "Who?"

"The woman," I say, thrusting the letter toward his face. "The old Weaver. *Fiona.*"

He blinks once, then understanding dawns in his eyes. "That old thing? She is probably dust and bones by now."

"What *happened* to her? What did you do?"

His hand presses to his breast, his eyebrows arching in offense. "I? *I?* Fiona was *you* four decades ago, my dear, and just like you she was small and mortal and clever. But she failed at her task, and there was nothing I could do to save her."

"What bargain did she make with you?"

He shrugs, squinting as if finding it difficult to recall. "A human she cared about was sick. I healed him. She knew the terms, and she agreed to them, just as you did."

"What did she offer as collateral?"

He sighs. "It's been so long . . ."

"Tell me!"

"Her time," he says, blunt at last. "Or her sense of it, anyway. At least that was how I interpreted it, which was *generous* of me, by the way. *I swear on what time I have left* were her exact words, and you can guess how I might have otherwise read that. But she was a foolish one from the start. That lad she loved—the one *I* healed for her—moved on to woo another merely a month after Fiona departed. The girl had no sense then either, tethering herself to such a faithless wastrel."

It must have been her Philip whom Lachlan had healed, summoned by a young Fiona out of desperation and terror. And to call due her debt, he'd then sent her on the same mission he has sent *me* on.

And she failed and paid a terrible price for it, living the same day over and over for forty years, still believing her beloved was waiting for her. How many of those pitiful letters did she write and never send, having no idea the years were passing her by?

I step closer to him, until I can see the dark-blue lines in his pale eyes. "Give me some other errand or task to perform. Not this, not anymore."

"I cannot."

"Release me, faerie, or I will—"

"What?" He steps closer, until his eyes are boring into mine and I smell the evergreen sprig he has pinned to his coat. His voice is as soft as the first wind of winter. "What will you do, Rose Pryor?"

I tilt my jaw, glaring at him.

"*You* summoned *me*," he murmurs. "Twelve years ago. Do you think I had a choice but to appear in your house? To offer you a bargain? I did what you asked of me. Now it's your turn. Forget Fiona. You're stronger and smarter than she ever was, and you will succeed where she did not."

"And if I do not, you will take my magic from me forever."

"I did not write the rules," he says. "I only play by them. And so do you. That is a choice *you* made. Now, you came all this way. You may as well give me a report."

I release a little breath as he walks back to the castle. For a moment I stay where I am, watching the way his hair moves when he walks, like water flowing.

I imagine pulling a silver strand from his scalp and Weaving it into a rending knot, to burst the heart in his chest. Then what would become of me? Would his death set me free? Or would this bond between us, this thread of my vow, destroy me along with him?

The very idea sends a cold shudder through me. I don't have the nerve for murder and dark magic, the kind Fiona turned to when she was desperate, draining the life out of birds to fuel her spells. And maybe Lachlan is right, and it is all my own doing, my own choices which brought me here.

In the castle, I find fae everywhere—lounging, eating, idly picking at stringed instruments. It takes me a second to realize there are more here than there were before. I remember counting near forty when we first left London; there are closer to sixty now. Fates, where did they all come from? Even as I watch, another arrives and is greeted with shouts and wine by her brethren. The fae have their own way of saying hello, placing their hands palm to palm and then resting their foreheads together while they murmur a low, synchronized phrase in their whispery tongue.

"Come and tell me what you've been up to," Lachlan says, gripping my elbow and steering me away from the scene. There are two armchairs tucked beneath a brightly woven awning, a low fire burning before them in a ring of stones.

"Well?" Lachlan sits lithely, throwing one leg over the other and flicking his ringed fingers at me. It occurs to me, suddenly and quite strangely, how very different he is from Conrad North, like winter and summer, like silver and gold. Faerie and human. Lachlan is an ethereal creature, all light and air, as if he might shift in and out of existence with a whisper. The laird of Ravensgate, on the other hand, is as solid as the earth, as much a part of the moors as its rocks and heather and rough, woolly sheep.

With a start, I wonder why I am comparing them at all, as if they were two racehorses I was thinking of betting on. It seems even here, Mr. North exists only to distract and delay me from my mission.

I tell Lachlan of coming across the laird in the wood, and of Mr. North's begrudging acceptance of my lodging at Ravensgate.

"This laird of yours," Lachlan says. "Is he handsome?"

With a start, I sit up straighter. "What?"

"It's only that, when you speak of him, the blood rises to your face, just here . . ." He leans toward me, one cool finger grazing the air by my cheek as if in a restrained caress. "How pretty you are when you blush. Should I be *jealous*?"

I pull back, my stomach tumbling. "What on earth is there between us, sir, that you should be jealous of?"

"You've done well, positioning yourself in this manor. Its proximity to the gateway will be a boon. Just remember, you are *my* little witch, Rose Pryor." With a half smile, he takes the sprig of evergreen from his lapel and tucks it behind my ear. "I found you first."

"I am my own, sir," I reply hotly. "And not a pet to be led on a leash."

He chuckles bitterly. "Imagine how *I* felt, twelve years ago, being summoned through the ether by a child of eight, with naught a say in the matter." He quirks an eyebrow at me, then smiles. "There you go again, blushing."

I lower my face, resisting the urge to cover my cheeks with my hands. "Mr. Murdoch—"

"Please." He grimaces. "Call me Lachlan."

"Lachlan, then. What if you had never asked of me this *favor*? What if I had turned twenty-one without ever having seen your face a second time?"

His eyes drift away, the smile fading. His features are as cool and still as carved alabaster. "Then you would have still lost your magic. So perhaps, instead of accusing me as if I were some sort of common kidnapper, you might try thanking me for choosing you to accompany me on this mission."

"Why *did* you choose me, a penniless teacher with unreliable magic?"

He gazes not at me, but at the horizon beyond me, turning ancient and unfathomable in that unnerving manner of his. "You possess qualities more valuable than magic."

"And what, do tell, are these? What talents, what virtues, what wiles do I possess that make me so *valuable* to you?" I'm not sure why I need to know. Perhaps the discovery of Fiona unsettled me more than I realized.

He stares at me now, looking a bit lost, his lips parted but no words between them.

"What am I to you, Lachlan of the fae?"

His hand rises again, this time to stroke one finger along the back of my wrist. Though his touch sends a cold shiver up my arm, I do not flinch. I can make no sense of the glint in his eyes, whether it is disdain or affection. I return his gaze, wondering what he wants. Who he is, really, behind his absurd clothes and mirror-gray eyes. What does he truly think of me? Am I just a tool to him, or something more? And if more . . . then what?

He gives me no answers. His hand falls away, and he rises to his feet with a sigh. I nearly reach out to stop him, then retract my hand, bewildered by my own reaction. How does he draw me in like this, stirring up . . . *something* deep inside me, then leaving me feeling twisted and confused?

"I am relying on you, Miss Pryor. We all are. When I sent Fiona in, things were not as dire. But now we are growing desperate, and you're the only hope we have. That is why I chose you. Because you were clever and fearless, a girl who wove like a moorwitch of old. I knew the moment I met you, twelve years ago, that you would be my finest investment . . ."

His words wash through me like a rush of wine down my throat, bringing warmth to my cheeks and a whirl of lightness to my head, but all the same, they leave behind a tinge of unease. For all that I've spent the last week in his company, I still have no idea how to read him, and how to winnow the truth from the flattery in his words.

"But now I must wonder . . ." He glances at me. "Are you still that girl?"

I reflect on that uneasily, unsure of the answer. "Why are you desperate?"

He extends his hand. "Come, and I will show you."

He leads me deeper into the ruins, where some of the old chambers are still intact, stone ceilings half fallen but the remnants sturdy enough. In one of these, on a bed of silk and evergreen branches, lies a faerie woman.

Her skin is ashen, flaking off her bones. There is not a drop of color in her; she is all grays and shadow, her cheeks sunken, her eyes hollows. I need only a glance to tell me she is dying. A few other fae sit around her, singing a strange, low song in monotone, Weaving charms between their hands and embroidering spells onto her green silk dress, but I sense their magic will not stop what is coming.

"This is what becomes of us the longer we linger in the World Above, among your iron and mortality," says Lachlan. "We call it our iron tithe."

He kneels by the faerie and takes her hand, kissing her fingers.

"My Lorellan," he sighs. "I was too late to save you, and that is a burden I will bear all my days."

The faerie seems too far gone to even acknowledge his presence. I think guiltily of the iron hidden beneath my skirt and back away a little, waiting for him to finish paying his respects.

We leave quietly, Lachlan subdued. He looks weary, his eyes shadowed. A cold wind wraps around us as we walk through the ruins, swirling his hair.

"Do you understand now?" he asks me.

"I think I do."

He pauses beneath a half-crumbled archway and studies me, the slope of the ground between us making him seem to loom. When the wind drags a length of hair from my braid, he tucks it behind my ear. I catch my breath, unable to look away from his glistening eyes. A single, silver tear beads in the corner of his left eye, then rolls slowly down his cheek.

Feeling half lost in a dream, I wipe it away with my thumb. He takes my wrist, trapping the knuckle of my forefinger against the corner of his lips.

"I know you think me a monster," he says.

"I don't." I did, once, but now . . .

"I have done monstrous things."

Briefly, I shut my eyes and see my aunt, scrabbling about senselessly in the padded room where I last saw her.

But it was I who summoned him. It was I who asked him to set me free.

"So have I," I whisper.

"Was I right about you, then?" he murmurs. "Did I put my trust in the right Weaver?"

"You did," I reply breathlessly. The words surprise me, bubbling out of some hidden well of confidence I was not sure existed.

Lachlan tilts his head, a sad smile playing on his lips as he releases my hand. I withdraw it, shaking a little, bewildered at the flutter of wings in my belly.

"Hm." He gives me a thorough look over that leaves me blushing yet again. "I must admit, when I saw the state of you in that wretched boarding room, I had my doubts."

A knot of desperation sticks in my throat, as I feel the sudden, bewildering need to prove myself to this faerie, the same way I needed to prove myself to Mother Bridgid. My magic is fading, but it is not *gone*. I still have my mind and its language of patterns. I have my twelve years of grueling education and teaching experience. I am not a lost cause.

"I will bring you that branch," I say. "You will return home, and Lorellan's fate will not be yours."

I try not to let myself pity him, nor any of his kind. I remember what he is, what he's asked of me, and what I will become if I do not carry out his bidding.

And yet . . . now I understand him better, in a way. He is desperate too, willing to go to any length to save his people.

For the past twelve years, I have viewed him as a shadowy menace lurking in the shadows of my youth, the monster I summoned from the dark and set loose upon the world. But he isn't a monster, really. He is perhaps more human than I gave him credit for, capable of fear, loss, and desperation.

Perhaps he and I are more alike than we are different.

"I will do it, Lachlan," I say again, more firmly.

He nods, seemingly to himself, and walks over to the Telarian tapestry, his back to me, his frame rigid as he gazes at the mesmerizing pattern of threads.

"Find the way into Elfhame, Rose," he murmurs after a long, cool moment. "You must. For both our sakes."

CHAPTER TWELVE

At breakfast the next morning, Sylvie North beams at me over her oats and milk. Notably absent is her brother, who has ostensibly set off to meet with some crofters in Blackswire to discuss spring plantings. I am a little surprised he is not determined to perch over Sylvie and me all morning, like a dark crow waiting to swoop down and peck my hands for so much as touching a spool of thread.

I soon find out my fears were not far off, however, when Mrs. MacDougal announces she will spend the day dusting the library, where it just so happens I planned to hold Sylvie's lessons.

So the housekeeper is to be Mr. North's spy.

"What should we do first?" Sylvie asks, curling up into a great armchair by the hearth. Mr. MacDougal lights a fire before stamping off to tend his sheep. The licking orange flames drive back the gloom of yet another rainy morning. Droplets run in pretty patterns down the arched windows, tracing down the glass like pale ribbons.

I take out a small list I wrote out last night to distract myself from thinking of Lachlan and Lorellan and the other faeries. The weight of their plight is an added pressure, entirely reframing my understanding of my mission here. Their lives apparently depend on *me* opening their way home. I can still feel the dampness of Lachlan's tear on my thumb.

I can still see the glistening, desperate hope in his eyes. How startlingly human he revealed himself to be.

And here is Sylvie North, with her large, similarly hopeful gaze fastened upon me, depending on me as well.

"I need some idea of how far you are into each subject," I say, running a finger down my list. "We'll do some informal exams on history, science, literature, arithmetic, geography . . ."

Sylvie's eyes glass over, the eager smile on her face turning to a grimace of dread. My finger pauses on the list, tapping thoughtfully.

"Let's start with geography," I say. "Does your brother have any atlases in here?"

We search the shelves, moving under the watchful gaze of Mrs. MacDougal, who dusts each book one by one as assiduously as if she were about to hand them to Queen Victoria herself.

"Ah!" Sylvie hauls a large leather-bound tome from a bottom shelf. *Maps of the Known World.* Is that what you want?"

"Good find." I hide my disappointment. I had been hoping for something closer to home. A map of Scottish faerie gateways, perhaps? The estate map I stole from this room two nights ago proved little use, and it seems today will turn up naught else of value to my search.

I take the atlas from Sylvie, and we open it. But inside, rather than neat pages of maps, I find a jumble of torn paper. Pieces flutter down and pile on the carpet, torn, their ragged edges pale as scars.

Every map within has been shredded to bits.

"Tch!" Mrs. MacDougal swoops in, her goose-feather duster all aflutter. "Such a mess!"

"No, wait." I raise a hand to forestall her. "It's like a puzzle, Sylvie. An excellent way to test your geography." Picking up a sliver of west Africa, I extend it to her. "Let's see how far you can get."

While Sylvie works at piecing together the maps, I notice Mrs. MacDougal watching her with a sorrowful expression. At my inquisitive look, the housekeeper clears her throat.

"It was one of Mr. North's favorite books, when he was a wain," she says. "Oh, he'd spend hours over those maps."

"Was he the one who tore them up?" I ask indignantly.

A sad smile tugs at her lips, but then she gives herself a small shake and turns back to her dusting. "Just you mind your student, Miss Pryor, and let the past be."

I realize then that Sylvie has stopped piecing together maps and is instead folding the torn papers into tiny swords. Finding she's been caught, she gives me a sheepish grin and smooths them out again.

By noon, with a bit of help, Sylvie's managed to assemble most of the maps. We discuss them for a while over lunch in the kitchen, and I find her more knowledgeable than I'd feared, but still a year or so behind where she should be for her age. After writing up a plan to help her catch up in her geography studies, I declare the subject done for the day. The rain has stopped, and though the world is wet and gray, we will take what escape we can get.

"You mean I can finally go outside?" She gives a relieved whoop and rushes for her boots.

"Outside to practice multiplication," I clarify. "We don't have apples this time of year, but I think we could scrounge up some rocks."

"Oh." Her exuberance diminished, she nevertheless puts on her boots and heads gamely out the door.

I follow, pausing to look back at Mrs. MacDougal. "Will you be joining us, then?"

The housekeeper, installed in her chair by the stove, groans. "Ach, get on with you. I am an old woman. I cannae be expected to traipse about the countryside all the livelong day! If Mr. North wants you watched, he can bloody well watch you himself!"

Smiling, I pull the door shut and catch up with Sylvie, who is pouncing on every puddle in sight. She grins when she realizes Mrs. MacDougal won't be shadowing us.

"Now you can show me some magic!" she cries.

"Sylvie." I glance at the house. "You know I can't do that."

She sighs and kicks a stone across the drive. "I know."

Taking her hand, I give it a squeeze. "Come. Why don't you show me which burn around here has the best rocks for counting?"

Her smile flashes back onto her face, and she drags me away over the heather. A small creek winds through the moors behind the house, feeding a series of small ponds where a few soggy sheep gather. While Sylvie collects stones, her skirts tied above her knees, I furtively Weave a subtle drying spell over a boulder, my back turned so she can't see. Once the water's evaporated from its surface, I sit and quietly let the ashes of the consumed thread trickle from my fingers into the scrubby brush.

"There," Sylvie says breathlessly, dumping an armload of stones at my feet. "I bet that would have been easier with magic."

"It would have been," I admit. "Now, multiplication is based on—"

"How old were you when you learned you could do magic?" Sylvie tosses a small rock from hand to hand, watching me.

"Sylvie . . ."

"You don't have to show me magic. Just tell me about yourself."

"I cannot."

"*Please.*"

"I gave my word."

She stares at me in a manner I know well—and dread—after my years of teaching. It is the look a particularly devilish pupil gives before she decides to do precisely what she's been told not to.

All at once, Sylvie jumps up and sprints away.

"Sylvie!" I start after her, hampered by my skirts. Lifting them over my ankles, I try to keep up with the girl's energetic pace. "Sylvie, come back!"

She runs over one hill and then another, as the wind picks up and rain begins to sluice down again. I slip and slide in the mud that seems to have no effect on Sylvie.

By the time I catch up with her, she's reached the south-facing side of Toren's Rise, the steep, rocky bluff as high as Ravensgate Manor's pitched roof. I call her name, only for the wind to steal the words from my lips.

Sylvie begins to climb the slippery rocks.

"No!" I reach for her skirt but grab empty air as she hoists herself higher. "Please come down!"

Sylvie gazes down at me, her eyes fierce. "How old were you," she calls, "when you learned you had magic?"

"This is no civilized way to conduct a conversation!"

"I am no civilized girl!" she hurls back, laughing.

Desperately, I look around, scanning the empty moors. We are completely alone, and Sylvie climbs ever higher.

"How old were you?" she shouts again.

It would be easier to deny her curiosity if I didn't see so much of myself in her. A lonely child, locked away from the world, denied freedom and education. Begging to be seen, to be respected. She may not have magic as I did, but she has all the same longing in her. The same hidden ferocity.

"I was six," I call out at last.

She reaches a small outcrop and drags herself onto it, perching there like a cat on a clock. Swinging her legs, heedless of the rain, she leans over and shouts, "And so your auntie sent you off to magic school?"

"No, that came later."

She props her chin in her hands, gazing down at me with those great, hungry eyes. "What was it like? Your school?"

"Can we *please* have this conversation on the ground?"

"I'll come down when you've told me about your school!"

Bloody-minded little . . . She is as infuriating as her brother.

I push my wet hair back and concede, if it is the only thing that will convince the mad creature to come down to safety. "It could be difficult, at times. As I told you, my classmates could be cruel. But many of them were quite nice." I think of my friend Orla, who went to Ireland to teach in Dublin, and of Lisette, who used to braid my hair and sing to me in French. She's in a convent in Austria now, I believe, devoting her life to the Fates and embroidering comfort shrouds for the dying.

"Despite the hardships, it was the happiest I'd ever been." I press my hands to the rock, beseeching her. "Please come down now."

She nods graciously and turns herself around to clamber back the way she'd come up.

But her boot slips on a loose crag of shale, the rock splintering under her weight.

"*Sylvie!*"

She yelps, scrabbling for purchase. Her fingers grip the wet ledge, legs swinging in midair. Any moment, she'll slip and plummet five yards—a potentially fatal drop.

"Hold on!" I cry, tugging thread from my pocket. "Don't let go!"

I struggle with the thread, its fibers already soaked in the rain. The wind pulls at the knot I Weave between my fingers, as if trying its best to undo the spell as quickly as I compose it.

"*Miss Pryor!*" Sylvie cries, as her left hand loses its grip. The other slips inch by inch.

"It will be all right! Just hold on!" The spell finally woven, I stretch my hands wide, and the threads snap taut. But soaked as the fibers are, it will take more magic than usual to ignite them. I reach out with all that is in me, curling invisible fingers around grass, heather, and bush, wrenching energy from their leaves.

Pain knifes through my chest, piercing lung and bone.

Above me, Sylvie screams, her fingers sliding free.

She falls.

I cry out, doubling over and forcing that tide of energy through the narrow, sharp point that is my constricting heart. It is like driving a blade into my own breast. But I channel relentlessly, and at last, the threads flare bright.

Sylvie jerks to a halt a half yard from the rocky ground, where her head would have split on a nasty crag of stone. Suspended in place, she gasps and stares up into the rain, as if she cannot believe she is still alive.

I can hardly believe it.

Breathless with pain, my head spinning, I reach out with ash-covered hands to grasp her skirt and pull her to me. A moment later, the spell releases and she drops into my arms.

I hold her to me, finally sucking in a sob of relief.

"It's all right," I whisper into her hair. "You're safe now."

Carefully I set her down and search for any injury, but besides a few scrapes on her knees and palms, she's blessedly unharmed.

"Thank the Fates," I breathe.

"Thank *you*," she says. "You saved me! With magic!"

I don't tell her how close it was. That had I faltered another heartbeat, she'd be severely injured or worse. I only squeeze her hand and tell her if she ever pulls a stunt like that again, I'll hex her with a month of warts.

"I'm sorry," she says, and to her credit, she does look it. Her gaze drops to her shoes, and I spy a bead of water on her lashes that I do not think is rain.

I sigh. "Come, let's get you dried off. And . . . shall we keep this our secret?"

Smiling, she loops her pinky around mine. "Definitely."

We make our way back to the house, a muddy, soggy journey that leaves us both spattered up to our knees. My heart still has not quite recovered from that painful channel, and I hope Sylvie doesn't notice how much I lean on her as we hobble along. Every step is a test of sheer willpower, and if she were not there to witness it, I might let myself collapse into the muddy heather and give in to the pain.

"I wish I could go to a school like yours," Sylvie says. "Somewhere far away, with other girls like me. Are there boys there too?"

"There are a few, though most boys join the Telarii, not the Moirai." Even there, they are usually outnumbered. A talent for Weaving and channeling has always been more common among women, in nearly every culture and time. I don't have the heart to remind her that without the ability to channel, no Weaving school of any order would take her.

"Well, I should make friends of them all, even the boys."

"Maybe when you're a bit older, you could—"

"No." She shakes her head. "Connie said *never*. He didn't go to school, he says, and I don't need to either. Just like I don't need to go to the seaside, or sail to France, or get married."

I stumble on a slick rock, nearly choking on my own tongue. "*Married?* He'll stop you from getting *married?*"

She shrugs. "Not too put out about that one, to be honest. But I wish Connie would get married. At least then I'd have a sister . . ."

She glances at me sidelong, her eyes narrow and sly, and I shake my head firmly. "No, Sylvie. Don't even entertain the thought. I've a life in London to go back to."

And I can think of beggars back in the Devil's Acre with more appeal than the insufferably arrogant Conrad North.

"Some days," she confesses, "I feel like a prisoner. Like our poor Queen Mary, locked away for no sin other than existing. Or like Elaine of Astolat, doomed in her tower to watch the world only in a mirror."

How lonely has this child been, that she would pour her whole heart out to a guest she's known for two days? My heart breaks for her, and not just because I see myself in her plight. But what can I do? What advice can I give her? Should I tell her to seek out a faerie and strike a devil's bargain, trading one sort of cage for another?

She wants answers I cannot give.

Back at Ravensgate, Mrs. MacDougal fusses over Sylvie while I dry off by the kitchen fire. The girl gives me a conspiratorial smile as the housekeeper bundles her off to her room, but the moment she is gone, I sag onto the hearth, gasping a little. Pressing my hand to my chest, I breathe out long and slow, willing my heart to calm. To unclench itself. It takes longer than usual, this recovery, and that terrifies me.

Fates above.

I must find the gateway to Elfhame, and I must find it soon.

◆ ◆ ◆

Later in the evening, after a simple but warming supper of potato soup and bread, I task Sylvie with some history reading in the library. In moments, however, she falls asleep in the great armchair, snoring softly.

On the floor beside her, I set about meticulously pasting the maps we assembled this morning, unable to bear letting the precious pages fall to pieces again. With the soft pattering of the rain at the windows and the soothing crackle of the fire, I catch myself yawning. Mr. and Mrs. MacDougal have already retired for the night, but Mr. North has still not returned from his trip to Blackswire.

As I fit the maps back together, I find tiny notes scrawled around the borders that I had not seen earlier. Childish script traces the outlines of the continents, penned in ink faded with age.

Here the Bedouin nomads pitch their tents! This is where the pyramids are—MUST see them first. On these islands, dragons can be found—but not the flying, fire-breathing sort, just big lizard things.

I am so engrossed in reading these little addenda that I do not realize I am being watched until a deep voice rumbles over me.

"Where the devil did you find that old thing?"

Startled, I drop the bottle of paste, and it spills across the carpet. "Oh, Fates!" I glare up at the laird in the doorway. "That's the second time you've nearly startled the heart out of me, Mr. North!"

"I hardly think you're in a position to judge, given the nature of our first meeting." Conrad North kneels across from me, taking a handkerchief from his pocket. Captain pads softly behind him and settles down on the warm carpet, his long tongue lolling. "Here. Let me."

"I can do it." I reach for the cloth, but he refuses to relinquish it, and for a moment our fingers tangle together. His are cold and damp from the rain, mine warm from the heat of the fire, and for a heartbeat, the temperature difference sends a spark up my arm.

He tries to snatch his hand away, but the paste on mine holds fast, and to my utter humiliation, I realize I have glued my hand to Mr. North's.

"Ah . . . my apologies," I stammer. "Um."

He stares at our hands. "Well. This is bloody hilarious."

"I can fix it. Just—hold still." I twist my hand.

"Fates, woman! Stop that wriggling! You're peeling the skin off my bones!"

"Oh, hush. You'll wake Sylvie. If you had just let me handle it—"

"I think we can both see how your *handling* turns out. What the hell is in this paste?"

"*Language*, sir!" I grind my teeth together, biting back a curse of my own. In attempting to wrest my fingers loose, I've only entangled us further. "I am not ordinarily this clumsy, I swear."

Captain rests his shaggy head on his paws and regards us both with a plaintive whine.

I study the situation as if it were a knot I am trying to unravel. I feel Mr. North's eyes on me, his steady gaze making the heat rise even higher in my cheeks. I must look stricken with rash by now, an absolute fright. His skin is hot against mine, his large palm enveloping the back of my hand. I find myself thinking, insensibly, of how gently and skillfully that hand had pulled a poor struggling lamb out of its mother.

The pattern of veins over his large knuckles reminds me of a vanishing spell I learned in my third year at school, useful for making small objects disappear for a few moments. I wonder if it would work on a small schoolteacher?

"Do you often solve problems by glaring at them?" he asks, interrupting my admittedly irrational line of thought.

I glare at *him*, just to see if it might work. "I was *thinking*. Which is more than you seem to be doing, laird. Have you got any bright ideas? No? I thought not."

Scowling, I go back to prying at my fingers, then his. Until he puts his other hand over mine, his thumb lightly brushing my wrist.

Right where the two circular burn scars gleam like white pennies.

"What's this, then?" he asks softly.

I instinctively attempt to wrench my hand away, which is, of course, impossible at the moment. Oh, but the Fates can be cruel.

"Nothing," I say. "Old injury. Hazards of a life devoted to magic."

He makes no reply, only gazes at me while I scrape at the glue between his thumb and forefinger. He's got calluses there to rival any farmer's, I suspect. What the hell *is* in this damnable paste?

"The important thing is to remain calm," I tell him, feeling a bit hysterical.

"Ouch," he says calmly. "You're peeling my fingernail off by the roots. Could you please stop?"

With a suppressed growl, I give up and sit back. "I do know a spell . . ."

"Of course you do," he mutters. "And how will you Weave it with one hand?"

A short laugh bubbles from my lips. "I have no idea."

For a moment we stare at our adhered hands, perplexed and about as awkward as two humans could be. The fire crackles beside us, and from her chair, Sylvie gives a soft snore. All at once, we both burst into laughter, his a deep, chest-borne rumble that vibrates the floor beneath us, mine high as a twittering sparrow's. I throw my other hand over my mouth to suppress the mad giggles, while he buries his face in his broad shoulder, his entire frame shaking. I feel completely absurd, the whole situation some ludicrous farce invented by a deranged playwright.

"Watch it!" I gasp out, as he leans to the left, toward the hearth. "You'll catch fire—"

Then it hits me. And, by the look in his eyes, it hits him too.

At the same moment, we both say, "The fire!"

"Of course," he adds. "Gently, now."

We raise our joined hands to the hearth and wait. In hindsight, this solution probably should have been obvious from the start, and perhaps I'd have realized it if I hadn't been so addled with horror and embarrassment. My laughter evaporates in the light of this new burst of rationality, and I self-consciously avert my gaze. He does the same, both of us struggling to look at absolutely anything but each other. The fire warms our hands, taking its precious time. But eventually, the heat softens the paste. We manage to peel our fingers apart without much damage.

At least, not the physical kind. My pride may never recover.

I clear my throat. "We need never speak of this again."

"A fine idea," he replies quickly.

I look down at my hand, the drying glue peeling on my skin, unsure what to say or where to put my hands or how to even sit properly in front of him. My legs seem folded in a terribly awkward angle. Why am I sweating so much? Can he tell?

And why is my heart halfway up my throat, making it suddenly difficult to breathe?

"So." Mr. North settles back, one long leg outstretched, the other knee drawn up to his chest with his arm slung over it. His hair is still damp from his ride home, his face still red from our regrettable . . . encounter. "I was going to ask how the first day of instruction went, but you've put your pupil to sleep, I see."

I glance at Sylvie, a bit startled at the fondness I feel for the girl after only two days. "Geography is hard work. It's no easy task, putting the world back together."

"'Tis not," he replies softly. He picks up one of the torn bits of map, rubbing the northern half of India between his thumb and forefinger. "Not my best work, I admit. In my defense, I was eight years old when I tore this up."

"Out of boredom? Or merely a wanton love of destruction?" I ask, still peeved at the idea of ripping up *any* book, much less such a beautifully illustrated, no doubt expensive atlas.

He sets down the piece, restoring India to its place. "It was rage."

"At the world, I presume?" I sweep a hand over the piecemeal map.

He gives a dry chuckle. "I was regrettably literal, as a lad."

For all that I find Mr. North to be a heartless brute, I feel a moment's softness toward the boy who tore up the atlas. I wonder what sort of childhood he had, and if he was as lonely as Sylvie is now. Is that why he keeps her so close? For fear of losing her and becoming that lonely boy again? At eight, he would have just lost his mother, and what child would not react so to such loss, clinging desperately to whatever family he had left.

"Eight is a hard age," I say softly. "All raw feeling and no control over one's destiny. One might make any number of understandable mistakes when eight years old."

Mistakes that might haunt one for the rest of one's life. I rub at my collarbone, just over my heart.

Feeling his eyes on my face, I look up and meet them. Mr. North's expression is enigmatic, an odd puzzle of curiosity and guarded suspicion. Does he suspect I am hiding something?

"Did you ever see them, sir?" I ask, raising a jagged sliver of Egypt. "The pyramids, I mean."

He looks at the fire, his eyes shifting from dark bronze to bright gold in its light. "Nay. They are a long way from Scotland."

"Mm. Most places are." Dipping the brush into the paste, I glue Egypt back together, concentrating on lining the edges up as precisely as I can. I feel Mr. North's gaze drift back to me, the weight of his eyes making my stomach tighten inexplicably. I ruin the Gulf of Aqaba and am forced to pry it apart to start over.

I remind myself of my conversation with Sylvie as we tramped back over the moor earlier today. This man has trapped her in his isolated little world, withheld her from friends, school, society. He is prejudiced against magic and intractable in his arrogance. I remind myself of all these things until a cool current of anger flows through me and settles the senseless fluttering in my belly.

"It is late," I say tightly.

"Indeed. Of course. I should put Sylvie to bed." He rises and lifts his sister into his arms, cradling her as effortlessly as a lamb. But at the door, he pauses and looks back. "Thank you, Miss Pryor."

I look up. "For?"

"Piecing the world back together." His eyes fall on the map. "Even if you did put South Africa upside down."

Startled, I look down, and he makes his final exit with a low, husky laugh.

Fates damn him, he's right. I *thought* something had looked off about the map. I stare at the inverted tip of Africa for a long while, my stomach in knots. Curling my hand into a fist, I find I can still feel the warm press of the laird's skin against mine.

"Truly, he *is* a most insufferable man," I murmur to the flames.

CHAPTER THIRTEEN

In the middle of the night, I lurch suddenly awake.

I lie still and listen, wondering what startled me. Nothing in the room stirs. The window is dark glass, without even the faintest moonlight to silver it. I breathe in the scent of the beeswax candles and the freshly laundered sheets and think perhaps my imagination has got the better of me. Absurdly, I think of Sylvie's ghost, and a chill prickles over my skin.

Then I hear it: a *thump* above, as if something heavy has hit the floor.

Sylvie's room.

I roll out of bed and land on my bare feet, already beginning to Weave a cat's cradle as I squint at the clock. It's two in the morning. Nobody should be awake, not even her.

I creep down the corridor to the first stair; the steps creak no matter how softly I tread. On the upper floor the hallway stretches into shadow. My feet are chilled by the cold floorboards. Light shines beneath Sylvie's door, but all is quiet again. In a tall painting beside me, a North ancestor looks down broodily; he has Conrad's dark brows and wavy hair. I give him a scowl and scurry past, every sense craning. The threads between my hands quiver; with a breath of magic, they'll release a spell to immobilize anything and anyone who might mean harm.

Another thump rattles Sylvie's door and is followed by a crash.

I break into a run, reaching for magic, prepared to stun unconscious whatever's on the other side of that door. Keeping my spellknot taut, I bend my thumb and little finger just enough to turn the knob—

—and stumble into a maelstrom.

Sylvie is spinning in midair, lit by the candles burning on her dresser, surrounded by a swirl of flying detritus: shoes, dolls, hairbrushes, vases, a great many wooden carvings of animals and warriors. It's all whirling around, faster and faster, objects crashing together and spinning away, bouncing off the walls.

"Rose!" Sylvie cries out. "Help!"

She flails around, tipping head over heels. Her window is open, and she's heading straight for it; she'll spin into the night and then, when the hovering knot around her ankle has worn out, she'll plummet to her death.

I lunge across the room, dodging flying objects, and then leap, grabbing her by her heel just as she floats through the casement.

With a grunt, I pull her back inside and rip the knot off her ankle. The thread turns to ash in my hands—she was only a second away from falling three stories.

Sylvie collapses onto me, and we both crash to the floor.

Keeping low, for there are still dozens of items spinning overhead, I unravel the unused stunning knot I'd woven and rework it into a settling charm.

My first attempt fails, leaving my heart clenching, but the second works. The charm seizes the errant objects and gently returns them to the floor.

A moment passes, in which Sylvie and I both pant for breath, surrounded by a mess of toys and candlesticks and broken vases.

Then she rolls to her feet and spreads her arms wide, her face flushed and her hair wild.

"Did you *see* that?" she asks. "Did you see what I did?"

I slowly sit up, looking around. Each of the items I brought back to the floor has a little hovering charm bound around it. Several of them are beginning to flake away, and the smell of ashes grows stronger. In an arrangement of glass jars, vases, and cases along one wall, a good many frogs are frantically jumping around, excited by the activity. At least she didn't try to send *those* flying about, nor did she draw energy from them. But the greenery in their cages—mounds of moss and weeds she'd planted for them to hide in—is all wilted and brown, sucked dry. A clear sign of a clumsy amateur's first Weaving.

"You can channel," I whisper.

"I can channel!" She claps her hands, giggling. "I knew I could! I always knew it!"

"Sylvie, you can *channel*."

"Aye." She frowns. "We just discussed that."

Rising to my feet, I pick up a carved oak Valkyrie, complete with a tiny wooden sword and cunningly shaped armor, and I recognize Mr. North's artistry in it. Picking at the hovering charm tied around the figurine's waist, I shake my head, speechless.

"The first few didn't go right," she says, anxiously peering over my shoulder as if I were a teacher grading her exam. "I had to work at it a bit. I forgot the loopy thing you did at the end."

But it's not her technique which steals my breath away—the knots are clumsy—but rather the fact she channeled *so many* at once.

I hold up the doll and frown at her. "Sylvie, have you ever channeled before?"

"I've tried, and I got a warm feeling all through me, but I never knew any knots. Nobody would teach me. I tried to learn battle spells from some spiders I caught in the larder, like Robert the Bruce did when he was fighting the English. But I guess they weren't the same sort of spider."

The question is, does Conrad know Sylvie has magic? He told me she'd been tested, and that nothing had come from it. Was the Weaver who tested Sylvie simply incompetent, or did Mr. North *lie*?

And if he did know she could channel, did he purposefully leave her untrained?

Because the only reason anyone would neglect a child's magical aptitude . . . is because they want it to go away.

If left untended, the ability to channel fades over time. A child fully capable of crafting a hovering charm at age five could lose the knack entirely by the time she is ten, if she is never taught *how* to control that energy. That's why it's so important that young Weavers are trained early. It's what, I believe, my aunt intended to happen to me. If I hadn't been taken in by the Order of the Moirai when I was, I'd have lost the talent entirely not long after leaving her house.

Heat sparks in my chest, a waking dragon.

"Sylvie." I keep my voice low and easy, so she can't see the rage building to an inferno inside me. "Did your brother ever let anyone test you, to see if you had magical aptitude?"

"What does that mean?"

I kneel opposite her. Then, pulling the spare thread from my sleeve, I twine it around her fingers and mine; a four-hand cat's cradle. She watches eagerly, eyes bright. The web is spread between us, threads quivering expectantly.

"It would have looked like this," I say. "Whoever was testing you—perhaps the schoolteacher in Blackswire—would have asked you to close your eyes and exhale very slowly, while thinking of these things: The wind pushing open a cracked door. A heavy cloud finally releasing rain. An oak shoot pushing up through the soil, finding the sunlight for the first time."

"Like this?"

She shuts her eyes and breathes out; at once the thread between us glows blue white and crackles with frost, all the way up my fingers and then my arms. Above us, flakes of snow begin to fall from nowhere, lacy white and soft. The air in the room turns frigid; my breath clouds white in front of my lips. The damask drapes on the window and bed creak as they stiffen, ice riming the fabric.

The thread burns through to ash, powdering our hands.

"I did it again!" she says, holding her palms out to catch the snow. "What spell is that?"

"It's a simple cold spell," I whisper. "And no one ever asked you to do that?"

"No."

So he *did* lie.

I look up at the snowfall, which begins to dwindle now. A few more flakes drift down and lace the carpet before dissolving into water. "You're *sure* you haven't done anything like this before?"

She scowls. "I told you I hadn't! What's wrong? You look angry."

What's wrong? What's wrong is that Sylvie is ten years old. She has magic, yes, but she's never used it before. Which means it should have faded away years ago. She shouldn't be able to summon a thimbleful of energy.

But to fill all those hovering knots, and to react to the test like that . . . I've only ever seen girls *barely* change the temperature of the thread, the difference all but imperceptible. I remember my own test, administered by Sister Elizabeth three days after Lachlan addled my aunt's mind. I'd summoned enough cold to frost the tips of the old woman's fingers, which had made her nearly giddy with astonishment.

Now, thanks to Sylvie, there is frost lacing my shoulders and collarbone, and cold water runs down my arms and face where the snow begins to melt.

I stare at Sylvie, at a loss for words, my mind vibrating between fury and wonder. She may be the most powerful Weaver I have ever encountered. Stronger than me, certainly, and to think for all these years, her talent has lain dormant, not only neglected but actively suppressed by her brother.

I rise to my feet and go to the door. "Sylvie, go to bed. It's late."

"What?" She blinks. "But—but we're only just getting started!"

"Started at what?"

"Well . . ." She raises her hands. "My lessons."

"Your lessons?" I shake my head. "I'm not here to teach you."

"But you *must.*" Her eyes begin to well with tears. "I was going to show you what I could do, once I'd got it under control. I thought for sure you'd be my teacher. I want this. I want it more than anything in the world."

I stand frozen in place, my pulse pounding in my ears. I glance at the shriveled plants in the terrariums and think of the damage an untrained Weaver can do.

"Please!" She clasps her hands together in supplication. "Nothing ever felt so right or wonderful or good! Please, Rose. I want to be like you. I want magic!"

I want magic, Aunt.

I have a right to it, same as anyone!

I shut my eyes, leaning on the door. I can hear my own voice, clearer than I ever have since that horrible night. My hands move subconsciously to my throat, to the burn scar on my neck.

"You have to teach me," Sylvie says, and I open my eyes with a shudder. "We can practice in secret. Just you and me. Connie doesn't ever have to know! Please?"

"You need a proper teacher," I whisper. "I can't—I'm not here to get involved. Even if I wanted to, I have my own—I have to go."

"But, Rose—"

I flee down the hallway, fists clenched, so angry I could scream. That anger is good; it is hot and powerful, and before it, the memory of my aunt disappears. It's so strong it's almost like magic coursing through me, filling me with strength.

I will find Conrad North, and there will be a reckoning.

CHAPTER FOURTEEN

I storm down the hallway, thinking of all the ways I'd like to hex the laird of Ravensgate for sabotaging his own sister's magical potential. The girl's pleas hammer at my ears as if she were hiding under my bed whispering them through the night.

Please, Rose. I want to be like you.

Mr. North's room is at the far end of the hall. I nearly burst in, but force myself to stop and draw a few breaths.

For all I know, he sleeps in the nude.

The notion leaves me flushed, and for a moment, I forget why I am here and that I should be angry. But it takes only a heartbeat for my fury to come rushing back.

When I knock and get no reply, I decide justice is worth the risk of exposed lairds.

I open the door softly and peer in. Mr. North's room is dark and silent, a jungle of dark furniture and a heavily curtained four-poster bed.

"Mr. North?"

I take a few hesitant steps inside, my eyes adjusting to the dark and picking out small details: a globe by the window, the spiky silhouette of his bagpipes on a chair, and a collection of seashells on the dresser by my hand. Another careful step takes me nearer to the still-made-up bed.

He is not in it.

I cast about at a loss, when a light through the window catches my eye.

Someone is walking over the moors, their lantern swinging gently. I freeze, thinking again of Sylvie's ghost—but then the figure turns, and the light illuminates his profile.

"There you are, you bastard," I mutter.

When I emerge from the house, I'm met by a low wind and a clear night. The darkness is only temporary; my eyes adjust quickly, and the waxing moon is bright, providing just enough light to find my way. Above, the stars are silver stitches in the sky.

I spot Mr. North a short distance away, walking not to the house, but in a wide loop around it. He walks unhurried and limping slightly, on one of the many paths crisscrossing the heather. Captain walks beside him, a low, dark shadow, and every few steps, Mr. North reaches down to scratch the dog's ears.

He hears me coming, because I don't know the paths well enough and end up crashing over the heather like a floundering sheep. I'm forced to walk for what feels like an eternity while he watches, his free hand in his pocket and his expression obscured by the shadows cast from his lantern. By the time I reach him, I'm breathing hard.

"Rose Pryor," he says, shaking his head slowly. "I suppose your unnatural stealthiness does not extend to moorland?"

"Not much heather growing in London these days," I pant. "Why are you out here so late?"

With a deep sigh, he raises his lantern, the light illuminating his frown in a wash of flickering orange light. "How have I offended you now, pray tell?"

Fury rolls through me like relentless waves beating against a stony shore. I trace the gold-limned lines of his face, noting the weariness in his eyes. Were we really laughing together by the fire, just hours ago? I was a fool to feel anything toward him, anything but anger. I let my guard down and nearly forgot what he was.

One moment of laughter does not erase the damage he has done.

"Why do you hate magic?" I demand at last.

"I beg your pardon?"

"There must be a reason besides bad family luck," I say. "Did something happen to you?"

"Hm." He begins walking; I trot to catch up. His course seems to more or less encircle the manor. It looms to our left, as if we are tethered to it by a long and invisible lead.

I remain silent. It's a trick Sister Elizabeth used to play on me—waiting, eternally patient, until I couldn't bear the quiet and confessed to whatever transgression I'd committed. I shiver and pull my shawl tighter, looking back at the house. All the windows are dark; it looks like a ruin from this distance.

Finally, he breaks. "I don't *hate* magic."

"Does it run in your family? Was one of your parents a Weaver?"

For a few seconds he only looks at me, then he curses. "What happened?"

"Nothing happened."

"Don't lie to me, not about *her*. Magic runs in families, and you've no doubt seen something in my house to make you think it runs in mine, and now you're wondering about Sylvie. What happened?"

"You never had her tested, did you?"

He turns his back to me, his hand raking his hair. "Mrs. MacDougal told me this was a bad idea, allowing you to stay. She said your eyes were too prying and your fingers too meddling, and of course she was right." Whirling around again, he asks, "Did Sylvie ask about your magic? Has she seen you Weaving? You promised me you wouldn't."

"If she doesn't have the ability, why does it matter?"

"Because I don't want her involved with any part of your craft."

My chest swells with anger, my breaths quick and short. "Is that why you've tried to sabotage her magic, letting it rot on the vine because you don't like its flavor?"

"Because it is poison!" His shout echoes across the heather and fades into the starry sky.

I take a step back, regarding him with wide, horrified eyes. He seems to realize then that he's confessed to everything, and he gives a low growl of exasperation.

"Miss Pryor—"

"So it's true," I whisper, my very bones curdling with disgust. "You knew she had magic, and you chose to neglect it."

He raises his hands, curling his fingers in the air as if he wishes he could shake something. "I chose to keep her *safe*."

"Safe. *Safe.* You haven't kept her safe. You've stolen her only defense from her. Her only means of protecting herself."

"Magic is a double-edged sword and I—"

"But it is a *sword!* She must learn how to wield it, or she could hurt herself again—"

"Again?" He draws in a slow breath, then releases it through tight lips. "So it's true. She did channel."

"And she nearly killed herself trying. If I had not got there in time—"

"If you had not been here, she would never have tried!" His snarl is half wild, and I take a step back, a splinter of fear striking me breathless.

"No! This is *not* my fault!" I push forward again, driving a finger to his chest. It is like prodding the side of a barn. "She is more powerful than any Weaver I have met. She is like a dry field, waiting for the smallest spark to set her aflame. And when she burns, Mr. North, she will not be able to stop."

He shuts his eyes and stands as still as a mountain for a long minute, breathing in and out. I watch his face as the tension slowly drains from the muscles of his cheeks. The deep furrow between his brows relaxes, and even his shoulders drop.

Fates, it worked.

I finally got through to him.

Relief flows through me, and my hand drops to my side.

"I understand your fear," I say quietly. "I do. But you will see. Magic will protect her. It will give her purpose and—"

"Purpose?" His eyes snap open, and I recoil from the rage in them. "You know *nothing* of my sister's purpose, nor of mine. You understand *nothing*. Magic is a curse in our family. It always has been. You just said it yourself—it nearly killed her!"

"That is not what I—"

"Mrs. MacDougal told me you went to the village. Well, didn't they tell you?" He gives a harsh laugh. "They love to gossip about us, tell stories of the mad Norths and their string of tragedies. Did they tell you about my father?"

I don't look away. I won't let him distract me from the enormity of his crime. "No."

"He was a Weaver too. And his magic led him down paths which should never be taken, and he paid for it with his life. I found his body myself, aye, out on the moors, half burnt to ash."

His voice nearly breaks, a hint of grief stabbing through his bitterness, and I am struck momentarily speechless. The horrifying image seizes my imagination: a younger Conrad, standing over a charred corpse . . . "I—I'm sorry. Truly. But surely you see why this is further proof that Sylvie must *learn* to—"

"Miss Pryor, stop." His tone is clad in iron. "This was a mistake. I should never have agreed to let you stay."

"This isn't about me!" I spread my hands wide, exasperated. "She will not stop trying! She needs to be taught how to channel safely!"

"She will stop. I will make her stop."

He starts to turn away, but I grab his arm. "Even if you could, you'd be robbing her of her power. And when she's older and understands that, she'll despise you."

The tension in his bicep is hard as rock. "Probably," he says, his voice so soft I can barely make out the word. "But she'll be safe."

"Oh, you impossible, stubborn man!"

I pull away in disgust and turn back to the house. But blinded as I am by darkness and fury, I trip over a rise and crash into the heather, scraping my arms and face. The hill is steep, plunging into shadow, and I roll hard until, with a startled shout, I land in one of the cold little ponds that dot the moors. The water is only waist deep, but I flounder for footing, sputtering. Captain barks and races up and down the bank in a panic.

Mr. North is there at once, wading into the water toward me, his lantern abandoned on the shore. Silver moonlight ripples around him, and he peels off his coat and tosses it aside to free his arms. I grab hold of his hand to steady myself, cursing.

"What is it you always say to me, Miss Pryor?" he growls irritably. "*Watch your language?* Fates, you curse like a sailor."

I tremble with anger. "Are you going to just stand there, or will you help me out?"

"Stop wriggling, and I might! You're only making us both sink deeper, you mad creature."

"I can't help it! My shoe is stuck in the mud. Which is fortunate for you, or I'd be clobbering you with it!"

His jaw locks, then suddenly he lifts me, and I find myself clinging to his neck while he trudges toward the bank. It seems to take a century, him slogging through chilly dark water and me shivering in his arms. Of course he has to be as strong as an ox. Of course he has to hold me against a chest like an iron slab. Fates damn him. I am intensely conscious of his hand, carefully positioned an inch below my breast. Of *course* he has to be bloody respectful, as if his honor meant anything to me after tonight.

"Do not expect an ounce of gratitude for this," I stammer through chattering teeth. "This was your fault. And that pond appeared out of nowhere!"

He lets me down at the bank, and I take a few steps, my wet skirts twisting around my legs. I am shaking with mortification more than the cold. My cheeks could light a match. At least the darkness hides most of it. Captain noses my leg, as if to be sure I'm unharmed.

Mr. North growls under his breath as he twists his shirt, water pouring from the fabric. It sounds suspiciously like "Troublesome, meddling woman."

"Don't think this erases our discussion!" I assure him.

"Discussion?" He looks up, his wet hair swinging around his temples. "Is that what that was? Because it felt like an ambush."

"Oh, no. You are *not* the victim here." I spread my hands wide, as if addressing an entire classroom of bloody-minded, boulder-chested Scotsmen. "And I am not finished with this conversation, sir."

"I can see that," he says in a strangely coarse tone of voice, as if a rock has lodged in his throat. "And I would be delighted to continue our argument indoors. We can shout till dawn if it would please you. But please . . . cover yourself first. Otherwise, it makes it very difficult for a man to stay angry."

He grabs his coat and thrusts it toward me.

I look down and realize then that the soaked linen of my nightgown is clinging in . . . deeply inappropriate ways. I wrap myself in his coat, feeling my face turn several degrees hotter. "Right. I'm going inside."

He picks up the extinguished lantern. "Shall I go ahead, in case any more ponds decide to appear out of nowhere? Savage things, ponds. Quite unpredictable."

I push past him and storm toward the house, fighting against the heather. He was right about one thing. It is difficult to stay angry when one is soaked to the bone, freezing, and stumbling through the dark.

"There's a path here, you stubborn thing!" he calls.

Ignoring him, I forge ahead, but he reaches the house first and opens the door for me. I go past him without a word and go straight to the kitchen, where the fire is low, but still warm. Captain flops onto the floor and pants, watching us with his eyes masked behind his long hair.

Standing in front of the fire, I let out a sigh and hold my hands to the coals, water dripping from my skirt and pooling on the floor.

Mr. North stands behind me, dripping and disheveled and looming like a great bear. I toss him a black look over my shoulder. "What?"

"Would you mind scooting aside a wee bit?" he growls. "Perhaps share a man's own hearth with him after he's just saved your bloody life?"

"I was hardly at death's door," I grumble. But begrudgingly, I edge to the left, and he fills the empty space beside me, his eyes closing as the heat from the low flames rolls over him. I eye him sidelong, my skin still prickling with fury. Water trickles down the thick locks of his hair and runs down his jawline. The soaked fabric of his shirt leaves little to the imagination, hugging the planes of his chest and outlining the rolling muscles of his back. The front of it is snagged on the waistband of his trousers, revealing a small triangle of bare skin and the dark, fine hairs on his stomach.

Fates.

The nerve of the man, honestly. How dare he be such a beast, and then stand there looking like . . . like *that*? And he had the audacity to ask *me* to cover up?

"Shall we strike a truce?" he asks softly, his eyes parting open.

I snap my gaze away, glaring instead at the fire. "A truce?"

"Until morning, at the least. Otherwise I feel I shall be forced to sleep with one eye open, lest you hex me in the night."

"Not an unwarranted fear," I mutter beneath my breath.

"Tea?" Mr. North asks. "To seal our truce and warm us up."

I harden my jaw, not wanting to give in. But the fire's heat can only reach so deep, and my bones feel limned in ice. "Let's call it a pause."

"As you like. And another thing . . ."

He leans toward me, and I catch my breath as his hand moves to my face. For a moment, I'm filled with the wild notion that he's about to kiss me. My eyes drop to his lips, and heat roars through me like wildfire. My body reacts before my mind can form a coherent thought, my toes curling on the stone floor, my breath suspending somewhere between my lungs and my lips . . .

"Just this," he says, and he gently peels some sort of pond weed from my neck and tosses it into the fire, where it hisses on the warm coals.

Oh. Rose, you fool. Of course he wasn't about to . . .

If he had, I would have slapped him.

Wouldn't I?

Yes, yes. I'd have definitely slapped him. I definitely would *not* have kissed him back. I am a respectable schoolteacher, and respectable schoolteachers simply do not go about kissing abominable Scotsmen with wool for brains and logs for biceps.

"Thank you, Mr. North."

"I wish you'd call me Conrad," he says. "Surely I've earned at least that, having saved you from a horrid drowning?"

I give an unmannerly snort.

Ignoring the stove, he hangs the kettle over the coals instead. Then he towels his hair before removing his shoes and stockings. His damp hair is already beginning to dry and curl. He pulls his shirt out of his trousers and wrings it, wincing at the puddle it makes on the hearth. His bare feet are pale on the stone, and for some reason, the sight of them makes me flush. I step closer to the fire.

"I'll take care of the water," he says, nodding at the puddles we've made. "I shudder to think of the questions Mrs. MacDougal might lob at me otherwise."

I let out a laugh, and he looks up.

"I think she dislikes me," I say. "Nearly as much as you do."

He glances at me, his storm-cloud eyes widening a fraction. For a moment, he seems at a loss for words.

"I don't dislike you," he says at last.

"Really?" I give a very unrespectable snort. "The day we met, I knocked you off your horse and gave you what seems to be a permanent limp."

He frowns, then thumps his leg. "What, this? This is an old injury. Not your doing."

"Oh. Well . . . what about later that night? You caught me red handed, snooping through your house."

"True, but I wasn't exactly gracious about it. You may be surprised to learn we don't get many visitors here, particularly of the female nature. My manners were—*are*—a bit rough at the edges. I am in fact aware of my shortcomings, whatever you may think of me. I know you consider me a monster."

"I . . . never used that word," I say carefully. "I have known monsters, Mr. . . . Conrad. And I do not think you quite fit the bill. But you *are* making a terrible mistake with Sylvie."

He doesn't reply, but gives me a sharp sidelong look, no doubt afraid I'll revive our argument. But what's the point? He isn't going to change his mind. He thinks he is doing what is best by his sister. How can I make him understand that magic isn't a curse, but a gift?

But I'm not here to get involved with these people. I keep forgetting that. No matter how much they need it, I cannot help them if I cannot even help myself. And pushing him further will only incite him to retract his hospitality to me, and what help would I be to Sylvie then?

So I keep my mouth shut, my teeth grinding together.

The kettle whistles, and Conrad removes it to pour our teas. I hold my cup close with both hands, soaking in its warmth. He finds a wool blanket somewhere and holds it up inquiringly, and with a nod, I let him drape it over my shoulders, replacing his now-damp coat. He wraps himself in another and sits on the hearth, back to the fire, his elbows on his knees and his face in his hands. The dog gives a little soft whine and lays his head on his master's foot.

I briefly consider telling him the truth: that I am bound to a faerie, losing my magic, trying desperately to complete a nearly impossible task in too short a time.

But how would that induce him to trust me more? If he knew the truth, he would only sink deeper into his conviction that Sylvie shouldn't learn to Weave. Even knowing she endangered herself trying to channel, he will not change his mind.

For her sake, I cannot come clean. At least, not until I've concluded Lachlan's favor and freed myself from him for good.

After a long moment, Conrad looks up.

"I love her more than anything in the world," he says quietly. "I just want to keep her safe."

I meet his eyes, seeing that every word is true, even if I can't agree with his methods of showing it. "Loving someone isn't only about knowing what's best for them. It's about letting them choose their own fate."

"Choice is a luxury." He grimaces. "Believe me, if I had another choice . . . but I am not unbound and free as the wind as you are. Some of us are bound by duties we cannot escape, our lives lived in debts we can never fully pay."

I swallow a bitter laugh. "I think I know more of your duties and debts than you may believe."

He gives me a curious look, which I return. He is hiding something. I am sure of it now. Neither of us is telling the whole truth. For a moment, his lips part and I think he will pry deeper into my words.

But then he looks away, his jaw clenching, and says nothing.

I stare at the dregs slowly circling the bottom of my cup. "I suppose I should go pack."

"I invited you to stay and I'll not go back on my word." He considers me with a studying eye. "I'll be away for a few days. More business on the estate, and 'tis too far to ride back and forth. Just swear you will not teach her so much as a wart hex."

"Well," I say. "That *is* a useful hex."

"Please. Rose."

It's the first time he's used my first name like that. The sound of it in his rough, low Scotsman's brogue unexpectedly startles me, like a cool wind over simmering coals.

"I swear it," I say softly. "By the soul of my dear aunt, who was like a mother to me, I swear it . . . Conrad."

He nods, satisfied, thinking all is settled between us. Thinking he has got his way.

Fault number five: *Dishonesty.*

I am a very good liar.

CHAPTER FIFTEEN

The next morning, I leave a note in the kitchen saying that I've gone to Blackswire to see if I might find word of my still-absent "employer" and his tragic, lingering, unspecified illness. Along with it is a list of assignments for Sylvie to occupy herself with, mainly arithmetic worksheets I wrote out before dawn. I finished them just as the sun rose tepidly over the moors, its light muted by a layer of pale clouds. From my window, I watched the laird of Ravensgate ride off on his big horse, his dog trailing after, toward the north. The opposite direction of the village, thankfully.

I was not able to sleep after bidding Mr. North—*Conrad*—a good night. Despite our truce, I found myself pacing my room for hours after, thinking of our argument, and of how young and lost he'd looked, sitting on the hearth with his head in his hands. Thinking of Sylvie kneeling in her room, threads webbed between us, her eyes glowing with delight as she brought snowflakes spiraling down from the ceiling.

I will help her as much as I can.

But I cannot forget the real reason I am here, nor the deadline creeping ever nearer. Another foray into the woods, in search of the gateway to Elfhame, is just the thing to clear the knotted tangle of the North family from my thoughts.

I have the stolen map in my pocket, but rather than thrashing about in the woods again, I decide to try a different approach. After all, someone else found the faerie doorway long ago—perhaps she left a clue behind.

I find Fiona's cottage easily enough, and shiver when I pass her grave. I realize I never found out *how* she died, and had assumed it had been old age. But what if it wasn't? What if some other fate befell her? If so, her belongings turn up no clues, but I do find something of interest—a sketch hidden among the pile of letters, showing a modified wayfinding knot.

"Clever old girl," I murmur, threading my string between my fingers to copy it.

It takes a true master of the craft to fashion new spells from old ones, rearranging threads in such a way as to alter their original purposes. This spell, when I've channeled into it, pulling energy from the abundant moss on the walls and roof, produces a hovering bead of light much like the north-finding spell that led me to the cottage in the first place. But this one burns red, not blue, and it zips around urgently, waiting for me to follow.

I am glad to leave the cottage behind, and I let the red light lead me into the trees and off the path entirely.

Over the crack and crunch of my footsteps, the woods seem to whisper, and I catch myself whirling more than once, eyes questing in search of some elusive follower. The shadows in the trees move furtively, giving the illusion of cloaks vanishing behind stones or eyes closing the moment I look their way. My arms are stippled with goose bumps that do not fade. I imagine the ghosts of the old moorwitches lurking in the gloom, their fingers Weaving dark magic.

After nearly an hour of tramping along over mounds of moss and carpets of pine needles, the wayfinding spell suddenly fades with a soft hiss, leaving me alone.

I stop dead, my heart missing a beat.

But there is nothing here. No door, no arch, no cave.

I must be close, or the spell wouldn't have fizzled out. That, or the spell was a dud to begin with.

Well, there's not much I can lose by forging ahead and hoping for the best.

The further I walk, the stranger the wood seems. It feels as though I have been walking for hours, and yet the sun never changes positions in the sky, and though I swear I walk in a straight line, I begin to see the same trees and rocks over and over again, until I'm certain it's not a trick of my eyes. The light here is weak and broken with shadows of jagged branches, and in the ravines swirl malevolent mists.

I press on, and twice pass a rock that juts from a high bank, shaped curiously like a turtle's head. The second time, I stop and grasp my threadkit.

I'm not lost at all.

I'm being misdirected on purpose. Someone has woven a confounding charm of some sort to nudge me away whenever I get close to my quarry—Fiona's wayfinding spell *had* worked, but the charm or some other ward must have stopped it before it reached its destination.

Finding a stump to sit upon, I take out white ounce-thread and a needle from my threadkit and begin stitching my shawl. The light here is poor, and I have to squint to see what I'm doing.

Overhead, a cold wind rattles the branches. I feel like a rabbit hidden in a hole while a hungry wolf prowls above, searching for a way in. I keep my head down and my eyes focused on my stitches, working as quickly as I can. The familiar *tink* of my needle against my thimble is little comfort in this dark forest.

"There," I say, after twenty minutes of embroidering. I hold up the shawl with its new pattern of knots curling up the hem like a vine. "That'll do."

I throw the shawl around myself and then draw a long breath before channeling, the memory of yesterday's hovering charm making my heart squeeze preemptively. It is as if I've touched a hot stove, only to force myself to touch it again.

"You can do this," I murmur to myself. "It's not always that bad."

I channel, wincing at the slight pressure it causes in my heart. But this time, thankfully, the pain is manageable. The embroidery on my shawl glows briefly, and then the spell is done.

"Counterwards," I say with no small measure of satisfaction. And to think, in our fourth year Margaret Appleby said they were a foolish waste of time because Moirene sisters, with their devotion to education and other social duties, didn't need to know battle magic.

Ducking my head, I pull my shawl tight and push forward.

Protected by the thin muslin of my shawl, I see the moment my spell takes effect, because the new stitches begin to glow faintly. I've stepped into some powerful wards and feel them prickling over me as I pass. My shawl grows hot, as my spell works to repel the magic pressing against it. The edges begin to flutter, though there is no wind to speak of this low beneath the trees.

I'm getting closer.

My stomach knots as my sense of foreboding grows stronger. Everything in me wants to turn back, to flee this place where the trees twist around each other like entwined serpents. Every step is harder to take, and I realize I've slowed to a crawl.

"Discouragement spell," I say through my teeth, feeling it lean on me with the weight of a horse.

Someone has been clever indeed, working with subtle yet intricate magics. This is not like the fae ward around Blackswire, but rather these spells were designed to escape notice. Only a Weaver might understand what they are, and only then if they were specifically looking for such magic. It took me far too long to recognize what was happening, that these trees are laced with power.

There are no counter-wards for discouragement spells; instead, one must marshal the willpower to press through and endure them. I need to rally my spirit by focusing on what I stand to gain if I make it through this ward; I need to fix my eyes on the greater goal.

That's simple enough: I think of magic.

I remember the day I stood before the Moirene Council in Westminster Abbey, the great cathedral roof soaring over my head. The triptych of the Fates, immortalized in stained glass, gazed down as I took my vows and stitched the trefoil knot into my collar. I remember my pride, my relief, my joy. For the first time in my life, I felt secure. *Safe.*

I think of how it feels to stand at the head of a classroom and guide a wide-eyed group of little girls and boys through their first spell samplers, their needles clumsy in their eager hands. To see the delight in their eyes when they complete a new, difficult spell.

And then, insensibly, another daydream finds its way into my thoughts like a stray bird flitting through an open window: myself sitting on the great steps in Ravensgate's grand foyer, teaching Sylvie how to Weave an illusion knot, to summon flowers of light, and when I look up, there is Conrad below, watching with the softest of smiles on his lips, mischief shining in his proud tiger-gold eyes.

Startled and shaken, I blink the vision away, and realize I've made it through the ward. The weight of the discouragement spell broke like a fever once I'd summoned enough willpower to force my way through it, and now I can breathe easier.

I hurry on, as if I might escape that last, unbidden image and the sudden eruption of butterflies it hatched in my belly.

I tramp up a hill, through more wards, but these are not as strong as the first ones. The threads on my shawl are beginning to burn away, ashes like dust on my shoulders, but the spell did its job.

I reach the crest of the hill, and there it is.

"Oh," I breathe, looking down in the shallow depression below. "Of course."

The door to Elfhame is obvious at once: a ring of standing stones, ten all told, tall and unnatural and silent in a clearing.

No insects here, nor birds or beasts. Not even the wind rustles the treetops. It's as if I've stepped into a cathedral at midnight, alone with only the Fates to notice me.

The ground below is velvet moss for nearly twenty yards in diameter, not a patch of mud to mar it. It feels like it's set outside time, in its own pocket of reality. It might have been a thousand years since another living creature set foot down there. And all around the clearing, the ancient boulders stand improbably balanced.

Carefully I make my way down the hill, sliding on the loose dead leaves and damp loam. Once at the bottom, I slowly approach the circle, feeling caught in a different sort of enchantment entirely—one of wonder. I draw near the closest stone, studying it for any sign of instructions carved into it, a clue of how to activate the doorway.

Lifting my hand, I reach for the stone, some primal part of my soul eager to feel its ancient face against my palm.

A flicker of movement catches my eye. I turn my head, eyes chasing a figure in my periphery—is that a *woman*, pale as dawn light?

Then my hand touches the stone, and I am thrown violently off my feet and hurled through the air. I collide into a tree with a shout, the wind knocked from my lungs. There I lie a moment, trembling from the aftershocks of the repulsion spell which still crackle through my body.

Gasping, I push myself to my knees and stare at the stones and the thing I'd missed in my dazed wonder: a very fine thread stretched taut between them.

Looking over my shoulder, I scan the trees. If there was a woman there, she is gone now. Though in retrospect, I feel sure I must have imagined the specter. It could have been a deer, or a shaft of sunlight.

That, or Sylvie's ghost is more real than I gave her credit for.

With a shiver, I put the apparition out of my mind and crawl forward to inspect the thread that knocked me off my feet.

It is a ward. A *strong* ward, and unlike the one surrounding Blackswire, this one is meant to keep out intruders of *all* species, human or fae, and likely animal too.

This is definitely the right place.

Lachlan's warning about the defenses which might surround the doorway were valid, it seems, and there will be more magic to counter here than mere discouragement charms. I rub my ribs and limp back to the stones, taking much greater care this time. Keeping a little distance and several rows of trees between me and the rocks, I follow the circumference of the circle and inspect every branch, twig, and trunk.

I begin to see more wards and hexes strung about, strings blending into the branches and grass. I narrowly avoid setting my foot in an immobilization hex. One stretches through the air at eye level, and I hold my fingers as close to it as I dare; most of these hexes will be activated by tripwires, so a simple touch, however light, will immobilize, shock, or even set me on fire. And these are no ordinary threads—they are thinner and lighter, almost invisible.

The spells are made, I realize with a chill, of spider thread.

Never have I heard of such a material being used to Weave spellknots. Never, that is, but in the old faerie tales.

It would take days to undo all these knots. They were not woven by an amateur, and many of the patterns are unfamiliar to me. Are they the work of the fae inside Elfhame?

I must clear my head—think, think, *think*.

How lovely it would have been to walk into this clearing and find the door here, open and waiting for me. But that's not how these things work, is it? There's always a secret, always a twist. There's always a dragon that must be slain or tricked.

Round and round I walk, inspecting the circle's defenses, as the sun tilts overhead and begins to decline, shadows growing longer. Even if I found a way through the wards, I'd still have to figure out which spell would open a portal to Elfhame.

Three more weeks until my magic is stolen from me. Three more weeks until every dream and hope I ever had slips through my fingers. Three weeks until I am no longer even a charity-school teacher, but just a girl with no money, no home, no name, and no other skill to make her way in the world.

Despair pools around my feet.

This *errand* of Lachlan's grows more difficult by the day, with layers of unexpected complications arising at every turn.

And after seeing the power at work to guard the stones, I can only wonder what—and *who*—waits on the other side.

CHAPTER SIXTEEN

At breakfast the next morning, Sylvie pushes her poached egg around her plate, her face downcast. Conrad is away still on estate business, and she is still angry with me for refusing to teach her magic. Upon returning from my walk yesterday, I graded her work and then set her to conjugating French verbs for the rest of the day, under Mrs. MacDougal's watchful eye. I've said nothing of the events of two nights ago, and how I found Sylvie Weaving in her room, a fact Sylvie seems keenly aware of. But there hasn't been an opportunity for us to talk. After our conversation, Conrad seems to have redoubled his efforts to have us chaperoned, to both my and the housekeeper's chagrin.

I chafe at being kept indoors. I should be at the stone circle, puzzling over the wards and attempting to find a way through them. My next report to Lachlan is due in two days; I have to have some notion of progress to show him. But I cannot spend another day "in Blackswire," or my cover will grow thin.

As I sit stitching one of my old stockings, I feel Sylvie's eyes flicking at me every few seconds, to see if I've noticed her black mood.

"Finish your breakfast, lassie," says Mrs. MacDougal to Sylvie, as she kneads a ball of dough on the table. "'Tis to be a long, hard day of sitting around the library, and you'll need your strength."

Mrs. MacDougal shoots me a glower. She knows it's on my account that she's been saddled with shadowing me about atop her other duties, and she doesn't love me for it. Despite Conrad's assurances to the contrary, Mrs. MacDougal has not liked me since I arrived and she learned I could Weave; I wonder if her ill favor of me is due to my magic, or if she thinks me guilty of some greater crime—such as lying constantly about my *true* purpose here.

"We will go back to your French this morning, Sylvie," I say. "I just need to finish darning this stocking . . . there." I set down the stocking and flex my cramped fingers. "All done."

I channel quickly, lighting the embroidered charm I've actually been sewing, and at once Mrs. MacDougal's head jerks up. She blinks twice, owlishly, then gives a great yawn and sinks into the chair by the stove. "Just a moment . . ." she murmurs, her chin dropping. "Then I'll finish . . ."

She draws a loud snore, her hands falling to her sides.

Sylvie's eyes stretch open, till they seem to take up half her face. "What just happened?"

I grin. "It's a four-hour sleeping charm. When she wakes, she'll go back to kneading her dough and never know the difference. We don't have much time. Hurry. Put on your shoes while I pack a basket."

Her mouth falls open and her hands lift to her cheeks. "You mean—?"

"It's stopped raining, your brother is away, and Mrs. MacDougal will be dead to the world until lunchtime." I take her hand, feeling only a small twinge of guilt. When Conrad learns I've gone behind his back like this, after swearing to his face that I would not teach her, he will surely hate me. But I cannot sit by and let Sylvie's magic wither, no more than I can let her injure herself or worse in attempting magic on her own. If Conrad will not be persuaded, he will have to be circumvented.

I give Sylvie a smile. "It's time for your first real lesson in the art of Weaving."

Sylvie tells me she knows the perfect place for the lesson, and leads me over the soggy moors to the east of the house. She can hardly contain herself, leaping and twirling and dancing around me as I pick my way over the brittle heather. The day is cool and still, with clouds like banners streaming across an iron gray sky. We see not a soul, save for a few errant sheep ambling over the rolling hills. I spot Apollo the lamb gamboling about his mother, who regards us uninterestedly as we walk by. She ignores my friendly wave and goes back to her meal of grass.

Finally, we come to a bluff that juts over a narrow stream. Atop it spreads an ancient oak, whose branches are just starting to bud with new leaves. Scores of ribbons and threads are tied to the limbs, so the whole tree flutters and rustles when the wind rises. Beneath the boughs stands an oblong rock twice as tall as I am. The sight of it makes the hairs on my arms rise. The color, the shape, the size—it might have been hauled from the same quarry and erected by the same hands as the ones in the fae circle.

"Here it is," Sylvie breathes, as we climb the hill. "The Moorwitch Stone."

I circle the stone, noting that unlike its forest counterparts, it has been carved with ancient, unfathomable runes, and with patterns that can only be ancient spells. There are images also, of people and animals and phases of the moon.

"What is it?"

"It's a magical, sacred place," says Sylvie. "Which means, obviously, Connie's forbidden me to come here. You're supposed to tie a ribbon to the tree as an offering to the faerie queen. They say she murdered a hundred moorwitches a long, long time ago, and if you don't pay respects, she'll send her servants to take your soul at Samhain."

A chill runs down my spine. "The faerie queen?"

She nods. "See?"

She points to the highest carving on the stone: it shows a severe woman in flowing robes, one hand raised as if about to render judgment, the other held out from her side; on her open palm stands a spider, and its web drapes over the crown on the woman's head.

I think of the spiderweb spells spun around the stone circle, and my blood turns to ice.

Sylvie's eyes glow when she looks at the stone. "They say the moorwitches were taught Weaving by the faeries. They could threadwalk—move themselves from Edinburgh to London in the blink of an eye, if they wanted to. They were awfully powerful, and completely wonderful. But the faeries killed them because they got to be *too* powerful, and the people put up this stone to remember them by, and as a warning that you should never meddle in the affairs of immortals. At least, that's what Mrs. MacDougal told me, when she got drunk on punch last Wintertide. She made me swear not to tell Conrad about it."

Wryly, I turn away from the stone. "Do you believe in faeries?"

"Of course!" She looks affronted, as if only a fool wouldn't. "And dragons and ghosts and all of it, no matter what Connie might say."

"What does he say?"

"That they're all stories and nonsense." She sniffs. "He's the best brother in the world, but honestly, sometimes he's no fun at all."

I squeeze her hand and smile, but feel the carved woman's eyes as if they are piercing my skin.

"Let's sit over there," I suggest, pointing to a mossy bank well away from the moorwitch stone.

Sylvie is too excited to eat and kneels with her utter attention at my command. She's practically shaking with eagerness.

I sit cross-legged on the blanket and open my threadkit. Sylvie sighs in appreciation, running her fingers over the little compartments with their spools, needles, and thimbles. With a smile, I remember touching the kit much the same way when I first held it, tracing the trefoil knot of the Moirai carved into the lid as if it were the key to heaven.

"Now, at its most basic," I say, as I take out the compartmentalized insert with all its accessories and set it aside, leaving an empty box, "magic is energy that we pull, or *draw*, from the natural, living world and then channel into the threads we Weave. It is strongest in animals and people, but only dark Weavers draw from such sources."

She nods. "Like Napoleon's Red Guard."

"Exactly." It wasn't so long ago that the French general sent out his infamous Red Guard, who sucked the life from their enemies and turned it into devastating spells. As I open the threadkit, folding its sides down to transform it from an empty box to a rectangular board, I continue, "The laws against drawing from humans are universal and punishable by death. In Britain and most other countries, it's also illegal to draw from animals."

I can't help but think of the birdcages around Fiona's cottage, and the grisly remains inside them.

The threadkit is fully open now, and Sylvie runs her fingertip around the circle of shallow holes bored into the wood. I hand her a few wooden pegs, then show her how to insert them in the holes to create a pegboard—a ring of spokes for Weaving complex patterns.

"So . . . where does our magic come from?" she asks.

I wave my empty hand at the hills around us. "The plants, mostly, but a good Weaver knows how to find it even in stone and soil and water, where the tiniest living thing can grow." I pick one of the few green blades around us and hold it out. "But you must be careful. If you draw too much from one source, it will die."

I wind thread around the pegboard, twisting around spokes in a simple but mesmerizing pattern. The threads crisscross, the spell taking shape layer by layer. Sylvie watches entranced, hardly blinking. When I am finished, I pause and stare at the pegboard, my heart beating faster.

A circle of pegs.

Like a circle of stones.

My mind snaps to the faerie gateway, and with a tumbling sensation in my stomach, I realize *why* the stones are erected in such a shape.

"Miss Pryor?"

With a sharp inhale, I pull my mind back to the present and meet Sylvie's eyes.

"Right. Where were we? Channeling, yes. Watch closely." I demonstrate by drawing on one of the blades of grass, held between my thumb and forefinger, and it withers quickly.

"Oh." She stares at the blackened grass, eyes wide.

I release the magic into the wind knot I have woven on the pegboard. Sylvie claps with delight as the threads begin to glow and a little breeze swirls through the grass around us.

"I'll teach you the most basic, but perhaps most critical, of skills today: how to draw from many sources at once. Instead of taking energy from a single blade of grass and killing it, you can draw a *tiny* bit from a thousand blades. They all live and regenerate that energy, and you get more than enough magic to complete your spell."

She nods, looking relieved. "But how does that make *magic*?"

"Well . . ." I Weave a cat's cradle to summon water, then, shutting my eyes, I relax my mind and *draw* on the green energy around me. It fills me like a flash flood, and I must quickly close myself again before I'm swept away. Then I focus on redirecting the energy inside me, through my heart, releasing it into the thread stretched between my fingers. Thankfully, this time, the pain is only faint, but then I'm only working with a very small amount of magic.

When I open my eyes, a thin flow of water from the stream is swirling over and around my hands like a playful otter.

"It's all about altering the flow of that energy," I murmur. "The heart acts as a catalyst, changing energy into magic. All magic flows into and out of the heart, but it's vital you do not hold it inside you too long. Always have a spellknot ready before you channel, because pulling in all that energy and giving it no place to go, or drawing more than you need, can result in terrible consequences. You can become a danger to yourself and those around you if you cannot control how much you channel."

With a sigh, I release the knot, and the water pours into the grass. I shut my eyes and massage my chest, breathing in and out slowly. The ache is dull, but persistent, and every breath makes my heart twinge a little worse.

"Like this?" asks Sylvie, and I hear a loud rushing noise.

I open my eyes.

Around us both, a great funnel of water twists and rolls to the sky. Sylvie stands with her hands spread, her spellknot sloppy but clearly effective. I turn and see a fish flicker by in a state of complete bewilderment, caught up in the maelstrom. For a moment, I am too stunned to speak and can only stare at the river circling us and rising thirty feet in the air. If anyone looked this way, they'd see an impossible tower of twisting water.

"Oh," I breathe, eyes wide. "Oh. Yes, something like that."

"I don't have to think about all that stuff," she says. "Water and grass and energy. I just sort of *do* it."

"Be careful. Summoning it all at once is one thing, releasing it is another." I clamber to my feet, lifting a hand.

"It's getting wobbly! Oh!"

The water crashes over us like a massive bucket has been upturned on our heads. I gasp, and Sylvie shrieks. Water runs over the hill and into the stream, leaving us both drenched.

"Sorry," she mumbles. But her eyes are bright and her cheeks flushed with excitement, and I cannot help but smile.

I remember what it felt like, discovering my power for the first time. Realizing I was capable of so much more than the world had ever expected of me. It was stolen moments of magic like this that helped me survive my aunt's stifling house. Magic will be Sylvie's salvation too, her respite from her brother's oppressive rule. If only she didn't have to hide it. If only she could embrace the fullness of her power—she could be a force of nature.

"It's all right." I set to work on a drying spell. While I Weave it, I study Sylvie.

She's strong for a girl her age, an *untrained* girl her age. Exceptionally strong. Her technique is rough, but that's only a matter of practice. I can't think of a single girl I knew at school who could have controlled that much water at once so early in her training.

"I can't believe you've gone this long without using your magic," I mutter, more to myself than her. "Your brother should have got you a tutor years ago."

"You mustn't tell him about our lessons," Sylvie says quickly. "He'd send you away."

"Of course. You have my word."

"Why are you teaching me?"

I pause, threads tangled between my hands, and consider her. "Well . . . because you need to learn. Magic is your right. It's as much a part of you as your voice or your thoughts."

She nods, her brow furrowing as she picks at some mud on her skirt. I wait quietly, twisting my threads, for her to say whatever is weighing on her.

When she does speak, her voice is fragile. "Do you think he will hate me if he finds out?"

My heart tugs in sympathy. "Oh, Sylvie. No, he couldn't hate you. He loves you very much. I think that sometimes, love can make us feel afraid. We want to protect the people we care about so badly, that that love and fear become a little bit like a cage."

"How do you break free, then, without hurting anyone?"

I lower my hands to my lap, not knowing how to answer her. The cage my aunt built around me was not one of love, but of grief and misguided hatred. And I had to sell my heart to break free of it.

"I don't know," I say at last. "But I promise you that for as long as I am able, I will help you find a way."

She meets my eyes, then suddenly wraps her arms around me. I gasp a little, startled, as the spellknot I'd been Weaving falls apart.

"I'm glad you came," she whispers. "I'm glad you're my friend."

After returning her embrace, I begin packing up my threadkit, shaking the wet ashes from the pegboard and reassembling the box. "Well, we'd better head back, before Mrs. MacDougal wakes up."

As I snap the threadkit closed, I exchange one last look with the faerie queen on the stone. She has been carved with an eternal smirk, slyness in her eyes.

Before we go, Sylvie and I both tie ribbons around the bough of the tree and leave them fluttering in the wind.

CHAPTER
SEVENTEEN

Two nights later, when I step through the tapestry in my room, I find Lachlan's castle camp lit by candlelight and song. On the damp stones, with the sky gray velvet above, I wait and watch, trying to understand what I'm seeing.

The fae are moving through the ruins in twisting lines, their heads bowed and hooded, their hands carrying slender black candles. They all sing, their voices strangely fragile and sweet, like the voices of children. If it is words they sing, I do not understand them; I hear only sighing notes which rise and fall like the chants of the priestesses in the chapels back home. It's beautiful.

Then, splintering the solemn mood of the scene, one of the faeries suddenly lunges at me, his hood falling and his pointed teeth bared. He grabs me by the throat and slams me against the ancient stone wall of the castle. I gasp but cannot speak for the fingers locked around my throat.

"*You,*" he hisses, his eyes glowing with rage. "You filthy, usurping mortals, poisoning all that was once good and pure in this land! *You* did this!"

I beat at him in vain with my fists. He squeezes tighter, until spots dance in my eyes and I strain for breath that does not come. None of the other fae come to my aid, though some stop and watch with luminous beetle eyes.

Panicking, I feel my head swimming into darkness, my lungs squeezing for lack of air. Then my hand closes on the iron snuffer I tied under my skirt, and I wrench it out. I smash it into the faerie's face, and he screams and jerks back, releasing my throat.

Gasping and coughing, I drop to my knees, but when he starts toward me again, I raise the snuffer.

"Clugh!" snaps a voice.

The furious faerie snarls, his hands raised to grab me again.

But then a hand seizes him by the neck and hurls him backward. Clugh soars twenty paces before smashing into a stone wall and collapsing to the grass, his expression glassy. I gape at Lachlan, who stands over me like a snarling wolf. For a moment, past and present pull together like fabric gathered in the Fates' hands, and I am a child again, quivering as Lachlan punishes my aunt. My heart pounds with a bewildering combination of terror and relief. With gratitude to my monstrous savior . . . and horror at his searing cruelty.

Clugh coughs and feebly clutches at the grass. His wheezing, pained breaths dispel the ghosts of my past, and I shudder.

"Away, Clugh." The calm civility in Lachlan's voice is jarringly at odds with the violence he just enacted, and it sends a chill down my spine. "Leave the girl alone."

The faerie grovels and slinks away, dragging an injured leg. The others retreat at the dangerous light in Lachlan's sweeping gaze, but a few spare me some final venomous glances.

Baffled and furious, I ignore Lachlan's proffered hand and push myself to my feet. His eyes fall onto the snuffer I'm still clutching. His lips thin.

"Cast that away," he says.

I squeeze it tighter, my voice a harsh rasp. "I think I'll keep it."

He looks at me, weariness dragging at the corners of his eyes. "Then keep it *hidden*, at least. They are all on edge tonight, and if a group decided to lynch you, there would be little I could do to stop them."

"What's going on?"

Lachlan watches the lines of fae; their candles make their eyes glint beneath their hoods. They continue singing, their voices rising and mingling in the air.

"Lorellan has died," he says. "They sing the long lament for her."

I rub my throat, my anger fading only slightly.

"I'm sorry for your loss." But I keep a hand on my pocket, where the snuffer is safely within reach should I need it again.

"Walk with me," he says, noting the placement of my hand with a frown.

We follow the last of the fae out of the castle and up a gentle slope. The moors rush and sigh, and the candles bob like will-o'-the-wisps in the gloaming, their berry scent sweetening the air. Off to the west drift wisps of honey-colored clouds, where the afterglow of sunset lights the horizon.

Lachlan inclines his head. "It is a hard thing, the death of an immortal. We are so few, and to lose even one . . . if we do not return home soon, we will lose many more."

At the highest point of land for leagues around, the fae gather around a pyre limned by the light of a hundred flickering candles stuck in among the mounds of flowers they've piled over Lorellan's body. I wonder where they found the blooms this time of year, black callas, white lilies, deep-purple dahlias, and velvet roses of every shade.

Lorellan is still and white as marble, her hair flowing around her shoulders, decorated with little white flowers. Her eyes are open, glassy blue and unseeing.

There are more fae here than there were last time I came to the castle; I lose count of their dark hoods, and then they seem to vanish entirely when, all together, they snuff out their candles. At the same moment, they cease their singing. Lorellan floats above us all on a cloud of blossoms and candles and silence. Only the wind may be heard, rushing over the grass and heather, stirring the faes' dark cloaks. The moors rustle like an unquiet sea, the hills in the distance darkening to deep purple and blue.

Then another light flickers to life—a thread glowing in the hands of the fae nearest to me and Lachlan. Then the light travels to the next faerie and the next, chasing a single thread that passes through the hands of each one. It moves in a great loop around the pyre, then spirals around again. They're all channeling into it, feeding energy into a great, collective spell.

All at once, the hilltop flares with light, as a great spellknot woven beneath the pyre floods with magic fueled into it by the long thread. I don't recognize the pattern, but I see its purpose soon enough.

The pyre, the body, and all the flowers begin to disintegrate; before my astonished eyes, they break apart with a sound like whispering leaves, transformed into many-colored sparks which swirl up into the air. In moments, Lorellan is gone entirely. The dazzling motes of light twist and wind their way up, up, up into the darkening sky, beautiful, strange, and terrible.

"A spell of unmaking," says Lachlan, taking in my expression of wonder with a sidelong look. "Few mortals have laid eyes upon such magic."

I breathe out a long, slow breath that mists the air before me. The hilltop is wrapped in silence, and then the fae begin to drift off, some back to the castle, others into the moors. They move solemnly, faces grim. The funeral is over.

Soon, Lachlan and I stand alone beneath the stars, and it's as if the fae had never been here at all.

"We are running out of time," Lachlan murmurs, after a long silence. "The humans are constructing a railroad from London to Edinburgh, did you know? All that iron strapped to the ground, poisoning the earth. I already feel it in my bones, like a disease sapping my strength."

My hand falls away from the iron in my pocket. I look at him, at the moonlight silvering the planes of his ageless face, while his eyes remain masked in shadow. His hood has slipped, and his loose mane of hair shines like nacre.

"Your world is changing fast," he says. "You would not see it, in your heartbeat of a lifespan, but I have walked the World Above for many decades, and I have seen the great change slowly coming, the scales tipping. And it seems that all at once the balance has shifted, and a new age dawns like an iron landslide, and the old ways are buried beneath it and crushed into myth. Magic will fade from the world."

"Magic is not affected by iron," I point out.

"Not directly." He looks up at the sky, his eyes angry and sad and terribly ancient. "But my kind are not the only casualties of your race's insatiable appetite for progress, my dear. You will feel it too. In a century, magic will be gone. You will see. Humans will find faster, cheaper, more efficient tools. And then your threads will turn to iron, your needles to guns, and humans will forget, as they have forgotten so much already. And then, Rose Pryor, it is *you* who will become a faerie tale."

"And what of your World Below? How long can you hide there?"

"Who ever said I wished to hide?" His tone frosts over. "Did you know, long before your kind came to these islands, it was *my* folk who ruled them? And before us, it was a realm of monsters, the Fomor, primeval things you could not imagine. We won this land from them and carved out a place for ourselves, the mighty Tuath Dé, but how merciless your race is. The old peoples, the ones like us, the creators and crafters of magic, have waned all across the earth. Do you think I have spent all these centuries in *England*?"

He laughs, the sound harsh as the bark of a wild fox. "No; I've crossed the globe in search of my kin, the demons and angels and djinn and all our cousins, the old ones, the forgotten ones, the ones you've reduced to talismans and put into your pockets. Even your beloved Fates you have cut down and reshaped to serve your petty purposes, while their true names have been forgotten. We lasted longer than most, up here in the corner of the world, but the mortals found us still. How curiously cruel you humans are, that you must first kill your gods before you worship them."

As he speaks, I slowly realize what drives Lachlan. It is the thing I have been trying to put my finger on since he appeared to me in that cold alley.

Vengeance.

He runs so very cold, it took some time to notice it. But he is angry, consumed with a desire for vengeance over being locked out of his own world, angry at being trapped in this one. Angry because of who his people once were and who they have become, casualties washed away by the tide of expanding humanity.

I feel a current of fear at the thought of what his anger might do once he regains his full power.

"Am I to make my report?" I say, hiding my unease in brusqueness. "Or have you further exposition you'd like to impart?"

He blinks, my words shattering his little reverie. His eyes, when they dart to mine, are icy shards.

"Go on, then." He turns and begins walking back to the castle, his strides so long I must nearly jog to keep pace with him.

"I found the stone circle, *and* the wards that guard it."

He nods. "I told you it would be defended."

"Yes, that is one of the precious few things you *did* tell me," I return dryly. "Lachlan, who is the faerie queen?"

He stops short. I take three more steps before I realize I've left him behind. Turning, I see his face set in grim lines. The night is only getting colder, and I shiver and wait for him to make his answer.

Then he sighs and flicks his fingers. "Come here."

I frown, immediately on guard.

"You're freezing, Rose. Come *here*."

Uncertainly, I step toward him. Then gasp as he takes his hands in mine, and the air around us stirs and sweeps in a whirl, whipping up his cloak and hair and my skirts. That wind is as warm as a summer day and melts the frosty chill from my skin. As far as I can see, Lachlan has woven no knot, but his pupils turn as silver as mirrors, reflecting my own wide eyes back at me.

Then his gaze clears, and the wind settles, but I remain as warm as if I were hunched over a fire.

"What . . . ?" I look around, then pull my hands from his.

"Better?" he asks.

"Where . . . where are your threads?"

"We didn't give you mortals *all* our secrets," he says.

He resumes walking, his hair tossing about his shoulders. The castle is filled with whispering fae and candlelight; they incline their heads to Lachlan as he walks past them.

He is trying to change the subject, distracting me with summer breezes and threadless magic. With a low growl of annoyance, I hurry to keep up with him. "The faerie queen, Lachlan. Who is she? What happened to the moorwitches?"

His lips twitch into a wry smile. "She rules Elfhame, and she ruled it when the moorwitches were slaughtered, their blood running thick over the fields of faerie. The queen of the fae is a fickle shadow, my dear, and if she catches you in her realm, she will make your death painful and slow."

I swallow hard; fear and anger fill me with a chill no amount of conjured wind could dispel. "Why didn't you tell me this in the beginning?"

"Would it have made a difference?"

My lips twist. "I would have liked to know what I was getting into! What if I'd charged into Elfhame with no idea what awaited me?"

"I could talk for days of my world, and you'd still have not an *inkling* what awaits you there. Forget this queen; she will never know you were there, if you play this right. Just don't *charge in* like a crazed ox."

"Well I can't charge, sneak, or so much as turn a jig into Elfhame if I can't even open the door. I found the stone circle—so what spell will open the way?"

"I don't know. It will have changed since I was last there."

"You must know *something*!"

"I know that to open the way to the faerie green, you must pay homage to its queen."

I grab his arm, stopping him. It is like grabbing hold of a tree in winter. "I ask you for help, and you give me nursery rhymes?"

He gives me look of a long-suffering teacher at wit's end with a slow student. "That has always been the way of Elfhame. There will be a spell to open the way, and it must be a spell of homage. What form that will take, I cannot say, having never paid homage to this queen."

"But that makes no sense! You're speaking in riddles!"

"It's not something that can be *explained*, silly mortal girl." He smiles, snatching a lock of my hair and coiling it around his finger. "If I had all the answers, I wouldn't need *you*."

"And how much happier we both would be."

He cocks his head, his lips slanted into a cunning smile. "Really? Do you believe that?"

I stare incredulously. "Of course I do!"

"You ought to look in a mirror then." Taking my hand, he spins me around, and there *is* a mirror, a massive thing in a gilded frame. Where the Fates did it come from? Lachlan holds me in place, his hands on my arms and his chin hovering by my ear, our reflections gazing back at us. "Look at her. She is not the same shivering, wretched thing I found in that boarding house. That Rose's cheeks are flushed and her eyes shine. She has come alive in this place, like an ember that required only a bit of wild wind to burst into flame."

Blinking, I try to think of a barbed reply but find none. I can only stare at myself in his inexplicable mirror, and to my surprise, I see the change he describes.

I am not who I was mere weeks ago. I *am* more alive, more driven. Perhaps some of that is desperation, the dread of losing my magic, but not all of it.

"Remember, sweet Rose," he breathes into my ear, sending a shiver down the back of my neck. "The whole world overlooked you, but not I. The world expected nothing of you, but not I. *I* see who you truly are and how dazzling you could become."

His hand traces down my arm, over my palm, leaving a tingling trail of ice.

"Sir Faerie," I say shakily. "Unhand me."

With a soft laugh, he steps back, his hands falling to his sides. "Who knows? Perhaps at the end of this, you'll wish to remain at my side."

"What?" I whisper, turning to face him.

"Clearly something here has awakened you. Is it my company?" He leans closer, until his face is inches from mine, tilted as if for a kiss. My skin prickles. "You are not like other humans, are you, my little witch? You see deeper. You feel the currents of the world."

"You're speaking nonsense, as usual."

But my heart beats fast against my ribs, with panic, revulsion, or intrigue I cannot tell. One moment, I feel like his plaything, a foolish pet he holds on a string. And then there are other moments . . . like now. His winter eyes are fixed on mine, probing and curious, and I feel for the first time as if he is truly seeing *me*. It is a startling sensation, to be seen by him, to hold the whole of this immortal being's attention. His gaze scours me to the depths of my thoughts, until I feel suddenly very exposed. And even though I want to look away, I find I cannot.

It's as if he's cast a spell, another clever threadless trick.

It is strange. All my life, there has been a part of me longing to be seen, to be understood and valued. Now here is this beautiful faerie, saying all the words my soul has craved to hear.

And I find I want nothing more than to hide.

"When this is over," he says, his voice soft as falling snow, "where will you go?"

My breath flutters in my lungs. "Back to London, of course. To my classroom and my students."

"And if you find you have outgrown such a humble position?" His jeweled eyes flicker, touching every part of my face. "What if—"

He is interrupted by a chorus of shouts across the ruins. His head snaps up, and the spell is broken.

"What's wrong?" I ask, but he's already walking away, moving with swift steps.

The fae are gathered around one of their own, a willowy creature with a mass of black braids hanging over his shoulders, dressed like the others in a mourning cloak. But he kneels and clutches his side, and even in the dim light, I can see that he is wounded.

"My lord!" he gasps out, when Lachlan reaches him. "I nearly had him! But he came at me through the boundary, with a pack of wolves at his heels! One of them bit me!"

"What are you talking about, Tarkin?" Lachlan demands, kneeling to inspect the faerie's wound.

"The queen's Gatekeeper! He was near the boundary line, and I thought—I thought to make him pay for Lorellan. They should *all* pay, every last one—"

"*Fool!*" Lachlan hisses, leaping upright, his lean form whip-fast and his teeth bared in a snarl. "You know the orders I gave! No one—*no one*—was to interfere!"

The other fae shrink back, eyes wide, leaving the bleeding Tarkin to grovel alone. "My lord! I—I thought if he were out of the way—"

"I've *told* you how delicate this endeavor is, you idiot." Lachlan pinches the bridge of his nose. "What happened?"

"I tried to burn him, but it got out of hand. The wood was drier than it seemed, the blaze spread . . ."

"Oh," I breathe, grabbing hold of Lachlan's arm again. "There!"

In the distance, on the eastern edge of Blackswire where the wood meets the moor, smoke rises thick, black, and angry, lit by the red glow of flames below. I realize at once, with a thunderclap of horror in my chest, that the fire is rushing west, toward Ravensgate.

"I have to go!" I cry.

"Rose, wait!" Lachlan says, but I am already gone, running back across the ruins. Lachlan calls my name, but I ignore him, throwing myself through the tapestry and landing in my bedroom in Ravensgate.

CHAPTER EIGHTEEN

"Fire!" I shout, as I rush through the manor. The hallways are dark, but I hear voices downstairs. As I careen down the foyer steps, Mrs. MacDougal emerges from the kitchens, her eyes wide.

"Miss Pryor! What on earth—"

"Wildfire, to the east!" I gasp out. "I . . . saw it from my window. Where is Sylvie?"

Fates, let her be nearby.

Thankfully, the girl herself appears, dressed in armor made of silver tea trays and a great many brooches strung together. She clatters as she walks. "What's going on? Where's Connie?"

"He's out doing an inspection of the grounds," says Mrs. MacDougal.

"What? In the middle of the night?"

"He said something about some missing sheep. He'll be out till dawn if he must, off to the east."

"East . . ." The same direction as Lachlan's camp. The hills there are steep, the land full of crags and crannies. If he's down in one of the ravines, he may not see the fire till it's overtaken him.

"Mr. MacDougal is down at the pub," the housekeeper frets, wringing her hand. "I cannot send him out to warn the laird."

"I'll go, then." I push through the front doors and pause on the gravel drive.

"Take one of the horses!" says Mrs. MacDougal. "Quickly!"

"Ariadne's the fastest," says Sylvie.

I push aside a wave of panic; I almost say I'd be better off walking than trying to stay atop one of Conrad's tall horses. But I go to the stable anyway, opening the stall door. Sylvie helps me saddle a gray-flecked mare, and I hastily Weave thread into her mane: a spell to calm her, a spell to speed her gait, and an empathy knot to make her pliant to my commands.

All too soon, it's time for me to mount up. Sylvie pushes a block my way, and I force myself into the saddle before I have a chance to think about it. The calming knots, or else the animal's good breeding, prove effective, and she waits placidly for me to find my seat.

"Find Connie!" says Sylvie. "Please, Rose!"

"I will."

I channel into the empathy knot, and Ariadne's mane begins to glow as the threads light. At once the spell takes hold of her, infusing her mind with my sense of urgency. I shout at Sylvie to stand back as the mare bursts from the stable. I barely keep my seat when the horse spins on the drive, her hooves flinging gravel as she turns east.

Ariadne thunders over the earth with me clinging to her back like an alarmed cat. When the reins tumble from my grip, I hold fast to her mane, my eyes straining to open against the wind. My threadkit jounces over my shoulder; I fear its strap will break.

In the distance, the dark sky brightens to an unsettling shade of orange—the fire is spreading fast. Ariadne's hooves crush the heather and rip up clods of mud, her muscles bunching and releasing beneath me as she skids down hillsides. My feet are knocked from the stirrups. Teeth clenched, I send up a silent prayer to the Fates that the horse does not snap her leg in the darkness, or my neck.

We approach the fire in mere minutes, a fraction of the time it would have taken me to reach the blaze had I been running even at my fastest pace. When we near the edge of the fire, close enough that the heat washes over me in a wave, Ariadne rears and whinnies, and will go no closer.

The flames before me are savage and frenzied, no ordinary fire. The blaze takes the shape of great beasts, like red-orange bears trampling the earth and swinging their heads about, throwing fire in all directions. Even the sound the fire makes is animalistic, the fire-bears' roars as deep and angry as thunder. One catches sight of me and Ariadne and rears up on two legs to bellow a challenge. From its mouth pours a torrent of hot sparks.

I recognize a curse when I see one and know this must be the work of either Tarkin or the queen's faerie servant—the Gatekeeper Tarkin attacked. Their fight has set the entire eastern moor ablaze, despite the snow and damp. And if these fire-bears are not stopped, they will reach Ravensgate in minutes.

Suddenly I hear a high whinny to my right and turn to see a black shape hurtling toward us, out of the flames.

Bell.

I recognize the muscled gelding from watching Conrad ride off on him each morning.

But where *is* Conrad? Bell's saddle is empty, his reins swinging loose. As he thunders past, I see the white of his rolling eyes; the horse is crazed with terror.

But there's no time to search for Conrad. I must stop the fire before it reaches the manor, with Sylvie and Mrs. MacDougal inside.

Hands shaking, I open my threadkit and take out the spool of sturdy twine. Hurriedly, I Weave a ward spell between my hands. Then I heel Ariadne and shout at her to run.

She does so with alacrity, nearly throwing me from the saddle. I grip her girth with my knees as tightly as I can and channel.

The magic is strong and eruptive; along the edge of the fire, the earth splinters, a crack following Ariadne's hooves. A similar crack shatters through my chest, gouged by the torrent of magic coursing through my heart. My vision blurs, and I nearly topple from the saddle with a shuddering spasm of pain. I slump forward, gasping, and grip as tightly as I can to Ariadne's sides with my legs.

When my twine turns to ash, I Weave another spell, and another after that, turning the horse back and forth across the wall of flames. Every spell drives spears of agony through my chest. I ruthlessly crush the voice inside me that begs for relief, even as I wonder how much longer I can keep this up. Choking on smoke, gasping as my heart seizes, my body and mind seem to separate. My fingers work by rote, Weaving spell after spell, while my mind screams within a cage of pure pain. But it is working. The ward spells slowly congeal, creating a shimmering barrier rooted in the ground and towering overhead, a great glassy curtain shot through with an auroral array of colors.

When the fire-bears reach the barrier, they rage but do not cross it. I pull Ariadne back, my skin and dress blackened with soot, my lungs choked with smoke. I cough and watch as the fire-bears spew flames, thrashing their paws, roaring in fury. A wall of flame builds up against my barrier like water behind a dam, flames sloshing and reaching higher, searching for any weakness.

"Oh, Fates," I breathe, my eyes widening, terror clenching my stomach.

The barrier begins to bow outward, and then it rips. Flames pour through.

Ariadne starts from under me, releasing a wild whinny. Unprepared, I tumble head over heels and land hard on the ground, the breath knocked out of my lungs. The corner of my threadkit jabs into my side. The horse bolts back to the manor, and I can't blame her.

I look up, just as a wave of fire rushes hungrily toward me.

I cannot even scream.

Then a hand grabs me and pulls me back.

"Get down!" Conrad pushes me behind him and then raises his hands. Strung between them is a wide net of silver thread, and all at once it begins to glow. Captain is snarling at Conrad's side, hackles risen along his back.

Silhouetted against that terrible orange glow, his hair and coat whipped by the hot wind, the laird of Ravensgate holds his ground. He strains against the raging heat, pushing his spellknot forward, his teeth flashing white as he bares them in a snarl.

I gasp as a powerful wind, cold as ice and called by Conrad's spell—his *spell*, which he is channeling with *magic*—rushes from the sky and attacks the flames. It carries with it gusts of snow and sleet, and wherever the enchanted flames rise, it bites down with wolfish savagery.

Conrad's thread turns to ash, and then he grabs me and we run from the fire, letting the cold wind do its work. The laird is limping, his pace slowed by his old injury, and my chest is a tight knot of fiery pain from the effort of channeling the wards. We lean on each other, struggling to get free of the elemental battle raging over the moor. Captain bounds all around us, still alert and growling, protecting his master.

At last we collapse onto a bank and watch as Conrad's wind-wolves harry the fire-bears, drawing them apart and leaping high to smother them to the earth. The two primeval forces clash again and again, and the sky is bright with clouds of sparks and hot embers, and despite the terribleness of it, I cannot look away.

"Are you hurt?" Conrad asks me, his voice hoarse.

"No," I lie. My heart feels like a pincushion, stabbed through with needles. Every breath is a battle. But the pain is familiar. I can bear it.

What I *cannot* bear is the revelation that Conrad can channel. Conrad can Weave. Conrad, who despises magic, just called upon it to save our lives.

In moments, the wind-wolves prevail; the last of the fire-bears is brought down and crushed to smoke, and then the wolves dissipate into a wind that rushes in all directions, flattening the grass and sweeping ashes everywhere. I throw my shawl up, shielding Conrad and myself.

Then it's over.

Stillness settles over the land, and the only sound to be heard is our own heavy breathing. The air smells of ash, and all the way to the horizon, the moor is black and charred. But behind us, Ravensgate stands safe, a dark silhouette against a deep-blue sky. A few faint stars flicker to life beyond it, watery blue through the haze of smoke still clouding the air.

I look at Conrad. He stares at the scorched earth, his eyes vacant. Captain sits beside him, watchful and silent.

My throat is tight with angry questions. I wait for him to defend himself, to order me to ignore what I just saw or to try to explain it away with some lie. But the damnable man silently avoids my gaze, looking like a dog that knows it's done wrong and is waiting to be judged.

Then I see the burns on his hands.

I take them in mine carefully. He sucks in a pained breath but doesn't resist.

"Let me help you," I whisper. I cannot keep the angry tremor from my voice, and he flinches at it.

I wait for him to resist, to pull away. But he only nods, and I see how hard he's trying to hold himself together. The pain in his hands must be terrible. After inspecting them, I set them gently upon my lap. Taking a handkerchief from my pocket and finding it not too dirty with soot, I tear it in half and wrap each piece around his palms. He watches silently, still dazed.

My heart still burns as if I swallowed the fire. Ash and soot are smeared all over my gown, shawl, and arms. Even my hair smells like smoke. I look down at the braid hanging over my shoulder and see the ends are singed.

Plucking the needle I keep tucked beneath my collar, I tear off a length of silk thread with my teeth. Then I remove my shawl and begin embroidering it, quick, neat stitches.

"What are you doing now?" he asks cautiously.

"It's a healing charm, slow working but with better results than those flashy, quick spells your usual cheap healers like to work. Makes them look good, to close up a wound all at once, but it's not so impressive when you get gangrene a few days later."

I stitch in silence after that, my thread illuminated by moonlight. Conrad bears his pain stubbornly, his jaw rigidly set. I pointedly say nothing of his Weaving, but I can sense the tension in him, waiting for the subject to come up. He's barely breathing for the weight of apprehension suspended between us. The longer the silence stretches, the heavier it gets, until it feels the sky itself will come crashing down on our heads.

You're a Weaver, is all I can think. *You denied Sylvie her magic, while all along you were wielding it yourself.*

He is a hypocrite and a bastard, and I should walk away now and leave him to tend his own damn wounds.

But he did just save my life.

"All right, it's done," I say at last, nearly ten minutes later.

I drape the shawl over him. The spellknot is cruder than I'd have liked, but I didn't have hours to work on it, and he doesn't have time to wait. It's best to tend to these things quickly.

Once he's covered, I place my hands on the embroidery and draw three deep breaths. Each one sends pain shooting through me, but I have to keep going or risk him getting infected and dropping dead in a few days.

The magic comes in fits and starts, my heart convulsing fitfully. I suck in a breath.

His eyes flick to mine questioningly.

"I'm all right," I tell him. "I just . . . breathed in a lot of smoke."

Conrad's burned hand closes gingerly over my own. "I can help."

He channels with me, holding my embroidery and exhaling slowly. My magic trickles in from one end, while his flows brightly from the other. He is nowhere near as strong as Sylvie, nor even as strong as I once was, before my debt to Lachlan took its toll on my heart. But in my current condition, his strength is more than enough to compensate for my weakness.

The light of our combined magic flows through the threads and finally meets in the middle. It illuminates us both and shines on the smoke still thick in the air, a ghostly corona all around us. Threads of his magic entwine with mine, until they are indistinguishable from one another. But I can feel his energy tingling on my hands, featherlight and warm. It makes a shiver run down the back of my neck. The sensation is as intimate as feeling his breath on my skin. Does he feel my magic the same way? Does my power prickle over his wrists and coil up his arms?

My eyes lift to meet his, and for a moment, I cannot breathe.

For the second time tonight, I am held in thrall by a pair of eyes, but unlike Lachlan's cold, immortal gaze, inscrutable as a lost language, Conrad's is warm and human, filled with pain. I expected anger, defensiveness, perhaps even hatred for my discovering his secret. But instead, he looks haunted. There are whole paragraphs behind his eyes, and he gazes at me as if begging me to read them, to understand the secrets, explanations, fears, and hopes dammed up inside him. Or perhaps that is a projection of my own swirling desires. I want to peel him open and get all the answers to all the questions piling on my tongue.

You are a Weaver, I want to shout, if I could only find my voice. *You are a Weaver who hates magic. Why, why, why?*

Conrad blinks, breaking his gaze away first. He looks down. Between our hands, the embroidered threads begin to fade as the magic sinks in.

"There," he says softly. "It's done. Are you—Rose!"

With a sharp cry, I pull my hands back and clutch them to my chest, doubling over. Searing spasms of agony knife through my heart, radiating through my shoulders, neck, and stomach.

Conrad stiffens, the shawl slipping from his shoulders. "Rose!"

I shake my head, unable to speak.

Then I feel his fingertips, gentle and hesitant, on my shoulder. He can barely touch me for the burns on his hands. "You are hurt. I'll go back to the house and ride for the doctor—"

"No," I whisper. "It's the smoke, nothing more."

"Then here. You have more right to this than me."

He removes the enchanted shawl and begins to place it around me. I shake my head, already knowing it's useless. I've tried every healing spell there is, many times over, in an attempt to stop or even just soothe the pain. Nothing works, but I can't exactly explain that to him.

"Let's share it," I say in compromise.

So we sit side by side, my shawl wrapped around us both, with the great, charred moor before us.

"Sylvie?" he asks.

"She's at the house. She's fine."

He nods, starts to speak again, then closes his mouth. His eyes are dazed with exhaustion, pain, or both.

"So," I begin, as the tension between us finally becomes too much to withstand. "You're a Weaver."

The corners of his mouth pinch downward. His fingers tense, as if he wants to curl them into fists but is stopped by the pain. "Swear you will say nothing of this to Sylvie. Tell her you put out the fire yourself."

I watch him sidelong, half angry with him for keeping such a secret while denying Sylvie her own magic. Half pitying him, because he looks like a man whose soul is in ruins, as if the ability to channel were a disease eating away at his heart.

That doesn't stop me from wanting to take him by the ear and shake answers out of him.

"I don't know much," he says. "Only a handful of spells, really. 'Tis not as though I went to a school as you did. Everything I know, my father taught me, at least until . . ."

"Magic took him from you?"

"Magic has taken *everything* from me," he snarls. He nearly clenches his hand again, but with a grimace of pain forces his fingers to open. Captain whines beside him and puts his head on Conrad's leg.

"Your mother?"

He nods. "I told you. 'Tis a curse in our blood."

I turn to the scorched land and scan the night; the moon, though unseen, casts the smoke-filled sky in a surreal shade of lavender. All around, the hills roll dark and endless.

"What started the fire?" I ask, drawing thread from my sleeve and winding it idly around my finger. "You and I both know that was no natural blaze."

"I don't know what you mean," he replies too quickly, too casually. "We often burn the moors to clear the old, dead brush and make way for new crops."

Is he seriously trying to deny what just happened? "Conrad, that was *magic*. I saw shapes in the flames that—"

"I don't know what anyone could see through all that smoke. It was just fire, nothing more."

My lips tighten, clamping down on the outburst simmering behind my teeth. *Why are you lying, Conrad North?* Controlled burns? In the middle of the night? I may not know much about country life, but I am not an idiot. I also notice he makes no mention of the supposed "missing sheep."

My fingers begin to dance, tapping restlessly, drumming my kneecaps. I feel as if Conrad's wind-wolves are trapped in my chest, howling into my veins.

Does he think me an idiot, to believe that fire was natural? I don't look at him, but stare straight ahead, my face stone, my heart throwing itself against my ribs.

Dread and suspicion blacken my thoughts. I feel I will fly apart. I want to rattle the truth from him. But I cannot, not if there is any chance he is what my instincts are telling me he is.

So I look at him and smile, and let him see me accept his lie.

"Your secret is safe with me," I say.

He glances sharply at me. "What, just like that?"

"Did you want to argue about it? I told you, I will say nothing to Sylvie."

"Why not? Why aren't you berating me with questions? Where is your infernal nosiness now?"

I shrug. "If I asked those questions, would you answer them?"

He looks away, the muscles in his neck flexing.

"I thought not," I sigh. "I'm tired, Conrad. I don't have the energy to drag answers out of you. I want to go wash my face and get in my bed."

He inclines his head, looking as weary as I feel. "Very well. Can you walk?"

He leans on me, and we begin the journey. My shawl is still draped over him, but his breath is ragged with pain. Halfway to the house, Mrs. MacDougal and Sylvie meet us, fussing and frantic. The housekeeper helps to bear his weight, and Sylvie tells us Bell and Ariadne arrived safely back at the stables, but that their empty saddles had given them both a terrible fright. She hugs Captain tight and stares at Conrad's burned hands, but the bandages I wrapped around them hide the worst of his wounds.

In the house, Conrad insists he is not that bad off, but lets Sylvie pat his sooty face clean with a damp cloth. He tells them of the burn gone out of control, but I see Mrs. MacDougal's lips purse, just slightly, and I know *she* knows. Of course she knows. She's run this house longer than he's been alive. She's complicit in all of this, whatever it is, however deep it goes.

Later that night, I pace my room, as tense as a cat in a cage. Is there more to Conrad North? Perhaps I'm wrong about all of it, leaping to foolish conclusions. My suspicions could be nothing more than heightened nerves.

I should just ask him.

Blunt and to the point.

What do you know of faeries, Mr. North? Are you in league with their murderous queen?

A few minutes more of this, and I've summoned the courage to open my door—

Only to duck in again, as Conrad goes stalking past, the manor creaking around him.

I hold my breath until he's gone down the stairs, and then, snatching my cloak, I follow.

Because no matter what explanation he might give, I know now that I could not trust it. I can only discover for myself who Conrad North really is, and what he is hiding.

And why he wove that mighty wind spell with spider's thread.

CHAPTER NINETEEN

Conrad moves with sure-footedness in the black night and does not light his way until he is well away from the manor. I see a knot of fire bloom ahead and hang back; it is no lantern, but a fire spell, the conjured flame twisting gently over his hand.

"Oh, you disingenuous bastard," I mutter. "You bloody-minded, lying hypocrite!"

I am still grappling with the revelation that he's not only *had* magic, he's been actively Weaving this entire time—after forbidding me, much less *his sister*, from so much as summoning a thimble across a room.

He has a great deal to answer for. But first, I must know where he is going.

His route is winding, following no path, but his direction seems assured. He pauses only a few times, and then I crouch low, melding into shadow until he begins to walk again.

The further he goes, the deeper my dread becomes, and the firmer my certainty. This is no idle wander, though he moves slowly, his limp and injuries paining him. He knows exactly where he is going.

It is a different wood into which I enter tonight than the one I first explored nearly a week ago. The trees are the same, the rise and flow of the land has not changed, but the spirit of the place has shifted. Before, I walked through it in awe, feeling small and intrusive, but not unwelcome. I was a mouse creeping along in fleeting insignificance, of no consequence to the wood's much vaster existence. It admitted me with indifference and let me go my way.

But tonight, the wood *pushes* at me. The wide spaces between the trees teem with festering shadows. It makes me think, insensibly, of the man who'd stood on the corner in Devil's Acre with his python wrapped around his arm. He would feed it mice and the children would gather to shriek as the lump of mouse slid down, down the snake's gullet. Now I am that mouse, being squeezed on every side, pushed deeper and deeper into the darkness, with only the distant flickering light of Conrad's fire charm to guide me. My thoughts tumble in a panic, and I wildly imagine that if his light were to go out, I would be swallowed up forever by this dark wood.

Not a long time later, Conrad comes to a stop, and I take up position behind a tree to watch what he will do.

The stone circle waits below, as I had known it would the moment Conrad walked past my room over an hour ago. As perhaps I'd known the moment I saw him raise his spell high and command the fury of the northern wind.

Conrad is connected to the fae. He may even be the "Gatekeeper" Tarkin mentioned—a servant to the faerie queen herself.

He steps precisely through the spider-thread wards, his movements calculated. As if he knows exactly where each one is stretched. And then, once he stands in the center of the circle, he puts out his light and begins to Weave.

The stones are, as I'd imagined, a great pegboard. He twines thread around and between them, but it is too dark for me to see the pattern he makes, though I can see that he does so with instinctive movements, working slowly but methodically. It is a pattern he knows well, has walked many times before.

I watch him carefully and hear nothing but the low, clattering wind. Conrad is lit only by the faint illumination of starlight reflecting off the stones. The moon is veiled behind a knot of black cloud; a storm brews in the east.

It takes him twenty minutes or so to complete the spell. I am half crouched by the time he finishes, my legs cramping from the effort of holding so still. My earlier panic has been replaced by bitter resolve. I am closer than I've ever been to my goal, closer than Fiona got in forty years. I feel like a predatory bird waiting high in a tree, immobile, all-seeing, waiting for the opportunity to strike.

Suddenly, the threads begin to glow. Conrad has finished and is channeling into them.

I pull behind a tree, heart in my throat, and watch.

The illumination is white and blinding, growing in the center of the circle like a star being born. I blink hard but do not look away, my pulse quickening.

The light spreads and grows, forms a shape like a great eye, broken only by the laird's silhouette. He stands at the epicenter of a massive, intricate Celtic knot, its complexity beyond my ability to memorize in the mere moments it is visible. It reminds me of the spells I glimpsed in my uncle's moorwitch book, a pattern ancient and terrible.

I hold my breath and step out from my hiding place just as Conrad North, who doesn't believe in faeries, steps into faerie land.

Behind him, in the circle, the eye of light is beginning to shrink. I wait as long as I can, letting him put distance between him and me. Then I rush forward at once, without a thought for what I might do beyond reaching that gate before it closes. I replicate his steps through the defensive wards and throw myself through the portal before it can close, unsure if I'm too late, expecting to only flop onto the mossy ground like a desperate fool.

Instead, I land in another world.

CHAPTER
TWENTY

The first thing I notice is trees.

There is nothing but trees in every direction. But they are unlike any trees I've ever seen; their trunks are pale and their branches spidery; the leaves are bloodred. Dragging myself to my knees, I press my hand against the nearest trunk and then withdraw it with a shudder; the bark is *warm*, like flesh.

What was the name of the tree Lachlan wants? The Dwirra. Could one of these be it? They are uniform in size and shape; I can see no feature which might distinguish one as being special from the others.

Conrad is nowhere in sight, nor is any other living creature. The stillness here is unnatural, like the stillness of the stone circle itself. No wind, no insects, no chittering squirrels. The light here is dim, faintly violet in hue, and I cannot tell the source of it. The sky above—if it is sky at all—is but blank shadow. No stars, no moon, no clouds. The spot where I landed is not marked or in any way distinctive. I remember what Lachlan told me about portal magic, and how every door needs an anchor to open to, but I see nothing here which might be the anchor to the stone circle. No doorway or portal back to my own world.

The ground is covered with scarlet leaves, and with dark-violet mosses and emerald ferns, but there is none of the scrubby undergrowth I would expect in any ordinary wood. Instead, I can see far between the trees, deep into the depths of the strange, silent forest. Trunks like white columns march in all directions, and in the far distance, they fade into a red haze. The only motion comes from the trees themselves, where the occasional leaf slips loose and drifts idly to the ground. The air tastes faintly of sweet summer wine and fills my nose with the ripe, dark scent of blackberries.

Slowly I rise, staying alert, lest my presence startle something or someone out of the shadows, and take a cautious step forward. Nothing moves. Another step. Another. Then I am walking, slow and careful, shivering even though the air is warm.

Is this really Elfhame, the enchanted faerie land? Then where are the faeries? Why am I alone?

With luck, I won't meet them at all. I'll slip right through, cut a branch from this damnable tree, and return to the human world, where I can finally free myself from this yearslong nightmare.

I struggle to hope it will be that simple.

How strange this place is. The further away things are, the more convoluted their shapes appear. Trees twist in unlikely forms until I get close to them, when they appear straight. But when I've passed by, I look back and see them warping again.

I come to a little brook, which ought to be babbling and splashing. But instead, the water flows sluggishly. After a moment's hesitation, I dip my hand into it. It feels like water, but it moves more like rolling honey. Parched as I am, I don't consider drinking; Fates only know what faerie water would do to me. I cross on stones and walk on.

A blur of movement catches my eye, like something low and lean streaking across the ground. I whirl, standing frozen in place as I scan the trees, but there is nothing there. I recall Lachlan's eerie warning about the faerie queen: *She will make your death painful and slow.*

Why didn't I ask him more about what to expect here? In hindsight, this should have been my first concern. But so focused was I on simply *getting* here I never gave much thought to what might follow. Or perhaps a part of me never truly believed I would make it this far.

Am I even going in the right direction? I stop dead at that, breaking into a cold sweat. I'd never considered which way to go, I'd just *walked*.

I look back, then side to side, but see nothing to break the monotony of the woods. I start to step forward but can't. What if it's the wrong direction? What if every step I take is leading me further from where I need to go?

"What's wrong?" whispers a voice. "Have you lost your way, dearest niece?"

I gasp and twist around, searching for her, but all I see are looming trees. The woods warp around me, mocking me. I lose my balance and land on my hands and knees. Scurrying forward, I find my feet and throw myself into a sprint.

All around me, her laughter echoes.

"You're not real!" I cry, hands thrashing at the branches which block my way. "It's just this place!"

Choking for air, I run and run, but her voice follows me, whispering. I can smell the tobacco from her pipe.

"Little bird . . ."

"No!" I shout. "I'm seeing this through, and you cannot stop me!"

She's only an illusion. It's this place, playing tricks on me.

But the panic in my breast is all too real.

I notice more movement flanking me; shadows run outside my line of sight, like wolves stalking prey. Always they vanish just as my eyes fall on the places they were. But once, I fully glimpse . . . *something*. A creature mottled gray, with burning red eyes and great, knobby legs.

Gasping, I crash through the woods. Every step I take, thorns push out of the earth and scrape my ankles. My skirt rips on a branch, a strip of cloth left dangling behind. The shadows hurry me along, and it seems they are getting nearer and bolder; I see a flash of dark fur, hear a snap of teeth.

Finally, unable to run any further, my breath scraping my throat, I stop and lean, panting, on a tree. Then, with a sob of horror, I see spiders crawling all over the trunk, and they swarm over my hands. I recoil, shrieking, batting them off my arms.

Despair overwhelms me, and I sink to my knees. I try to think of what to do, of some spell to light the way. But my thoughts disintegrate before they can lead anywhere. The shadow-creatures lurk just out of sight, but I feel them circling, circling. My scent is in their noses.

"Please," I whisper. "Someone help me."

From behind me, slithering and sly, comes a reply.

"My *dear*," she says, "you had only to ask. Turn around and face me, girl."

I rise slowly, my soul emptying of panic, of courage, of defiance. I become dread. Black, vast, consuming. When I turn, I know whom I will see, and she does not disappoint.

Tall and skeletal, my aunt looms before me in terrifying detail. She wears a black gown, her hair high and elegant, her long-stemmed pipe perched delicately between her fingers.

Horribly, she smiles at me.

"Wicked Rose," she hisses. "I told you that you would come to no good end. I did tell you."

I run, but every step I take, thorns grasp at me. I trip and go on hands and knees, sobbing, the terror rabid, gnawing at me. I cannot get enough breath. My vision shrinks to a pinpoint. I hear her following behind, a whisper, a susurrus of dry paper over leaves. I can feel her awful smile.

Something lunges out of the trees and takes a snap at my skirt; it rips fabric away with a tear. Spinning, I see a terrible sight: a wolfish thing with eight long, hairy legs and a too-wide mouth, every inch of its expansive gums studded with long, glinting teeth. It scurries away with a scrap of my skirt in its mouth, and I stumble in the other direction, mind bursting with terror. Wherever I go, I hear my aunt's laughter.

I will die here.

I know it with certainty, and terror infuses me. No matter how fast or far I run, she will follow. As she has *always* followed. She has been waiting all these years, knowing I would return to her.

"The tree," I whisper to myself. "I just have to reach the tree. Then it will be over."

"Fool child!" She appears before me, blocking my way. "You think you can escape what you did to me? You are not worthy. You are nothing! Nothing!"

She stabs her pipe at me, its bowl flaring red.

I cry out, landing hard on the ground and curling up, trying to hide from the coming pain. It's as if she's reached into my chest and dug her nails into my heart and is pulling it from me. From every side, the wolf-spiders lunge, hissing and snarling. Their jaws open, their teeth seeking my flesh.

I scream.

All at once a blinding white light floods the trees, so brilliant it banishes every shadow and throws into startling detail every vein on every leaf, a scouring, searching, violent light that passes through trunk and through me, for a moment wiping every thought from my head, filling me with its radiance. My aunt vanishes like smoke before a gale, nothing more than an illusion. The wolf-spiders retreat, whining, and vanish into the woods' depths.

When the light fades, I see a woman looming over me, her silhouette outlined by the fading glow, her crown tall and jagged.

"Little witch," she sighs, "what have you done?"

She reaches for me, and at the touch of her cold and lovely fingers, I faint.

CHAPTER TWENTY-ONE

When I wake, I find myself sunken into a pool of luxurious textiles—silks and velvets, satins and cashmeres. For a moment, I simply relish the textures and the exquisite warmth, like being wrapped in a cocoon.

Then I bolt upright, remembering.

The portal. The wood. My aunt. The monstrous, wolfish spiders.

There's no sign of any of it now. I'm in an ornate room, every wall a burnished mirror. The ceiling is peaked, and from it hang many chandeliers—all broken, chipped, and faded, but a few candles burn between them. The bed is a nest of blankets and cushions, most of them frayed. But despite the raggedness of the objects, the room is elegant, a shabby memory of grandeur. And it's drenched in cobwebs.

On a silver-plated credenza, a small music box plays an endlessly repeating melody, and with a start, I realize I know the song. I've heard it recently, sung in the sweet voice of Carolina, my former student:

> In the shadows 'neath your bed,
> She spins her spells with spider's thread,
> Her hair is black, her eyes are red,
> If she sees you, you are dead.

I swallow hard and draw up my knees, feeling itchy all over. Spiders are everywhere, in the curtains around the bed, in the corners, swinging from chandelier to chandelier. It is their silken strands which form the translucent canopy overhead.

"Do my pets unsettle you?" asks a voice.

I jump, then spot her—sitting so still in the far corner that I'd completely missed her at first.

She is dressed in a thin silvery gown, cobwebs in her black hair, and watches me with eyes as green as polished emeralds—not red at all—smiling as if she knows a terrible secret. I do not have to ask to know at once, with dreadful certainty, who she is.

I sit absolutely still and watch the faerie queen watching me.

Her face is pale as milk, her features all slightly more elongated than a human's would be, her cheekbones thin and swooping like filigree to ears that arch to graceful points. Blue shadows pool beneath her eyes and in the hollows of her cheeks and throat.

I remember her in the cursed wood, banishing my nightmares with a flare of white light. But I cannot believe she did it to save me. She must want me for something else.

If she catches you in her realm, Lachlan's warning sounds in my mind once more, *she will make your death painful and slow.*

Her head cocks. "Little witch, little witch, do you know what laws you've broken, coming here?"

"W-what?"

In a singsong voice she recites, "*Saucy mortals must not view what the queen of stars is doing, nor pry into our faerie wooing.*"

She rises, smooth as silk, and glides toward me, her fingers wrapping around the bedpost. They are gray tipped in black, as if she's been dipping them in ink. Her eyes are larger than a human's, more pupil than whites, and her teeth and ears are as sharp as a cat's. And for all her strangeness, she is the most beautiful creature I have ever seen. I find myself staring half out of terror, half out of awe. Is it some spellknot which makes her seem so alluring? Or is it an older, stranger magic, something beyond my mortal ken?

"Yet here you are, saucy mortal," she murmurs. "Insatiable and bold and so very, very stupid. Why are you here, in Morgaine's realm?"

Morgaine.

It is a name which stirs at the bottommost depths of memory; a name whispered in a storybook, glimpsed between the lines of myth. *Morgaine, Morgana, Morrigan, Mag . . .*

I open my mouth, remembering suddenly why I came here and intending to demand to see the Dwirra Tree. But my voice fails, and I can only gape like a fish.

Her fingers close on my jaw, shutting my gaping mouth for me. Then they linger, tracing my cheeks, my brow. She studies my face as if she is about to either kiss it or devour it.

"How frightened of me you are," she says. She smiles, displaying each of her pearly teeth. "Like a butterfly caught in a web."

"*Please,*" I whisper, but I cannot seem to summon more than that.

"Don't you mean *thank you?* I could have let you wander the Wenderwood until you were old and gray, but I did not. I could have turned you into a spider on the spot, but I did not."

I nod wordlessly, sensing the best course now is to play along, to show her I am no threat. Which is, of course, the utter truth. She perches on the bed and tilts her chin, her inhuman eyes studying me.

"Little witch," the queen says again. "Why have you come here? What do you seek? Who sent you, or are you merely a witless lamb lost in the dark?"

I want to ask her what her connection is to Conrad North, and why he is Weaving wards around her doorstep. I want to demand that she show me this Dwirra Tree Lachlan craves. But I lack the courage for any of these queries. I feel like I am dreaming; the surfaces around me are all slightly blurred and indistinct, nothing quite real, as if the curtains or the mirrors or the chairs might turn to mist if I reached out to touch them.

"Are you—" I whisper, then pause to collect my voice. "Are you enchanting me?"

"Why?" she asks breathily. "Do you feel enchanted?" She pulls back with a soft laugh. "It is easy to forget how young you humans are. Your passions run right beneath your skin."

She rises and goes to a gilded sideboard, where she pours something from a crystal pitcher into a burnished brass goblet. This she hands to me, and I take it but do not drink. The liquid is coppery gold and smells of acrid smoke. I stare at it, wondering if it's poisoned, if I will transform into a goblin if I taste it.

Morgaine watches me while she pours her own glass. "Go on. Ask me the question tingling at the tip of your tongue."

"The Wenderwood," I blurt out, though that's not at all what I'd intended to say. "I saw things in there . . ."

"What did you see, witch?" She drains her wine in one long draft; I realize I'm staring at the muscles in her graceful neck, working as she swallows. I look away, my face hot.

"Nightmares," I mutter. "That's all it was."

"Was it?" She lies down beside me, on her side, head propped on one hand while the other reaches out to stroke my forearm. I pull it away, the hairs rising on end.

"My watchers were real enough," she says. "And they would have torn you limb from sinew if I had not stepped in. Naughty girl, leaping through portals, tossing herself into people's lands as if she had any right. My watchers watch, and they defend my borders. But they were not *all* you saw, were they?"

I shake my head, my mouth dry. "My aunt."

"Ah." Morgaine grins. "That is the nature of the Wenderwood—to reveal your deepest fears and most shameful secrets. I know the heart of every mortal who enters my lands. For when you know what a person fears, their will becomes yours to control."

She grabs my hand suddenly, so fast and tight I cannot recoil. Her nails dig into the tender skin of my palm. Her eyes spark like green fire. "You are trembling still. How very afraid you are."

"I'm not afraid."

"You're afraid of *being* afraid, and that's the most powerful fear of all. Haven't you heard? Magic is not for the faint of heart."

I shiver with recognition at the simple phrase, which had once seemed so banal printed on the opening pages of *The Westminster Weaving Primer*. On her lips, the words are insidious, a dark prophecy spoken by a cruel oracle.

With a sigh, she rises and pulls her hair over one shoulder, studying me as if disappointed. "Come, then. I will show you my realm, and you will see what becomes of mortals who trespass here."

My stomach drops. "Are you going to kill me?"

Her expression never changes as she steps backward through the door, her nails trailing on the frame. "Come, now. Hurry!"

I clamber out of the bed, and when my feet hit the floor, I see I'm still in my muddy dress, and my feet are bare. My threadkit is sitting by the wall, seemingly untampered with.

Dragging my fingers through my hair, I find it tangled with ribbons and white feathers and strings of pearls. With a shudder, I realize the faerie queen must have been playing with my hair while I slept, as if I were her doll.

"Is this . . . spider silk?" I ask, pulling fine, sticky strands from my hair.

Looking up, I see Morgaine has already gone, through a mirrored door on the far side of the room. I grab my threadkit and run after her.

"Hurry," she says. "You must change at once. The others are waiting."

"Change? The others? What—?"

She snatches my hand and tugs me out of the bedroom and into a large dressing room, the walls hung with ornate burnished and warped mirrors. Chandeliers hang overhead, all jumbled together, cooled wax hanging from their arms like icicles. The air smells of sweet jasmine and honeysuckle, a heady scent that soon becomes cloying. Three large wardrobes, each looking plucked from a different century, line the furthest wall, and Morgaine throws each of these open. She settles on one garment and flings it at me, her eyes gleaming.

"Put it on," she says.

Then she sits in an armchair upholstered in a patchwork of fabrics and waits.

I clutch the dress, my head whirling and cheeks hot. "N-now? Here?"

She raises one hand, and I spy thin silver threads tangled in her fingers. "Do you require encouragement, little witch?"

"You're mad," I whisper.

"Darling," she says, "I am the *queen* of madness."

Gritting my teeth, I begin removing my torn dress, trying to cover myself with the other, which is an awkward affair. Morgaine seems to have no concern for modesty and watches with open interest.

Cursing beneath my breath, I wriggle into the dress she forced on me and glance around, looking for exits. There is only the one door, and I find I lack the courage to make a run for it, not with her ten paces away, staring straight at me.

The dress is exquisite in the same faded way everything in this strange palace is; the skirt is gray silk, covered in gauzy, layered petals, like a wilted rose, dusted with glittering flecks of silver. The bodice, embroidered with tiny silver stars, is tight and low cut, leaving my shoulders and collarbone bare. The slippers are stippled with white beads. Finally, I pull silk gloves up to my elbow. It all fits perfectly.

I feel like a doll, a plaything, to dress up before the queen cracks me open.

She studies me with a strange little smile for a long moment. Her fingers idly twist her spider threads, hypnotically graceful as they twirl and bend.

Then she says, "Come."

She rises and presses a mirror; it opens outward, a hidden door. Morgaine does not wait to see if I follow, but I do, on trembling legs, my borrowed, opulent gown whispering along the floorboards.

I step into a curved corridor paneled in white wood, Morgaine several steps ahead. I run my hand over the wall, feeling in the grooves and whorls that same pulsing warmth that lived in the trees of the Wenderwood. Shivering, I move on. On and on I walk, with only glimpses of Morgaine to guide me—a slither of her silk dress, a flash of black curls.

Her court contains many hallways and many closed doors, all of which look as if they were stolen from a different time and place. One might look like any humble wooden door from any poor alley in London; the next might be gilded and decorated with a crumbling mural, as if plucked from some continental palace. The hallways bend and twist in impossible ways, at times slanting downhill or up, or spiraling in seemingly infinite loops. Many of the walls are covered in mirrors, throwing my own distorted reflection back at me. In some of these, I appear to be smiling a mad, horrible smile. In others, I am screaming. Shuddering, I try to look directly at none.

Finally, a great doorway looms in front of me, arches of white wood carved like delicate trees. Morgaine waits beneath it, watching me approach. Her expression has turned solemn and aloof, and somewhere along the way, she picked up a crown. It is tall and made of many jagged, asymmetrical points of silver, and between these slender prongs her spiders weave their glistening webs.

"Well, little witch?" she whispers. "Would you look upon a faerie realm?"

I nod, breathless, my skin crawling with terror. But I didn't come this close to turn back now. Perhaps I will find an opening when her attention is diverted and I can slip away, find the tree, and escape.

She leads me down a wide, shallow stair that opens to a vast, mossy floor. Looking up, I see no sky, only a great roof of white branches all woven together. Among those branches hang spheres of light, lanterns white and lavender and gold. They flood the faerie court with a soft twilight glow.

The fae enclave is spread below in a cradlelike valley, ten times the size of Blackswire, almost a small city. The houses are like nothing I've ever imagined; they rise from the mossy earth in white domes and hills, irregular shapes with circular doorways carved into them, and childlike handprints and patterns are stamped across the walls. From these black openings, I see hints of faces—pale, inhuman, with bulbous black eyes and sharp teeth. These fae are even less human than their queen, even less than the ones attending Lachlan outside the great ward. We walk among their houses, and I hear them chitter their teeth.

I stick close to Morgaine, fearing what would happen if I were left alone out here, with those dark, glinting eyes watching me hungrily.

The Wenderwood borders the fae enclave on three sides; looking back, I see her palace rising over it all, a jumble of towers and walls and impossibly thin spires, all white wood. It looks like something from a dream, a house of melted wax, or what you'd get if you splashed white paint onto a canvas and then let it run. It doesn't look as if it could truly be real; certainly it doesn't seem capable of standing on its own, but there it is.

Then we turn around a bend, and I see what stands on the other high end of Elfhame, a tower to mirror the palace, and yet no tower at all.

"Oh," I breathe. *"Oh."*

Morgaine looks back, coming to a stop. "Is it not magnificent?"

It is a tree, a tree taller than any structure I've ever seen in my life, its trunk curved naturally into the shape of a woman. It is white, like the smaller ones in the Wenderwood, and it arches high over the enclave. Its arms are lifted up, morphing into the branches which form the canopy overhead, thick and tangled and shivering with scarlet leaves. Its head is tilted so that the face gazes down at the dwellings of the fae, and the eyes are blank white wood. Vines trail over its trunk, forming a kind of stringy gown. Its limbs arch over the whole of Elfhame, until they reach the borders and there droop low like the branches of a great willow tree, forming a scarlet curtain of leaves that encircles the whole of this little queendom. I sense if I were to push through that curtain, I would tumble into the void beyond the earth, the nothing between the worlds. At its base, new growth springs up, branches clustering at the ankles and calves and knees, slender young stalks gradually melding into the greater tower of the main trunk.

The Dwirra Tree isn't *in* Elfhame.

Elfhame is in the Dwirra Tree.

Everything around me, all the odd shapes and patterns, now begin to make sense. The fae houses are roots protruding from the ground, and into which they've burrowed to create homes. Even Morgaine's palace is part of the tree. All the little paths tracing through the enclave seem to lead here, up a slight incline, toward the main trunk.

I feel very, very small before it.

This is the tree I must take a branch from?

"Come," Morgaine says, watching me. It occurs to me that she never blinks. "They are waiting for us."

"Who?" I walk forward in a daze, my pulse a hammer in my temples.

We follow a narrow track through the thick moss; it weaves up the hill and ends at a wide green clearing. There are odd shapes there, hidden by blankets of moss and ivy—tables and chairs, a broken loom, a spinning wheel. Morgaine walks through them, her head high, but her expression seems . . . sad.

"This is where they came," I whisper. "The moorwitches."

The moorwitches who were, according to the legend Sylvie told me, slaughtered by the queen of the fae. I glance sidelong at her, my skin clammy, my throat sticky with dread.

"Yes." She presses the tip of her finger to a broken spindle. "This is where they came."

"Why did you bring me here?"

She stops, her back to me, the lines of her sharp shoulder blades visible through her gown. Her head is slightly bowed, her dark hair parted over her shoulders so that the pale column of her neck is exposed.

"It is not often a mortal visits my realm. With the exception of my Gatekeeper, of course."

I think of Conrad stepping into that glowing portal but say nothing. I still do not know the entirety of his part in this strange drama, and I want to know more before I make him a topic of conversation with the most dangerous creature in—or below—the earth.

Now Morgaine turns, just enough to peer at me over her shoulder, one glinting emerald eye fixing on my face.

"We are to have a revel," she says. "There will be dancing and feasting in homage to me, and you, my little witch, my stray lamb, are invited to join."

"I don't want to dance. I want to leave. When can I go home?"

She laughs, low and soft. "You have trespassed on my lands, set foot in my faerie court. You have looked upon the Dwirra, the most sacred of trees." Her head tilts, and she leans closer, until for a dizzying moment, I think she will kiss me. I meet her green eyes and find myself transfixed.

"Little witch, did you think I would ever let you *leave*?"

CHAPTER TWENTY-TWO

A faerie revel, as it turns out, is something like a human ball—if all the humans were punch drunk and half dressed and the musicians hexed with a hastening spell. It is a chaotic jumble of noise and limbs and light.

Morgaine leads me down a narrow stone stair that wends down the back of the Dwirra Tree's hill, to a wide clearing of moss ringed by craggy standing stones, much like the ones that circle the portal in the human world. Trees grow around the perimeter, their branches glowing brightly with clusters of those strange fruit-like lamps, and between the lights wend vines of ivy and fragrant purple wisteria. In the center of the clearing burns a large crackling bonfire.

Gathered there are hundreds of fae, dancing and shrieking with utter abandon. Linked hand in hand, they form several rings around the fire, moving at a rapid, reckless pace. If any of them tripped, they would be trampled by the others. Their shadows, cast from the bonfire, twist behind them with lives of their own, flickering over the oblong stones.

The fae are dressed in revealing, almost nonexistent garments, thighs and waists and shoulders bare, their skirts and tunics ragged, petaled things that resemble crushed roses, not unlike my own gown. Colorful painted patterns ring their eyes and curl down their cheeks, necks, and arms, vanishing beneath their sheer, many-layered garments.

Hanging from the hems of their clothing are tiny baubles, beads and buttons and keys and thimbles, human things, the sort of trinkets that one might drop on the road—none of iron, of course. The fae have turned the objects into glinting jewelry, and the result is a glittering, tinkling spectacle. They have even studded their wild, tangled hair with them.

Faerie musicians blow, pluck, and pound on instruments I do not recognize, though I can guess at their human counterparts—flute and fife, fiddle and cello, drum and harp. The music is furious and fast, a fever dream of a song, played with no regard for harmony. The notes clash and writhe in the air, and yet somehow emerge symphonic, beauty born of chaos.

"My people are beautiful," sighs Morgaine. "Their songs a tribute to my ears, and their steps an homage to my rule."

The music scurries beneath my skin and bursts behind my ribs, tugging at my heart.

"Do you wish to join the revel?" asks Morgaine, her voice sibilant in my ear.

"Yes," I say, before I can stop to think. My thoughts are beginning to blur; I catch myself leaning forward in anticipation. Music shivers over my skin, pulls insistently at my hair.

"Then go," she says. "Dance, little witch, and forget the world above."

I move forward in a daze, descending the rest of the stairs and setting foot in the mossy clearing. Everything spins around me, fae and tree and fire, and before I know it, hands grasp my arms and drag me in, linking me into the dance, submersing me in their dream.

Round and round I spin, clutching a faerie on either side. There is thread woven in their hair and on their clothes, I dimly realize. Spells upon spells, magic layered over magic, until the air is so thick with it I can barely breathe. The smell of it burns in my nose, smoky and sharp, blended with the sweetness of the wisteria overhead and the earthen aroma of trees and moss. Vaguely, I wonder what spells they are, but

I cannot clear my thoughts to focus on any one Weave. Instead, my head is full of pounding drums, and I let myself be pulled and spun the length of the revel, handed from faerie to faerie. Their long fingers, with those extra joints, trail down my arms and twist my hair, and their eyes study me with a range of expressions—curiosity, delight, hunger, rage. In those glimpses the fae fragment, no longer a tribe of faceless, vibrant creatures, but individuals with different reactions to the human in their midst. Not all of them welcome me. Some look keen to take a bite of me. But I linger with none long enough to truly understand what they see in me, and the longer I dance, the less I notice. Like ink on a rain-spattered page, the whirling, twirling fae begin to run together and blur. I blink hard, trying to focus, but less and less makes sense. I'm not even sure if I am dancing anymore or sitting; the world wheels relentlessly around.

Then I find a familiar pair of eyes locked with mine: Morgaine has me in her arms, and for a moment, my head clears a little. The dance has splintered, the great rings of fae breaking up into pairs and trios who dance together, the steps seeming to consist only of holding tight to one another and whirling as fast as possible.

But Morgaine spins me slowly, her hands tight around my wrists.

"Did he let you in?" she asks softly. "Or did you sneak through like a mouse?"

I cannot answer her; my throat is too dry. My head is pounding now not only from music, but with pain, and my legs shake. I realize, dimly, I've been dancing for hours.

"My Conrad is loyal," she says. "But he has his weaknesses. What are you to him, little witch? What spell have you woven over him?"

I can only shake my head.

She pulls me closer, her hands sliding around to lock behind my waist, so we spin close enough I can see the spiders in her hair.

"If he has fallen for you," she whispers in my ear, "I can see why."

"No," I manage to return at last, my voice a rasp. "He had nothing to do with my coming here."

If she hears me, she doesn't show it, for she only spins away and laughs, lost to the crowd. Another faerie steps in and sweeps me away, and my head fogs once more.

How long can I keep this up? How much more can I endure before I collapse? Does she mean to *dance* me to death? It is a curious way to die, and not the worst, I suppose.

Like a bird trapped beneath a heavy blanket, panic sparks in the back of my mind. The past, only hours behind me, recedes like a shoreline in a sea fog, and the harder I try to define it, the less tangible it becomes. I forget how I came here; I forget what I came here *for*. And the need to remember dims; these questions—who, what, why, when—become meaningless and silly.

All that matters is the dance.

All I want is to *dance*.

I am drowning, and I relish the waves closing over my head.

I whirl from one faerie to another and feel a hand close on my waist, another slide against my palms, our fingers entwining. Unlike the others, this one's skin is warm.

"Wake up," whispers the faerie. "Damn it, lass, keep your head."

Not a faerie.

Conrad.

His face sharpens in my vision: human, gloriously human, his skin sun-warmed bronze, his tiger eyes reflecting the glowing lights all around us. His tailcoat is black, the lapels and shoulders crusted with dark jewels and silver embroidery; his cravat is white silk chiffon tied in an elaborate knot; his dark hair is dusted with silver. Lacy cuffs cover half his hands, and a sprig of elderberry and juniper is stuck on his lapel with a raven pin. He looks like a groom, or a faerie prince.

We are a matched set.

I smile dreamily, reaching up to twist my fingers in his hair the way I've been dreaming of doing. Just as I'd imagined, the dark locks are luxuriously thick and buttery soft.

"Dance with me, laird." I tilt my head, smiling coyly up at him.

He curses and disentangles my hands from his hair. "You should not have come here, you daft wee menace. What were you *thinking*?"

I sigh and rest my cheek against his chest, feeling him tense. I imagine cracking through that gruff exterior of his, breaking through his wall of secrets and finding the soft center of him. The real Conrad. My hand plays across his shoulder and then down his arm, tracing the magnificent curves of muscle beneath the sleeve.

His voice turns ragged. "Rose . . . you're not thinking straight. Stop that."

"Why should I?"

"Aren't you a Moirene sister? Don't you have celibacy vows or something?"

I giggle. "That's the stuffy old Edgithans you're thinking of. My order makes no such vows. I don't have to be celibate *at all*."

For emphasis, I rub my hand down the front of his coat.

His heart thumps against my ear, racing faster and faster. I feel a rumble deep in his chest, a suppressed groan, as if he is fighting against himself. He pushes at me, but the effort lacks conviction. I lift my eyes to his again and drag my finger along his jaw, finishing with a tap of his lower lip.

"Always so grumpy," I pout. My gaze remains fastened on his lips, as heated visions fill my head and tingle through my veins. I imagine his mouth closing on my throat, his tongue dragging over my skin . . . finding my lips. With a moan, I shut my eyes and nuzzle into his neck.

Only to feel his fingers tug at something in my hair. They pull away a tangle of spider's thread, destroying the spellknot.

All at once, clarity bursts over me like a splash of cold water. I freeze in place, gasping.

"There you are, lass," Conrad murmurs. "Welcome back."

I blink at him, heat flooding my face as fragments of sensual fantasies still swirl about my head. Fates, if he hadn't stopped me, I might have . . .

"What happened?" I whisper, rigid with mortification.

Fae cavort madly about, the music higher and more feverish than ever. Conrad and I blend in with the immortals. His hands, I see, are whole and healthy again. Someone has healed him. But then my eyes wander away, back to the fae, their whispers and glances and whirling bodies reeling away my every thought.

"Stop looking at them," Conrad says. "'Tis their spells that are muddling your head, the threads they've woven into their hair and clothes. Do not look, and they'll have no power over you. Keep your eyes on me, Rose."

My muffled panic breaks free and sends spikes of alarm vibrating through my body. I start breathing sharply, my heart fluttering too fast.

"I have to get out of here," I whimper.

"Gently now," Conrad murmurs. He pulls me close, his lips against my ear, which sends a wave of heat rippling over my skin. Those blasted visions of him kissing me come roaring back to the front of my thoughts. "We cannot leave just yet, or they will take notice. We must be subtle, and you must stay clearheaded."

"She means to kill me," I gasp. "She'll drain my life force to fuel her own, or drink my blood, or—"

"You're speaking nonsense. Morgaine doesn't do things like that." He pauses, then adds, "Not usually."

That doesn't make me feel any better. I twist around, looking for her, but Conrad gives me a little shake.

"Don't look!" he says angrily. "Do you ken how close you were to losing your mind entirely? Once you forget who you are, you can never leave this place. And they are *drenched* in forgetting spells. 'Tis how they survive immortality, by constantly wiping away the past. But their magic is too strong for you. It would obliterate your mind entirely. Not that you wouldn't deserve it, blundering into places you've no business. Honestly, why must you be so profoundly *nosy?*"

"What about *your* mind? Or are you one of them?"

"I am as human as you are," he replies, his jaw tight. "But I am also more used to this place."

"You're a bastard. You've been lying all this time. To me, to Sylvie."

"I'm the bastard who's going to get you out of here," he returns roughly. "Whatever I say or do, Rose, you *must* play along as if your life depends on it. Because it does. Remember: Keep your eyes on me."

But my eyes dart upward, to the Dwirra Tree on the hill, and the smaller saplings shooting up from its roots like children gathered around their mother's feet. Those slender limbs would be within my reach, if I could slip away unseen.

But Conrad is tugging me away, through the dancing fae. I resist, glancing at the Dwirra, wondering how I could reach it, if I might create some sort of distraction.

"Rose," he whispers urgently.

Who knows if I'll get a chance like this again? I pull away a little more, until he has me by the wrist and we are stretched apart, clearly not dancing anymore, and it is this which gives us away.

She is on us in a blink of the eye, black silk and spiderwebs, inhuman eyes crackling with anger. Her arm snakes around me, gripping my waist tight as if I were her wayward child, and Conrad's hand falls from mine. He meets her gaze silently, and the three of us stand locked in a terrible tableau as the dancers whirl around us. My head swims; I watch Conrad's face now in earnest, as I feel the tug of fae memory spells wash over me again, stronger and sharper, like flowering vines turned into venomous snakes.

"Are you trying to steal my pet away, Connie?" Morgaine asks.

Conrad's jaw is hard, his face schooled to calm. He does not flinch away from her.

"She is a guest in my house," he says after a moment. "She only lost her way."

"Is that it?" Morgaine looks at me. "Did you lose your way, little witch?"

"I am responsible for her," says Conrad. "Let me take her home."

The queen's fingers creep up my arm. She slides her hand up my neck, toying with me, letting me feel her strength. She smells of magic;

it glitters on her skin, tingles at her touch. One of her spiders crawls over my shoulder.

"You know I don't like it when you keep secrets from me, Connie."

"She's hardly a secret. She's a terrible meddler, aye, but she's just passing through. She's no one."

"You don't look at her as if she's no one. You don't *dance* with her as if she's no one."

He looks at me, anger sharpening his cheekbones, souring the line of his mouth.

"You're right," he mutters. "I didn't—I hadn't planned on telling you like this, but I suppose we cannot hide it any longer. Rose and I . . ." He steps forward, takes my other hand. I feel like a rope being pulled by two dogs. "We plan to marry."

My eyes open wide; I stop myself just in time from blurting out a prickly denial, remembering his whisper to me moments ago. *Play along as if your life depends on it.*

So I pry apart my teeth and say in a strained voice, "Yes. Of course."

Morgaine's head tilts, a faint smile on her lips. "Is that so."

Conrad's hand is clammy in mine; other than that, he gives no outward sign of his nervousness, of his lie. He matches her gaze and nods. "It happened suddenly, but so strongly. The moment I saw her, I . . ." He glances at me, swallows, his eyes aflame as if holding back a wall of fury. He grips my hand so tightly it hurts a little. "It was as if I'd been enchanted."

Morgaine looks at me, clearly waiting for me to add my side of the story.

"Yes," I confirm, and I squeeze his hand back, letting my nails dig into his palm until he winces just slightly. "Truly, I was astonished to find myself so very much in love. I can hardly believe it true."

"I'd intended to bring her to you, for your blessing," he says. "Just not so soon, but I suppose her *curiosity* got the better of her." He raises our joined hands, his eyes hammered gold. "My beloved, I must confess, is something of a snoop."

"Indeed, I find I must be," I reply through my teeth. "For my *dearest*, most darling Conrad keeps so many secrets."

He gives me a sweet smile that clashes with the glower in his eyes.

"My Connie," Morgaine purrs, her other hand sliding to comb through his hair with her long fingers. "After all these years insisting you would never wed."

"Yes, well," he grumbles. "I suppose the Fates have made a joke of me."

The faerie queen's predatory grip on my shoulder releases at last. She steps back, pulls us with her, calling out, "So this is no ordinary revel, my mortal lovers. This is a revel of celebration! We shall hold a handfasting."

Conrad inhales. "I don't think that's—"

"Dance!" she cries. "Drink! *Love!* My fae will dote upon thee, and sing for thee, and fetch thee pearls from the deepest depths of the sea."

The dance changes, the fae responding, breaking apart, rearranging. More of them appear; those from the enclave come bounding and howling to the revel. More musicians add their instruments to the band, until a full orchestra of immortals drape us in their mad waltz. Others twirl in with platters of fruit and sweets, none of which I dare touch, but Conrad drinks from a goblet some faerie gives him. It smells unmistakably of whiskey.

We are thrust onto the queen's dais; two more chairs have been added beside hers, seats made of twisted willow branches, strung through with ivy and flowers. I perch on mine in a daze. The fae spin and leap and perform daring acrobatics for our amusement. Conrad has not let go of my hand, gripping it tightly on the arm of my chair. Morgaine stands in front of us and calls out commands, sending fae scurrying this way and that to fetch more food, more drink, more gifts. They pile things at our feet: pearls still in oyster shells, heavy jewelry, gemstones, lace, small mirrors in jeweled frames, a magnificent rose-colored conch.

Conrad leans to me, smiling as if besotted, but his whisper in my ear is heated: "At least *try* to look as if you can tolerate me, will you?"

"By Atropos's needle—*what* are you playing at, Mr. North?"

"Playing at? I'm *playing* at saving both our necks."

"You might have consulted me first as to the method of your salvation."

"Consulted!" His smile is strained, nearly a grimace. "Tell me, Miss Pryor, where does *ungrateful* fall on your list of faults?"

"Number six, if you must know."

"You trespassed into Elfhame, and she would have stolen every memory from your head and kept you like a silly, empty pet. And *I* would have paid the price for failing to keep you out. I am her Gatekeeper. Intruders from the human world are *my* responsibility. Of course this is all a charade, but if you don't convince her you're in love with me, she will destroy us both."

The fae are watching us; even as they dance and spin, their eyes return to us hungrily, and I cannot quite tell if it is displays of our affection they want, or if they hope we will falter so they can swarm on us and drag us down.

Morgaine returns to us with ribbons of blue and red and gold. Her eyes are smug as she orders us to hold out our hands. I swallow hard as Conrad raises them, his fingers knitted through mine. Morgaine gazes into his eyes then mine as she winds the ribbons around our wrists, binding us together. I cannot tell if she is convinced by our playacting, or if she is mocking us with ceremony, building up to a bloody conclusion in which she takes off both our heads.

"May the road rise to meet you, young lovers," she murmurs. "May the wind always be at your backs. May the sun shine warm upon your faces, and may your threads never break."

The ribbons are tied so tightly my wrist begins to throb. Conrad's knuckles are white, and he stares at our bound hands as if the ribbons were snakes and not silk. The blood has drained from his face. I feel I must be as pale as he, my head spinning and my breath stilted.

"Well?" says Morgaine, stepping back. Her viper's eyes flit between us. "Go on, then. It's not every happy couple that begins their troth with a faerie queen's blessing. Seal it with a kiss."

Conrad inhales sharply, his eyes flooding with sudden panic, and all the color which had leached from his face now comes rushing back to shade his cheeks a violent pink. He looks as though he's about to stammer a protest and ruin everything.

So, forcing softness into my smile, I lean over and kiss him quickly, softly, on the corner of his mouth. It is as chaste a kiss as was ever shared between two people, but it seems to startle him. He stiffens, blinking at me as his lips part. Then his fingers catch my cheek before I can pull away, and his eyes fall to my mouth.

"Conrad—" I start, but he swallows the rest of my words as his lips crush against mine.

Startled, I stiffen . . . then slowly melt, my bones trembling as I take in a thousand sensations at once: the warmth of his skin, the softness of his lips, the scent of whiskey and juniper, his hand clutching my hand, his strong, nimble fingers knitted with mine—

And his mouth, *Fates*, his mouth, pulling at my lip with his teeth.

I forget the queen. I forget the fae. Every thought in my head frays down to nothing until I am an empty void hungry for more, desperate to be filled. All the fantasies my enchanted mind dreamed up minutes ago come thundering back, possessing my limbs. My free hand grabs hold of Conrad's coat and drags him closer, as my tongue scrapes his teeth.

He gasps against my lips, and the sound snaps my mind back to attention.

I jerk back, my skin blazing and my hand going to my cheek, feeling utterly disoriented.

Conrad stares at me, his lips swollen. I look away, unable to bear the honey-gold fire in his eyes. Feeling the gazes of all the fae, I cover my face with my hand in attempt to hide my mortification.

Morgaine watches, eyes glinting. "Well, well. *That* was a kiss, indeed. She is small, Connie, but there is fire in her. She'll bear strong children."

"Oh," I breathe, my voice high and tight.

Conrad's face turns scarlet. He sinks back into his chair, his grip on my hand going limp. But he attempts a smile for Morgaine's sake, until she turns away again and he flashes me a brief apologetic look.

"As the newest Lady of Ravensgate," Morgaine says to me, taking the seat on my other side, "you of course will have certain obligations. Which I am sure your betrothed has informed you of."

"He has . . . hinted," I reply carefully.

"You know of his duty to Elfhame and to me?"

I nod mutely. *Play along, play along, but do not give your own secrets away.*

"You know he must stand watch over the stone circle for the duration of his life, as his father did, as his children will?"

I swallow, glancing at him. His face is pale; he does not seem to be breathing. He will not look at me.

"Of course," I whisper.

"We should probably go back," says Conrad gruffly. "It will be morning soon, and though my absence might not be questioned, Miss Pryor's certainly will."

The faerie queen studies me a moment longer, then nods. "Go then, dearest Connie. Take your bride and have joy of her."

He rises, but Morgaine suddenly reaches out and grips his chin in her hand. She leans toward him, her eyes locked with his. "Just remember, your first duty will *always* be to me."

My stomach roils as I think of Lachlan, his hands tracing along my skin. *You are my little witch. I found you first.*

What is the nature of Conrad and the queen's relationship, exactly?

Is he more like me than I could have imagined?

The muscles in Conrad's jaw tighten; he meets her gaze steadily. "Always, my queen."

She finally releases us, smiling slyly. Conrad pulls me down the platform and out of the circle, as fae whoop and toss flowers and leaves on us.

"Hurry," he whispers in my ear. "And whatever you do, don't look back. Eyes on me. You're not out of danger yet."

He drags me away by our bound wrists, as if worried Morgaine will change her mind. I can only run with him, still angry, but much preferring his company to the fae. We hurry through the strange root village and up a narrow stair that ends at the queen's palace. He knows the passages well, taking every turn without hesitation. Doors and corridors and stairs flick past, Conrad breaking into a full run now, and I pant to keep up.

"That was some very fine acting back there, Miss Pryor," he growls. "Where does a schoolteacher learn to kiss like that?"

Acting. Yes, I was certainly acting. I snap back, "If you recall, sir, I kissed you once and would have left it at that. *You* kissed *me* the second time."

"Lucky for you, or you'd be a mindless puppet by now, dancing for Morgaine's entertainment. She wanted a show, and I gave her one."

"Oh, is that all it was? A *show*?" I scrub at my lips and glare at the back of his head.

He turns to me so suddenly I nearly walk smack into his chest. "Why?" he asks, his tone dangerously low. "Did you want something more?"

His eyes crinkle slightly at the corners, enough to give away that he is mocking me. I knot my hands into fists and lift my chin. "Of course not."

With a snicker, he turns and continues walking.

The bloody-minded arse.

At last we burst into a round room with an open floor; in the wood walls are set a series of alcoves, each one holding a large circular frame of silver, as if they once held mirrors. But they are all empty and covered with cobwebs now, except for one, in which is set a smooth pane of murky glass. It reflects not our own faces, but a watery image of the stone circle in the wood.

This is the anchor, I realize. The place the portal *ought* to have led me when I followed Conrad through.

"Go on," Conrad says roughly.

I put a hand on the glass and find it soft as jelly. With a little gasp, I pull it out again, but Conrad has no patience for my dawdling. He steps through, yanking me along. We burst out into the dark forest, the ring of stones all around.

"Conrad North!" I shout, panting. "I demand an explan—"

"Quiet, lass," he replies, and he raises a small spellknot twisted between his fingers. I realize it's a sleeping spell at the same moment blackness swims up and swallows me whole.

CHAPTER TWENTY-THREE

I wake in a narrow cot in a one-room stone cottage. Across a rough wooden floor sits a small hearth. A low blaze burns cheerfully in it, with a pot of fresh-brewed tea set nearby. The place smells of woodsmoke and bergamot shaving soap—Conrad's scent. It startles me how easily I recognize it.

Pushing out of the bed, I find my limbs languid; the sleeping spell he put on me had cast me into a deep and dreamless slumber, and my mind struggles to emerge from it. I'm still in the elaborate gown Morgaine had thrust at me. In this rustic place, I feel completely ridiculous in it. My wrist bears the slight indentations of the ribbon that had bound Conrad and me together. But for these details, I would think the events of yestereve a strange dream.

My hand flies to my lips and finds them no longer swollen, but the memory of Conrad's kiss is no less dim in my mind.

Fates, I *kissed* him.

And . . . I did more than that.

The night's events come swimming back like a bad dream, including the part where the faerie's mind-altering spells had sent me spiraling into a lustful frenzy.

Did I really rub myself all over Conrad North like a cat against a tree?

Oh, *Fates.*

Blearily I stumble to the door.

The tiny cottage sits in a forest glen awash in nodding snowdrops. The delicate white blossoms rustle all around me, growing in thick patches up the banks and around the trunks of the oaks. Their fresh, cool scent gently sweetens the air. Waves of them roll off through the trees where they vanish into banks of fog. The light is weak, the day barely begun, and the stone circle is nowhere in sight.

Conrad sits on a mossy stone nearby; he seemed to be drowsing, but his head rises when I sit up, his eyes grimly fixing upon me. In his hands is clasped a tin cup of tea. He no longer wears his faerie suit, but a tweed waistcoat, plaid kilt, heavy boots, and a scarf and coat of the same brown wool—the clothes he wore when I shadowed him to Elfhame.

"Good morning, Miss Pryor," he says, and he sips his tea, as if this were any ordinary morning. But his eyes never once stray from me, dark with mistrust.

I stare back at him speechlessly, trying to reel in my spinning thoughts. Trying *not* to remember the way my lip had been caught between his teeth just hours ago . . .

Snatches of faerie music still tumble through my head, measures and melodies only half remembered, already fading. But when I think of the faerie queen, she is searing and vivid in my memory, unforgettable.

As is the memory of Conrad's hand gripping mine, his eyes locking with mine, his fevered whispers in my ear.

"You hexed me," I say, my voice a dry rasp.

He has the decency to at least seem chagrined. "How are you feeling?"

"What is this place?"

"'Tis an old hunter's shed, not far from the circle. I stay here, sometimes, when my work demands I stay close to the fae."

"What is going on? What *happened* last night? Who are you and what is your business with the fae? Why did you *hex* me?"

"You were riddled with memory-erasing magic," he explains calmly. "The effects didn't fade just because you stepped out of Elfhame. The only way to be sure your mind repaired itself was to put you into a deep sleep, and it had to be done quickly, or your mind would have unraveled like an old frayed hat."

I bite my lip; he's right about sleep being the best recovery from a mind-altering spell, but still, anger at his methods courses through me.

"I demand a full explanation," I say. "Shall we start with the fact that there is an entire faerie realm hidden in your back garden?"

He rises, putting down his cup. There are dark circles around his eyes, the whites around his irises bloodshot. I gather he hasn't slept at all, not since before the attack by Lachlan's servant. There is still a faint dust of silver in his hair, and as he rakes his fingers over his head, it rains onto his shoulders.

"I will be asking the questions, Rose. If that even is your name."

"Of course it's my name!"

"Are you truly from London?"

"I am."

"You went to the Perkins Charity School?"

"I did."

"And why are you here, on my land?"

I start to reply, then realize how easily he's pulling answers from me, how I'm giving them without a thought. I become aware of a slight tug at my navel, as if a hook has been sunk into me, and I look up then and see it: a wide complicated knot strung between the rafters of the cottage.

A truth knot.

My stomach twists. I lurch forward, but Conrad crosses to me in an instant, stepping into the doorway just as I am trying to leave it. His hand meets my waist, and he traps me against the jamb. When I try to break past, he only gives a grim smile and holds me more firmly in place.

"Be still, Miss Pryor, and let me do my job," he says gruffly. Framed in the doorway, he looms over me, unmoved by my glower. "Forgive me. But I cannot allow you to leave just yet. Now, why are you here?"

I resist. But my abdomen is tightening, making me nauseated, and before I can stop it my mouth opens and words spill out, drawn by hooks of magic. "I am here because *you* won't let me *leave!*" I point furiously at the spell strung above. "I did not agree to this interrogation! Take your hand off me!"

Truth knots are powerful and difficult to Weave, and also entirely illegal without a court warrant.

His hand remains on my waist, gentle but unyielding. "This will not take long, and if you have nothing to hide, you'll be free to go."

I try to think of a way around the magic, but he doesn't give me the chance. His questions fire as rapidly as arrows, and I am forced to deflect as best I can, giving him only just enough truth to satisfy the spell's demands.

"Did you seek out Ravensgate and my family on purpose?"

"No. I had never heard of you, nor this house, before I met you on the road that day."

"Do you mean me or my sister any harm?"

"Of course not!"

"Did you know of my association with the world of Elfhame?"

I shake my head. "I knew nothing of it, not until I saw you open that portal."

"Why are you in Blackswire?"

"I am awaiting my . . . employer." I expect the truth spell to stop the word cold, but it slides off my tongue anyway. And I remember, then, before we ever left London, Lachlan telling me to Weave warming knots into his carriage in exchange for my new wardrobe and threads. It had been such a little thing, a moment I'd forgotten as soon as it was over.

"And who is your employer?"

"His name is Murdoch, Lachlan Murdoch."

"And what is his business?"

I manage to think my answer through before replying truthfully, carefully: "He is a cloth merchant. Can I ask a question now? What about: How many strong children shall I give you, oh laird of Ravensgate?"

His cheeks flush again; for all his sternness, how easily he blushes.

"That's not the issue," he growls. "What do you do for this Lachlan Murdoch?"

"I fetch things. Run errands." Even as I say the words, growing more confident in them, a feeling like eels crawling through my body makes me squirm. I have all the answers. They come so easily now, every lie carefully packaged in truth, smuggled through the web of the knot strung above me.

As if that had been the plan all along.

As if my cover story had been particularly crafted *just* to pass this test, purely to satisfy Conrad North.

"Why were you in Elfhame?" he asks.

"I followed you. After the fire, I was curious where you might be going in the middle of the night, injured as you were." I find if I speak slowly, I have more time to think, to pry up enough truth to satisfy his questions. "I went in and those wolf-spiders chased me and . . . it's a blur after that. Did *she* heal your hands?"

He brushes aside my question, not to be distracted. "And what are your intentions toward the fae?"

"Toward the fae?" I laugh. "I intend to have as little to do with them as possible, of that I can assure you. I have quite had my fill of immortals." That, at least, is the pure truth. "Why do you guard the faerie queen's door like a dog? How thoroughly under her thumb are you, oh *Gatekeeper*?"

Conrad tugs me closer, his hand gripping my hip. His face is inches from mine, his eyes probing me. Does he imagine I am lying, despite his truth knot? "Are you acquainted with a faerie named Manannán?" he asks. "He is also called Oirbsen, and Mac Lir."

"I've never heard any of those names."

"The Briar King?"

I shake my head. "No."

A crease deepens in his forehead. I wait in silence, clutching my ridiculous skirt, wondering if he's satisfied. If Lachlan's defenses have held firm.

Then he relaxes, letting out a breath, and I know it's over.

"Is that all?" I ask thinly. "Are there any other intimate details of my life you'd like to pry out of me? Or are you going to take your hand off my hip?"

"I apologize," he says. "But I have one more thing to check. May I touch your hair?"

"My . . . ?" I realize then what he means. "There are no spells braided in my hair."

He gazes back impassively. "May I?"

"Oh, help yourself, then!" I have nothing to hide. At least, not there. And it's not as though he hasn't already helped himself to my lips.

As if you didn't offer them up to him like ripe berries in your palm, a traitorous voice whispers in the back of my thoughts. I brush it away, irritated and flustered all over again.

It was only for show. We were literally kissing for our lives. Conrad made it clear that it didn't mean anything more.

His free hand slides up the back of my neck and into my hair, his fingers cradling my skull. Even with warning, I find I am not prepared for the intimacy of his touch, and I go rigid, my spine rising off the doorframe.

"Easy, lass," he says, as if I were a restless mare. "I'll be gentle."

His eyes stay locked on mine as his fingers conduct their search, carefully and thoroughly examining every strand by touch.

With his other hand gripping my hip, I have no choice but to endure. Unable to withstand the accusing heat in his eyes, I lower my gaze and find it snagging on the warm pink cushion of his lips. Fates. I'm not making *that* mistake again. Defiant, I meet his eyes, unwilling to let him see me flinch.

The sensitive skin of my scalp prickles under his fingertips, shivers racing down the back of my neck, running straight to my core. My nerves light like threads flooded with magic. I find myself glancing at the thick dark waves of *his* hair, wondering what it would feel like to . . .

I wrestle my thoughts back to safer ground, glaring harder at him.

His fingers move to the hair behind my left ear, softly riffling through it as if he were thumbing the pages of a fragile book. If I had tied any spells in my hair—counter-wards against truth knots, for example—he would have found them.

There are, of course, none.

He concludes his thorough examination with a gentle stroke through the hair at my temples. By now my neck is hot, and I can feel sweat tracing down my spine. I realize I've stopped breathing, my stomach drawn taut as bowstring, and it seems something more than just his hand is holding me in place.

Something warm and fluttering behind my rib cage.

Something that terrifies me down to the toes curling in my faerie shoes.

"See?" I whisper. "I did not lie."

"Aye, but I had to know," he murmurs, his hand against my neck, the hot pad of his thumb on the soft, sensitive skin below my ear.

"Are you satisfied, laird, or is there more of me you *have* to search?"

His gaze drops to the low neckline of my faerie gown, his fingers tightening ever so slightly on my hip. My heart flutters treacherously, and I inhale the snowdrop-scented air, my beaded bodice glinting as it rises and falls with my shallow breaths. I watch his face as his lips part and a low, soft sigh rumbles in his chest.

Then he pulls back, releasing my waist and rubbing his thumb over his fingertips, as if they've gone numb from pinning me against the doorframe for so long.

Breathless and flushed, I rake my hair over my shoulder, smoothing it out. "Is it my turn now? Who is the Briar King? What is your business with the fae? Would *you* like to have a sit under the truth knot?"

There is another question pressing against my teeth, but I bite it back. *Why did you kiss me a second time?*

He glances away, his mouth twisting. "I didn't want to question you. But I have a job to do, and I had to know if you were any threat to my family. I'm sorry, but I can't let anything, or anyone, put Sylvie in danger." Before I can ask another question, he slips out the door, rubbing his palm on the rough plaid of his kilt. "I'll leave you to tidy yourself up. Your old clothes are folded by the bed. Leave the gown and other fae things here—I cannae have Sylvie asking questions about them. And don't dawdle. Breakfast will be served soon, and Mrs. MacDougal will be expecting you."

I clear my throat, my head still spinning. "Where are *you* off to?"

"I must patrol the estate."

He looks so weary, his eyes dogged by shadow.

"How long has it been since you slept?" I ask, in a slightly gentler tone.

He leans in the doorway, every bit of his exhaustion evident in his face and his limp. "I have a duty to perform. My feelings about it are quite irrelevant. You would not understand."

I do understand, as he would know if his truth knot had been more successful. Though I would not call my obligation to Lachlan a *duty*, his will nevertheless binds my own. He drives me half mad with his surly attitude and his prejudiced ideas, but I suspect I understand Conrad North more than he could possibly imagine.

"Is this about the fire-bears?"

"Aye, if you must know. Someone is testing the border, trying to get in. I must find out who, and how many they are."

"Why—?"

"Enough." He glares at me irritably. "If you know what's good for you, lass, you'll march yourself down to Blackswire and take the first coach back to London."

"What?"

He drops a coin purse into my palm. "That will cover your fare and beyond."

"You want to get rid of me?"

He looks away, his face taut. "The queen of the faeries knows your name. You've seen her realm; you know where her doorway stands. So now you must get as far away from here as possible. She is not to be trifled with."

"You're saying goodbye."

He stares at me, his eyes weary. "I will walk with you back to Ravensgate, and then, Rose Pryor, aye. We must say goodbye."

CHAPTER
TWENTY-FOUR

Lachlan is not in the castle when I step out of the portal tapestry that afternoon, and I find myself instead surrounded by a dozen blinking fae, all lying about on sofas and carpets, still half asleep despite the fact it's nearly noon. It strikes me then how different they are from their kin in the World Below, in their coats and shoes and cravats, however fantastically adorned with lace and gems; as different as dogs from wolves. I think of what Lachlan told me about them having sojourned in the human world too long, and now I see what he meant.

Remembering what happened the last time I set foot here, I put my hand on my skirt, feeling the weight of the iron snuffer beneath it. But I see no sign of the faerie who attacked me, and no others come reaching for my throat.

"Where is he?" I demand.

They goggle, until I step to one and yank on his lacy cravat. Then he starts and says, "The waterfall, north of here."

"Take me to him *now*."

The faerie hisses, baring pointed teeth in irritation. "Look, the human is hysterical. Typical mortal, overstating its importan—"

The faerie cuts off in a yelp, thanks to the stinging knot I Weave in a trice. He rubs his shoulder, where my magic pricked him like a needle, and glares at me.

"I could snap your neck, girl."

"Go on, then. I'm sure your master will look leniently upon you for it."

Snarling, he relents and stalks away. I follow at his heels, reaching threateningly for my spool whenever he slows. In a way, dealing with these sulky, strange fae is not dissimilar to handling a classroom of surly ten-year-olds.

We trek for several minutes over a rise; the land here is a jumble of rock outcrops and tumbling ravines, with little foliage higher than my waist. A brittle wind grazes among the dry heather and seems to startle and flee at our approach, setting the moor to crackling.

Soon the sound is drowned out by the rush of water, and we come to a stony, glacial blue stream carving its way through the land in a frantic rush. A short distance upriver, my escort gives an indignant wave, then departs the way we'd come.

I squeeze through two sharp boulders and see a bright but small waterfall pouring into a round basin, the spot quite hidden by high crags of rock. Lachlan sits beneath the water, his head tilted back so that it drags at his hair. When he sees me, he rises, and with a curse, I turn around.

He's completely naked.

My cheeks flame; I fold my arms and try to forget what little I saw as he approaches from behind me. Spotting a cashmere robe slung over a rock, I grab it and toss it blindly back, then stare very hard at a patch of silver-blue lichen clinging to the boulder in front of me.

"*You* burst in upon *me*, Rose dearest," he says in my ear, making me jump. "Such blushing modesty—how exquisitely mortal you are."

I turn hesitantly and am relieved to see he has covered himself. His white hair hangs nearly to his collarbone, as silk smooth as ever and dripping with freezing water. The cold doesn't seem to affect him in the slightest; he truly is a creature with winter in his heart.

"I'd nearly forgotten," he says, as he runs his fingers through his wet hair, shaking water from it and leaving it in a tangle. "The water up here is less tainted than it is in the south. Its teeth still hold a wild bite. You ought to give it a try. Let it wash the mortal stench off you."

I only look at him and feel a seething anger rise behind my eyes. How did I ever feel a stir of warmth at his touch? How did his flattery ever bring a blush to my cheeks? How could I have been such a fool?

Lachlan takes one look at me, and his expression sobers. "You saw her."

"Saw her!" I shout, a dam bursting. "I did a good deal more than *see* her, you lying snake! You *knew*, you knew from the beginning what Conrad North was, and that I'd meet him and he'd tie a truth knot over me and you *meant* for me to meet him. All of this was some grand, devilish scheme to which I *never* agreed!"

"Sit down and cease with this shrieking. Let us talk as reasonable—"

"I will *not* sit down!" Surprising even myself, I plant my hand on his chest and give him a shove. His eyes widen in astonishment. "I will take no more commands from you, *Manannán*, or the Briar King, or whatever you truly call yourself, not after you've done nothing but lie and manipulate and use me. I didn't meet Conrad by chance. You *threw* me into his path."

His face warps, anger contorting the cool line of his mouth. All civility, all gentility is gone as his mask drops completely. "Of course I used you. Was that not evident from the beginning? Did I not make it clear I had a use for you? And as for the rest, you can thank me. Oh, yes, *thank me!*"

I scoff, and he raises his finger, like a scolding schoolteacher.

"Oh, think it through, Rose. You are no idiot, despite this display of irrationality. Conrad North would snap your neck before he let you set foot in Elfhame. Or what do you think happened to poor old Fiona?"

My eyes widen.

"That's right," he continues. "She ran afoul of the Gatekeeper, that's what. Liam North killed her, and his son would not hesitate to kill *you* if he knew your true purpose."

"No," I breathe. "He wouldn't."

Would he? After all, how well do I know Conrad? Not nearly well enough, given he's been hiding the fact he's the fae queen's Gatekeeper all this time.

Who knows what he might be capable of or the extremes to which he might go? I touch my lips, feeling his kiss again. Just a show for the queen's sake, he'd claimed.

Oh yes, he seems capable of *great* extremes.

Lachlan continues. "I told you just enough to set you on your way, and it *worked*. You're behind Conrad North's defenses. You're in his confidence."

I look beyond him, to the waterfall, my thoughts an angry snarl. I'd known before I even came here what his defense would be, but it doesn't soothe me in the least.

"Now tell me about Morgaine," he says. "Did you speak to her? Does she have any idea you work for me?"

Now that I study him, I see his similarities to Morgaine. His coloring is entirely different, but their bone structures are very much alike, long and finely carved, able to go from snow-soft to ice-sharp in a moment.

"You're related," I realize.

He nods once. "The faerie queen is my sister. Or was, before she betrayed me."

I always figured him for a faerie lord; now I know he is faerie *royalty*. And that brutal savagery is a family trait. As is manipulating mortals like marionettes.

I see Conrad as if in mirror to myself. He is caught up with the faerie queen in the same way I am bound to Lachlan. The how and why of it may differ, but we are both but tools to immortals far older and stranger than I could imagine. Whatever the nature of the game between Lachlan and Morgaine, I see now that Conrad and I are the pieces they have selected to pit against one another.

"Did she threaten you?" Lachlan asks, likely misreading the horror on my face.

"She was going to erase every memory from my head," I say shakily, "down to my very name."

Lachlan gives me a grave look, then sighs and flicks his fingers. "Walk with me, and start at the beginning."

For a moment, I hesitate. I cannot trust him, of that I have no doubt. I want to tell him nothing.

But I cannot dismiss the reality of my predicament. I am alone in the wilds of Scotland, with no way out. Even if I turned and walked away now, I would not make it far.

No, I need time to plan and think and find out what's really going on here. And so, for now, that means playing along.

We follow the burn through the rocks, leaving the silver waterfall behind. I tell Lachlan of how I found Conrad battling Tarkin's firebears, and how I followed him into Elfhame. Lachlan's eyes narrow when I tell him how I met the queen of the fae, and he nods knowingly when I tell him of the revel and the memory-altering spells.

"It is disgusting," he half snarls. "The way they lull themselves into forgetting, spreading a veneer over the past as if that could erase it. As if it could save them. They are like drunkards drowning their woes. Pathetic."

"What are you, really?" I ask. "Why were you exiled from Elfhame, and all these other fae with you? I want the truth. Can't you just give me something real?"

"Like what?"

"Your *name*, for starters. Your true name. There is no reason to keep secrets from me now, is there?"

He blinks, and a fog masks his eyes. His gaze fixes over my shoulder, and his terrible age drags at the corners of his mouth. He will not answer, I think at first. He will think it beneath him to explain himself to a mere mortal, and one who has so grandly twisted up the finely laid strings of his scheming.

But then he stirs, like a gargoyle shaking off its stone casing. His eyes, when they meet mine, hold something I would call *sorrow*, if I thought him capable of it. Instead, I suspect it to be another manipulation.

"I have many names, so many I cannot recall which was the first. Manannán, Oirbsen, those are only a few. And once, I was king of Elfhame." He lifts his chin, his eyes going to the sky. "Morgaine was my sister, and together we were the last of our kind, the Tuath Dé, with the last of the aos sí, the lesser fae races, relying on us for their survival. The humans had pushed us back and ever back, and we knew we faced a choice: stand and fight . . . or diminish and burrow into the earth, like so many others of our kin had done across the world. Morgaine was weak minded and swayed by her affection for the mortals who came to worship her. She did not have the stomach for war. So we planted the Dwirra Tree and nourished it with magic older than the race of men, and we built a haven on the outside of the world."

"The tree . . . it was like nothing I'd seen before."

"There are many trees like the Dwirra, all over the globe. If this place is a tapestry woven by the Fates or the Norns or Matrones, or any of the countless other names the triple goddess has been given, then the Dwirra and its kin grow on the *wrong side* of the cloth, rising out of a chaotic tangle of threads, and in their shade our kind have found refuge. But instead of withdrawing completely, Morgaine wanted to leave a few pathways open, through the stone circles. That is how the moorwitches came to Elfhame long ago and learned our magic, such as moving from place to place in an instant by navigating the very fabric of the world—powerful magic, and I knew it would bring us trouble if they ever turned against us. But Morgaine wouldn't listen to reason."

"It was *you*," I whisper, horror tangling in my rib cage like a viper. I think of the broken looms and spinning wheels moldering at the foot of the Dwirra Tree like rotting bones. "*You* killed them, not her."

The earth and sky seem to change places, the world reordering itself in my mind as I see Lachlan truly for the first time.

He is a monster.

He is a villain.

I should have listened to my instincts from the start, that inner voice which whispered he could not be trusted; he must be feared. But then he threw Lorellan in my face, and that damnable *tear* rolling down his cheek—he played me like a fiddle. He strummed the strings of empathy and humanity in my heart until they sounded *his* tune. And I, fool that I am, let him. I wanted to believe there was something noble in him, some redeemable heart as desperate as my own. But it was all a manipulation.

And Conrad—oh, Conrad. I have been wrong about him too. He knew what Lachlan is. He must know the truth about the moorwitches and Morgaine too.

"I defended my people against those whose very existence had destroyed us." Lachlan's voice is terrible and cold, his eyes shadows beneath ice. "I had those dangerous women killed, yes, and for it, my fool sister turned on me and cast me out. But it was too late, and the humans she'd once doted upon turned against her in retaliation for their women. They attacked Elfhame itself, led by your Conrad's ancestors. Morgaine was forced to close all the gates between the Worlds Above and Below, all but the one, with the great ward around it to keep me out. I think, even after all the grief they've caused our people, she cannot entirely let go of humanity."

It is all I can do to still my feet, to not burst into a run. I wouldn't get far from him, I know, but the urge is primal, that of a rabbit who feels the shadow of a wolf. He is worse than I had feared, worse than I could have ever imagined.

I think of Morgaine's sweetly venomous glances, her fingers in my hair, how she seemed to balance between a kiss and a kill. A faerie queen who once loved humans, and who betrayed her own brother to protect them, only to see herself take the blame for his heinous crime.

"*Rose.*"

I suck in a breath, realizing he asked me a question. "What?"

"I asked, How did you escape?"

I stare at him, wide-eyed and unblinking, my hands clenched at my sides. I wonder how many moorwitches he killed, and how he killed them. Was it by his own hand, or did he send his lackeys like Tarkin to do it?

I cannot let him see my horror at this glimpse behind his mask. I must play along as if nothing has changed, at least for a little while.

"Conrad," I say at last. "He told the queen we were . . . betrothed."

Lachlan's brows flick up. "Did he, now? Clever man. It was, perhaps, the only thing that could have saved you. He knows Morgaine needs him to wed, to produce more North Gatekeepers for her. If Morgaine had figured out you were working for me, you'd be worse than dead—she'd be torturing you for information. And worse, I'd be set back by *years*. I hadn't planned on her finding out about you so soon, but it's done now, and we must adapt."

Of course his inconvenience would be more concerning to him than my *torture*.

"What *did* you plan, then?" I demand. "Was my near obliteration part of your plan? I am a capable enough Weaver. If you'd told me the truth from the beginning, I might have tied a truth knot over Conrad the first day and had the spell in hand to open the way to Elfhame myself."

"Don't be obtuse, Rose," he says with a sigh of annoyance. "If it were that simple, would I not have accomplished it years ago? Do you think Morgaine would leave herself so easily exposed? Fiona had the same idea as you, and that's how we learned it would never work. After picking away at the circle to no avail, year after year, she finally managed to trap Liam North. But he could not tell her how to open the portal, no matter what spells she worked, not even when she held a knife to his child's throat."

"Conrad," I whisper. I picture him small and wide-eyed, held in the clutches of a half-mad old Weaver.

"It is part of the Gatekeepers' contract with Morgaine that they cannot open the way for anyone, no matter how threatened. Vowknots, as you've come to realize, I'm sure, are binding indeed."

"You never expected me to enter Elfhame at all, then, did you?" I whisper.

He inclines his head, affirming my suspicion. "I'll admit, you making it through surprised me. But you were lucky, and you'll not get another chance like that again."

"Then why send me at all, if . . ." I look away, at the storm rolling in, feeling the air begin to stir with anticipation of the coming thunder. The horizon is curtained by a dark sweep of rain.

Understanding strikes me like a bullet. My head whips around, my eyes locking on his.

"You mean for *him* to do it," I breathe. "You want Conrad to fetch the Dwirra branch, to betray the queen. And you think he would do it for *my* sake?"

He says nothing, but I see my answer in his chilled gaze. I feel bile in my throat; all of this, from the beginning, has been his orchestration. We were all puppets in his play, dangling on his strings.

"No." I shake my head, backing away. "No, I wouldn't ask that of him. Never! If he were caught—"

"If he *succeeded*, dear Rose, he would be free."

My breath stops.

"Him and his sister, and all the other North descendants they might produce. For when Morgaine falls, their duty to her will end. You see, the boy's contract might forbid him from telling you how to enter Elfhame or taking you there himself, but *he* is free to come and go as he likes."

"No. He wouldn't listen to me. You didn't see how he reacted when he even suspected I might be playing him false." I think of warm fingers tangling in my hair, and shudder.

"Oh, have a little faith in yourself. Why do you think I chose you? Why do you think, of all the talented Weavers I could have compelled to undertake this task, I chose *you*? Pitiful, lovely, kind Rose, with your soft lips and your passions flashing in your eyes."

Before I can pull away, his hand goes to my face, his long fingers twining roughly through my hair, wrapping it around his hand as if it were a rope. My body reacts to his touch involuntarily—with a shudder of horror, my throat constricting. Even when he suspected me of plotting against his family, Conrad only ever touched me with respect and gentleness.

Lachlan touches me as if I were a thing to be controlled, a wayward dog jerked at the end of a tight leash.

"*Let go,*" I snarl.

He pulls on my hair, forcing my head to tilt back, and presses a finger to my lips. I freeze, my heart racing, revulsion thrashing like a caged eel in my belly. Lachlan looks at me with a predatory smile, but his eyes are soft, melting snow that trace the shape of my nose and jaw, as if he were inspecting a painting he'd just finished, searching for flaws.

"You were irresistible to him," he murmurs. "To put you in the path of that lonesome young man was my grandest stroke of genius. The day I first saw him, years ago—a wretched, lonely boy on the cusp of manhood—I knew exactly what his weakness would be. And I was right."

"No," I whisper against his finger. "Your plan failed. He means to send me away."

"Does he? Good. Then he cares for you even more than I'd hoped. But you'll go back, and you'll twist him up in your threads until he'd *die* for you. Then, together, you and he will bring me the Dwirra branch, and the balance of power will shift. I will be strong enough, then, to face Morgaine and end her tyranny. Then I can finally save my people."

He releases me at last.

I back away from him until I can go no further, the tumbling river behind me, its freezing spray stinging my skin. I cannot reply; words stick in my throat, my mouth too dry to speak. He used me as *bait.* All this time I'd thought I was special, that my cleverness or my Weaves were what made me valuable to him. But all along it was empty, petty things. It was never me he needed; it was my youth, my face, my sex. He played on my pride, identifying my desire to be seen and rewarding it just enough to entice me along, feasting on the crumbs of his attention like a pathetic lost puppy.

"Now go back to that house," he says, his tone hardening, "and whatever you do, don't sabotage your position there. Bide your time, spin your threads around that man's heart, and don't report back unless it's urgent. The Telarian tapestries only have two uses left, and I don't have another set."

"You're forgetting one thing," I manage to choke out. "I could walk away this moment. I don't have to be part of any of this."

He scoffs. "Go on, then. Say it. Say that you wish to break your contract with me. Tell me you would sacrifice your magic here and now."

Nausea churns in my stomach. The scar on my neck pains me as it has not since I was a little girl.

"*Say it,*" hisses Lachlan. "After all, magic isn't for the faint of heart. Perhaps you don't deserve it. Perhaps you've always been too *weak*. Too afraid. A mouse scurrying from her aunt and her pipe, hiding herself away in holes and cracks. Perhaps that's what you really crave—to go back to that dismal, pathetic existence before I came along and set you free."

The words are there in my throat, yet I cannot speak them. My tongue ties itself, balking. Chills of guilt and shame prickle over my body.

"See?" Lachlan murmurs. "You'll hurt whomever you must in order to protect yourself. For you and I both know: Without magic, you are nothing."

My hands will not cease their trembling, no matter how hard I clench them.

"Go back, Rose Pryor. Be genial, be charming. Be *coy*. Slide into his bed, if that's what it takes. Twist him round your pretty finger like one of your threads, and when the moment is right, all you have to do is *ask*."

I don't want to go back.

I don't want to be Lachlan's bait, his spy, his puppet. I don't want to be a string twisted between his fingers, a conduit for his dark will.

But if I refuse, that's it—the end of my quest. The breaking of my contract with him. My magic will be forfeit, and without it to anchor me, the world will wash me away.

I will become nothing, and he will win anyway.

But if I am canny, I can pretend to be his tool a little while longer. I must only put aside my pride and my dignity. But Fates help me, I will not make Conrad his puppet too. I tell myself it is because that's the right thing to do—not because I simply cannot bear the thought of confessing my duplicity to the laird. If I help Lachlan, and he breaks Morgaine's hold on Elfhame, then Conrad and Sylvie will be free too. We can all escape this madness and let the fae fight their own battles.

I agreed to bring Lachlan a branch from the Dwirra tree, and that is what I will do. He may not believe me capable of accomplishing the task on my own, but I've already proved him wrong once.

I'll bring him his thrice-damned branch, and by the Fates, I'll do it myself.

CHAPTER
TWENTY-FIVE

I step through the tapestry with my heart thumping and Lachlan's words ringing in my ears. *Without magic, you are nothing . . .*

Fates damn him! And Fates damn *me* for a fool to be taken in by him. And for coming back to this house, slinking in like a traitor behind city walls, waiting for the enemy to come knocking so she can open the gates.

Well. I won't be his puppet. I will succeed, but I will do it *my* way.

The afternoon has ripened, Conrad no doubt having ridden off hours ago on his usual patrol of the estate. He likely believes that I am on my way to Blackswire now to wait for the London coach. I can hear Sylvie running up and down the halls of Ravensgate, yelling about the Nile and Marc Antony, engaged in one of her grand dramas.

I don't have a minute to waste, not a heartbeat to squander.

The spell to open the stone circle *must* be in this house somewhere. A spell that complicated would need to be written down; it would be too risky to leave the only copy in Conrad's head. Maybe he cannot tell it to me, but perhaps his vows to Morgaine never stipulated he couldn't write it down for his own use.

I take half an hour to change my dress and wash my face, then pull the snarls out of my hair, courtesy of Lachlan's rough grip. I sit at my dressing table and brush it over and over as if I might comb out the memory of his touch. When I am done, my eyes burn with tears. I let my head fall forward into my hands, my fingertips slowly tracing over my tender scalp. But that makes me think of Conrad's soft if untrusting explorations, and with a strangled cry, I wrench my hands away.

I must keep moving.

Composing a wholly false expression of cheer, I step out of my room and go looking for lunch; after my conversation with Lachlan, I have no appetite, but I need to keep my strength up now more than ever. It will take all my cunning and magic to return to Elfhame without Conrad's help.

Mrs. MacDougal finds me in the kitchen minutes later, an apple between my teeth and a scone in my pocket. I give her a little wave and try to slip out, but she catches my arm in the doorway.

"You were gone all night," she says in a low tone.

I freeze, blinking at her over my apple. Then I slowly take it out, my teeth marks two white crescents in its crimson skin.

"Yes," I reply. "I went to Elfhame and danced with the faeries."

She hisses and pulls me into the kitchen. "Watch your mouth, girl! Sylvie's about!"

"I understand now. You want to protect them. Well, so do I."

We match gazes for a moment, her surprise evident. "He is a good lad, our Connie."

"And I swear to you, if I can help him, I will."

"He told me you'd be leaving us today. Mr. MacDougal has prepared the cart to take you to town, but when we knocked on your door, you did not answer."

"I was asleep. And I . . . cannot go just yet."

Her mouth is a sour line, the wrinkles at the corners of her eyes deepening with her frown. "What is your aim, Miss Pryor? Do you think to win Mr. North's hand by hanging about?"

"I—no! That is not my intention, not in the least." My skin flushes; I feel the phantom warmth of his palm in mine as the faerie queen bound our wrists together. I curl my fingers into a fist. "But . . . what if there were a way to end all this? To set him and Sylvie and all of you free? I am a Weaver. I know a great many spells—"

"You're a meddler," she spits, "just like Vera."

"Who—"

"Conrad's mother. She tried to flee Ravensgate with him when he was a boy. She was killed by the fae a league from here, and only by riding hard and fast did Liam find the babe in a ditch and save his life. Some curses cannot be broken."

"Conrad doesn't deserve this."

"Nay, none of them did. But his only hope is to go the way of his father. Liam accepted his lot and was happier for it. He was forever in Elfhame, gallivanting with immortals. Even took a faerie lover for a time, until . . ." She presses her lips together.

"Until he was also killed," I say. "And how long before something similar befalls Conrad?"

"If you've been to Elfhame, and if you've spoken to Connie about all of it, then you know this house has seen few stories with happy endings. The best we can do is to help him last as long as he can."

"That's not good enough."

She gives me a strange look, as if she pities me as much as she loathes me.

"Well, you won't be breaking any curses today, lass." She gestures at the hall window, where a soft rain has begun to fall, misting the moors. I spot the cart, which Mr. MacDougal is now pulling back to the stable, out of the damp.

For once, I am glad to see the rain. I'd half worried Mrs. MacDougal would *force* me into the cart and back to London. But now I have a little time, and I intend to use it.

"Hm." I study the shuttered windows, the canvases over the paintings and furniture, as a plan begins to flicker in my mind. The air is stale, the frames of the paintings rimed with dust. In some places the grime is a finger's-width thick. It's as if we've been shut up in a tomb, in one of the great pyramids, wives of a pharaoh doomed to wander in darkness until we die at his side. "Very well, then. While I am stranded here, may I at least be of some use to you?"

Her brow furrows with suspicion.

"Don't look so askance, Mrs. MacDougal. There are some foes which can be beaten with the commonest of weapons. Where do you keep your brooms and cloths? And where is our Cleopatra? Let me keep us both out of your way for a few hours. Honestly, what harm can I do with a broom? I'll even leave you my threadkit, if you like."

And who knows? Perhaps in dusting off some old credenza, I'll find a folded bit of paper with the portal spell of Elfhame scribbled upon it. The chance is certainly worth a day of scrubbing and sweeping.

The housekeeper presses her lips together, as if this task were even more impossible than outwitting the queen of the fae, but she shows me to the cleaning cupboard and lets me raid it as I please. She tracks down Sylvie for me in the meantime.

"We're going to *clean the house?*" Sylvie asks, her eyes wide.

I brace myself for an argument, but before I manage a word, she adds, "This is the *best day ever!* I'll be just like Cinderella, slaving away before my evil, jealous stepmother!"

Mrs. MacDougal sputters and waves her hands. "Off with the pair of you, then! And Fates bless, don't *break* anything!"

In minutes, I've armed myself and Sylvie with brooms and dustcloths, and she giggles when I tie back her hair and cover it with a handkerchief. Next we tie on aprons. We have buckets of water, lye soap, and an absurdly ornate tea cart to push it all on.

"Will we get in trouble?" she asks. "Connie doesn't like things being moved around."

"Connie isn't here," I say. "And besides, a little fresh air and sunlight can cheer even the grumpiest of brothers."

We scurry up one hall and down the next, tearing down curtains and canvases. I can hardly blame the housekeeper. The place is simply too vast for any one person to keep up with. Whenever I find a window that isn't jammed shut, I open it and let in cool breezes which chase us down the corridors and clear out the musty smell, while rain spatters the sills. Everywhere we go, Captain lopes along, then throws himself onto the carpets to watch us with a perplexed expression.

"Wouldn't this be easier with magic?" Sylvie asks, leaning on her broom handle.

"It would." Thinking back to my first conversation with Conrad, I smile. "But sometimes the body needs honest hard work."

Though that work is taxing, it's something to *do*. It alleviates my feeling of helpless panic, which had threatened to leave me flattened on the floor for the next week. But no matter how hard I scrub, I cannot wash away Lachlan's poisonous touch or his silken whispers in my ear.

In a cherrywood chest, I find a partially unraveled shawl folded up. It looks as though a mouse has been nibbling at the hems, drawing away threads for its nest. When I unfold it, I find tucked inside an untitled oil portrait of a woman in bright Romani clothing, barefoot on a hillside; by her olive skin and black hair alone I know her to be Conrad's mother. If there were any doubt, he has her amber eyes. I am struck by the vividness of her gaze, glimpsing the bright and joyful spirit she must have been. It saddens me to think of her struck down by faeries, for simply wanting to be free of them.

"Good on you," I whisper to the portrait. "At least you tried to fight back."

Something about Vera North's face makes me think she would hate her portrait being shut up in a chest. I polish the frame and respectfully set it on a shelf, where her tiger eyes can gaze out the window. Around her shoulders is what appears to be the very same shawl in which I found the portrait.

I run my fingers through the mess of tangled threads, then quietly tuck the shawl into my cleaning basket for later, more careful inspection. That done, I turn back to polishing picture frames with Sylvie.

We unveil portraits of Sylvie's long-dead relations, and she puzzles out their names and we work out how, exactly, they fit onto her family tree. The North clan was once quite vast, spread around Blackswire in several large houses, but I'm guessing only Ravensgate is still in the family. Many of the Norths, I note, died quite young. It saddens me to think how lively and full this house must have once been.

In one hung frame, hidden behind a canvas sheet, we find an almost life-size image of Liam North, Sylvie's father.

"Oh," she breathes, clasping her hands on her chest and staring up at the stern figure. "Da."

"Do you remember him?" I ask gently.

She shakes her head. Wisps of hair have escaped her kerchief and cling to her face. Dust smudges the end of her nose, where she pressed it against dirty windowpanes. "He died when I was a bairn."

He was a striking man, with strong features and thick dark hair peeking out from beneath a formal white wig. His kilt boasts the North tartan, and tucked into his knee-high stocking is the same sgian-dubh his son now carries. Despite his rigid pose and solemn face, he has a glint of mirth in his eye, as if he possesses some wonderful secret.

Conrad North looks quite like him.

I regard the man with conflicted feelings. He killed Fiona, a fellow Weaver, after all. But if Lachlan's story was true, he had good reason.

"You have his nose," I tell Sylvie, and she raises a hand to her face, looking awed. She spends fifteen minutes polishing the frame.

Sylvie works like a fiend, taking particular joy in perching atop my shoulders so we can reach the high ceilings, startling the spiders who have no doubt founded long dynasties and expansive kingdoms there, undisturbed for decades. We dash them away in moments, and they scuttle into the cracks, defeated.

In her zeal, Sylvie accidentally knocks over a fine vase. It shatters into bits on the carpet, and for a moment, I freeze in place, eyes fixed on the shards. The chill of old, familiar terror crackles over my skin, my stomach clenching with dread. I swear I can smell the faintest wisp of tobacco smoke wafting down the hallway.

Then Sylvie laughs, and the sounds banishes the senseless, icy terror gripping my heart.

"Whoopsie," she says.

I give a weak smile and remind myself this is not my aunt's house. Conrad is not Lenore. Sylvie can break a vase without fearing for her life.

Suppressing laughter, we hurriedly gather up the broken pieces and hide them in a large urn before the housekeeper can see.

After a few hours, Mrs. MacDougal brings us tea, which we lay out on the foyer floor as if we were picnicking. The front doors are open, giving us a grand view of the rain sweeping across the drive.

So far, I've found nothing which might help me open the way to Elfhame, but the difference in the house is staggering. Pale light floods the once gloomy hallways, striping the carpets and walls. Ravensgate is like a winter field showing the first signs of spring.

"All right, troops," I say, setting down my empty teacup. "Top floor cleared, on to the attic!"

Sylvie's eyes grow wide, but before she can reply, Mrs. MacDougal cuts in. "Absolutely not."

"Oh, come," I tease. "We've got our momentum now. Right, Sylvie?"

But Sylvie looks into her cup and says nothing.

"We do not go into the attic," Mrs. MacDougal says.

"Why?" I lean to Sylvie and prod her with an elbow. "Be there dragons?"

But seeing her serious little face, I realize this might not be a battle I can win. Mrs. MacDougal is entirely unamused. She picks up our brooms and cloths, holding them as if they are contraband. "Sylvie, you've quite ruined that dress. Come, let's get you changed before your brother gets home."

"But—"

"Go, lassie! Now!"

Sylvie sulks but obeys, driven to her room by the housekeeper.

When they're gone, I quietly put away the tea and then go to the attic stair door, which is firmly locked with three different bolts, but my unlocking Weaves make quick work of them.

I creep up the stairs with caution, unsure what waits. But I *will* find out; if it's important enough to merit three locks, then maybe it's important enough to get me into Elfhame.

The air here smells dusty and stale, like an old wooden chest that hasn't been opened for years. The stairs go on and on, further than it seems they ought, as if I've climbed out of the manor entirely and entered an invisible floor. I drag my palm along the wall for guidance, for the darkness here is nearly absolute, even in this late afternoon.

But then I turn a narrow corner and see a rectangle of pale light; a doorway. Quickening my steps, I go through it and find myself in a vast room raised by mighty beams, on a floor gray with dust. The space is massive and entirely empty—except for a large, silent loom.

It stands in the center of the chamber, lonely, resolute. I breathe out as I approach it, eyes wide and fingers itching to touch the tapestry hanging upon its frame.

The piece is exquisite, and judging by the faded colors, it is decades or perhaps even more than a century old. The closer I get, the more detail stands out in its tightly woven threads: little buildings, hills, rocks, roads, streams, and lochs.

Blackswire.

I stop a half yard from the tapestry and let my hand linger over the village, while not daring to touch the old threads. It is not just Blackswire I find, but the rolling hills around it, the rivers tumbling through it, the forests and moors . . . and Ravensgate.

It is a map of the entire surrounding area, wrought with exquisite craftsmanship by some bygone Weaver of masterful skill. A border of Celtic knotwork frames the piece, gorgeously intricate. And I need only close my eyes to know it is humming with magic: I feel it simmering on the air, like steam off a boiling pot of water. It bubbles over my skin and prickles through my hair. This is no common spellpiece, and no ordinary magic.

It is the heart of the great ward which surrounds the township, and which has repelled Lachlan and his followers for centuries.

I wonder if Lachlan knows it is here, tucked into the eaves of Ravensgate. He certainly never mentioned anything of it to me.

For several long, wondering minutes I marvel at the tapestry's design, then I circle the loom to study the far messier but even more impressive back. Here threads tangle in a seething mess, but the longer I look, the more the pattern of it appears; in the loops and knots and wads of weft, there is a kind of harmony. It is the same image as the one on the front of the tapestry, but fragmented. Unraveled. The world unmade and raw. My fingers hover over it, and I think of how Lachlan described the Dwirra Tree as growing out of the backside of this world's tapestry.

I can find no sign of recent work on the loom. The spell was completed long ago, and now it only needs to be guarded. Its woolen thread is thick and sturdy, spun to hold magic for many, many years. Eventually, of course, it will disintegrate into ash and will have to be remade, but not in my lifetime.

Pulling my hands out of reach, resisting the terrible temptation to touch it, I retreat regretfully. Awe-inspiring as the loom is, it is not what I am looking for.

And I'm not about to fool with it. If that spell broke, Lachlan and Tarkin and a hundred other faeries would be clamoring at Ravensgate's doorstep within minutes.

CHAPTER TWENTY-SIX

After dressing the next morning, I arrange my threadkit and then step into the hallway, intending to search Conrad's study before breakfast while everyone is occupied downstairs. The laird did not return home yesterday, and I can only guess he spent the night in Elfhame.

But I make it not five steps down the corridor before I hear a shout from Sylvie in the foyer. "Connie! You're back!"

Biting back a curse, I toss my threadkit back into my room.

When I step out again, I see Sylvie dragging her brother down the hallway, showing him our cleaning progress from the day before. He stops short when he sees me, his face grim. My eyes search his hair and clothing for souvenirs of Elfhame—cobwebs or glittering bits of crystal—but if he did spend the night in Morgaine's realm, he has brushed away all signs. He's wearing a rough tweed suit, and his hair is damp from the outside, his long, thick curls shining not with faerie magic, but with earthy dew.

Sylvie, still holding tight to his hand, glances between us curiously.

"Miss Pryor." He inclines his head in a formal nod, but his eyes pierce me from beneath his dark lashes.

"Mr. North."

"You're still here." There is nothing in his tone—no accusation, no inquiry, no disappointment. It is as if he doesn't yet know how to feel about my presence, so he can only state a blank fact.

"So I am," I reply. "It was raining yesterday, after all."

We hold gazes a moment longer, and my heart quickens a pace. This is the first I've seen him since Lachlan confessed his true plans, and I cannot help but see Conrad in a different light. Oh, I'm still indignant over him interrogating me with a truth knot, and I still absolutely condemn his withholding Sylvie's magic from her. But I understand him a little better now, and know that he is not, perhaps, quite the villain I first cast him as.

If anything, I am more the villain in *his* story than he is in mine.

"Oh, Connie, come *on!*" Sylvie urges, pulling him away.

I trail behind the Norths as they stroll through the hallways. Conrad walks with one hand in Sylvie's, his air distracted. He keeps glancing at me, as if to be sure I am there.

"And that," Sylvie declares, "is where I killed forty spiders at once with a smack of my broom."

"Forty!"

"And here," Sylvie says breathlessly, "is our da."

We stand before the great portrait in silence.

Conrad's eyes soften. A curious expression passes over his face—sadness, regret, a little anger.

"I'd almost forgotten," he murmurs. "The way he would scowl with his lips but laugh with his eyes."

He raises a hand to touch the portrait's frame, then pulls it back, his gaze falling upon the portrait of his mother I found and set out. He blinks, as if he doesn't recognize her at first. Then his lips pull to the side, in either wry smile or grimace, I cannot tell.

"Fates be," he says. "I thought this painting was lost years ago."

He picks it up, the entire frame small enough to fit in his palm.

"She was beautiful," I say.

"Aye. She was." He seems held in a trance. "I have no memories of her but her songs. Her face I cannot picture, save for this likeness. But her voice . . . she sang traveling songs, of the lands her people had walked before they swept through this one, leaves on the wind."

I am not quite sure how to respond. He seems lost to himself, speaking as much to memory as to me. Sylvie glances at me, her eyes wide, seemingly as unsure what to say as I am.

"She was like a bird that soared into a fisherman's net, my da used to say," Conrad murmurs. "She tried to adapt to a life without wings."

"No wild thing can long survive a cage," I say softly, and he glances at me as if startled from his reverie.

"Aye," he replies. He studies my face, and though I try, I cannot discern the emotion behind his dark gaze.

His sister narrows her eyes. "What are you two talking about? I can tell you're hiding something, you know."

Conrad clears his throat. "Sylvie. Go and fetch a block from the woodpile, and I'll carve you another wolf."

"But I want to show you—"

"*Go*, now."

She huffs but skips away, her hair swinging.

Then Conrad turns to me.

I draw myself up, meeting his gaze squarely. But my heart feels untethered, knocking against my rib cage like a frantic pendulum. Lachlan's words slither through my head.

To put you in the path of that lonesome young man was my grandest stroke of genius.

"Why are you still here?" Conrad asks. "I thought I was clear. I thought . . . after that night . . ."

"That I'd be so terrified out of my wits I'd have been halfway to London by now? I hardly thought you cared. After your interrogation, you vanished entirely."

"I had business in Elfhame."

"What, did you have more innocent maids to kiss for your queen's amusement?"

His lips curl at one corner. "Would you be jealous if I had?"

I scoff, hoping he can't see the blush that heats my ears.

His expression turns grim. "I cannot guarantee your safety here once she realizes I lied about us."

"Why must you serve her? What hold does she have on your line?" Lachlan and Morgaine had both made it sound as if the position of Elfhame's Gatekeeper were a hereditary one, passed through the North generations like a bad heirloom. But why? Did Conrad have any choice in the matter?

He shakes his head. "I only stopped by the house to eat, and now I must go out again and see how the south planting is proceeding. I do have an estate to run, ye ken."

I'm torn for a moment; him leaving will give me the opportunity to search his study. But the chance to glean more information from him is enticing too. If he were to let slip some secret, perhaps how he learned to Weave the portal spell, it could be as useful as finding the pattern itself.

"I'll come with you," I say at last. "We can talk as we ride."

He gives me a doubtful look. "Last time, you rode as if you'd never even *seen* a horse before."

"But I *have* ridden one, now, haven't I?"

"I wouldn't call what you did—"

"Will you lend me a horse, or shall I be forced to run alongside you? Because this conversation is far from over. It's no use putting me off, sir. My seventh fault is *stubbornness*, you know."

He groans. "Don't be absurd. You can't ride dressed like that anyway. All those skirts and skirts *under* your skirts—you won't fit in the saddle."

"I'm sure you can scrounge something up for me. Besides, we're supposed to be getting married, are we not? What if Morgaine is watching? Shouldn't we let her see how blissfully inseparable we are?"

His lips thin; he looks ready to argue it further. I put a hand on his arm, feeling his skin contract at my touch.

"After that night," I say softly, "you owe me an explanation."

"After that night," he returns, "you owe *me* your life."

I only stare at him until he relents, his hands tossing in the air. "Ach, all right! But I won't hear a single complaint about sore legs or the damp, because I've got a great deal of ground to cover, and I won't be slowed down."

Muttering about the stubbornness of city lasses, he stalks off to recruit Sylvie's help, then goes to ready our horses. She is more than glad to hunt through the wardrobes of Ravensgate, assembling a riding kit for me.

She pulls out clothes from various drawers and armoires—riding skirts and gloves and a straw hat with a gray ribbon around the brim. When she's done, I have to admit Sylvie has more than one way of working magic. I regard the stranger in my mirror, a well-dressed, if slightly out-of-date young woman ready for a day of upper-class sport. Washleather trousers beneath a voluminous charcoal skirt and matching habit, the straw hat, chamois gloves, and gleaming boots that, though a bit big, look as if they've never been worn, and even a little pocket tucked in the bodice of the habit, where a skein of thread might be kept and quickly accessed. Whatever North woman wore this dress last was a Weaver too. I tuck a bit of waxed white thread into the pocket.

We walk down the hall, toward the stairs, and Sylvie slips her hand into mine.

"Are you in love with Connie?" she asks.

I blink, startled. "What?"

"You're going riding with him. And you two always seem to be whispering."

"Sylvie . . . I am only a guest for a short time. I must soon leave, you know."

"You *can't* leave us," she says, dragging me to a stop and planting her small frame in front of me. "Don't you see you make us better?"

"Better?"

"You gave me magic, and you make Connie laugh. Anyway, I know *he's* in love with *you.*"

My stomach lurches; it's as though I can *hear* Lachlan's insidious laughter in the back of my mind. "You—you do?"

"Oh, aye. He's played his pipes more in the past week than in the last year altogether." She smiles with satisfaction. "He's just *busting* with feelings. What other explanation could there be?"

"I—I'd better go on out there," I say, rattled. "Before he rides off without me. Sylvie, don't talk of this again. Please. I'm not . . . I'm not what you think I am, all right? And I cannot be what you wish me to be."

I rush past her before she can say another word, pressing a hand to my twisting belly.

In the drive, Conrad holds the reins of two horses, Bell and a white gelding with a proud head. He's beautiful, more sculpture than horse, with a white mane and a tail raised like a banner, his gleaming coat specked with gray flecks.

Conrad is checking the horse over obsessively, making sure all the straps and buckles are in the right places and tight enough. For a moment, I must catch my breath, struck by the smile on his face as he laughs, pushing Bell's head away when the horse tries to nibble his windswept hair. It is one of his rare smiles, reserved only for animals or Sylvie, with no hint of reserve or sardonicism. It brings out not just his left dimple, but the more elusive one on the right. He's changed too, wearing only a loose linen shirt, the sleeves rolled to his elbows, the hem tucked into the high-waisted riding trousers that hug the hard muscle of his thighs and backside.

And . . . Fates, here I am, ogling a man's arse, no better than a wanton maid in a public house.

"Connie!" Sylvie calls out, and he turns, his smile dimming slightly. The spell is broken, and I manage to finally breathe again.

When I come down the steps with Sylvie, Conrad takes in my attire. At first, I think he disapproves. His face pales a shade, and he drags a hand over his mouth and chin, where a shadow of stubble gives him a somewhat disheveled look. I suppose between serving wicked faerie queens and interrogating innocent maidens in the forest, he didn't find time to shave.

"You, ah, found the clothes, then." He clears his throat. "Well. Shall we?"

Conrad locks his hands together to help me into the saddle, but he must see the apprehension in my face.

"Roman's a good horse," he says. "I made sure of that. Even-tempered and obedient, and easier to handle than Ariadne. He'll stick with Bell."

I put my boot in his hand, and he lifts me into the saddle, only for my other boot to be left planted on the ground.

"Ah." He bends down and picks it up.

"They're a bit large," I admit, flushing a little.

"May I?"

I swallow, then extend my stockinged foot. He takes my ankle gently and slides the boot on, then ties it more securely. I wait in silence, watching the top of his bowed head, as my heart flutters up my throat.

"Better?" he asks, stepping back.

Not trusting my voice, I nod in thanks.

Conrad gives Sylvie a hug and a kiss on the top of her head, tells her to mind Mrs. MacDougal, and then he swings easily into his own saddle and clicks his tongue. At this, both horses start forward, and Captain takes the lead, barking happily. I pointedly avoid Sylvie's gaze; she watches us from the steps, her hands on her hips.

It takes a few minutes to get accustomed to the rolling pitch of Roman's gait, but before long, I find myself exhilarated. The horses trot side by side over narrow paths cut into the heather, leading us south. The land turns stony, boulders jutting up from the ground. Moss and roots hang scraggly about them, and in their cool, damp shadows bright ferns have begun to unfurl their leaves.

We ride along the scorched perimeter of the moorland that Tarkin's enchanted fire had ravaged, and Conrad grimly surveys the damage without a word.

After an hour, we come to a silver cascade. The water tumbles away, bright and quick. Musical birds dart through the sky like arrows. Both land and sky seem on the verge of bursting into life, spring building up like water behind a dam. Captain sniffs out rabbits and then gleefully pursues them over the heather.

To the east, fields of dark soil blanket the hills, and I spot a few small figures driving mule-drawn plows, gouging furrows into the earth, preparing them for spring planting. Conrad rides nearer, stopping to chat with a few of the farmers. They seem surprised to see me, but Conrad doesn't mention me at all, focusing instead on the plans he has for the fields, whether they will plant rye, barley, or potatoes. I sit by and try to unknit the coil of impatience in my belly, my fingers idly Weaving warming knots into Roman's mane. When Conrad glances at me, I still my fingers and pretend I was simply combing the horse's coarse hairs.

Finally, Conrad leads me to a high hill overlooking the field, where he takes out a small notebook and begins jotting down numbers and lists, taking stock of the crofters' progress.

"I do love these hills," I sigh, the words slipping free before I can catch them. "They unfurl like a tapestry, as if you could gather them up in your hand and wrap them about you."

Conrad gives me a wry glance. "I suppose I have spent more time looking at the horizon. Dreaming of what lay beyond it."

Oh. Of course. I think of the torn maps, bits of continents and shredded dreams scattered across the floor. Casting him a sidelong look, I wonder how I might get him to stop taking notes and open up about Elfhame. I am not here to learn more about the North estate's agricultural practices, after all.

"You must have been a child when you learned your fate," I say. "A boy destined to serve a queen . . . it's like something out of a story."

"Aye."

His pencil scratches away at his notebook, except for when he pauses to think, and he taps it against his lower lip. The simple gesture reminds me of how that lip had tasted against mine down in Elfhame . . .

Oh, no. I will not go back to that moment. For one thing, thinking about it will make my face turn red as an apple. For another . . . ever since Lachlan revealed his twisted plan to me, that kiss has stuck in my memory like a stone in a shoe, painful and wrong. That kiss was not *ours*. It was a sham, performed for Morgaine's benefit and Lachlan's scheming.

Granted, it had been a very convincing sham.

One that had nearly persuaded *me* that there might be more between us, some hidden, tenuous thread woven not by faerie fingers, but by my own heart's dangerous curiosity.

Was any of it real? What if we had met by chance, and not by Lachlan's machinations? Would Conrad have noticed me if we'd passed as strangers on a London street? Would the accidental brush of his hand against mine have made me catch my breath?

What would it be like to kiss him with no eyes upon us?

The question startles me so that I cough. I tear my treacherous eyes from the laird's lip and try to recall what it was I wanted to ask him.

"You can't leave, can you?" Yes, that was the question. "Is that why you tore up those maps? You learned your duty to the queen would confine you to the estate."

His eyes flicker to mine, wary. He places the pencil in the spine of his notebook and shuts it. "Very well, then. If I satisfy your curiosity, will you go home to London?"

"I might."

He sighs and rakes his hand through his hair. "What do you want to know?"

"How did your parents meet?" I ask. "Considering her background, and his being confined to this place and the fae queen's service, I find it odd their paths ever crossed."

His gaze drifts to the moors. "My mother's folk often camped on the estate. In most places, Travellers are not often welcomed. But my father always gave them safe passage on his lands."

"Do they still visit?"

He shakes his head. "Not after she died. There was mistrust between us, thanks to some wholly false rumors that my father had . . . been involved. Nonsense, of course. Her horse threw her. 'Twas an accident."

"That must have been hard for you. Her people were your people, after all."

His eyes lift to the distant hills, the worry seam between his eyebrows deepening as he frowns.

"Aye . . . foolish lad that I was, I dreamed of joining my mother's people and traveling the world with them. I would sit on the roof of Ravensgate and watch their caravan pass over the moors, chafing at my father's refusal to let me even visit their fires." He gives a short laugh, heavy with bitterness. At last, he shuts the notebook and tucks the pencil behind his ear. "When my father finally told me such dreams were never to be, I did not take it well. It was the first time I realized my fate was never my own to decide."

"You thought you were free, only to find a leash fixed round your . . . throat," I murmur. Fates, I'd been about to say *heart*.

"Aye . . . exactly." He gives me a sidelong look. "'Tis strange, confiding in someone about Morgaine. The MacDougals prefer not to discuss it, and of course I cannot confide in Sylvie yet. Since my father died, there was no one else who knew."

I give him a tight smile, feeling ten ways a traitor, wishing he'd used any word but *confide*. It is too close to *trust*, and if only he knew how unworthy of that trust I am. "Earlier, in the cottage, you asked me about a certain person. A . . . Briar King?"

He goes very still, a dangerous glint in his eye. "Aye."

259

I have to force the words through my dry throat. "Who is he?"

"He is Morgaine's enemy," Conrad replies tensely. "There is a great ward around Ravensgate, Blackswire, and the surrounding land. It keeps the Briar King out, but every few decades he tests us. When I was a boy, he sent a Weaver to try and force my da to open the gate to Elfhame. *Fiona.* She put a knife to my throat, but my father would not give her what she asked for." His eyes pinch, as if the memory leaves a sour taste on his tongue. "My da killed her instead, to save my life. And that was the day I learned faerie tales were real, and that they were nightmarish."

The contempt in Conrad's tone when he said Fiona's name turns my stomach.

I am his Fiona. I am the knife sent to be put to his throat, and when he discovers that . . .

I suppress a shudder.

Conrad continues, "My father took me down to Elfhame for the first time and told me the story of my ancestor, a man who attempted to kill Morgaine after the fae murdered his wife and a bunch of other women."

After *Lachlan* murdered them, I now know, and left his sister to take the blame for it.

"The moorwitches?" I ask. "You're descended from them?"

He nods. "Aye. And in exchange for sparing my ancestor's life, she charged him and his entire line with guarding the gate to Elfhame. We've spent generation upon generation of North blood paying for that one man's rash attempt at vengeance."

Well, that answers one of my questions. His obligation to Morgaine does go back generations. And from the sound of it, he had little choice in the matter.

"What happened to your father?" I whisper, dreading the answer.

"Years later, when I was twelve, my father went on patrol and never returned. I found his body on the other side of Blackswire. He'd been burned to death with magic." Conrad's voice grows thick.

I imagine him at twelve, stumbling across his father's corpse. Realizing he was now completely alone, with a little sister to protect, and that great house.

"Morgaine came to me in the wood shortly after that," he goes on. "Sometimes she walks in the mortal world, says she likes to *remember*."

That catches my attention, and I think of the two times I thought I spied the ghost of a woman in the fields—Sylvie's ghost.

Could that have been the queen of the fae?

So many threads are finally falling into place, revealing the pattern I've been straining to understand.

"That very night," Conrad continues, "she had me kneel at her feet and Weave a vowknot of fealty to her. So you see, my servitude is bound by magic as well as by my word."

"I see." I shiver, seeing him in mirror image to myself, only a little older than I was when I made my vow to his father's murderer. *Upon my heart I swear, a favor for a favor . . .*

We both bargained our lives away when we were too young to understand the weight of those vows. Mere children, manipulated and used by beings far older and crueler, made to dance upon their strings. And now, though Conrad does not know it, here we are set against one another, proxy soldiers in a centuries-old conflict I barely understand.

My heart aches to tell him my own truths, to show him how alike we are. But I know the truth would break the fragile trust we've built, and my mission would end at that moment. He would never let me near Elfhame again, if he did not drag me to Morgaine himself. Or kill me outright, as his father killed Fiona. Though I cannot bring myself to fully believe him capable of such measures, I remind myself of what measures *I've* gone to lately. I've done things I never dreamed possible, all out of forced fealty to a faerie lord. Perhaps neither of us yet have reached the limits of how far we will go to fulfill the bargains we've struck.

"Do you know anything else about this Briar King, or why he might be trying to return?" Does Conrad have any idea that the exiled fae are dying out, that they need to return home before they are all lost? For all that I know him to be a villain, Lachlan's intentions seem true. He wants to save his people. Morgaine would abandon them all to die.

Conrad shakes his head. "I know only that he is devious, and Morgaine will do anything to stop him from taking back the throne of Elfhame. And it is my duty to see he does not slip through our defenses." He pauses, then says, "I met him once."

My eyes snap to him. "You . . . did?"

"'Twas some years ago. He was standing mere inches outside the ward, just . . . *waiting*. He was like winter bound by skin and velvet. His eyes were empty, as if no soul were left in him. When I demanded to know his business, he only said he'd come to have a look at me, and then he said I looked just like my father. I realized then that *he* had killed my da, and likely my mum too, when she tried to run away."

Lachlan killed his father.

Fates, I should have guessed it. But all the same, the horror of it punches me in the lungs. I shut my eyes for a long moment, overcome with a wave of dizziness that threatens to knock me from the saddle.

Conrad leans forward to run his hand over Bell's neck, his eyes dark as the pools which dot the moors. "I'd never been so angry in my life. I rode through the ward just to get my hands around his neck, to make him pay for what he did." He shudders. "He killed my horse, Julius. My father had given me that horse, trained me to ride on him. I fell and shattered my leg and had to crawl back through the ward before he could finish me off. I paid for my stupidity, and nearly paid for it far more dearly than this."

He thumps his bad leg.

Nausea rolls in my stomach; I picture it all as if I'd been there myself. The hands which nearly killed Conrad—those hands have held mine a dozen times. They've stroked my hair, twisted it, tilted my chin so he could look into my eyes.

"He is a monster," I whisper.

"Aye."

"I don't understand," I say. "If this is the creature you face, if you live in such danger, why do you forbid Sylvie from practicing her magic? Why deny her the ability to protect herself?"

He stiffens; as he always does when the subject arises, he closes himself to me, sitting straighter and hardening his jaw. "It would be better if she lost her magic and was of no concern to him or anyone else, than for her to become a threat. Or a tool."

I start to argue with him, then remember how useless it was the last time I tried. At least I know Sylvie hasn't lost her magic at all. Her spirit is strong and her mind sharp. Whatever it takes, she'll fight for her magic, now that she knows how to wield it.

Unless . . . she didn't *need* to fight for it.

As Lachlan told me, if Morgaine were to fall, the Norths' duty to her would end. Would Conrad see the opportunity in that? Would he ever consider betraying the queen?

When the time comes, said Lachlan, *all you'll need to do is ask . . .*

My stomach clenches with revulsion. I'd sworn to myself I couldn't—*wouldn't*—use Conrad that way. But before I know it, I find myself asking, "Wouldn't it be . . . to your advantage, to see another take over rule of Elfhame? Even someone as reprehensible as the Briar King?"

He stares at me.

"All I'm saying is, Wouldn't you be free then?"

"If Manannán took the throne, I'd not live long enough to find out. He'd kill Sylvie and me both."

"What if . . . you came to an arrangement with him?"

Conrad gives me a sharp look. "With my parents' murderer? You think I should strike a pact with their *killer*, as if he didn't have my family's blood all over his hands?"

"No," I breathe. "No, of course not. You're right."

Shame eats at me like acid, tearing down all the defenses and excuses I've built up around myself to make my own treachery more palatable. I may not have known the details of all his monstrous deeds, but I knew what Lachlan was the moment I met him. I saw what he did to my aunt, and regardless of whether she deserved it, the faerie never flinched in his punishment of her. Even knowing his depravity, I let him draw me in. I let myself believe his lies, searching for humanity where none lay.

I will *not* let him make a monster of me. I swore to myself I would finish this mission my own way, and that is precisely what I will do. I will not use Conrad's heart against him, even if he were foolish enough to give it to me.

"We will never be free of her," he says. "Some of my ancestors fled as far as America, only to find themselves kidnapped in the night by fae and dragged through the underworld back to Morgaine's feet. And their punishments, Rose, were not light. You've seen my family portraits. The Weaver outside your bedroom door? She lost her eyes to Morgaine after she tried to run away to France." He shakes his head, his brow dark with anger. "Our best chance, my da said, is to let our line die out. And so I never intend to marry or have children."

"So that's it, then? That's your life's grand ambition? To die alone and miserable with your lonely, miserable house crumbling around you?"

He scowls and heels Bell, trotting ahead to evade the question.

"Oh, Conrad. If there were a way—"

Conrad reels his horse around, Bell tossing his head in annoyance. "Just *stop*, will you? You cannot seem to stop meddling!"

"I am not—"

"You're *always* prying. Into me, into my affairs, into Sylvie."

I sputter. "Prying!"

Conrad shifts in his saddle, fingers raking his hair in agitation. "You burst into our lives like an autumn wind, changing things. You rearranged my entire house to your liking!"

"I opened a few curtains."

"You let the light in. You stirred up the dust. You unveiled things that should have . . . stayed hidden." The way he says it, it sounds almost like an accusation. He looks wretched, bitterness in his eyes, like there's another voice trapped inside him, unable to speak freely. Unable to *dream*.

"Have you really given up?" I ask softly.

"I'm a pragmatist, Rose. I am what I had to become, for Sylvie's sake. My life was bargained away from me long before I was born."

Our horses have taken us to the peak of Toren's Rise. We gaze out over the ancient forest toward the bluff in the distance. Somewhere below, the stone circle waits, and I think of how many Norths have died as sacrifices to guard it.

"Will you send me away, then?" I ask.

He frowns at the forest below for several long moments, as his hand idly scratches Bell's mane. "It isn't safe for you here."

"I am sure my employer will recover soon, and then I will be out of your way for good. But until then . . . give me a fortnight," I plead. "Let me continue to teach Sylvie. She has made such progress in mere days; it would be a shame to waste that. I can write out lessons for her, a guide for the next year or more of what she should study. It would help you to prepare her in case . . ."

Our eyes meet, and I see he understands me. In case Sylvie can be freed from Morgaine's service. So he hasn't given up entirely, at least not where she is concerned.

Sensing his hesitation, I press him harder. "She will need a firm foundation if she is to have a future. I can help with that."

"The risk to you—"

"Let *me* decide what risk I am willing to accept."

He studies me, his eyes so intent I feel them like the touch of fingertips to my skin.

"Why?" he asks at last. "For what reason would you risk your freedom, even your life, to help one child you barely know?"

"Because I was just like Sylvie, once. I was a lonely child filled with longing, desperate to learn." I do not add the part about an overbearing guardian who tried to withhold my magic from me. Besides, I no longer see Conrad in the same light as my aunt. His intentions are wholly different, despite their similarities in method. And while I cannot agree with that method, I can understand his reasoning now.

That doesn't change the fact that Sylvie has a right to her own magic, and I promised her I would help her as long as I can.

And I *need* access to the stone circle if I am to have any hope of completing my mission for Lachlan. Leaving Blackswire now just to ease Conrad's mind is not an option.

"A fortnight," he says at last. "That is all I can give you. It will be difficult enough to maintain this sham of our engagement for that long. Morgaine is no fool, and she has seen too much to believe any lie for long. She is older than you can imagine."

I think of Lachlan and resist the urge to inform Conrad that my imagination is far more capable than he knows.

"Thank you," I reply. After all, it's only a fortnight until my birthday. Just two weeks left to finish this.

"I have one condition," he adds.

I incline my head, waiting.

"Teach me as well."

I draw in a breath, frowning at him. "You want me to teach you?"

"Is that such a repulsive prospect?" His lips quirk amusedly. "As I told you, my arsenal of spells is limited. My father did not have time to teach me much, and the fae . . . are unreliable tutors. Their magic is very different than ours, and my clumsy hands cannot Weave half the spells of which they're capable. The more I know, the better I can protect Sylvie."

I hesitate, fearing where this may lead. I should be spending less time with Conrad, not more. He's already *confiding* in me, by the Fates. If Lachlan were here, he'd be ordering me to say yes, to use this as an opportunity to gain more of Conrad's trust. That alone is enough reason to turn him down flat.

Then again, perhaps I am overestimating the laird's regard of me. He mistrusted me enough to Weave a truth knot over my head. He knows we will never agree on Sylvie's magic. And he was very clear about that damnable kiss being nothing more than for show.

Never mind that to me, it had *felt* like more.

I do owe him *something* for the way I'm using him and his house in order to access Elfhame. Teaching Conrad wouldn't be nearly enough penance to assuage my conscience, but it could be a start. It doesn't have to have anything to do with winning his trust. This is merely a business transaction and a chance to atone, in some small measure, for the ways I've already betrayed that trust without him even knowing it. And if all goes as I plan, I'll be well away from here before he ever *does* know it.

Conrad clears his throat, and I jump, realizing I've been going back and forth in my own head for several minutes now.

"If it is *that* offensive a notion, Miss Pryor—"

"No," I say quickly. "That is, *yes*. I think it's a fair trade. A fortnight of lodging for my instruction, in general studies for Sylvie, and in Weaving, for you."

"But no longer than that," he states firmly. "After a fortnight, you *must* go, Rose. I won't have you caught up in this."

I force a smile. If only he knew it's far too late for that.

"Yes, I'll be gone soon, then, and you need never see me again," I reply, knowing whether I succeed or not, it is the truth. "Will that please you?"

Now his eyes shift away, the gray sky turning them a stormy shade of topaz. For a long moment, he makes no answer, but stares at the horizon as the wind rises higher and faster, and the forest below stirs with a great rushing sigh.

"Of course," he says at last, in a strange, low voice, as if he is speaking more to himself than me. "Of course you must go."

CHAPTER TWENTY-SEVEN

A warm light burns in the stables when I reach their doors that night. Behind me, a restless wind sweeps over the moors and carries with it the scent of snowdrops and the call of a lonely nightjar.

I stand for a moment outside, waiting for the tingling in my stomach to stop. As far as anyone else knows, Conrad is asleep in his bed, and I in mine.

This is no different from the night he first startled me in his study, or when he interrogated me in the cottage in the woods. Except, this time, our meeting is planned, a secret I've carried close all day. Dinner was tense with anticipation, as he sat at one end of the table and I at the other, Sylvie between us.

For me, the dinner hour had passed on a tightrope. There was Conrad, glancing at me over his mutton every few minutes with a secret glint in his eye, as if to silently remind me of our later plans. Then there was Sylvie, idly drawing spellknot patterns on the table and shooting me wicked little grins when I noticed. I felt stretched between them, wondering when I'd say the wrong thing and spill every secret I carried.

But we made it through the meal, and Conrad had departed with a yawn, saying he'd turn in early. His last, sidelong glance had been for me, an unspoken *See you soon*.

For some reason, that look sent a shiver over my skin.

Now here I am, fist raised to knock, my heart already knocking against my ribs.

It's not as if we are breaking any rules. This is his house, and he may do as he likes. Of course, the impropriety of meeting any man alone like this is obvious, but who will know? We are both independent people, fully capable of conducting ourselves with decency.

So why do I feel as if we are engaged in some great criminal act? Why are my nerves buzzing like one of the hives I found on the moor?

I remind myself I am a professional and that this is a business transaction, and nothing more.

I knock twice, to let him know I am here, then push open one of the doors. It swings silently, letting in a current of wind that rustles the hay strewn on the floor.

Conrad stands in the center of the stable, his horse Bell nudging his shoulder. His coat discarded, he wears a white shirt beneath a brown tweed vest, still in his fitted riding trousers, his boots dusty from the stable's hay and dirt floor. When he sees me, he gives the gelding a scratch beneath the chin before walking over.

"Are you sure this is all right?" he asks. "I didn't even consider that perhaps you're tired. If you wish to go to bed—"

"Nonsense." I set my threadkit on a three-legged stool by Ariadne's stall. The mare nickers, and I take a cube of sugar from my pocket and extend it on an open palm. She plucks it with velvety lips and snorts in appreciation. "You won't get out of your lesson that easily. Now, I think we should start with a simple deflection knot and work our way up to the wards."

"Right." Conrad gives me a small bow. "Whatever you say. Tonight, I am not your employer but your student. Equals."

"I beg your pardon?" I raise a brow as I open my kit. "I believe that as your teacher, we are *far* from equal, sir."

"Aye." He coughs. "Indeed. I am your humble inferior in all things, Miss Pryor."

With a laugh, I take out all the spools from the kit and set them aside, so the box is empty, then open a compartment and pull out twelve little wooden pegs. "Please just call me Rose. Every time someone calls me *Miss Pryor*, I have to check to be sure my hair has not gone gray. It makes me feel like one of my old teachers."

"Nonsense. You are beautiful no matter what you're called."

I freeze, my hands full of wooden pegs, and feel my face catch fire.

Conrad coughs. "I . . . I spoke without thinking, Miss Pryor. Ach, I mean *Rose*. That is—not that I dinnae believe what I said. I do. Very much." His embarrassment seems to thicken his brogue until he's nearly unintelligible. "What are you doing now?"

"If you're going to practice wards," I reply in a carefully controlled tone, "it's best to have something to ward *against*."

Opening the threadkit so it forms a flat square, I begin inserting the pegs into the ring of holes set into the inner walls of the disassembled box, creating a pegboard. Conrad watches curiously, keeping his mouth firmly shut, as I twine sturdy worsted yarn around it.

As I Weave, I try to ignore the guilt pricking me from within. If I were really trying to prepare him to defend against Lachlan's schemes, I would show him more truth knots, as well as spells to reveal a person's true intentions. I would teach him how to see lies hiding behind pretty faces. I would warn him to guard his heart, trust no one, and above all else, save his kisses and his dimples and his fitted trousers for someone who is worthy of them.

"Is everything all right?" he asks, shaking me from my spiraling thoughts.

I smooth the scowl that inadvertently crept across my face. "Yes. Of course."

It takes nearly ten minutes to Weave the illusion knot. Yarn winds between the wooden pegs, building in layers, forming an intricate pattern not unlike a snowflake or a Hindu mandala. Woven with bright crimson worsted, it reminds me most of a sunburst, flames radiating outward and then spiraling back in, an infinite, mesmerizing dance of color and lines.

"You are full of wonders," Conrad murmurs, watching my fingers work.

I sit back and shake out my hands. "Go shut that window," I tell him, nodding to an open casement at the back of the stable. "I don't want any of the wisps to escape."

He does as I bid, and I take the opportunity of his absence to channel. Just as I'd feared, the first attempt goes awry, my heart spasming and the magic lancing through me like a hot knife. With a little gasp, I swallow a cry of pain and try again, desperate to complete the spell before he returns. I don't need him to see me like this—it would invite questions I don't have ready answers to.

It works the moment he turns back from the now closed window; I feel a surge of relief as the magic rushes from my fingertips to light the worsted. The pattern flares brightly, its light faintly tinged by the red dye in the wool.

"Now," I say, rising with two spools of white thread in hand, "defend yourself."

Tossing him one spool, I pull thread from the other and Weave a slow cat's cradle; he rushes to mimic my movements, managing to create his ward knot just in time—a series of bright red lights suddenly burst from the illusion spell on the pegboard. Shaped like small fiery dragonflies, trailing sparks in their wake, the wisps dive and dart, attacking Conrad. I know from experience that where they strike him, they'll leave sharp stings that take a few minutes to fade.

Conrad discovers this right away, when he fails to channel quickly enough and a wisp stings his neck. He yelps and finally lights his Weave, generating a flash of blue light that spreads like a web in front of him. The five remaining wisps collide with it and explode in a shower of glittering sparks.

"That's it!" I say. "Now move quickly—there are more!"

Six more times my illusion knot sends a burst of wisps into the air, and six more times Conrad manages to Weave the ward spell, each time faster and more sure of the movements. Then the yarn on the pegboard burns away to ash, and he is left breathing harder, flushed and triumphant and looking to me with shining eyes for approval. There are a few red marks on his neck and face where the wisps stung him, but he seems hardly to notice. His dark hair flops over his eyes, and when he rakes it back, the collar of his shirt flexes open, revealing a plane of muscled chest.

"Fates," I breathe, my throat suddenly knotted.

"What's that?" he asks.

"I said, *great*! You did great."

"I did, rather, didn't I?" Looking entirely too satisfied with himself, he tosses the spool back to me. "C'mon, now. *Really* test me."

Feeling a flicker of mischief, I smile sweetly and pick up my pegboard, brushing the ashes off. "If you so command."

Minutes later, Conrad abandons his threads with a yelp and scurries into an empty stall, where he is forced to take refuge under a horse blanket as my band of enchanted broomsticks attempts to clout his ears. When the animating knots I tied around their shafts disintegrate and they drop harmlessly onto the floor, he emerges, panting and wide-eyed. "I wasn't ready that time!"

With a shrug, I channel into my next Weave—and the bale of hay beside me suddenly rises up and forms itself into the rough shape of a man. It jolts forward, rushing across the wooden floor with a dry, raspy sound. Conrad shouts and struggles out from under the blanket, lunging for his threads. He manages to Weave another ward spell, but not before the straw man thumps him a few times, knocking him into the walls and floor.

"Mercy!" he bellows, as the straw man finally bursts apart and rains down on him. "Have mercy!"

Leaning against the wall, presenting nonchalance to hide the fact I'm on the verge of collapsing after all that channeling, I let out a laugh. "If you so command."

"'Tis not a command," he says, thoroughly out of breath. "'Tis a plea."

Straw sticks out of his hair, and half the buttons on his shirt are undone. But for all his dishevelment, he looks to me in that moment as bright as a sunrise. His smile hides no secrets, his laugh unfettered by weariness. This, I think, is who Conrad was meant to be, before he was ever chained to his duties to Elfhame. He was meant for breathless horse races over a sunbathed moor, for hearty rowing on the Thames with a dozen other bright and ruddy boys, for raucous nights in the pubs with an ale in his hand and a song on his lips.

He was never meant to be shut away in a moldering mansion, away from the world. His life is a shadow of what it might have been, as he is a shadow of himself. This Conrad, the one before me now, is one that must be stowed always in the back of a closet, like a costume worn once a year, while the grimmer, older Conrad must bear the yoke of the Gatekeeper of Elfhame, with so much suspicion in his heart he has no room for mirth.

"What's wrong?" he asks, and I realize I've been staring for too long, while my frown deepened and my brow furrowed.

Smoothing my features, I smile and say, "I think you're ready for the bigger wards now."

He brightens, but then his smile drops away.

"Do you hear that?" he whispers.

Footsteps. Right outside the stable door.

"Sylvie?" I ask.

"Quick—hide!"

He points to Bell's stall. Pulling open the door, he lets me go in first, then he blows out the lantern and shuts the stall behind us—just as the stable door swings open and someone with heavy footsteps plods in.

Conrad and I duck into a pile of hay, with Bell snorting over our heads. Breathing in hay dust, I hold back a sneeze, gripping Conrad's arm so tightly he winces.

Conrad lifts his head a bit, then ducks down again. "'Tis only Mr. MacDougal. He must have argued with his wife and got himself kicked out again."

Mr. MacDougal lights the lantern Conrad just extinguished and begins shuffling around, muttering to himself. He fiddles with the lantern, sighs, and then the stable fills with the smell of sweet pipe tobacco. Something heavy scrapes along the floor, and Mr. MacDougal grunts.

"He's pulling out a cot," Conrad whispers, rubbing his face with an expression of weary disbelief. "We're trapped until he falls asleep."

"You're not serious."

He shrugs helplessly.

I reach into my sleeve, but it's empty. I left my spare thread atop my threadkit and abandoned all of that when we darted into the stall, so there's no chance of Weaving a spell to assist Mr. MacDougal in falling asleep.

I glance at Conrad, at the door, then pinch my lips together and sit deeper into the hay. He sits beside me, grinning apologetically.

"I'm sure he'll nod off soon," he says.

If we had stopped to think and simply let Mr. MacDougal find us Weaving, he might have thought it perfectly innocent. But by losing our heads and hiding, we've doubled the suspicious nature of our meeting.

Bell nudges me, asking for sugar. I feed him the last cube and prop my head in my hand. I drum my fingers against my cheek and try to ignore how Conrad's shoulder is pressed against mine, and how every time he shifts, his thigh bumps against my knee.

"Once," I whisper, desperate for some distraction, "I spent two whole hours inside a desk cabinet."

Conrad slowly looks at me. "I . . . beg your pardon?"

I shrug. "It was life or death, or so I thought at the time. I was only seven years old. I'd stolen a book of magic from my uncle's library, but my aunt came into the room, and I was so frightened and out of my wits that my first thought was to hide in the desk. She sat the whole afternoon in there, muttering to her cat and complaining about the strength of her tea."

He leans forward and looks at me over his shoulder, his arms folded over his knees. "I never asked you about your childhood."

I stare at Bell's silky blond tail, wondering how the horse would react if I plucked a hair to Weave with.

"There isn't much to tell. My aunt and I did not exactly get on. My uncle caught an illness from me, and though I recovered, he soon died, and she never forgave me for it. I thought she might discard me entirely the night I learned I could Weave."

"How did you learn it?"

"I was reading a book of spells I'd found in my uncle's library, shortly after he'd died, and I thought I'd try one. I don't think I ever actually expected it to work, but there it was—a little butterfly made of ice, conjured by twisting a few threads into the right shape." I open my palm, lost in the memory. It occurs to me I've never told anyone this story. It's not like me, to go prattling on about the more painful parts of my past. But then . . . perhaps that is because I've never had anyone so eager to listen. Conrad watches me closely, his head cocked, waiting for more.

"It was so beautiful," I murmur, "hovering over my hands, sparkling like crystal. I thought if my aunt saw it, she'd be pleased. She was no Weaver, but my uncle had been, and I thought it might make her like me to know we shared the gift. But I was wrong, of course. I think it made her hate me more. She forbade me from having anything to do with magic."

"Ah." Conrad lets out a long, thin breath, his head falling back against the stall door. "So that's it."

"That's what?"

He looks down at his hands, his fingers twisting a piece of straw. "I wondered why you despised me from the moment we met. It's because I remind you of her, isn't it? Of course I do. You must think me a beast."

"I . . . well, at first, yes." The admission makes my ears burn. "But you're not like her. Not at all. She believed in . . . firm punishments, for one thing." I look down at my hands, trying to hide the ugly truths of my past from him. But then I feel his fingers, light as silk, on my jaw, with his thumb just brushing the scar on my throat.

I freeze, my gaze fixing upon his, wondering if he can feel my pulse quicken in my neck.

"Did she give you this?" he whispers, his eyes fire trapped in amber glass.

My mouth parts, breathless, and his thumb traces its way up my neck to follow the curve of my jaw, as his gaze tears at me like the northern wind I saw him conjure, threatening to strip away every secret in my body. My treacherous mind flashes back to our night in Elfhame, of his mouth warm on mine, our hands entwined.

No, no, no, I want to scream at him. *You don't want this. You don't know what I am!*

My skin heats, a chill running from my scalp to my navel. I sit as one transfixed, his thumb working a magic unlike anything I learned in school.

But no; that is not my imagination—the air is moving, stirring the hay around us. Feverish heat rolls off Conrad, who I realize is drawing energy in by the pail. I can *feel* it, like water flowing just beneath the floor, rushing toward him. The horses feel it too. Bell stamps and snorts, and across the stable, Ariadne whinnies.

"Conrad," I whisper, placing my hand on his wrist. Is he even aware of what he is doing?

His eyes burn. "What happened to you, Rose? Did she hurt you?"

I'm on my knees now. I pluck a hair from Bell's tail and begin to Weave a wind knot, something for him to pour all that energy into before it—or he—combusts. Needles of straw are spiraling higher, caught up in the power rolling off Conrad, his magic uncontrolled and dangerously volatile. If the lantern threw a spark, it would catch the air like a flash of lightning and set all this hay on fire. Unspent magic simmers all around us, the air boiling and taut, ready to explode.

My eyes begin to burn; tears fall before I can stop them.

"It doesn't matter," I whisper. "She's far away now. You're losing control. You have to stop! Quick—take this!"

I thrust the wind knot into his hand, and he gasps, channeling all the energy at once.

A mighty gust of wind rushes through the stable. The lantern sputters out as the doors crash open with a bang. Mr. MacDougal curses and runs to them, and I take the opportunity to scramble out of the hay and over the stall door, scooping up my threadkit. Conrad follows, and we dart to the rear door while Mr. MacDougal struggles to shut out the gale. Now it is not Conrad's wind which pushes the front doors open, but the wind of the moors, wild and angry, the howling vanguard of a coming storm.

I stumble into the night, my hair coming unbound in the wind. I cannot even see the house for the leaves and debris blowing about. Conrad puts his hand on my back, turning me toward it, and I follow his guidance until we reach the kitchen door. Behind us, lightning splits the sky. Thunder growls on the horizon.

We burst through, and Conrad throws himself against the door, latching it with a wooden bar to keep the wind out. We both breathe hard, disheveled and covered in straw.

Mrs. MacDougal is standing over the stove with a cup in hand, making herself a late-night tea.

She blinks at us as the kettle begins to scream behind her. But she doesn't turn. She watches Conrad and me, her eyes wide.

I stand frozen in place, mortified, extremely aware of how we look and what she must think we were up to. But Conrad simply greets her with a nod, speaking over the howl of the kettle. "Mrs. MacDougal. Big storm coming in."

Thunder breaks again, and I flinch. Mrs. MacDougal's eyes shift to me, her expression unchanging.

Conrad straightens his waistcoat and bows to me. "Well, then. Good night, Miss Pryor. Thank you for the lesson."

He waits so that I can leave first, and I can only think it is because he doesn't want to leave me to face the housekeeper alone. I scurry away as quick as I can, feeling Mrs. MacDougal's eyes follow me all the way out; she doesn't remove the kettle until I am out of sight. My blood is pumping fast. It's as if a piece of the storm lodged in my lungs and is raging in the cavity of my chest.

I pause on the stairs, holding a hand to my fluttering stomach.

What *happened* in that stable?

One minute, everything was going well enough. I was teaching, he was learning, we were making innocent scholastic progress . . . and the next minute, he was putting his fingers on my neck while I poured out my deepest secrets. I made one mention of my aunt's abuse, and he began drawing in magic as if he were about to charge into battle.

I knew agreeing to teach him would be a mistake.

Just as I know I am too weak to put a stop to it.

I can practically hear Lachlan's sly laughter dancing on the wind.

CHAPTER
TWENTY-EIGHT

Bagpipes awaken me at dawn.

Again.

Upon hearing the first keening blast, I groan and pull my pillow over my head, cursing Conrad North.

It has been two weeks since my last meeting with Lachlan, two weeks since Conrad agreed to a fortnight's deadline for my departure from Ravensgate.

Tomorrow is my final chance. The day after that, I will turn twenty-one.

I am supposed to have the Dwirra branch for Lachlan by tomorrow night, but I've come no closer to finding the portal spell. The deadline draws tight around my neck, and panic lurks like a kraken beneath my bed, waiting to devour me the moment I set foot on the floor. I have no idea what I will do, but I know I must act soon. Today, if possible. I must find a way into Elfhame or lose my magic forever.

I haven't visited Lachlan again. With only two uses left, the tapestry is too precious a tool to use unless necessary. It is a relief not to see the faerie, but every now and again, a strawberry will appear on my windowsill, a reminder that he is waiting. How it gets there, I have no idea.

Conrad has said nothing of my leaving Ravensgate. I'm almost inclined to believe he'd forgotten our deal. It doesn't seem to matter much anyway; one way or another, my time at Ravensgate will end tomorrow. Either I'll have acquired the Dwirra branch or not. Either I'll have saved my magic or not. No matter which outcome, I'll have no more reason to stay here.

Desperation makes a knot of my stomach.

But Fates, a body cannot *think* with that Fatesdamned noise rattling the windows! Conrad is not so much playing the bagpipes as he is murdering them. And for the past two weeks, he's begun every single morning like this, startling us all awake with a dreadful racket. Every note is an assault upon the eardrums, sharpened by the unbridled zeal with which they are played.

He only plays his pipes when he's in a very good mood or a black temper, Sylvie had told me.

Unluckily for the rest of us, the laird's moods swing without much warning from black piques to bright bursts of energy in which he and Sylvie race about the house, roaring and stamping and sliding down banisters. On these days, Mrs. MacDougal fusses and huffs and tells Conrad to mind his age. But Sylvie comes fully alive with him, her eyes warm and adoring, her laughs tumbling up and down the halls. It is easy to tell she worships him utterly.

But other times, he grows dark, and I come upon him gazing out a window, clenching the sill as if he might break through and take to the sky, a wild, dark raven like the ones carved on his front doors. He yearns to escape, that much is clear. Sylvie thinks this place a prison, but Conrad *knows* it is.

In the evenings, after Sylvie falls asleep, we sneak to the stable and I teach him wards, defense spells, blinding hexes, anything which might help him protect his family. But half the time we simply end up sitting on bales of hay, talking. He asks me to tell him about London, and I describe the bustle of the markets, the bells of the Westminster School, the ragged children of the alleys and gutters. He listens as if

I were spinning tales of gods, not of the poor and common people I grew up around, his eyes hungry for the outside world. I even tell him stories of my aunt and my punishing school days, though I soften the details. I don't want a repeat of the episode in the stable, with Conrad channeling uncontrollably.

He doesn't touch me again like he did that night. Perhaps this is because I am very careful to keep distance between us—no more squeezing into tight places together, no more physical contact than is strictly necessary for the sake of our lessons. Every time I am tempted to pick a piece of straw out of his hair or take hold of his hands to correct his cat's cradle, I think of Lachlan's sly laughter, and I resist. Every time I feel Conrad's eyes are lingering too long on mine, I look away. When he finishes a particularly demanding lesson, with his sweat-soaked shirt clinging to his chest and his cheeks dimpling with proud laughter, I close my eyes and pray to the Fates for strength.

Then again, perhaps I only imagined the heat in his eyes and the softness of his fingers on my skin during that first lesson, and there was never anything to guard against in the first place. Perhaps he really does see me as nothing more than a temporary guest with some useful knowledge to share before we part ways for all eternity. Perhaps when he told me that kiss in Elfhame was purely for show, he was telling the truth.

But I cannot deny that something has changed in him since that night. He is easier around me, almost comfortable. He thinks all is open between us, that I know his deepest secrets and he knows mine. I play along, letting him think so, unable to fathom how I could possibly break it to him that I am a tool of his father's murderer.

And despite my best efforts to remain aloof, I find myself lulled, pulled into this quiet, eccentric world he and Sylvie have built, a world of playacting and horses and books and sudden, wild stampedes down the halls in their stockings. But when his mood turns, it is like a thunderstorm rolling across a clear sky, darkening all in his shadow.

Even Sylvie cannot reach him then, and he locks himself in his study and broods.

When he goes away for an afternoon here and there, to patrol the border or, I assume, to visit Morgaine, Sylvie sneaks in, and I tell her the difference between a chain stitch and a close stitch, and she makes little samplers. If Conrad were to discover us like this, I know he'd throw me out at once. There is one line he will allow no one to cross, and that is anything which might endanger Sylvie. She seems to understand the risk we take and is very discreet with her lessons. She listens like a sponge, soaking up every word, and though her stitches are messy and her threads tangled, I can see her improving by bounds day by day.

The sound of Conrad's bagpipes goes on longer than usual this morning, and no amount of pillows will block them out.

Finally, I hurl myself out of bed, yank my shawl over my clothes, and go downstairs. Sylvie and the MacDougals have emerged from their rooms and gathered atop the foyer steps, blinking and hollow-eyed, even Sylvie looking irritated.

"He's having *feelings* again," she groans.

Mrs. MacDougal presses her fingertips to her temples and releases a small whimper. "It's never got this bad before." Then she glares at me as if it were all *my* fault.

"That's it!" I cry. "I can't take another minute of that bedlam he calls *music.*"

No one stops me as I throw open the front doors and stalk over the drive. Conrad stands with his back to the manor, his pipes blasting to the sky like a bloody rooster crowing at the sun. He doesn't hear me approach, so he is doubly startled when I wrench the bagpipes right out of his hands.

"Rose Pryor!" he cries. "You cannot just snatch a man's pipes away, you harpy!"

"I can, I did, and I will again, if you don't let up!"

"Give those back, you madwoman!" He lunges at me, and I dance out of reach, the pipes clacking in a way that makes the color drain from his face.

I turn and walk briskly back to the house, still clutching his pipes. He follows with a stream of curses. Brushing by the MacDougals, Sylvie cackling in the doorway, I storm upstairs into my room and slam the door shut.

Moments later, I hear a timid knock. "Rose."

"Go away!"

"Rose. *Please*."

I sigh and go to the door, to find Conrad standing like a wounded dog. The top of his head rests on the doorway, and he looks up at me through the dark fringe of his eyelashes. He is wearing a sprig of juniper in his collar today, just like the one he wore the night of the faerie revel.

"Rose. I'm sorry. I did not mean to make you cross with me. Please, give them back."

I glance across the room at the great clock on the wall, its hands inexorably creeping toward tomorrow's midnight, my final deadline. Mouth dry and stomach clenching, I turn back to Conrad.

There is one last resort left to me, a terrible one, and I feel my conscience squirm as I reply, "I'll give them back, if you take me out riding again, after I've finished Sylvie's lessons. I feel I've been stuck indoors for days."

His face brightens. "You've a deal, Miss Pryor."

That afternoon, we ride far and wide over the moors, beneath a sky thickening with clouds. It will rain soon, but we are determined to make the most of the fair weather we have left. The air is springlike, warm enough that I didn't need my shawl.

Conrad talks of Elfhame, and in any other circumstance, his tales of wild revels and faerie-court intrigues would hold me fully enthralled.

But I can only half listen, distracted as I am by the gnawing guilt in my belly. I am glad for my bonnet, which allows me to look slightly away whenever he glances at me, the brim obscuring the treachery in my gaze. I left my threadkit behind for once but carry several spools in my pockets. The borrowed riding clothes are sewn with many such hiding places, and I keep one hand wrapped around a skein of black silk thread, trying to work up the nerve to use it.

After an hour, we stop atop Toren's Rise to rest and eat the sandwiches Mrs. MacDougal packed in Bell's saddlebags. The moors spread magnificently below us, dramatically cast in pools of light and shadow by the clouds and late-afternoon sun.

Conrad stands at the very edge of the jutting rock and gazes out at the landscape, dressed in a loose white shirt, the sleeves rolled to his elbows, and tight riding breeches tucked into his boots. The wind breaks over the bluff like a wave, ruffling his shirt and hair. He's just finished telling me another story of faerie exploits, this one involving two angry fae dueling one another with spoons, after Conrad convinced them that was how disputes were settled in the human world.

"I would like to see it again," I say.

He glances over his shoulder at me, surprised. "What's that?"

"Elfhame. You know, I remember so little of that night," I go on. "Perhaps if I returned with you again, it would further convince Morgaine that you and I are . . ."

"Nay," he says, his tone brusque. "You don't understand, Rose. I *can't* take you there, even if I wanted to. My vow to her does not allow it."

I grimace with disappointment, even though I'd known that would be his answer. But a part of me had hoped, pathetically, that there still might be some easier path.

"Well, I suppose it does not matter," I say stiffly. "After all, I'm meant to leave in two days' time. We had a deal, did we not?"

He looks away, his back straight, and gazes over the moor toward the purple hills sloping in the distance. All around us, a dark ring of clouds is slowly closing in, congealing into thunderheads.

I rise from our picnic blanket and walk to his side, to see another storm gathering in Conrad's eyes. His mood is turning again, sun to shadow.

"There is no rush," he says at last. "When I said a fortnight, I meant it . . . generally."

My hand shakes as I take hold of the truth knot in my pocket. It's a smaller one than the great net Conrad wove over me in the cottage, meant to last for only a minute or so, but that will be all the time I need. And though I half wish my heart *would* choke for once, it gives me no trouble at all when I channel into the thread.

Conrad stands up straighter, his face smoothing slightly, the only indication I have that the spell is working. But there is no awareness of it in his eyes. Even if there were, I am already prepared to Weave the memory spell which will erase this conversation and my treachery from his head.

I open my mouth, knowing I have to get straight to the point while the truth knot still holds, and find some way to pry the portal spell from him. He cannot tell me it straight out, but perhaps he can tell me where a drawing of it might be hidden, or at least what sort of spell it is.

But he speaks before I can.

"I don't want you to go," he says.

My breath catches; I turn my face fully to him. Conrad's eyes, glazed from the truth spell, nevertheless fix me in place until it feels I am made of stone. The wind pushes at us both, twisting my skirts and dragging his dark hair over his forehead.

"You said you would go if it would please me," he says. "But nothing would please me less. These past weeks with you have been like . . . waking after a long sleep. Not since my mother was alive has Ravensgate been so full of life. I'd forgotten it could be like that. Like a *home*."

"You know nothing about me," I whisper. As if I haven't already shared more of myself with him than with anyone I can remember. As if there aren't a thousand more things I want to tell him, if they weren't buried behind a wall of secrets. But if he knew everything . . .

"I know you're an excellent teacher. I know you're passionate and clever and stubborn as a mule, but that in that stubbornness is a strength I cannae help but admire. I know that you care fiercely for your students, for their futures and safety, and for defending those who cannae defend themselves. And for all that you stand no taller than a spring colt, you will go toe-to-toe with any bloody-minded bastard you deem unjust."

I look away, my cheeks warming, unable to bear the directness of his gaze. "What, like you?"

"Like me." He smiles. "And if you leave now, I'll never have the chance to learn more. I *want* to learn. I want to know where you go in your thoughts when you look out the window and your brow furrows. I've noticed how you drift away. Who captures your mind so? Is there someone else, someone you've left behind?"

My mind flashes to Lachlan, and a chill scurries up my spine.

Conrad seems to notice my hesitation. He lifts his chin. "There is someone."

"No. That is, not in the way you think. I have obligations, Conrad. My employer—"

"Your *employer*." He twists the word on his tongue. "You rarely speak of him. And when you do, your voice shakes."

"Nonsense."

"Who is he? Why did you leave your teaching post—which you speak of with such pride and passion—to follow a cloth merchant around the backwaters of Scotland?"

"I needed a change. I wanted to travel." I hear the defensive edge to my tone and know he is not fooled. "Surely you can understand that. My employer offered me the opportunity, and so I took it."

Conrad's jaw flexes. "Does he have some claim on your heart?"

My hand moves to my hair before I can think, remembering the feel of Lachlan's cruel fingers. "It's nothing like that."

"So you've no obligation to this man."

"I—I do, but not in the way you imagine." What is happening? *I'm* supposed to be the one asking questions, not him. But I feel as if he has turned my own magic against me. This is not at all the sort of truth I'd hoped to steal from him!

Hands shaking, I fumble with the truth knot, tugging desperately at the thread.

"Rose," he says. "I cannae let you slip away from me. Damn me, for it's foolish and selfish, but I believe I'm falling—"

"Stop talking!" I cry, my voice ragged. My fingers finally work into the tight knot, pulling the threads apart and collapsing the spell.

Conrad blinks once, slowly, then shakes his head a little. The glaze in his eyes fades, and I breathe out in relief.

He looks around, confused. "I . . . I'm sorry. I don't know what came over me just now."

"It's all right," I reply shakily. "We should probably go back, don't you think?"

I nod at the encroaching clouds.

"Aye," he says, but he still seems slightly baffled.

We pack up our dinner and mount the horses. To avoid Conrad and his dangerous confessions, I ride ahead for once. My thoughts whirl with panic and dread. I relive the past two weeks, turning over every moment Conrad and I spent together, searching for where I went wrong.

I've been so careful. I've kept my distance, even when it felt like I was locking my heart away. Even when I ached to touch him, I stopped myself, because I would not—*will not*—let Lachlan use me against him. I will not be his undoing.

Have I failed so miserably?

No matter how fast I ride, I cannot escape his words: *"I believe I'm falling . . ."*

No, no, no.

I won't let him make that mistake. I am not who he thinks I am, and I should never have agreed to stay at Ravensgate after I learned Lachlan's true plans. This has to end.

My resolve hardens. I will go to Elfhame tomorrow night, one way or another. I'll get that damned branch, and I'll be gone by the next sunrise. Conrad will never see me again, I will go back to my humble classroom where I belong, and I will do my best to forget everything that happened here.

It is the only way I can escape this place with both my magic and my soul intact.

We don't get far before the clouds break and release their rain. We are still miles from the manor, and it is a long and soggy ride over the moors. The horses plod miserably, and Conrad apologizes repeatedly for getting us caught in the downpour. I only shake my head and clench my hands around the reins, my bedraggled hair swinging in wet ropes.

At last, we reach the stable and Conrad helps me down. I'm so exhausted and drenched I can't even refuse him; I just slide awkwardly into his arms, and he sets me on the ground, then wraps a horse blanket around me. While I stand in the hay and shiver, he unsaddles Bell and Roman, gives them a thorough currying, and then fills their troughs with sweet oats. I find a barrel and perch on it, watching him work. How at ease he is with the animals; they respond to him with soft, affectionate nudges.

Once the horses have been seen to, we head into the manor. I walk quickly ahead, determined to go straight to my room.

"I am truly sorry," he says.

"It's just rain. I'll dry off."

"Not about that. Well, not *just* that. Rose. *Rose*, can we please talk?" He catches my arm and holds me fast. We stand in the narrow kitchen doorway and face one another, his eyes pleading, my heart rioting.

"I'm fine," I insist.

"No, you're not. You're angry, and I am sorry." Rain drips from the lintel and drums steadily beside us, a curtain of water. There is a lantern lit inside, and it strikes one side of his face, while casting the other into shadow. "For what I said out there. It was wrong of me. You owe us nothing. Of course you must go, and I am just a fool for wishing otherwise."

"You're not a fool," I whisper. "But you're right. I must go."

I should turn away now. I should put one soggy foot in front of the other and take myself upstairs, putting an end to the whole affair.

But I don't.

I stay frozen, unable to force my body into motion. My back is against one side of the doorway, his against the other. He lowers his face, trying to get me to meet his eyes.

Finally, swallowing hard, I do.

Looking caught in a dream, he lifts a wet lock of my hair from my forehead. A spark seems to travel from his touch down my spine. The blanket slips off one of my shoulders, leaving my collarbone bare. I could easily pull it up again, but I don't. I watch his eyes fall to the raindrops glistening on my bare skin. My mind is a hopeless snarl of threads, nothing making sense.

"You come in here like a summer storm," he says softly, "and you change everything. Why? What drives you?"

"I can only be what I am."

"And what are you?"

Traitor. Spy. Puppet. The acidic truth tingles on my tongue.

Conrad is but a touch away. A tilt of the head. A lean. A raised hand. He could be mine. I feel it in this moment, as surely as I have ever felt anything. But if I close that distance between us, giving us what I can no longer deny we both want . . . and then, when he finds out all the secrets I've been keeping and sees me for what I truly am . . .

His hand drops from my hair, instead trailing up my sleeve, then, hesitantly, his fingertips brush the bare skin of my shoulder. A shiver of heat runs down my back, and I gasp a little. That small touch threatens to set fire to every ounce of resistance in my body.

So what if I have secrets? a traitorous whisper asks from the back of my mind. *So what if he learns them? Let the future sort itself. Live for this moment.*

He waits, as if wondering how I will react. If I will pull away or tell him to stop.

I don't.

Instead, I tilt my head, my cheek brushing the back of his hand. My eyes never waver from his. I wait for him to make the decision I am too terrified to make, knowing if he does, I will be helpless to resist.

"*Rose,*" he breathes warningly, as if he weren't the one who started this.

He was the one who kissed *me,* down in the realm of faeries.

Thinking of that night brings a flush of heat to my middle, and my gaze lowers to his mouth. My reason unravels more quickly than I can gather it up. My guilt gives way to longing. The need to touch him pulses through my body, a physical, primal ache so strong it makes my chest hurt in a way no spell ever has.

"Well?" I whisper. "What is it you want, Conrad?"

He doesn't have to speak. His hungry eyes say everything. He leans forward and brushes his lips against my throat, and my breath, my heart, my very thoughts all stop—

"By the Fates!" squeals a voice.

We rip apart. I hadn't realized how close we'd been until Mrs. MacDougal bursts from the kitchen, a lantern swinging in her hand.

"Look at you! Come inside at once! You'll catch your deaths of pneumonia. Mad, mad creatures!"

Before either of us can speak, she tugs us into the house, shutting the door. Then she pulls me further away, her hand too tight for me to believe she is merely concerned about my health.

"Now you go upstairs, lass," she says, her eyes boring into mine, "and dry yourself off. Then straight to bed, lest you catch cold. Riding off into a storm, what nonsense! Ach!"

"Good night, Rose," Conrad says, his voice ragged. He is flushed and wide-eyed, watching me with an intent expression.

With another warm shiver, I plod up the steps, thinking the best thing for me now would be a dash of cold water to my burning face, and I hope the basin in my room isn't empty. But then whispering from the kitchen catches my ear. I stop where I am, holding my breath.

". . . is not your concern, Mrs. MacDougal." Conrad's voice is as brittle as ice.

"I'm trying to help you, lad. That girl is trouble. I don't trust her. Something about her just doesn't add up. She *disturbed* the peace of this house, as if she had a right to it. I have it on authority she broke a vase and hid it in a bureau!"

"A vase? *Really?* That's what all this is about?"

"Someone has to shake some sense into you! What are you doing, lad? You can't get distracted. Not now, with the Briar King rattling the windows."

"You think I don't know that?" Conrad's tone is hard. "I'll do what I must, as I always have. But when do *I* get to be happy?"

The ensuing silence stretches so long I begin to pull back, fearing they suspect me of eavesdropping.

But then Mrs. MacDougal says in a low, weary voice, "I know your passions are getting the better of you, just as I know *she* is the cause of it. Remember where your duties lie, and remember—no one from the outside can be trusted."

"Aye, I know where my duties lie, and I know I'll never experience anything of the world beyond this moor. I've accepted that, with all the misery and frustration that goes with it. But I want to do what brings *me* joy, just for once, and maybe Rose makes me happy. In any case, it's not your decision to make, ye ken?"

The kitchen door slams shut; I can hear Conrad's heavy footsteps as he storms away, off to his wing of the house. Mrs. MacDougal sighs and begins moving toward the stairs. I gather my skirts and flee as silently as I can, my cheeks burning.

That girl is trouble.

And the worst of all, the words which had pricked my heart like poisoned thorns: *Maybe Rose makes me happy.*

Back in my room at last, I sink onto the chair by the low, flickering fire and wrap my arms around my knees. My heart is tumbling against my ribs, and my skin is feverishly hot.

I hear his footsteps as he walks down the hallway, and I hold my breath, heart pounding, when he pauses at my door. Will he knock? What will I do if he does? Invite him in?

Don't knock, I think. Then, *No, please do.*

But he moves on, footsteps receding, and I press a pillow to my face and scream into it.

Closing my eyes, I feel the hungry warmth of his lips on my neck; I envision his eyes poring into me, heat and energy rolling off his skin and crackling through my hair.

I'm falling in love with him.

My cheeks flush, the heat of the room suddenly too much to bear. I go to the window and throw it open, pushing my face into the cool night air. I draw in the rain-washed scent of the moors and stare at the glimmering stars marching across the horizon.

On the edge of the windowsill, crimson as blood, rests a single strawberry.

I pick it up with trembling fingers and turn it over. A bite has been taken out of it, and the wound leaks red juice onto my fingertips.

I hurl it outside, watch it disappear into the darkness, then lean weakly on the sill.

"Just a coincidence," I whisper. "He doesn't know."

But I can't make myself believe it. Does Lachlan have some way of watching me? Did he see me moments ago, ready to surrender to my treacherous desires? To become the trap he meant me to be?

Lachlan sent me here to be Conrad's undoing; and even *knowing* that, I've let myself fall for the laird. I thought I was so careful, so clever, and all the while, my heart was betraying me.

I can't do this anymore.

I'm tired of sacrificing more and more of my soul just to keep my magic. I thought I could complete my task and leave Conrad out of it, that somehow I could still keep separate these two threads. But what a fool I've been; for all this time, they've been tangled together, and every time I looked at him, heard his voice, that knot only pulled tighter. Despite all the lies I told myself, I cannot possibly pay my debt to Lachlan *and* protect Conrad.

I have to choose one or the other.

Another storm is rolling in. The sky to the east is as black as spilled ink, and I hear another sweep of rain approaching, like a herd of wild horses thundering over the moor.

I grip the stone windowsill and shut my eyes, feeling the vanguard wind howl through my hair and grip my dress in its teeth.

I know then, in that cold wind with the shadows prowling the room behind me, what I must do, what I should have done from the beginning, the very moment I first felt a spark flicker within me when Conrad fixed me in his tiger gaze. It's the only thing I *can* do, and the only way I possibly walk away from this with my soul still intact.

I must leave this place and never return.

I must break my contract with the faerie king.

CHAPTER TWENTY-NINE

I put it off all night, and then linger in my room the next morning, pacing and twisting threads until they snap. Breakfast comes and goes, and Mrs. MacDougal does not come knocking; I am sure *she* does not miss me overmuch. But neither does Sylvie come looking for me as she usually does, which I suppose is for the best.

I tell myself I'll write to her, to find some way to encourage her to continue learning her magic, whatever her brother might say. But I'm not sure it's an intention I can keep. After today, I have no idea what course my life will take. Where I will go, what I will do . . . nothing is certain. But I know I cannot stay in this house another night.

Picking up my valise in one hand, my threadkit in the other, I turn and face the tapestry.

It will be left behind, and Conrad will know the minute he sees it what I was, who I worked for. He'll know the truth and he'll burn the tapestry, and he'll curse my name to the skies.

At least I won't have to see his eyes when he learns how I've lied and betrayed him.

But today, I'll set things right, or as right as they may be set. I hope he will come to understand that and hate me a little less.

Drawing a few deep, bracing breaths, I start toward the tapestry—and freeze when someone pounds on my door.

"Rose!" Conrad calls, all out of breath. "Is my sister in there?"

In one motion, I pull down the tapestry and shove it beneath the bed. As an afterthought, I stow the valise too. Then I throw open the door.

Conrad is wild-eyed and unkempt, an unshaven shadow on his jaw. He has one hand on the door, the other gripping Sylvie's fur cloak. Raw panic burns in his gaze.

"What happened?" I ask.

"We argued this morning, and then she ran into the moor. I set Captain on her trail, but all we found was this." He raises the cloak. "Her trail *ended*, Rose, in the middle of nowhere. I tried a finding spell, but the trail just *ended*. What does that mean?"

"Where did the trail stop?"

His face hardens. "Southeast. At the ward's edge. It's as if she vanished."

The blood drains from my face as a stifling wave of foreboding rises in me, a storm cloud of dread.

Southeast is the direction in which Lachlan's castle lies.

Fates, no. Please no.

"Go," I say. "You search east, and I'll go south."

"She left. She took her bag with her." His eyes are hollow. "My father left, and he didn't come back. My mother—"

"We will find her," I say firmly. "Go, and I'll set out once I've put together my threadkit."

The pain in his eyes tears at me. It takes all my strength to shut the door, to shut him out. I hear him walk away, his breathing tight and panicked.

I drag the tapestry out from beneath the bed and hang it up again, then take hold of the guide thread. With a deep inhale, I push into it, parting the fibers with my free hand and shutting my eyes against the swirling, writhing chaos beyond it. The whispering roar of the threads fills my ears, and I do my best to shut it out and follow the guide thread to the other side.

Stepping into the castle, I exhale and shiver, still feeling the effects of the passage. It always takes a few moments to clear my head, even when I've kept my eyes shut the whole time. Once the dizziness passes and the roar of the threads fades from my ears, I look around.

And find the castle entirely deserted.

Lachlan is gone, as are all his fae. And they've taken everything with them: the carpets and tents, chairs and tables. Not even the grass is flattened where they lay. Only the Telarian tapestry remains, exactly as it had before, hung on the old stone wall.

It's as if they never were.

I stand in the center of the collapsed great hall and listen to the wind whistling through the cracks in the stone walls. My scalp crawls, and my stomach tumbles with alarm.

Where did he go? Did he abandon his mission? Did he abandon *me*?

No; Lachlan wouldn't give up this easily. Perhaps someone came upon the castle and found the fae, and they had to retreat to another camp. If so, he would have left some way for me to find him.

I look around more carefully then, this time searching for some hidden message. It isn't long before I find it: a silver thread wrapped around the half-fallen archway into the upper rooms. I take hold of it and follow, just as I'd followed the guideline through the tapestry portals.

The day is fair but won't be for long. Clouds brood in the east and cast a malevolent eye on these sunny hills, plotting rain. With no houses or fences in sight, and even the ruins lost to view behind me, I feel I've reached the end of the world. Lachlan's silken thread slides over my palm, a whisper against my skin.

I must walk two miles before I see his tent, a small simple pavilion of white linen draped over wooden poles, with ribbons fluttering from the corners and a silver banner streaming sinuously from the highest point, like a dragon's tail snapping in the breeze. Below it sits a table and two chairs.

Him in one.

In the other, Sylvie.

I break into a run, dropping the silver thread and shouting until my lungs feel raw. I call her name, my stomach clenching and fear shooting through my veins. My feet fly over the heather with a nimbleness I did not know I possessed.

"Sylvie! Sylvie!"

When I am near enough to see the blue ribbon in her hair, she turns and smiles.

"Hello, Rose."

Slowing, my hands going to my knees as I pant for breath, I gauge the scene. Lachlan sits easily in his high-backed, upholstered chair, watching me passively. Sylvie's legs dangle; she kicks them happily and sips from a dainty teacup. There are sweets on the table, with tea and strawberries and a little bouquet of snowdrops, their soft petals as white as Lachlan's hair.

"Tea?" he asks me. "We've eaten all the berry tarts, I'm afraid, but there are still some butter scones."

Lurching forward, I grab Sylvie's hand and pull her to me. She drops the cup, and it shatters on the gleaming white carpet laid beneath the tent.

"Rose!" she cries. "I am having tea with my new friend! Don't be rude."

Putting myself between him and her, I face the faerie with my fury scorching my skin, a tide of curses simmering behind my teeth. "What did you do? How did you find her?"

"She found *me*!" he protests, spreading his hands innocently.

"Aye, I did," Sylvie affirms.

I turn around to stare at her, then notice a battered valise sitting by the table. "Sylvie . . . you were running away?"

"It was only for a little while," Sylvie says. "To make Connie understand how much I want to Weave magic. I'm tired of hiding it from him! He only needs to miss me for bit. Then I would come back, and he'd change his mind. I want to show him what I can do, how I can raise a river from its bed and make boulders fly and even do magic without—"

"*Sylvie*. Enough." I squeeze her shoulder and glance furiously at Lachlan.

"Do you not see the pain you cause me?" He gives an innocuous shrug. "I find a little girl lost on the moors, and I save her, and yet *I'm* the villain?"

I turn to Sylvie. "Did he touch you, or do anything—?"

"He was *going* to show me some magic, until you interrupted," she says. "He's a Weaver like us!"

"Indeed," agrees Lachlan, eyes glinting. "Watch closely, little Miss North."

Before I can get a word out, his quick fingers twist his silver threads, and with a sigh, Sylvie slumps to her knees, then curls up like a sleeping cat.

I cry out and catch her, checking for a pulse.

"She's only sleeping," Lachlan says. "And I assure you, she is entirely unharmed."

Slowly, I reach for my spools.

Lachlan gives an imperious click of his tongue. "You know you cannot best me in a battle of threads, Rose Pryor."

I try anyway, thread hissing as I wrench it loose. But I don't even have time to break a length of it off, because Lachlan twists his fingers in the air, Weaving without thread. Invisible hands take hold of my hair and drag me down, bashing my head against the ground. I cry out, grasping at the white carpet, tears pricking my eyes as the roots of my hair scream in pain.

"What do you want with Sylvie?" I gasp out.

"I am telling you the truth when I say I found her. And what a *fascinating* creature she is."

I look at Sylvie, unable to reach her for the spell gripping my hair. She lies so still, her face porcelain, her dark curls unbound and spilling over the carpet. She is dressed today in a white frock, lace down the front and grass stains on the skirt.

"Where are all your fae?" I demand. "Why is the castle empty?"

"The hour is late," he replies. "Events move apace, and I have dispatched my people to the four winds, to prepare themselves and gather the rest of our kin."

"What does that mean? What are you plotting now?"

"Were you going somewhere?" Lachlan catches my question and turns it back on me, like a knife plucked from my hand. "You are dressed for travel."

Did he know I would come to him today? Did he know what I intended to say? He couldn't have, and yet why else would he have lured Sylvie to the edge of the ward, where he could lay hands on her? I cannot believe his finding her was a mere accident.

"Do you intend to use her as leverage against her brother?" I ask.

His eyes narrow. "That depends, I think, on what *you* came here to say."

My skin heats. "I—"

Lachlan twists his invisible threads again, and the cords of magic seize my hair and drag me to his feet. Gasping with pain, I push myself up, only to feel his cold fingers under my chin. He raises me to my knees and bends close, the tip of his nose grazing my cheek as he puts his icy lips to my ear.

"I tried to do things the civil way. But now I see I must resort to more brutal methods."

My voice flutters weakly. "Let. Me. *Go.*"

His teeth seem to sharpen into points as he hisses, "Do you really think you can still walk away? After all I've invested in you—the gowns, the shoes, the thread, not to mention the *time*? Do you think it will be so easy for me to find another blushing maid with which to ensnare Conrad North? No, it must be *you*. You have the Gatekeeper's confidence—even, dare I say it, his heart." He puts his face against mine and inhales deeply. "I can *smell* him on you. And yet you think to *walk away?*" His laugh pelts the air like sleet. "You would not make it ten steps before one of my fae snapped you in half, witch."

The breath leaves my lungs in a rush. He brought me here for one purpose, and he will tolerate no insubordination. And he will use any means he must. His people are dying. Of course he will not let his plans be stymied by the conscientious objections of a common schoolteacher.

Did I truly dream I could escape him? In my twelve years of being haunted by him, did I never learn my lesson? This is the creature who killed Conrad's father, who had a knife put to Conrad's throat when he was a child. I've seen him lie and manipulate and use, use, *use* everyone around him, feeding them to the fires of his rage until he's built himself into an all-devouring inferno.

Such devils always come for their due.

All my plans crumble to ash, like cheap string burned through before it can complete its spell. In the back of my mind, I hear my aunt's hollow, mocking laughter.

My eyes close. I draw a shuddering breath, and then release it.

"All right," I whisper. "You win."

He cocks his head, waiting.

"On one condition," I continue, and the words burn through my tongue like hot coals. I spit them out anyway. "If I bring you the branch and you dethrone Morgaine, you will give the Norths to me. Swear they shall not be harmed or touched in any way. Swear you will not let the queen harm them either. You will do all within your power to see that they are safe."

His expression doesn't change, but his eyes seem to gleam with cold disdain. He drops me at last and flings his arms over the sides of his chair, his long pale fingers dangling like icicles. "Are you reneging on our previous agreement?"

I sit back on my heels, hands clenched on my knees. "I am asking . . . I am *begging* for new terms."

"Renegotiation was never an option. So I ask you again: Are you breaking our original contract?"

I look down at Sylvie. She looks so young asleep, her face unlined by trouble. Will she remember any of this tomorrow?

"I'd lose my magic," I whisper. "For good."

"And you'd secure my promise not to harm your precious mortal Norths instead."

His eyes are as expressionless and ancient as two frozen mountain lakes. The Lachlan who greeted me in London weeks ago is slowly disappearing. He is less and less recognizable every time I see him, as what I know now to be his true self—Manannán the Briar King—is emerging. And that creature is utterly a stranger, unpredictable and terrible.

I cannot believe I ever pitied him.

I look down at my hands, at my fingers, nimble and quick from the thousands of spells they have woven.

But then I close my eyes and think of Sylvie, tearstained but triumphant in the road outside Blackswire as her tormentors fled. I think of Conrad, barefoot in his kitchen, telling me he'd do anything for his little sister.

I never had anyone like that, who would have died for me. My uncle had liked me well, but I wasn't with him long enough to form much of a bond. I barely recall my parents, who I am sure loved me, but who were stolen from me so early their faces are watery blurs in my memory.

But Conrad and Sylvie . . .

I could set them both free, if I were willing to pay the price for their freedom. They would never have to fear Morgaine or Lachlan or any other faerie. They could leave this place, that crumbling old house, and find a new and better life. With Morgaine dethroned, Conrad's duties to her would end. And Lachlan would be bound by his vow to never touch them.

I came here to break my vow, in order to be free of Lachlan and his schemes. But he has cut off my last escape route, and now I see only one choice before me:

I must sell my soul to him all over again, only this time with much higher stakes.

With a long, slow sigh, I take a spool of thread from my pocket and unwind a strand, feeling it run over my fingers, small and fragile. How easily it can break, yet how easily it can become anything: a sword, a shield, a suit of armor. In that slender and delicate thread, the whole of my being sings.

Closing my hand over the spool, I hand it to Lachlan.

"Faerie," I whisper, "I break our bargain."

With breath held, I knit my fingers together and hold them to my stomach, waiting for . . . *something*. A twist of pain, a tingle over my skin, some physical, undeniable evidence of what I've just surrendered.

Nothing happens. Perhaps that is how magic dies, then—in silence, without a single note of farewell. It seems more cruel than the sharpest pain.

Lachlan's countenance darkens; I think he did not believe I would actually do it. But he takes the spool, his fingers searing mine for a moment, and then he pulls off a length.

"Then I vow to you this, Rose Pryor: I'll not harm or in any way exert my will over your precious mortal Norths, *if* you bring me a branch of the Dwirra Tree by midnight tonight. Succeed, and you will go free. Fail, and I will spare none of you."

I cannot speak; I can only nod. Midnight—that is no time at all. But what can I do, with Sylvie lying here, both of us wholly in his power?

He Weaves the vowknot, a complex web spun between his hands and mine binding our oaths, then breathes a little magic into it, and it is done. Ashes trickle through our fingers.

Tears burn in my eyes. I am nothing to him. I have always been nothing to him. And now I have proved him right, groveling before him, defeated and begging. He's taken my magic, my integrity, and now my pride. I wonder what more is left, and what more he will take.

"The clock's ticking, my dear," Lachlan says. "There's really not much time for sulking."

Then he lifts my hand, opens it, and places the spool in my palm.

"K-keep it," I say, unable to keep the tremor out of my voice. "I don't need it anymore."

He only leans back, his arm slung across the back of the chair. "Do you really think you can bring me that branch without it?"

"I'll find a way."

He shakes his head. "I'm not taking your magic from you, girl, not yet."

"But . . ." I clench the spool. "What are you saying? I broke our agreement. My magic was the collateral."

"No, it wasn't."

"Yes it was! I said . . ."

"*I swear on my heart,*" he says mockingly, mimicking a child's high-pitched voice.

My voice fades as I realize my error.

Cold, choking horror clots my throat. My body seems to sink, heavy as lead.

He is a card charlatan, performing sleight of hand at every turn, always hiding his truths and purposes and only revealing them when it suits him, and even then, I can never trust my eyes.

"And so it is your heart you leave behind."

He stretches out his hand, tenses his fingers—and I scream as a torrent of pain opens in my chest. Letting go of Sylvie, I curl up on the ground, certain I am dying, wishing I were already dead.

It was not my magic I put up as collateral. At least, not according to *his* interpretation.

It was my *life*.

He holds my heart on a string, my life's thread his to snip at the time of his choosing.

The pain fades, but the echoes of it remain, reverberating through my body and sending spasms through my bones. I remain locked into a fetal position, breathing raggedly, the tears I'd held back now flowing freely.

Lachlan leans over me, putting his hand on my head as if I were a dog.

"There, there," he says, but there is no soothing note in his voice, only terrible, hollow indifference. "Play nicely and there will be no need to harm you."

"You *bastard*," I choke out.

"Every choice has consequences, my dear, and make no mistake about what you chose here today: Your heart belongs to me, and with it, your magic, your freedom, your *life*. The only thing saving you right now is the fact that you may be of some use to me yet."

He pulls me up by my chin, till I'm on my knees, trembling and horrified. "Now bring me what I desire, dear Rose, or I'll have no more use for you at all."

CHAPTER THIRTY

I carry Sylvie halfway back to Ravensgate with no aid from my magic; my chest still radiates pain from Lachlan's twisted demonstration. She seemed not very heavy at first, no more than a few skeins of cloth, but the further I walk the heavier she becomes until at last, I sink to my knees and lay her carefully on the grass. It is an open spot, with a great view of the land around, the forest outside Blackswire a dark smudge on the horizon. To our left, the hills are still blackened and scorched by the fire Tarkin started and which Conrad put out, but the first new blades of grass are starting to soften the charred land. The moor is awakening from its wintry dormancy, adding new shades of green to its quilt of browns and golds and reds. Fresh growth pushes up through damp soil, curious and bright, providing a soft carpet for Sylvie to lie on.

Out of breath, I sit beside her with my back against a rock and stare up at the blue sky, where fragments of cloud glide smoothly on a high wind. Their shadows run over the earth, pools of deep blue gray ever shifting, strange to watch. It is as lovely a day as one could ask for, the temperature pleasantly cool, the wind lazy and low, ruffling the tufted golden grasses in a perfunctory fashion.

None of it does anything to soothe the tempest in my breast.

Stupid.

Stupid, stupid, *stupid girl.* My aunt's voice creeps into my thoughts. *You don't deserve magic. Your soul is too twisted, your sins too great. May your threads be your curse as you have been mine.*

I draw one hand up, place it over my pounding, aching heart. My weary, battered heart, beating away despite all the torment my naivety and foolishness has inflicted upon it. I wish I could pull it from behind my ribs and cradle it in my hands like a wounded bird; I wish I could set it free, watch it soar across the moors.

I might have been free, if Lachlan had not had Sylvie to leverage me. Whether he'd known I'd intended to break my vow today or not, I suppose the end result is the same. While I'd been pondering my escape, waffling in indecision, he'd already been in motion, laying down the final pieces of his plan. Putting me in an impossible corner, cutting off my last avenue of escape.

I try to imagine why he hadn't simply kept Sylvie and used her as a hostage to control Conrad. It makes little sense, but that only puts me on my guard. Lachlan cannot touch a thing without tying a dozen strings to it, to turn it to his use.

After a few minutes, I gather enough strength—and courage—to attempt a Weave. The magic comes when I call it, but only a thin stream of it, a strained trickle where it had once come in a rush. It takes all my effort to channel it into my smoke knot, which I have strung on my pegboard. The threads catch and hold the energy, then dissolve to ash, the magic converted into a pillar of magenta smoke that twists high into the air. I can only hope it will be a large enough signal to catch Conrad's eye, wherever he is. Then, exhausted, I lean back and close my eyes, too tired to even think of attempting another spell, or carrying Sylvie any further.

She wakes some ten minutes later, with a soft exhalation of surprise. I sit up and watch her very carefully, as she rubs the haze of Lachlan's spell from her eyes and looks around.

"Oh," she says. "I fell asleep!"

"What were you doing out here?" I ask gingerly. "What do you remember?"

She stares at me, her eyes still a bit vacant, but there is no flash of remembrance in her, no sudden gasp as she recalls the faerie lord who gave her tea and strawberries.

"I . . . ran away," she begins. "I was angry at Connie."

"And?"

"And . . ." She frowns, as if encountering a foggy patch in her memory. "I must have got tired. I must have laid down."

"Indeed you did." Memory-altering magic, much like glamours, is a fickle thing, and does not stand up well to pressure. Prod the holes in your memory hard enough and the magic will collapse like a castle made of sand. "Come home, Sylvie. Your brother loves you with all his heart, magic or no magic."

Tears glisten in her eyes. "I love him too, more than anything. I just wish he would understand me."

I squeeze her hand. "He does, better than you know."

Moments later, Conrad thunders up on Bell, his eyes finding Sylvie at once. The blood drains from his face and he flings himself at her, gathering her up and checking her all over for injury, despite her annoyed protests.

"What's the matter with you, Connie?" she asks, shoving him away. "I'm all right."

"What have I told you about wandering off? There are—"

"Highwaymen, aye, I know," she drones. "Perhaps I wished to join their band."

He groans, then glances at me in silent query. I stare back blandly and tell him how I found her asleep on the moor, safe and sound, and that all his worries had been for naught.

He knocks at my door that evening.

With a shiver, I put my shawl over my gown and go to the door. I hesitate a moment, my hand against it.

"Rose?"

I flinch away.

His voice is soft and cautious. "I know it's late, but you didn't come to dinner, and I wanted to be sure you were feeling well. And I . . . have a gift for you."

I glance at the tray of uneaten mince pie Mrs. MacDougal had delivered to me. I'd had no appetite for food, and even less for company. *His* company, in particular. I can't trust myself around him anymore; I'm not at all sure whether I might hex him or kiss him. And after the violent turn in my fortunes today, my greatest fear was that I'd blurt it all out, tell him everything, and earn his eternal hatred.

"I was just going to bed," I say. A lie, of course. I was about to climb out the window and set off for the stone circle, to find my way into Elfhame by whatever means necessary. The clock on the wall ticks out the remaining hours of my life, every second making Lachlan's string around my heart tighten.

"Oh." He sounds disappointed. "Well. Tomorrow, then. My apologies."

He begins walking away.

I rest my head against the door and let out a breath, my pulse drumming in my ears. Then I pull it open.

"Conrad."

He turns, his face brightening. He's combed his hair and put on a clean coat and kilt, even had his shoes shined. He looks a proper laird.

I bite my lip, torn between the ticking of the clock and the warmth in his eyes.

"Come in," I say at last.

Conrad steps into my room. I face him, wondering if he can hear the hammering of my heart. Just being this close to him is like standing by an open furnace. Heat warms my skin; the hairs on my arms stand on end. He smells of hay and horse beneath the bergamot of his shaving soap.

"I brought you something." He takes a small box from his pocket. But then his eyes fasten on something folded on the dresser by the window, and he slides the box back into his coat. "Wait a moment. Is that . . . ?"

I suck in a breath, about to stop him, but he's already moving across the room. I still my hands and wait as he picks up the folded cloth and lets it unfurl between his hands.

The ever-present worry lines in his brow ease for once as a look of realization, then wonder, steals over his face. The knitted fabric bunches in his hands as he lowers them to gaze at me.

"My mother's shawl," he says.

"Yes . . ." I reply haltingly. I'd planned for him to find it after I departed, a farewell gift . . . and an apology. Now I can only watch helplessly as he surveys my handiwork, the result of many late hours' toil by candlelight in my room.

The colors are vibrant again after a gentle washing, the dust rinsed from its fibers. Threads of yellow, blue, green, and red swirl and dance across the shawl, a dizzying chaos of color. The longer I stare at it, the more the chaos reveals order, the riot of threads transformed into intricate flowers and vines, like a garden slowly coming into focus.

"I should have asked," I say. "Before I touched it. I apologize if I overstepped."

He says nothing for a long moment. He pulls the shawl through his hands, studying the patterns. "You repaired it."

"Yes. I think a mouse had been at the edges, and half of it had come undone. But I was able to find the pattern and knit it back together."

I watch, resisting the anxious urge to wring my hands as he sits on the velvet settee under the window. My eyes flit again to the clock, the seconds draining away.

The shawl ripples across Conrad's thighs and spills over his knees. His large hand smooths the fabric as if it were delicate gossamer at risk of tearing with his touch. It won't. I was meticulous with my work, knitting strength back into the threads, restoring the pattern to its original durability.

"It's been years since I . . ." He raises the shawl to his lips and breathes it in. "It still carries her scent."

I nod. I'd been careful to use no soaps on it, hoping to preserve the gentle fragrance of jasmine that had been embedded in the fibers.

"What do they mean?" he asks. "Are they spells?"

I sit delicately beside him, intensely aware of the inches between us, and trace the whirling patterns that curl around the edges of the scarf. They are mesmerizing, reminiscent of Sanskrit, but all formed from a single continuous line.

"Not spells," I reply quietly. "I puzzled over them for a while until I realized what they were. I had a teacher in the Order who specialized in hidden Weaving languages, used in times and places where magic has been forbidden in the past. It was a way of communicating safely between Weavers. I believe your mother's people used something similar to the Weaving dialects of the northern Indian subcontinent, and if I am correct, then this appears to be a record of your mother's travels."

His eyes lift to mine, wide and hungry. "How do you mean?"

The clock's hands creep onward, its ticking a hammer against my skull. But Conrad is looking at me with such desperation. He reminds me of Sylvie that night I caught her Weaving, begging for magic. Pleading for answers.

Once again, I find myself torn between the teacher and the Weaver. My two halves have been at constant odds since the moment I arrived at Ravensgate.

"Well, look here." I scoot closer and spread the shawl so it covers both our laps like a treasure map. "See, this pattern marks her birth in Turkey, but she traveled all through Europe and the Mediterranean before coming to the British Isles. Each section of the design corresponds to a different country." I point out each one woven into the scarf, tracing the journeys of Vera North through Damascus, Crete, Rome, Paris, Lisbon, and more. But after a while, I become conscious of Conrad's eyes on me, and not the fabric.

I pause, looking up at him, and find myself unprepared for the heat of his gaze. His eyes catch the lamplight, threads of gold twining through his irises. His thigh rests against mine, the heat of him sending warmth rolling up my hip to pulse in my belly. I feel nearly sick with it, the quiet, soft nearness of him making me lightheaded.

"You did this for me?" he asks softly.

The warmth in my abdomen travels up my neck as I look down at the scarf. "I suppose I've a weakness for tattered, forgotten things. I couldn't bear to see it left to unravel."

He watches me still, the crackling fire and the ticking clock the only sounds in the room.

"You are a North, Conrad, and this manor is your home." I slide my hand over the record of Vera's travels until my little finger comes to rest against his. "But this is your story too. A story woven in thread across continents."

Breathless and still, I watch his little finger graze over mine, his knuckle exploring the sensitive skin of my fingertip.

I clear my throat. "You, er, said you had a gift for me?"

He blinks, pulling back as if freed from a spell. "Yes. Yes, of course."

He raises the little box, extending it to me. I stare at it, and my stomach turns over.

"'Tis an apology gift," he says, his tone rough at the edges. He does not quite meet my eyes. "For being such an arse, after . . . the revel. And it is a thank-you gift. For everything you've done. In finding Sylvie. And for the house."

"For the *house*."

His voice is as soft as a settling leaf. His fingers curl in the scarf. "And for me."

I look down at the box; it's tied with a thin gold ribbon. "This isn't necessary."

"Well, are you going to open it, or shall I cast it into the fire and be off?"

"Fates, must you be so dramatic?" I pull the ribbon apart and tuck it in my nightgown pocket, then lift the lid of the box.

And gasp.

"Is this . . . ? *No.* It can't be." I touch the slender skein of yellow-gold thread. "Conrad. *Conrad.*"

I jolt to my feet and begin pacing, my heart thudding against the wall of my chest.

He looks at me shyly, a boyish flush to his cheeks. "Do you like it?"

"I—I'm not even sure I should be touching it." But I do, reverently, letting it slide over my hands and savoring its smoothness, its weightlessness. The fibers in the thread are finer than the hairs on a newborn's head.

"Sea silk," Conrad says. "The rarest and most powerful thread in the world."

"I know," I whisper.

I remember the sea silk I saw in the King Street Threadshop, kept under glass with its own guard to stand watch over it.

The skein in the box Conrad gave me is thirty times the length that one was.

"This is worth a king's ransom," I say. "Conrad, how did you—?"

"Morgaine's had it lying around for centuries. It was an easy matter to slip it in my pocket. She won't even remember she ever had it." He looks down at his mother's shawl, his thumb tracing the hidden language in its hem.

I suppress a shiver, imagining Lachlan's laughter. If Conrad would steal sea silk for me, would he steal a branch from the Dwirra tree?

No. I won't find out. It won't come to that.

"What on earth am I to do with it?" I ask.

"Save it. For something special."

My voice sticks in my throat. I can only shake my head, letting the thread fall back into its box with liquid fluidity, where it coils like spun gold. I cannot take my eyes off it. I cannot quell the butterflies panicking in my stomach.

This is not the sort of thing you give a guest. This isn't the sort of thing you give your sister or mother or best friend.

This is the sort of gift you give a queen . . . or a lover.

I cross the room and sit heavily on the armchair, putting down the box because my hands are shaking, and I fear I'll drop it. Leaning forward, elbows on knees, I run my hands through my hair.

"Oh, Fates," I whisper.

"You have no idea what you've done, do you?" He rises to his feet and looks at me directly, his eyes fevered. The shawl drapes over his arm. "You've made me *want* things; don't you realize that? Things I should never have wanted. How much easier my life would be if I had never met you!"

I stare at him.

He growls, rubbing his face. "That's not what I . . . I didn't mean that. It's only that—damn it, Rose, why is it so difficult to speak around you? You've ruined everything: my plans, my expectations, my very *idea* of the world." He raises the shawl, giving it a small shake. "You made me want to go beyond the borders that have measured out my existence, to experience things I never dared dream . . . *Rose.*"

I am a curse on his lips, and a prayer.

"This place is too small for me now," he says helplessly. "Do you understand that? I can never go back to the way things were. I was content, and you rattled me out of my contentedness. I was safe, and you made me want to fling myself off cliffs to see if I might fly. Never did I ask anything for myself, until you came along, with sunlight in your hair, and inspired in me a great and terrible selfishness."

"What are you saying?"

"I'm saying that just for once, I'd like to do what makes *me* happy." He turns away, pacing restlessly, eyes boring into the carpet, as if searching for words among the curling shapes there.

"What are you asking of me?"

"I'm asking . . . What about you? Might we both want the same thing? Is that why you stayed here, even after learning the truth about me, when anyone else would have fled to the other side of the world?" He stops and gazes at me from across the room, like a starved pauper begging me to save him. "Might I be half so constant in your thoughts as you are in mine?"

I rise with a rustle of skirts; my own shawl slips, and I let it pool on the chair. The box of thread I set on the table.

Conrad walks to me slowly, his eyes gauging my expression, searching for my answer. But what do I tell him? That yes, he *is* constant in my thoughts, that I've begun to expect his footstep outside my door for nights now, hoping to hear his soft "Good night" through my door? That I've come to anticipate our nightly trysts, eager not just to teach him, but to watch him work, his brow furrowed in concentration as he tries to make sense of the thread in his fingers? That I've come to dread his going away, and when he leaves, that I long for his return? That I relive our kiss every night until I'm soaked in sweat and half mad with need?

How do I tell him that I am his enemy's tool? That my heart is in the clutches of the monster who killed his father?

My kiss would be poison to him.

"We lied to Morgaine about what we were to each other," he says. "But what if . . . what if our lie became our truth?"

He stops a step away from me. If I moved a little closer, our toes would touch and our breaths would meet. Even here, I can feel his heat, see the expanding of his pupils. His eyes are soft as dark, sweet honey.

He is still waiting for my answer, dangling at the end of my string, his entire world holding its breath for me.

If I just took one step forward, if I only tilted my face, he would kiss me. I feel the certainty of it in my marrow. The smallest movement, the slightest invitation, and he would open to me like a leaf unfurling to the sun.

"Conrad . . . there is something I must confess."

"Confess that you hate me, and I will go now and never ask again." The shawl slides from his grasp and drapes over the footboard of the bed. Then his hands take my waist, drawing me closer, forcing me to tip my head back to hold his gaze. "Confess you do not feel as I feel."

I cannot, and he knows it.

His hands rise up my bodice, his thumbs tracing slow, tentative circles, small questions that sink through the fabric of my dress and curl like fire over my skin. Even if I told him I hated him—*I don't*—that I did not want this—*I do, oh Fates, I do*—my lies would be betrayed by my body, which trembles at his every touch.

We turn slowly, eyes locked, until my hips rest against the edge of the bedframe. Then he lifts me, gentle as if I were a spring lamb, and sets me on the bed.

It is like the faerie revel, only this time, the urges controlling my limbs come from within, not from some cobweb of spells. It is my own heart driving me, my own desire flushing my skin with heat and desperate, primal need. I need *him*, his touch, his lips on my bare skin.

My hands slide up his arms, his neck, to his face. My fingertips trace the rough stubble on his jaw and the softer skin under his eyes, exploring every inch of his face as if he were a complex pattern I were trying to unravel. The details of him hold all my attention: the creases of his dimples; the small bump on the bridge of his nose; the coarse, dark hairs of his eyebrows. I sink my fingers into his hair, pulling him closer.

His hands similarly explore my body, the ridge of my spine and the curve of my hips. He smooths my skirt over my thighs, and I shudder, my hands knotting in his hair. My knees fall apart, and he fills the space between them, and still, still it is not enough. I need him *closer*. Warm and dark as embers, his eyes trace my features as if I were the first human he has ever seen and my every change of expression were a wonder to him.

I have never been touched like this. Held so tenderly, so intimately. It is the sort of thing the older girls whispered about in school, between giggles and blushes. Those were never the sort of conversations I felt part of, for I could never imagine being *wanted* in such a way. I closed myself to the possibility of it, resigned to a life that would be as solitary as its beginnings.

But oh, Fates, the possibilities that flare in my mind now.

They bring heat rushing to my cheeks and neck and stomach, my skin drawing tight with feverish want. I pull him closer until his body folds over mine, and I am enclosed in his arms with his mouth on my neck. He kisses my throat, and a soft sigh slides from my lips. His nimble fingers trace up the buttons on the back of my dress, undoing buttons one by one, until the fabric parts and I feel his palm against my naked back . . .

When the time is right, hisses Lachlan in my memory, *all you'll have to do is ask.*

The faerie's voice strikes me like an arrow, and I gasp.

Fates damn me, I never meant for any of this to happen. How was I to know, when I found him unconscious on the side of the road weeks ago, that I would become his undoing? How was I to know that as our souls were slowly being knit together, that I would be the very instrument by which Lachlan destroyed him?

Everything was so much clearer before. I knew what I wanted. What I *needed*. And I wasn't going to let anyone get in my way.

But now here I am, with him looking at me as if he were the desert and I the rain. And there he is, ready to give me the world if I asked for it.

It is just as his lips bump softly to mine, the first, tender invitation to a kiss, that I push him away, my hands on his chest.

Conrad blinks, his brow knitting inquisitively. "Rose . . . ?"

"The Briar King sent me here," I whisper. "He sent me to help him destroy Morgaine."

Conrad doesn't move; not a single feature on his face changes. He only stares at me in exactly the same way, as if he's been turned to stone. For half a heartbeat I think perhaps he did not hear me, that I only thought the words and never spoke them. Fates damn me! I did not intend to blurt the truth out like that, but to ease into it—to explain my reasons, my desperation, to make him understand I had no other choice. I was driven by forces more powerful than me. I am no more than a pawn.

But then, I know these would only be more lies, as much to myself as to him.

I had a choice from the very beginning, the moment Lachlan put his cold hand on my shoulder in my uncle's study and told me his terms. I had a choice then, and fear made it for me. Years went by and I thought I would escape the consequences of my choice, but when he appeared in my boarding house, I'd made *another* choice, and again fear spurred me in the wrong direction. The entire road from there was paved with wrong choices and I, driven by fear, leaped headlong from one to the next. I cannot put all the blame on Lachlan. As he has told me time and time again—*I* chose all of this.

When the change in Conrad does come, it is slow and terrible, like watching the sun go dark at midday. The corners of his mouth sink lower, and shadows crawl into the hollows of his face. The very room seems to darken around him, the fire in the hearth shrinking to embers and the candle flames flickering. A shudder rolls through him as he steps back, his hands withdrawing from my waist.

I see every moment we ever spent together scroll through his mind, every touch between us, every soft word, every lie I told. I can *see* his opinion of me shift like a rockslide, slow at first, a few loose stones tumbling, but then faster and faster, until it is a thunderous roar echoing through him.

He inhales sharply, the first breath he's taken since I spoke, and steps back again. He looks at me as if I'd stuck a sword in his belly, with my hand still upon the hilt, twisting.

"I have no excuse," I say, hot tears burning in my eyes. "Only my story. I was eight years old when I met him. I was alone and terrified for my life, and he helped me. He offered me a bargain and I took it. And now he's come back for his due and I—"

"The truth knot," he says, his voice a strangled breath. "No one could have beaten it."

"I did tell you the truth then, or at least . . . enough of it. I didn't know who you were, Conrad, I swear. He never told me about you being the Gatekeeper, or that he was this Briar King. He intended it that way, so that I would win your confidence even without realizing I was doing it."

"My *confidence*," he scoffs, in a horrid dry voice, his hand dashing caustically through the air. Here is a Conrad I've never met before, not even the morning after the faerie revel. He is wholly the Gatekeeper now, defender of Elfhame and bondsman of the faerie queen.

He is her weapon as I am the Briar King's; we are the swords they raised against one another.

I slide off the bed and raise my hands beseechingly. "Conrad, I regret every second of it. I know it is no excuse. I deserve every ounce of your hatred. I know that I am the villain here. But I swear, had I known the depth of Lachlan's—the Briar King's—cruelty and cunning, I would never have agreed to this. He is not what I thought him to be."

Conrad's acidic laugh underlines the irony of that statement. He turns away, his anger an iron rod down his back. Around him, the air simmers, and a candle at his elbow flickers out with a sputter of hot wax.

He's drawing in energy, just like that night in the stable.

"Did he send you here to kill me?" he asks.

"No! In fact, if I fulfill my mission, he's sworn that you and Sylvie—"

"Sylvie!" He whirls, and the door creaks and slams against the wall; the drapes around the bed and windows gust as if on a strong wind. Sparks dance from the fire and skitter over the carpet, singeing the fibers where they land.

"Conrad, be careful! You're channeling—"

"What of Sylvie?" he demands. "What business does he have with her?"

I open my mouth to tell him how I found her with Lachlan only this morning, but then clamp my teeth together. That will only make him lose control completely; he'll burn up this room and Ravensgate itself, all that wild magic rushing into his veins. I have to calm him down, get him to release it safely. My hands fumble for a spool from my pocket, but he knocks it away as he advances on me. I back up until I hit the wall, and he looms terribly, his eyes burning with golden heat, his teeth bared.

"Tell me what he wants with Sylvie."

"Nothing!" I say. "He swore to not harm her or you if I bring him a branch of the Dwirra Tree by midnight. Don't you see? We could set you free for good!"

He lets out a short breath and steps back, still staring at me as if I'd stabbed him. The room settles slightly, the candle flames still fluttering but the drapes falling still.

"A branch from the Dwirra. Why? How does that help him?"

"He said it would restore his power. And, Conrad, if he dethrones Morgaine, you and Sylvie will be free. You won't be the Gatekeeper anymore. You can leave this place."

"And you trust this creature to keep his word?" He says it as though I would be a fool to do so, and I suppose I have proved myself to be no more than that. But I nod anyway. What other choice do I have?

"Help me," I whisper, my heart pulsing as though Lachlan were listening in on us now, approving my words. I feel like a puppet as I step forward—his hands lift my hands in supplication; his whisper in my ear softens my gaze; his magic pulls a tear from my eye and sends it rolling down my cheek.

"We can all be free," I say. "If you'll just help me."

Sweat dampens his collar. His face, his neck, even his lips have gone pale, those lovely, soft lips which only minutes ago had been about to open to mine.

How terribly the wicked truth cuts; how mightily it transforms.

He will do it, I think. He will see the same path I see, leading us all out of this land of fae and duty and curses. Together we will find our way out.

But then, "No," he says. "You understand nothing. Not about me or Sylvie or Morgaine or the Briar King. He is not trustworthy. And Morgaine is not the monster you think she is. And Sylvie . . ." He shakes his head. "No."

"Conrad!"

"Enough!" he roars, and suddenly he channels into a knot he had hidden in his pocket. Somehow he'd woven it there, one handed, while I was too distracted to notice.

It's an immobilization spell, one *I* taught him, and it pins me to the wall, my hand slamming into the wainscoting. A brass sconce unfurls to wrap around my wrist and hold it fast above my head. The other is seized by a peeling of wood trim from the mantel, secured wide from my body. The magic releases then, but though I can twist and buck, I cannot pull my hands free.

He watches me struggle with a strange look on his face, half fury, half regret. Perhaps there is a part of him which does believe me, but it is not strong enough.

"What is his plan?" he asks.

"I don't know! He tells me so little. Put a truth knot on me if it will convince you."

He shakes his head, his eyes going to the window and the black velvet moors.

"When you get yourself free," he murmurs, "you should leave. This time, I mean it, Rose. Get away from this house."

"But—"

"You don't understand, do you?" He looks back at me, his eyes agonized. "What you've done, what you've cost me? I put myself on the line for you. I gave her my word."

I stare at him. "What do you mean?"

"I must go to Morgaine," he says. "If the Briar King has been behind our defenses this long, she needs to know. She needs time to prepare."

"No! Wait! Conrad—"

"I have a job to do. I never should have thought that I could . . ."

"There's still a way out," I whisper.

"No. Mrs. MacDougal was right," he murmurs. "You were trouble all along, and I . . . I wanted too much."

He sweeps out of the room, still drawing in ropes of energy, and with his exit, every candle in the room and even the fire goes out, as if he pulled out all the air with him. He leaves me in darkness, tethered to the wall, my heart ripping in two.

CHAPTER THIRTY-ONE

I shout and kick the wall, but neither Sylvie nor the MacDougals come running. I wonder if he placed a muffling charm outside my room, or a sleeping charm on theirs, to keep them from hearing my pleas.

In either case, I realize I'm the only one who can possibly free myself. I look around at everything within my grasp; there is nothing. Conrad's mother's shawl has slipped off the footboard and piled on the floor, its threads just out of reach. My hands are securely fastened, and though I pull and twist and curse, they will not come free. I keep trying until my wrists are raw and stinging.

Then, gasping out a sob, I slump over, strands of my hair stuck to my lips and my neck from sweat.

What will Morgaine do to him?

He may claim she is not the villain I think her to be, but I saw the dread in his eyes when he turned to go. She took one of his ancestor's *eyes* for simply trying to run away. He swore to take responsibility for me, and yet I fooled him. His love for me put her rule at risk. What punishment will she exact? An eye? A hand? His life?

I have to reach Elfhame and explain myself. Perhaps I can offer her information on Lachlan in exchange for Conrad. More deals. More bargains. Fates, I'm a fool, but I am a desperate one.

With renewed vigor I struggle, thrashing and yanking my wrists until they bleed. Finally, panting and sore, my heart a hot coal in my breast, I force myself to draw even breaths and think.

There is not a chance of reaching my threadkit; the box lies out of my reach by nearly a yard. Nor could I reach the tasseled edge of the Anatolian carpet, or the ribbon tied around the window drapes.

Only one potential material lies within my grasp, I realize.

Steeling myself, I grasp several strands of hair and yank them loose. The pain is sharp but fleeting, and nothing to the pounding mallet of my heart. My ribs feel like they're beginning to splinter, as if one more fit of pain might shatter them entirely and pierce my heart through with their jagged ends.

Concentrating hard, eyes shut against the darkness, I rely only on my sense of touch, on my five nimble fingers and the impossibly fine hairs twisted around them.

The first attempt I fumble at once, and the hairs fall from my fingers without so much as a whisper. Growling, I pull out more. Fates, if at the end of this night I have a bald patch—

Oh, you fool, if there was ever a worse time for vanity . . . !

The next attempt goes better. I manage half a knot before the hair snaps.

Taking a moment to recenter myself, I try again.

I close my eyes and picture the hair, one single strand finer than any thread, pinched between my thumb and forefinger. My wrist stings where it chafed against the manacle of the mangled sconce. I push away the pain, pack it down and stamp on it until it's nothing more than a dull prick at the back of my mind. Slowly, carefully, I catch the hair with my little finger, securing it taut against my palm. Then my middle fingers go to work, dipping, looping, pulling. Twisting themselves as no finger is meant to twist.

I can barely feel the hair at all, so light and thin it is, as insubstantial as the faerie queen's spiderwebs. Will she kill Conrad with magic, I wonder, or will she resort to a more traditional method—a knife, poison, a garrote?

No, no, I cannot lose my focus now.

Third loop from the left. Pull taut. Wind behind middle finger, pull through fifth loop. Pull taut.

It is no complex spell, really; with thread and two hands and good light I could Weave it in a heartbeat. Curse Conrad! He could have at least left me one free hand.

Thread beneath sixth layer. Over the fourth. Pull taut—

The hair snaps.

A feral cry of frustration rips from my throat before I can stop it.

But I still have the rest of the knot woven, and a finger's length of hair left pinched between my thumb and little finger. If I can only manage to loop it over my middle finger . . .

There!

I don't wait a moment to double-check the knot; I channel fast and recklessly, pulling from the ivy just unfurling new leaves outside my window. They wither and go dry, a shoddy bit of work on my part, but I don't care much about the rules right now.

The hair crumbles to ash almost as soon as it flares with magic. That is how thin and poor a material it is. But it works.

The nail holding the sconce to the wall pops loose and drops with a soft *tink* on the floorboards, helped along, no doubt, by my wild thrashing earlier.

With a sob of relief, I pry the wooden manacle off my other hand and then pitch forward onto my knees. It takes me a moment to rise again. I hadn't realized how much strength I'd expended in my struggle, unless my weakness is in part due to the draining of my heart. It pulses red hot as I lurch upright, every beat driving the pain deeper, as if it were working its way to my soul.

"Right," I say through my teeth, as I wrap the ribbons from the drapes around my bloody wrists as makeshift bandages. The sea silk I bind around the left, over the ribbon. "Now for the difficult part."

The circle is deserted when I reach it. Roman dances beneath me, withers shifting as he sidesteps nervously just outside the stones. I slide to the ground and pat his haunch, giving him permission to run home. He bolts with his tail raised like a white silk banner, though he pauses at the tree line to give me a guilty look.

"Get out of here," I say, waving a hand. And either his fear or the empathy knot I tied in his mane does the trick. He vanishes into the trees, a ghost into the night.

The unnatural stillness of the circle is a smothering pall on the air. The stones themselves loom defiantly, mottled gray under the full moon that hangs above. The grass is as thick as fur, silver and long, the stalks already bending beneath pearls of dew. My skirts are soon damp.

The wet grass proves to be my advantage: I see the imprinted traces of Conrad's boots in it. He passed through not long ago and unwittingly left a path for me.

I make my way through the spider-thread wards, careful step by careful step, placing my shoes in Conrad's prints. I brace, ready to be hurled off my feet as I was the first time I snooped around the circle. But I make it through unharmed and let out a relieved breath.

Striding to the center of the circle, I keep my chin high, as if to prove to the stones that I am not afraid. They are like a silent ring of judges, gazing into my soul, my past, my purposes, draining the truth of me from my bones. They are so very impassive, like the Sphinx from the old stories, or the Delphi oracle.

"If you've any wisdom to share," I say, glaring at the largest of them, "don't be stingy about it."

I shiver as I feel the sudden sense of pressure in the air, as if the stones were *leaning* toward me.

On second thought, maybe I ought not provoke them.

Instead, I sink onto the ground, my dirty, damp gray skirt pooling around me. I look up at the stones, the budding branches of the oaks and yews, the soft glow of the moon. The cool air of the forest seeps into my skin and wraps around my heart like a balm. I savor it, drink it in, let it soothe the pain in my wrists and chest.

I think of Conrad North.

I think of him standing in this spot, weeks ago, thread unspooling between his fingers. But I cannot remember the pattern, only the shape of him against the dark, dancing among the stones . . .

Dancing.

I recall with a start when he put his hand on my waist and spun me on the floor of Elfhame, to the furious drumming of the immortal band. That night, beneath the glowing fruit of the Dwirra Tree, he'd been more than a laird—a prince, his hair glittering with faerie dust, his eyes holding secrets like candle flames behind dark windows. How sure of the steps he'd been then, how sure of his place in the dance, even though he'd been not at all sure of me. I think of him that night, remembered through the smoky haze of the fae forgetting spells, so that the edges of the memories are all faded, soft paper handled over many years. I feel the heat of his hand on my waist, the strength of his grip, the command in his eyes. He did not have to intercede for me that night. He could easily have let Morgaine expunge my memory and keep me as her pet or servant or footstool.

But he hadn't.

Instead, he'd risked *his* life to speak for mine. He'd bought my freedom with his troth, and it was my faithlessness and foolish fears which had deceived him, made him think me worthier than I am.

I will not let him die for me.

I will not let these stones outwit me.

With the memory of that dance sharpening in my thoughts, I rise and take up a spool of white thread.

I know that to open the way to the faerie green, Lachlan had told me, *you must pay homage to its queen.*

Now I understand, and I unwind the thread as I begin to dance.

I cannot think beyond the moment, beyond a single step. I don't know the full measure of the faerie's dance, how it begins or how it ends, I only know what it felt like to dance those steps with Conrad holding me fast. I only know how I felt when he bent his head to mine and whispered in my ear, so that I could feel the heat of his breath on my bare neck.

Keep your eyes on me.

I imagine him here with me now, the fire in his tiger eyes, the warmth of his skin, the smell of the juniper in his lapel and his bergamot soap, as he guides me from stone to stone, his hand on mine as thread feeds through my fingers.

No matter what, keep your eyes on me.

The faerie queen had called the revel an "homage," her people's celebration of her rule. I had forgotten, but now the words echo through me again. Of course Lachlan would not know these steps, he who was thrown out of Elfhame on the day Morgaine became its queen. I doubt he would bend his pride to learn them, for it would mean acknowledging the crown on his sister's head. No doubt when *he* ruled Elfhame, the spell was some other form of homage to *him*, a dance or some other pattern that would only be known to those who had paid tribute to him before.

I dance round and round the circle, hardly paying attention to the thread, not thinking of where I will spin next or what stone I will twist my knot around. It just *happens*, the spell part of the dance, the dance part of me.

Soon there is a web strung across the circle, layers of thread glittering like spun silver. The dance takes even these into account, spinning or lowering me just at the right moment, so that I pass within a handsbreadth of the threads without disturbing them.

Faintly, I wonder how I must look. If someone came wandering out of the wood and saw me whirling about in silence, eyes half shut, spinning thread like a spider, they would think me possessed.

The dance is accelerating now, reaching a crescendo. The steady flow of it becomes a heady, tumbling cascade, faster and wilder, more demanding. I must leap over threads, then duck beneath them, keeping my line taut. Some stretch above my head; others so low in the grass I cannot even see them, but the dance knows they are there. The dance guides me deftly over them. I sense now that if I faltered for a second, if I lost even an ounce of trust in my memory of that night, I'd lose all sense of it entirely. The dance would abandon me and leave me standing in the middle of the dark wood with nothing but a pile of strings. It is as much a test of faith as a pattern for magic. It will show me the way, but only if I am worthy of it.

My wrists are feeling the exertion, the bandages loosened by my movements. One ribbon unwinds entirely and drifts to the ground; the other hangs in loose tatters.

I can't stop for them, or for anything else. My heart, strangely, has stopped paining me. I wonder if Lachlan knows I am here and approves of my efforts. Perhaps so long as I stay on his ordained path, it will not trouble me at all.

Ruthlessly, I wrench my thoughts away from the pains, or lack of pain, and scour every conscious thought from my head. I've come too far to fail now due to a wandering mind. I let the dance take full control of my limbs, until I am a puppet operated by memory and instinct alone.

And then, all at once, it is done.

I whirl and then stop, my hands above my head, my feet spread, my chest rising and falling as I pant for breath. The spool in my hand is empty, but the last length of thread is caught between my thumb and forefinger. The spell is complete; all it awaits is magic to fuel it. The dance ended with me in the center of the circle, a spider at the middle of her web, surrounded on all sides by crisscrossing white lines, taut and trembling. My exhalation fogs the air and dissipates into the threads, pale and then gone.

Carefully, I tie off the knot, then let the empty wooden spool drop to the grass. Then I reach wide, take hold of the thread to my right and left, and channel.

The old magic of the forest rises to meet me, as if it had been waiting impatiently for this moment, and my invitation. Like a gust of wind through an open doorway it roars into me, and I gasp.

It has been *years* since I felt a power like this.

Lachlan must have released his hold on me almost entirely, giving me full access to the energy around me for the first time since . . .

Since before I ever met him.

I cannot ever recall a strength like this, a torrent of magic rushing through me, with only the slightest reproach from my heart, just enough of a squeeze to remind me that somewhere, leagues distant, the exiled faerie king is still holding the other end of the string that binds me.

Well, curse Lachlan and his plans. It occurs to me that not once since Conrad left me in my room have I thought of how I'll acquire a branch from the Dwirra.

I'm going to reach Elfhame, I know that now.

And as I release the flood of magic swirling in my heart, my fingertips glowing where it wicks into the threads, I know that when I step through the portal, I will do it not for the faerie king or his followers, or for my stolen heart, or for all the magic in the world. I will do it for the man who gave me silk from the sea. I will save him, as he saved me.

No matter the cost.

No matter what the queen of Elfhame might demand of *me*.

CHAPTER THIRTY-TWO

My second trip through the portal is nothing like the first, for I do not throw myself headlong but rather step through cautiously. I pass through a shimmering film of light, then turn and see it harden into glass, a great round pane held in a silver frame. It is a much faster and more pleasant experience than telepestry, and I cannot help but wonder how the magic of it works. It seems to be another of the secrets Lachlan has hinted at——the powers fae wield that they do not share with us mortals.

I end up not in the Wenderwood, but in the faerie queen's palace, in the chamber where Conrad and I escaped the night of the revel. The portal room is deserted, the empty frames in their alcoves the only witnesses to my arrival. I suppose If I'd not come through at the last minute before, I would never have got lost in those horrid trees, hunted by Morgaine's spider-wolves. I would have arrived here, as the portal intended.

The glass shimmers behind me. Nearly opaque enough to be a mirror, it reflects my pale, startled face back to me, and I see how bedraggled I am, with tears and blood and mud on my dress and arms. I look as if I crawled off a battlefield.

The same warping, impossible hallways wait for me, and I follow blindly, my hand trailing along the left wall so that I do not end up going in circles. Every door I find, I open; all the rooms are deserted, though cluttered with the most absurd collections. Pianofortes and suits of armor, looms of gold and beds of silk, indoor gardens, statues of Greek gods, fountains, piles of exquisite clothing, empty birdcages, burning braziers, crystal jewelry; none of it organized, all of it tarnished and faded.

Stopping short when I reach a mirrored dressing room, I step in and find the first thing I recognize here—the gray silk gown with the skirt layered in gauze petals. Conrad must have brought it back after the revel. Hurriedly I wrench off my torn, bloody dress and put on the gown, then pull white gloves from a drawer and tug those over my sore wrists, all the way up to my elbows. At least I don't look as though I'd been brawling behind a pub. As I finish with a pearl-and-crystal comb to hold up my hair, I glance in the mirrors and think I might just look like a girl capable of bargaining with a faerie queen. The only thing I cannot find are shoes. I leave my filthy boots behind and continue in bare feet.

Hurrying onward, I make out voices echoing ahead, stretched and warped as if heard through a tunnel. I walk more quickly, starting to sweat, my instinct for self-preservation pulling at me like a frightened rider trying to rein in a galloping horse.

What are you doing, you stupid girl? Don't you know what will happen to you? Go back. Go back now!

But I cannot go back. If I did, Lachlan's ultimatum would catch up to me. My time runs out tonight, no matter what I do. So perhaps it is this which gives me the courage to go onward—I have nothing left to lose, but something which I might still save.

The hard wooden floor of the palace begins to squelch under my feet, turning into a path of moss and damp soil. Along the wall sprout ferns, and green vines heavy with purple, bell-shaped flowers wend up the walls and crisscross the ceiling. I brush my hands through them, and they tinkle like chimes and faintly glow at my touch, then fade when I've walked on. The wall begins to break apart from one solid sheet of wood to individual trees, grown so close together I can barely see between them. Are they connected to the Dwirra?

No, that's not why I'm here. Not anymore.

No more passages branch away now; this tree-lined corridor winds round and round with single-minded purpose, sweeping me away to some preordained destination. It seems I am walking in a great spiral like an old Celtic spellknot, the sort I found carved onto the ancient memorial stone where I first taught Sylvie how to Weave.

Then, abruptly, I turn a corner and there they are—Conrad, Morgaine, and *hundreds* of fae.

I pull back sharply, catching my breath, my heart nearly bursting out of my chest. I am tucked behind a wide trunk. Another of equal size stands across from it, their branches forming an ancient doorway.

Peering around more cautiously, I see them: a crowd gathered, facing the throne at the back of the room. Rows of trees form columns down the sides of the hall, and their branches rise into a magnificently vaulted ceiling, the space between them filled with clusters of glowing Dwirra fruits, but unlike the soft pastel lamps I'd seen elsewhere in the World Below, these shine violently red, bathing the room and all in it in a bloody glow.

The throne upon which the faerie queen sits is high above the crowd, at the top of a wide wooden staircase blanketed in mosses and ferns and small white flowers. The seat itself is white wood grown organically out of the tangle of moss-covered roots which undulate around the throne. The back of the seat shoots upward and then branches wide, limbs heavy with leaves and red lamp-fruits. Scraggly beards of moss and ropes of bellflower vines hang from them, forming a green curtain across the back wall.

Morgaine sits imperiously there, her face stone, her back rigid. On her head sits her high, jagged crown, and her red dress shimmers like scales, hugging her form and pooling at her feet. She looks down at Conrad, who is kneeling halfway up the stairs, his head bowed, dressed in a dark fae suit. The crimson light of the fruits shines on his black hair.

"I will ask you only once more, Gatekeeper," Morgaine is saying, her voice reverberating through the great chamber, "how came you by this information?"

"My answer remains the same," Conrad replies, his voice a murmur I can barely make out. "I saw another of his fae on the outskirts. He boasted to me of his master's plans."

"And from this one foolish servant you were able to discern that the Briar King is on the move?"

"I know that he is here, and that this time, he has a plan."

"What plan is that?"

"He wants a branch from the Dwirra Tree. Though I cannot fathom why—"

"A branch from the Dwirra?" Morgaine rises to her feet, so suddenly that the fae in the front rows draw back.

Conrad nods.

Morgaine hisses something in the fae tongue, then descends the stairs and seizes Conrad by his throat. She lifts him with preternatural strength, until he stands on his toes. My hand clenches; I half step through the doorway, still unnoticed.

"Where is she?" Morgaine asks.

Conrad doesn't struggle, but I see his frame stiffen. "Who—"

"The *witch*, boy, the too-clever girl with your heart on a string?"

I shrink back, pressing myself against the tree.

"Did you think me a fool, Connie? Did you think for even a moment that your little charade at my revel could convince me? My mistake was in believing you would discover the truth of her and act accordingly. Not that you would *dare* to hide her from me!"

"Rose has nothing to do with—"

"I knew what she was the moment I laid eyes on her: she was a trap meant for *you*, and I see now that you know it, that you fell for it, and that still you'll try to defend her."

Conrad pulls away; I catch at last a glimpse of his face, just enough to see how pale he is, and yet his eyes are defiant. "She's long gone now, Morgaine. You'll never catch her."

Morgaine strikes him, fast as a lashing snake. Her nails open a deep cut in his cheek.

"Bring me my sword!" she calls out, and a fae bursts forward with a blade in his hand, offering it up to her.

Morgaine looks down at Conrad without an ounce of compassion. "For your crimes, Gatekeeper, I demand an ear. You choose. Right or left."

Conrad blanches. "I—"

"The left ear it is!" Morgaine announces.

Two faeries seize Conrad and shove him to the floor. The queen raises her sword.

"Stop!" I cry. "I'm here! Fates damn you, I am here!"

They all turn: fae and queen and mortal man, to stare at me, a thousand beetle eyes and Conrad's dismayed expression.

"Rose—" he begins, but he is cut short as the queen sweeps by him. The fae part, forming a corridor that leads to me. I feel as small as a sparrow in that grand, ancient doorway, facing down the advancing queen of the immortals, but I keep my chin high and do my level best not to pass out from sheer terror. My heart throbs, as if Lachlan senses my treachery and does not like it, not one bit.

She reaches me faster than I could have anticipated, crossing the hall more quickly than any human could. I brace for her touch, expecting some curse or her silver sword in my belly. But she only stops before me and looms.

"It's not his fault," I say. "I tricked him, but still he came to you to warn you. Don't you see? He would not betray you!"

She only watches me, her green eyes nearly black, sharp as a hawk's. I look around her, to Conrad standing on the stairs, one hand half extended, as if he's afraid of moving beyond that lest he inspire some savage reaction in the queen.

"Your brother sent me to take a branch from the Dwirra to restore his strength."

"To restore his strength," she echoes hollowly.

I nod. "But you see, I have not brought him so much as a twig. The moment Conrad learned my true intentions, he imprisoned me in his manor. He stood by his duty to you, and the only one here who deserves blame is *me*. I am just what you say I am: a liar, a trap, a *tool*, only I did not know the extent of it until recently. But all the fault is my own, not Conrad's. Please—"

I cut short with a gasp of pain.

Morgaine's sword point finds my shoulder; its sharp edge presses into my collarbone, as her eyes flutter briefly closed before opening again. "So that's the way of it, then." She looks at me differently, not with anger, nor with pity. Only . . . blankness, as if I am of no consequence at all. "You foolish child," she murmurs. "Did you know what the cost would be, when you struck your bargain with the King of Exiles?"

I press my hand to my heart.

"How long do you have?" she asks.

"Until midnight," I whisper.

"What?" Conrad's eyes snap to me. "What are you talking about?"

Morgaine shakes her head. Slowly, she lowers the sword, resting its point between her feet. "You poor witless naïf." She turns to two faerie guards. "Lock her away, and let her own mistake do the rest."

"What are you doing?" Conrad cries. "What will you—?"

"Nothing," she says, turning and giving him a hard look. "I need do nothing at all. For in a few hours, she'll be no threat to us anymore. She has sold her heart to the Briar King, and by midnight, she will be dead."

He stares from her to me, his eyes wild with confusion and horror.

"You should be glad, Connie," Morgaine says, her voice flat. "By coming here, the treacherous little witch has touched my merciful side. You may keep your ear, Gatekeeper. This time."

I close my eyes, feeling a tear drop to my cheek. I'd thought I could take any risk for the sake of magic—for the chance to live free of the fear my aunt beat into me. All I ever wanted was to be free and unafraid. I knew. I *knew* what I was risking, and I had thought myself strong enough to beat the odds.

But what I hadn't known was that there might be one thing—*one thing*—I would find more precious to me than magic.

One thing I would not be able to sacrifice.

I look up and meet Conrad's gaze for just a moment, and then the faerie guards pull me away.

CHAPTER THIRTY-THREE

The room is small and peculiar, the walls ribbed with wooden beams which bend overhead and meet in a high apex; it takes me perhaps twenty minutes of staring blankly up at that ceiling before I realize the room is shaped to resemble an ornate birdcage.

A simple narrow bed, a broken harpsichord, and a faded carpet are all that furnish the space. I sit in the center of the room with my knees drawn to my chest, my hands wrapped around my legs, still wearing the resplendent gown and silken gloves. How ridiculous I feel now, to have thought dressing up as one of them could possibly have made a difference. How ridiculous and small, and every other wretched quality I saw reflected back at myself in the faerie queen's emerald eyes. Her very glance had diminished me to nothing more than a bird with a broken wing, fluttering pitiably on the floor. And now she has put me in a cage, to let my foolishness finish me off.

I feel Lachlan's touch even here, his hand squeezing my heart, his fury at my failure scorching my ribs. I wonder if he knows the exact nature of my circumstances, or if he only has the general feel of them, or if perhaps he knows nothing at all and his cursed hold on me is simply following its natural course, the pain increasing as my sand drains from the hourglass he set on my life.

Bring me what I desire, dear Rose, or I'll have no more use for you at all. At midnight, my time will be up, and he'll consider me to have reneged on our second deal as I had on the first. He'll wring the last miserable drop of life from my heart, and I will drop dead, right here on this floor.

At least my failure will not put Conrad or Sylvie at further risk. He will be more vigilant now and ensure his sister does not return to the border where Lachlan can touch her. They will remain in Morgaine's service, though, bound to her will as I have been to Lachlan's. How arrogant I was to have imagined I could set them free.

Well. At least I will finally be free of Lachlan.

The thought is bitter and no comfort at all.

I want to *live*, Fates damn me! I don't want to waste away in this room, not even in my own world, alone and miserable and racked with pain! I want to live. I want to unravel the minutes back to my bedroom, and again feel Conrad's hands on me, his breath warm on my neck, his hair twisted around my fingers. I want the future we would never have.

They took my threadkit from me when they locked me in here. So I yank out a strand of my hair and attempt to Weave it into a fire knot. If I set something ablaze, maybe they'll let me out. Maybe I can still find a branch—

The hair snaps.

So does the next, and the next, and the next.

The sea silk is still tied around my wrist; I cannot bring myself to use it. I pull a thread from the carpet and Weave that, but my heart is thrumming with so much pain I cannot begin to channel any energy into it. And when I manage to push through the wall of pain, I encounter an unfamiliar current of energy, the magic of Elfhame entirely foreign and unbending. It does not answer me the way the energy of my own world does. Instead, it seems to hiss and recoil, offended I should even try to touch it.

Suddenly a great shudder runs through the walls. I shout and scramble up, the floor rolling beneath me, the light of the fruit-lamps above flickering. Is this because I tried to channel?

The tremor ends as soon as it began, but the guards outside yell to one another. The lights are dimmer but burn steadily again.

With a shiver, I slump over onto my side. I cannot seem to stop shaking, and soon my thoughts become consumed with horrible speculation of what will happen to me in the end. Will I know when I draw my last breath? Will I feel my soul leave my body? Will I see the Fates bending over me, Atropos's shears gleaming as she snips my life thread? Or will there only be darkness and nothing, not memory, not consciousness? Will I simply end and know nothing more at all?

These thoughts send chills racing down my body, and another clench of pain causes me to curl up tighter. My teeth begin to chatter. All my wanting turns to ash, and the fury and fight melts from my bones. Despair howls in like a frigid wind to fill the cavern of my body.

I find myself wishing the end would just come. That it would all be over, because waiting for it now seems to me to be ever so much worse.

Then I hear a knock on the door.

My head lifts, and I unfold shakily, keeping a hand on my heart as the door opens and Conrad slips into my little birdcage of a cell. His face is pale and drawn tight, with shadows pooling beneath his eyes. His hair is a dark tangle dusted with cobwebs, and the crystal-embroidered faerie suit is ragged at the hems, with a froth of white lace at his throat. He's wearing his own boots, but they're splattered with mud. He looks terrible.

"Rose," he says.

I shrink away, curling against the far wall in a miserable knot of despair and shame. Whatever condemnation he is here to deal out, I deserve.

He approaches slowly, his hand raised, and I cower deeper into myself.

"I did not come to hurt you," he says, sounding pained. "Rose . . ."

"I have ruined everything," I whisper. "Conrad, I am so sorry."

I bury my face in my hands, my tears pouring out into my palms. He kneels and without a word gathers me into his arms.

I let out a sob and grip him tightly, as if merely holding on to him by strength of will could tether me to life. Relief and confusion burn behind my eyes, spilling out in tears that Conrad wipes away with his thumb.

"I did not know," he murmurs into my hair. "Forgive me for not understanding you earlier. For not hearing you out. I should have listened, instead of running off to Elfhame like the dog that I am."

"I should have told you the truth sooner."

"Why did you do it? Why did you give him control of your heart?"

"I thought I could save us both, and Sylvie too," I whisper. "I deceived you, and I deceived myself most of all." I brush my fingers over the cut on his cheek. "Oh, why did you not tell her it was me? That none of this was your fault? How you must despise me."

He pulls back, holding my face between his hands and gazing at me as if I were the most precious and yet perplexing thing in the world. "Despise you? Fates, Rose Pryor. I could as easily despise the sun for rising or the stars for gleaming."

"You don't hate me?"

He combs his fingers through his hair, his features twisting into a grimace. "I know how it seems. What a bastard I've been. When Morgaine struck me, perhaps she knocked some clarity into my thick head at last. We are both of us bound by *their* threads, and to be angry with you is to dance on their strings. I will not do it any longer. I will not accept that we cannot choose our own fates." He weaves his fingers through mine. "So damn my oaths to Morgaine. I have broken them."

"What do you mean? How did you even get in here?"

His eyes dart to the door. "I caused a . . . distraction. Come. We must hurry."

I shake my head as he pulls me to my feet. "No. Even in the World Above, his hold on me cannot be broken. If even Morgaine can't—"

"You don't need Morgaine, or anyone else."

"But—"

"Hurry!" He pulls me through the door and to the left, and I have no choice but to follow. Dread and despair sour in my stomach, knowing it's useless.

"You're going to get yourself in more trouble," I point out.

"I've taken care of it."

"Care of what?"

"*You*, Rose. I'm taking care of you, as I ought to have done an hour ago, instead of running off to Morgaine. Damn her and damn my duty and damn this *place*. You will not die tonight. Faster, now!"

He knows these hallways in a way I thought they could not be known. What seem to me to be ever-shifting passages, he follows with surety, like a boy in his childhood home, following narrow corridors and stairs I would not have noticed. But strange as this palace is, it's getting even stranger. A thick drop of red liquid splashes on my bare shoulder.

"Conrad—the ceiling!"

We slow and look up and see cracks opening over our heads. From them, a liquid the color of blood runs and drips.

"What is it?"

He shakes his head, looking mystified. "'Tis . . . Dwirra sap."

"What's happening?"

"I believe my diversion is working. Come. We must go faster."

Onward we race, through a palace that seems to be ripping at its seams. Gaps appear in the walls, jagged and ugly and fleshlike, bloody sap running from the openings.

"Something is wrong," Conrad pants.

Suddenly he stops, and I run into him. He puts out an arm to steady me.

We are standing in the portal room. The great round glass waits where I left it, but the reflections on it waver as the room shakes.

"Conrad!" I look up and see a crack splinter across one of the support beams. "What did you do?"

"I made my choice," he says breathlessly, and he turns to me, opens his coat, and takes out a white branch as long as my forearm, tipped with a few red leaves. "And I chose *you*."

I gasp as he places the branch in my hands.

The moment my fingers close around it, the biting pain in my chest stops.

I breathe in deep, feeling cool relief roll through my body, my spine straightening, the tension draining from my muscles. I stare at the branch, and somehow, I *know* Lachlan knows I am holding it.

"This is what he meant to happen," I tell him hoarsely. "This was it all along. He wanted you to steal the branch for my sake."

Conrad places his hand against the side of my face, his thumb caressing my cheek. "I don't give a damn what the fae want. I only care that you live, and that Sylvie be protected. If you don't take this stick to the Briar King, you'll die. If you do, and he dethrones Morgaine, then you will live. That's all I need to know."

"You'd betray her?"

His face contorts; he glances at the doorway, a tear of Dwirra sap running down his temple. "As terrible as she seems, she is neither good nor evil, neither kind nor cruel. She just *is*. Like a force of nature, like a storm. My father even . . . Fates, I think he loved her. I don't want to betray her, but I had to choose, and I choose you and Sylvie."

"Then let's go. You and me and Sylvie. We'll deliver this wretched branch to Lachlan, and then we will be free of them all."

He gives a little laugh. "And where will we go?"

"Somewhere warm." I give a half sob, half laugh. "Turkey, perhaps. Where your mother was born. We will sail the Mediterranean and live as pirates."

"We'll rescue stray children for our crew, and you can teach them to Weave."

"Oh, yes. We'll make terrible mischief."

He smiles until both dimples flash. "I should like to commit mischief with you. I have a feeling you'd be very effective at it."

"Well, it *is* my eighth fault."

"Nonsense." He shakes his head, his hands cradling my face. "To me, you are faultless."

I tilt forward on my toes, as his lips part and his breath draws, about to speak, and I kiss him.

Just a touch, a brush of lips, a question asked.

I hesitate, waiting for his reaction. Will he pull away? Tell me I am too late?

He stares at me, his dark eyes startled, his brows lowering. He doesn't breathe, and I fear the worst.

Then his hands close around my waist and draw me to him. His lips find mine, and I abandon inhibition.

I kiss Conrad North as if I am ice, and he the fire to melt me. I kiss him knowing that while I thought I had nothing more to lose, I find I could still lose *everything*. Maybe the only thing that ever mattered.

My gloved hands are crushed between us, still gripping the branch, feeling his heart quicken. His lips are warm and yielding; they rove from mine to follow my jaw and the skin below my ear, sending chills shivering down my body.

It feels like channeling magic, only without the pain.

"They'll be looking for us," I whisper.

"Just one more minute" is his reply, his voice rough and yet as soft as velveteen, and I gladly relent.

He pushes me back, crushes me against the white wall, and presses his lean body into mine. I tilt my head, exposing my neck to his lips, and weave my fingers through his hair. His hand rises to cradle my head, and his other hand follows the soft skin on the underside of my arm, tugging my glove down to my wrist, then pulling it off altogether. He laces his fingers through mine; my palm conforms to his. I can feel his heat seeping into me, his smell—of saddle leather and open moor and clean hay—intoxicating. My soul cracks open like an ember, flaring hot and white.

His mouth returns to mine, opening for me. I meet it hungrily, every nerve in my body drawing taut, thrumming as if flooded with magic. His thumbs trace lines of fire over my breasts, leaving me dizzy with need. My knee rises, and I wrap my leg around his, then feel his hand on my bare calf, then gripping my thigh, grinding his hips to mine. My head spinning, I break from his mouth to gasp down air and moan into his ear.

The Dwirra branch slips from my hand, forgotten.

My fingers tear at the buttons of his coat, fumbling and clumsy. I let out a strained breath when it finally opens and my hands are on his chest, soaking his heat in through my palms. Our mouths meet again, tongues pressed together, my lip tugged between his teeth. He groans weakly as my hands trail down his muscled abdomen and my fingers tug at the waist of his trousers.

"*Rose* . . ." he murmurs. "There's no time. Fates, if I had time . . ."

I claim his lips and stop his words, then his breath, as I dip my fingers below his belt.

Every sense I have is afire; every spot of bared skin he finds and kisses, down to my collarbone. But suddenly he stops, breathing hard, and rests his forehead against mine. Staring into his copper eyes, I feel I have known them all my life and yet no time at all. I want to keep going, to unravel him down to his core.

"Rose Pryor," he whispers, his breath heavy, his chest heaving. He pulls my hand from his hip to his mouth. "I should have kissed you like that weeks ago, when the notion first crossed my mind."

I run my finger along his rough jaw, then over his lower lip.

"And when was that?" I murmur.

"The moment you walked into that damned pond, your nose pointed to the sky like a proud wee empress." He cups my face, tilting my lips to his for another soft kiss. "I could spend years kissing you. But it's time to go."

"Yes," I agree regretfully.

He steps back, holding me at arm's length. Then he picks up the broken Dwirra branch and presses it into my hands. "I'll see you on the other side. Hurry, now."

I draw a deep breath, then step through the glass portal. The surface shimmers and parts for me, sliding over my skin like cool water. My foot falls onto dewy grass; my lungs inhale the fresh, clean scent of the forest. Turning, I see Conrad standing still in Elfhame.

For a moment, we stand on opposite sides of the portal, I in the forest behind Ravensgate, he in the world of the fae. I press my hand to the glass, and his palm meets mine, but our skin cannot touch; the pane has gone rigid.

"What are you doing?" I ask. "Come, you must hurry."

But Conrad only stares at me.

My stomach plummets, as I realize what he means to do. Why he made me go through first. Why his eyes were full of such sadness when I kissed him. Why he pressed me to him as though it were our last kiss, not our first.

I chose you and Sylvie.

No mention of himself.

I slap my hands against the glass, trying to open the way again. He watches, his eyes hollow.

"Conrad!"

He shakes himself, then says, "I must give you time to escape. Without the portal, she'll be slowed down considerably. I'm so sorry, I . . ." His voice breaks. He shuts his eyes for one heartbeat, then opens them, his gaze blazing. "Promise me this: You'll take care of Sylvie. Whoever triumphs—Morgaine or Lachlan—they may come for her yet. You *must* get her away from here. Take her to the Telarii, perhaps, or some other powerful guild that might protect her. Mrs. MacDougal can explain once you're away."

"No!"

"Go east from the circle, and you'll find Bell tethered to a tree. He'll carry you back to the manor, then as far as you can run. There's money enough for you all to live on, wherever you go. Mrs. MacDougal will know where to find it. Promise me, Rose."

"I won't leave without you!"

There are tears in his eyes. "My sister. Please."

I begin to sob, leaning into the glass.

"I promise," I whisper. "I promise."

"Thank you." He breaks off a bit of beam that has already splintered away from the trembling wall and raises it.

My heart cracks. *"No!"*

He swings the beam and shatters the portal. I watch in horror as shards of glass rain down, his image fragmented in their jagged pieces, and then the portal, Elfhame, and Conrad all vanish entirely.

I stand alone in the black wood, an hour from midnight.

CHAPTER
THIRTY-FOUR

I cannot Weave another portal knot, for my threadkit is still in Elfhame. And even if I could, I know it would not work. Conrad broke the portal glass, the anchor to the standing stones, so that Morgaine could not follow me, and so that I could not return for him.

The way is entirely shut.

Conrad could not have issued a more final farewell.

I let out a scream of anger and splitting, searing sorrow, on my hands and knees on the damp earth, my fingers driving into the dirt. The wind tears through the clearing, disturbing the once sacred quiet of this place, driving home the knowledge that the connection between these stones and Elfhame is shattered. They are only rocks now.

A glint in the grass reveals one triangular shard of the portal glass which somehow followed me through. I pick it up and stare at it venomously, as if all of this were *its* fault. The glass reveals no image of Conrad or Elfhame, only a twisting, vague mass of threads—the strange place the Telarian tapestry led me through, I realize, when I traveled to and from Lachlan's camp. The raw warp and weft of the tapestry of the world.

Finally, I put the shard in my pocket, as if somehow it might still help me reach Conrad. It is the only tie I have to Elfhame, now.

That, and the Dwirra branch.

I look at it sourly, the pale bark and dark-red leaves hateful to my eyes. It seems such a paltry thing to have cost so much.

After a few minutes, I force myself upright and into the trees, clutching the branch with all my strength. If I get it to Lachlan in time, perhaps he can somehow reach Elfhame and overthrow Morgaine before she can harm Conrad.

It seems a desperate fool's hope, but without it I do not think I could stand.

I'm still barefoot, stepping painfully over rocks and roots, but I push myself anyway, until I find Bell among the trees, where Conrad said he would be. The horse is so tall I must lead him to a rock so that I can climb atop it and then onto his back. I give him his head and whisper encouragement in his ear; he takes off at a trot, picking up the pace once we leave the wood.

The night sky festers with fitful clouds. They roll and boil across the stars, swallowing the moon whole. A black wind rushes over the moor, and on it I smell smoke.

My stomach twists with foreboding.

"Faster, Bell," I say.

I see the fire a full minute before I realize it is Ravensgate I am looking at.

The manor is ablaze, orange and angry beneath the brooding storm clouds. Horror opens like a pit in my stomach, and I dig my heels into Bell's sides. He throws his head forward and gallops hard, sweat hot on his withers.

I slide off before he comes to a full stop and sprint to the house. About a third of it is on fire—the wing where Sylvie and the MacDougals sleep. There is no sign of anyone outside, which means they may still be within.

Throwing open the door, I stumble back as a wall of black smoke rolls out. Then, coughing and gasping, I hold my skirt over my nose and plunge into the manor.

The grand foyer is aglow with flames; they eat the drapes and gnaw on the banister and have completely filled the passage to the kitchen. The roar of the blaze drowns out my shouts for Sylvie and Mrs. MacDougal. The floorboards are hot under my bare feet.

Charging up the stairs, I come to the MacDougals' room first and pound on the door. When no one replies, I wrap my skirt around the hot handle and open it.

The old couple is still asleep; a muffling charm is hung on the door, pale threads wound across a thin hoop, as I'd suspected one must be when I'd tried to escape Conrad's entrapment spell earlier. I wrench it down and tear it apart.

"Wake up!" I shout.

Their eyes are only starting to blink open as I run out of the room again, then up the stairs to the floor where Sylvie sleeps. The flames are thicker here, and I push through a corridor lined with them, dizzy from the heat and smoke. I cannot shout for Sylvie; I can barely breathe. Even if I had all the thread in the world, I could not put out this fire. It would take twenty Weavers together to have a hope.

When I reach her room, I open the door only to see a torrent of flames rushing out. I leap back with a dry gasp.

I'm too late.

Her entire room is filled with fire.

For a moment I stand frozen in place, my mind utterly blank with horror. All I can think of is Conrad, begging me through the portal glass: *Promise me, Rose. Please!*

Something grabs my skirt, and I shout, turning, ready to bludgeon whoever it is.

But then I see a familiar furry face, and I let out a sob and reach for him. "Captain! Come!"

He evades my hand and instead tugs at my hem with his teeth.

"What is it, boy?"

With a bark, he turns and bounds away.

"No!" I shout. "Come back!"

I run after him, determined to carry him over my shoulder if I must. He barks again, his hackles raised high, then darts through an open door leading to the attic.

Cursing and teary, I follow him up. The air is choked with smoke, but I look back and see the flames pursuing me with ravenous hunger. I cannot go back down.

So I climb, coughing and dizzy. At the top, I stumble to a halt, and stare.

Sylvie stands in the center of the attic, her back to me, before the great ward loom. Fire licks the frame, and the corners of the tapestry begin to wither and blacken. Captain lies at Sylvie's feet and whines.

"Sylvie!" I rasp, lunging for her.

Grabbing her arm, I turn her around and find her gazing blankly at me. But her hands are moving, tying a fire knot.

I knock the thread from her fingers, horrified.

"*You* did this?" My voice is a croak in my throat.

I shake her by her shoulders but get no response. It's as if she cannot see me at all. Otherwise, she seems unharmed save for the singe marks on her nightgown and soot smeared on her skin.

The flames on the loom leap up suddenly, catching the tapestry. I pull Sylvie back, eyes wide as the beautiful ward spell begins to shrivel and flake to ash. Captain growls and retreats, staying between us and the flames.

Dreadful understanding bursts in my mind.

Pulling the girl to the window, I knock out the glass with my elbow and give us a thin flow of fresh air. I turn Sylvie around, looking over every inch of her, then my gaze settles on her thick dark hair.

"Oh, Sylvie," I whisper.

I run my fingers through her locks and find them—tiny, subtle knots tied in the fine hairs at her nape, nearly imperceptible. There are dozens of them—the same knots woven over and over again.

Puppetry spells.

They're illegal, and extremely difficult to Weave. But I know Lachlan is likely more than up to the job. He must have the mirror versions of these knots tied up somewhere, waiting to be thrummed to life and then manipulated, triggering Sylvie to carry out the task he would have whispered in her ear, planted in her brain like a poisonous seed while serving her tea and strawberries. The moment Conrad put the branch in my hands, Lachlan would have activated them, setting her to her terrible task of destroying the warding tapestry and Ravensgate with it.

I curse myself for not finding the knots sooner. I'd searched Sylvie's dress that day, but not her hair. Stupid! It is the same sort of trick Conrad once suspected *me* of. I should have seen it.

There is no time to undo each knot one by one, nor to wait for their magic to burn her hair to ashes. Already Sylvie has produced another thread from somewhere and is trying to tie another fire knot. I wrench it away, then plunge my hand into my pocket, nearly cutting my palm on the shard of the portal glass as I pull it out.

"I'm sorry, Sylvie," I whisper.

I slice the shard roughly through her hair, sawing it off at her jawline, cutting through the awful puppetry knots.

The moment they fall away, Sylvie starts, blinking and looking around. Then she grabs hold of me, eyes wild.

"I didn't mean to!" she cries. "I couldn't stop myself! It's like I was trapped in my own head!"

"I know," I whisper, wrapping my arms around her. "It's all right. You're safe now."

But she isn't. None of us are. The manor is on fire, and we're trapped up here with no way down. The window is too small for even Sylvie to squeeze out, even if I could manage to Weave some spell to slow her descent to a survivable speed.

Through the window, I see the MacDougals standing in the drive, clinging to one another, Mrs. MacDougal sobbing. I wave but cannot catch their attention.

Turning back to Sylvie, I hold her shoulders and look her in the eyes.

"Is there any other way out of the attic?"

She shakes her head, pale as a ghost. "I don't know."

"Sylvie, *think*."

She begins to cry.

"Do you have more thread, then?"

She nods and pulls a strand from her pocket, pushing it into my palm. It's pitifully short. I look at the sea silk tied to my wrist and know it's pointless. I don't have enough to get us out of here, and it would take too long to unravel our clothes or Weave hair, even with the mass of Sylvie's dark locks on the floor.

But I Weave the thread Sylvie gave me anyway, and a simple wind charm is all I can manage to get out of it. A gust blows through the window and out again, clearing the smoke just enough for us to catch our breaths.

The fire has spread from the loom on one side of us and spilled from the stairway on the other. We're trapped between two walls of flame that are closing in. I look at the sea silk and wonder if there is enough to Weave a heart-stopping spell, to end it quickly and save us both from the pain of the fire.

But just as I begin to untie it from my wrist, Sylvie pulls back.

"I can stop it," she whispers.

"You don't have thread."

"I tried to tell you before," she replies. "I don't *need* thread."

She begins to channel, her eyes shut, hands in fists. I shout and reach for her.

"You'll burst your heart!" I say, though I'd been about to Weave a spell to do just that. "Sylvie—"

"I can stop it," she says through her teeth.

The walls, ceiling, and floor groan around us. The flames flicker and warp. The world seems to twist around Sylvie as she wrenches energy from it, wrings it from every leaf and branch around. I feel behind me and find the Dwirra branch stuck through my sash has gone brittle and dry, its life force sucked out of it.

With a cry, Sylvie throws her arms wide and opens her eyes.

I watch in shock as her pupils turn silver, the tips of her ears stretch into graceful points, and the very bones in her face sharpen and grow longer, her body transforming before me. It reminds me of a glamour spell fading away, revealing a true form, but this is a different magic altogether.

I remember at once a dozen whispers, a score of subtle hints: Sylvie's way with animals, her astonishing power, Conrad's mistrust of her magic, Mrs. MacDougal's mention of Liam North's faerie paramour.

My father, Conrad had said, in those last, awful moments I was with him, *I think he loved her.*

Sylvie's ghost, her silent watcher, glinting like silver mist in the trees.

I look at Sylvie's black hair and emerald irises, and I know then who she is.

All around us, the flames begin to wither and shrink, reduced by Sylvie's strange, threadless magic until they are nothing but smoldering ash and plumes of thick, dark smoke. I have no idea how she is doing it, but I know I've seen this type of spellwork before, woven by Lachlan when he'd warmed me on the cold night of Lorellan's funeral. I can only watch as the girl channels by some instinct deep within her, beyond my ken.

Then, spent, Sylvie pitches into me with a soft cry.

I catch her, as silence falls over the manor. The blaze is out, leaving smoke thick enough to kill us still.

So I lift Morgaine's daughter in my arms and carry her, pressing her face into my shoulder so she doesn't inhale too much smoke, and holding my breath as long as I can until we reach the front foyer, where it is a little thinner. Captain races ahead of us, barking.

Finally I push through the half-gaping front doors and stumble into the drive, falling hard onto my knees and gasping for air. Sylvie rolls from my weakened arms, coughing and choking, looking herself again, but for the still slightly pointed tips of her ears.

It is only after several minutes of coughing and wiping tears from my burning eyes that I look up.

And see Lachlan and all his fae standing in the drive, watching us.

On the Briar King's brow rests a crown of silver thorns.

CHAPTER THIRTY-FIVE

Lachlan is dressed in armor, his silver breastplate exquisitely engraved with stars and moons. His hand rests on a sheathed sword, and his white hair hangs down his back in a long, tight braid. He is glorious and terrible with all trappings of the human world cast aside. And with the ward destroyed, he wasted no time closing in on us. His host of exiles are also dressed for battle, silver and shining all, like something out of a story. They carry scarlet pennants that snap in the lowering wind and magic torches with silvery flames.

Sylvie sees Lachlan and gasps with remembrance, the sight of him enough to shatter the fog of the memory spell he'd put on her. She pulls close to me, and I put an arm around her as we both rise. Captain plants himself in front of us, his fur coated in ash, his hackles high as he snarls. The MacDougals stand to the side, solemn and pale, looking between us and the faerie king.

Lachlan steps forward and slowly claps, his eyes black ice.

"Well done, my little witch," he says. "Well done indeed."

I reach behind my back to grasp the Dwirra branch. I wonder if he knows it is withered and dry thanks to Sylvie's channeling. I wonder if that will matter to him.

"You enchanted her," I spit. "She nearly died for it!"

"Nonsense." He looks at her, his eyes greedy. "My niece is strong, despite her regrettable human blood."

"*Niece?*" Sylvie whispers.

"Did you know who she was all along?" I ask.

"No," he says. "She was the one variable I hadn't accounted for, and it was cleverly done for Morgaine to hide her here, in the mortal world, with her magic suppressed to hide her. But the moment I touched her, I knew. I felt the fae in her stir, her blood weak and undernourished, but beginning to awaken—thanks, I believe, to your influence, Rose."

A cold hand grips my heart, as the threads connect in my mind, the full pattern of events finally coming together. I understand at last why Conrad has so vehemently denied Sylvie her magic. Her faerie blood must be tied to her power, and as long as she did not channel, it remained dormant. Then I came along, thinking I knew what was best for her, seeing too much of myself in her eyes, and in teaching her to Weave, I unwittingly exposed her. I look at Sylvie in dismay.

"Now," continues Lachlan. "I believe you have something for me?"

Yes. The reason Conrad sacrificed himself. The only hope I have of saving him. I take out the branch; its white bark has turned gray and the leaves are gone. Will it still be enough to restore his power so he can stop Morgaine before she hurts Conrad—if it isn't already too late?

"Give it here," Lachlan says. "Give it to me, and your debt will be paid."

But something pulls at my mind, a whisper of hesitation. There is more to this pattern. He always has schemes within schemes. Nothing is what it seems with him.

"*Rose.* It is minutes to midnight." He holds out his hand. "What are you waiting for?"

The whisper grows, the unfinished pattern wild and desperate and screaming to be understood, louder and louder until, in a burst of clarity, I *do* understand.

Sylvie.

Horrified, I step back.

The pattern's final thread snaps into place. I see at last the terrible twist hidden in his words and how he has trapped me yet again.

According to the deal we struck, if I give him the branch, he will be unable to harm Conrad. But I remember all too well his words: *I will not harm your precious mortal Norths.*

I look at Sylvie. If I'd known then what she was, I'd have seen his words for what they were, and the poisonous barb he'd hidden in them.

If I give him the branch, I might save Conrad and myself.

But the cost would be Sylvie, with her immortal blood. I see that as plainly as the ring of thorns engraved into Lachlan's breastplate. When his full power is restored, nothing will stop him from killing her or bending her to his dark purposes.

Once again, I find the cost too high.

The only hope she might have now is to escape while he is still in his weakened state. And I made a promise to Conrad, and I will keep it.

Looking the faerie in his silver eyes, I unwind the sea silk from my wrist and wrap it thrice around the branch.

"Rose . . ." he says, his tone warning. "Give me the branch."

"No."

I channel fast, my heart clenching at once, but I force the energy through my body and into the precious sea silk even as my fingers are still Weaving the fire knot.

The branch ignites at once. I drop it and step back as it blazes up, then crumbles to ash. A thin trail of smoke curls up between us, sinuous and pale.

"Foolish," sighs Lachlan.

"I won't help you conquer Elfhame." My heart begins to writhe, the pain returning with hungry vengeance, creeping from the edges of my vision, his anger in every stab. "You'll remain weak and your power broken, and you'll diminish and fade like a . . . a *mortal*, like a—" I gasp and clench my breast, my strength draining from me.

Lachlan only laughs.

"You ought to have given it to me," he says.

"Without your power—"

"My power? Witness my *power*," he scoffs, then spreads his hands. He begins to channel the way Sylvie did when she put out the fire, his pupils silvering over. Wind stirs; the ashes and soot layered over the ground shiver and then begin sweeping toward him. Captain barks, snarling like a wild wolf.

Hearing a sudden crash behind me, I whirl and see vines springing from the earth. They grow up and over the half-destroyed manor, thick as ropes, then thick as trunks. They push into the broken windows and wind over the eaves like the tentacles of a kraken consuming a ship. Mrs. MacDougal cries out, and Sylvie gasps.

"You still don't understand," sighs Lachlan, still channeling, as his vines wrap and weave over Ravensgate. "It was never the branch I needed, it was the *breaking* of the branch."

I remember the way the queen's palace had begun to splinter apart, red sap leaking from the walls.

"The Dwirra," I realize.

"It is dying," confirms Lachlan. "Such was the weakness of the Dwirra—that no mortal should harm it, lest it wither like a blighted stalk. Morgaine's fragile haven is collapsing, and she and all her fae will soon be driven out into *this* world. The Dwirra will fall, and with it, the World Below will be destroyed entirely."

"How can you rule it if you destroy it?" I cry.

"Oh, Rose." He smiles. "I never wanted to rule *it*."

Understanding dawns; of course I should have seen it sooner. The way he spoke of Elfhame, with disgust and disdain, disparaging his people for withdrawing beneath the world and hiding like rabbits. It is not Elfhame he wishes to conquer at all.

It is *our* world.

The World Above, London and Edinburgh and Liverpool and these moors.

The lands the fae once reigned over as near gods, their original kingdom. That is what Lachlan covets most—the glorious lost days of his people's zenith, when mortals existed to bow and serve and sacrifice themselves for their beautiful and terrible overlords.

I gaze at him, feeling horror and anger, but most of all, surprisingly—pity. I feel, for the first time, as if our positions were reversed. Even as I stand dying before him, the weight of his cursed debt crushing my heart, I look at him and see that for all his might and beauty, he is small and desperate and destined to fail. It is a strange thing, to look on a god and see only a fool.

But he is a fool who will kill thousands of people before he realizes how impossible his dream is. And I will be the first casualty.

"You have to know that will never happen," I cry. "There are not nearly enough of you, even if you were all at the height of your power. We have rifles and bullets now, Lachlan. We have iron enough to nail down the sky. You said it yourself—magic is fading from the world."

He glowers; I've angered him.

"There is still time to change that," he snarls. "The tide can yet be turned."

Looking down at the broken bits of the Dwirra branch, I realize it doesn't matter whether I can talk him out of his mad venture. The damage is already done. By destroying the Dwirra, he is forcing the other fae to join him. With nowhere to retreat to, they'll have to either fight with him in hope of taking back their old lands, or else die like the mortals they despise, sickened and poisoned by our iron world. In destroying the one safe haven they had left, Lachlan has thrust all his kind into a battle for their survival. That is what he meant by restoring his strength—his strength of numbers, all the fae united under his banner, and Morgaine left with no one to rule at all. Would she join him, I wonder, seeing no other alternative but a slow and painful demise? Likely he would kill her outright no matter what, and Sylvie too.

I sink to my knees and cry out, my vision blackening, my consciousness slipping. The pain is sharp and pointed, and this time I know there will be no more fending it off. My heart is shattering piece by piece, and the shards drive into my lungs.

Lachlan's eyes move on to his niece, as if I am already forgotten, as if he considers me already dead.

"Come here, Sylvie North," he says.

"No!" She blazes with defiance, holding fast to my hand still. "Fix Rose now! Whatever you did to her—"

"You've awakened to your immortal self, beloved niece. Don't you know what you are? Pledge fealty to me, spin a vowknot of loyalty, and you will reign as a queen."

"I don't need to bow to some nattering old fool to be queen," she snaps. "I'll be and do whatever I please, and right now, I'm thinking I'd like to smash your ugly nose in."

He blinks, looking taken aback, and that is all the time Sylvie needs, apparently.

She's been Weaving all the while, I realize, pulling thread from a tear in her skirt, hands behind her back. It is the knot I taught her to animate a broom, which makes sweeping a dusty floor a moment's work.

But Sylvie doesn't use it on a broom.

Instead she turns and channels fast, before any of us have finished digesting the fact she wove it at all.

From the rooftop of the manor, a dozen stone gargoyles launch themselves from the eaves with stony rumbles. They dive, shrieking, at Lachlan. Captain barks and lunges at the faerie too, but Sylvie shouts his name, and he turns back to us.

While the faerie scrambles to fend them off, drawing his silver sword and knocking one from the air with a metallic clang, Sylvie pulls me up and the MacDougals run forward.

The old couple help drag me into the house, and Sylvie slams the doors shut behind us and the dog. The air here is still smoky, and everything is charred and covered in soot, but now great swollen vines twist through the house as well, like fat snakes.

"He's coming!" Sylvie shouts, glancing out a window then pulling back as a silver-tipped arrow slices through it and impales a vine with a squelch.

Leaning heavily on Mr. MacDougal, I follow Sylvie and Mrs. MacDougal up the stairs, clambering over vines and spaces where the steps burned through entirely. Charred bits of wood fall from the ceiling, the house groaning as if it is doing all it can to hold itself together. Captain snuffs the doors and singed drapes, his hackles still raised.

The front doors crash open, one coming entirely off its hinges, and I catch a glint of silver armor in the doorway before we turn down another corridor.

"It's no use," I gasp out. "There's nowhere to run."

"We're not just giving up!" Sylvie says.

We press deeper into the house, hearing the fae advance behind us. They hack at vines with their swords and kick down doors. I hear a crash and hope the ceiling caved in on Lachlan, but then I hear him shout out, "You cannot possibly elude me, niece!"

"Is he really my uncle?" Sylvie asks Mrs. MacDougal.

"Aye, lass." The old woman shoulders open another door and ushers us all through. "It's why your brother withheld your magic from you. He and your mother knew if you began channeling, it'd only be a matter of time before your faerie blood stirred."

Sylvie looks delighted, even as her murderous kin pursues us deeper and deeper into the ruined bowels of her house. "My faerie blood! I *knew* it! I knew I was terribly special!"

Mrs. MacDougal groans and drags her down another corridor, then up a stairwell. I'm so racked with pain, my eyes dancing with dark spots, I cannot even tell where we are. Lachlan is getting closer; I hear him knocking at the walls, sweetly calling out my name and Sylvie's, toying with us now.

In my fevered, anguished mind, his voice warps into a gross imitation of my aunt's; his sword hilt thumping on the walls becomes the rap of her heeled boots. Terror courses through me, tangling the years into a great, impossible knot, until it seems I am eight years old again. Where is my hidden passageway now? Where is my tunnel through the walls that will carry me to safety?

Then I realize: I know exactly where it is.

CHAPTER THIRTY-SIX

"Wait!" I cry, pulling Mr. MacDougal's arm until he stops. "I know what to do!"

He and his wife look at me askance, perhaps thinking, rightfully, how *I* was the one to cause all this mess in the first place.

"My room," I say. "Go to my room, and I think I can save us."

Whatever doubts may linger in Mrs. MacDougal's mind, she seems to brush them aside, and she grimly nods. "We're nearly there anyway."

Two hidden servant's doors lead us directly to the hallway where my room is, but we have to scurry under a fallen beam to reach my door. While Mr. MacDougal shoulders it open, I listen to Lachlan calling out further down the corridor, sounding angrier now.

The door finally opens; it had been blocked by more burnt rubble. My stomach lurches, thinking the fire might have destroyed everything in here, but then I see it—the corner of my valise, where I'd dropped it on the other side of the bed.

"Open it!" I cry. "Hang up the tapestry inside."

"What good will that do?" Mrs. MacDougal demands, as Sylvie unlatches the valise.

"You'll see," I tell her.

I lean against the door and hear footsteps coming down the corridor. My slippers are set against the wall, remarkably unharmed, and I pull them onto my dirty, scraped feet.

The MacDougals hang the tapestry on the curtain rod, then look at me. I nod, then push forward, Sylvie helping me along. Every step, every breath, is a knife of unbearable pain. Tears run from my eyes; they taste of salt and soot.

I take the guide thread in one hand and Sylvie's in the other; she in turn holds Mrs. MacDougal's hand, Mrs. MacDougal takes hold of her husband, and he grips Captain's collar.

"Ready?" I say, my voice strained.

At that moment the door to my room bursts from its hinges and Lachlan appears in the doorway. His sword shines in his hand, and his eyes are angry blue flames.

"Stop—!"

I don't hear the rest of his shout, because I push through the threads of the tapestry. They part once more for me, and I pull the others along.

We spill into the strange world of the shifting threads, a tangle of limbs and hands, keeping hold of each other. But another hand comes too—Lachlan took hold of Mr. MacDougal's coat, and I turn to see his head and shoulders pushing through the tapestry, with the rest of him soon to follow.

So I do the only thing I can: I let go of the guide thread and lunge at him. I grab Lachlan by the rim of his breastplate and then push with all my strength. He gives me one startled look before I shove him through entirely, back into the bedroom.

The tapestry crumbles the moment he's gone, its magic spent. It'll be no more than a pile of ashes, now.

Turning back to the others, I see them watching me with clear terror in their eyes. Captain whines, his tail between his legs. I remember my own overwhelmed senses the first time I walked through the thread-world and know they must be feeling the same thing. Even Sylvie, for all her bravado, looks afraid.

"It's all right," I say, my voice warped and distant in my ears, as if sound does not operate by the same rules here as in the real world.

"Where are we?" breathes Mrs. MacDougal.

"The world is a tapestry woven by the Fates," I tell her. "And we have crossed to the other side of it."

"Bloody hell. Well, can you get us out again?"

"I . . ."

I look all around for the guide thread that would have led us to the ruined castle—no further out of Lachlan's reach, in the end, but with more time to think of something else.

But the thread is gone, lost to the flow of millions around us. Nothing is familiar here; this place is always changing. One might as well search for a familiar ripple on a river's current.

"Come on," I urge queasily. "And whatever you do, *touch nothing*. These threads are forbidden to all."

At least we are alive. At least Lachlan cannot reach us here.

But what if I never find a way out? I have only minutes before Lachlan's debt comes due and I pay for it with my life. Will that leave Sylvie and the MacDougals to wander the wrong side of reality until they die?

"If we just keep going," I say, "we have to find a—*ugh!*"

I squeeze Sylvie's hand as a mighty splinter of pain opens through my body; I feel I am cracking in two, head to foot. The spasm lasts longer than any have before, and I hear the distant, rattling sound of my own scream echoing back to my ears.

Lachlan must be doing this, wrenching the noose he's tied around my heart. I can feel his fury in the fire that spreads through me and know I don't have much time left before I succumb entirely to it.

I pry my eyes open, feeling nauseated. The others are clustered around me, alarmed and at a loss. Captain pushes his nose against my arm, as if trying to spur me to my feet.

"Help me up," I croak.

I hobble onward, shuddering and fighting to stay conscious, the pain a swirling red whirlpool sucking at my feet. All it would take is a single moment of weakness and I would tumble into it for good, sinking deeper and deeper until I am obliterated entirely.

Deliriously, I begin to think the thread-world is no true place at all, but a manifestation of the pain inside me, and that I've dragged all of us into the pit of my own madness. I stumble forward, onward. And all around us, all the while, the threads of the world pulse and writhe.

I gradually become aware of a hand in mine, and I look down to see a small girl, not Sylvie, holding on to me. Her brown hair hangs in loose curls, her freckles stark against her porcelain face. She is so familiar, from her upturned nose to her clever little fingers to the spool tucked in her pocket.

"We're going to die in here," she says.

I shake my head. "Have to keep moving."

"It was always going to end this way for us. Alone, powerless, and—don't you remember our ninth fault?—*fearful*. Perhaps that's all we are. Perhaps when you unravel us down to our weft, fear is the only thread left."

"I still have my magic."

"No, we don't. We couldn't summon a thimbleful of energy now. What point is there of going onward? Even if we make it out, what good are we to anyone? We are what *she* said we always were: a mouse. Weak and stupid and unworthy. Magic is not for the faint of heart."

Her words whittle away my courage. "Please stop!"

But she clings to me like a leech. "We should hide. Bury deep into these threads. Let go of the others. Let them find their own way through. We cannot help them."

"I'm not you anymore. I stopped being you the day I left the house on Wimpole Street."

"Wrong!" Her voice is shrill in my ear. "I've been your truest self ever since that day! Every decision you made, *I* made for you. I kept you *alive*, till you went and bungled off in your own direction. Why didn't you just give the branch to the faerie? Then we would be free! I could have kept us safe!"

"Some things are stronger than even you," I whisper.

"What, like love? What's the point of falling in love if you're too *dead* to enjoy it?"

I lift my head and realize I haven't moved at all since she took hold of me. Instead I've sunk into the threads; they're up to my knees now, swirling, coiling, sucking me down. But I look at her—my eight-year-old self, small and terrified and alone—and I know her for what she is: She is the fear which controlled me all these years. She's been with me forever, making every choice for me, ruling me, driving me away from the small chances I'd had at happiness and love and true freedom.

You're afraid of being afraid, Morgaine had said, seeing to the heart of me in a matter of moments.

But it wasn't for fear that I destroyed the Dwirra branch, and it wasn't for fear that I danced the spell of homage to open the way to Elfhame.

"It was love," I whisper. "I love Conrad, and I love Sylvie. More than I fear death. More than the loss of magic."

"Without magic, we are nothing!"

"No." I shake my head. "That . . . is the lie I told myself, isn't it? It is the lie Lachlan exploited to control me. But I am so much more than my magic. I am . . ." It is Conrad's words which weave through my thoughts, tethering me to myself, helping me to see clearly. "I am a teacher. I am passionate and stubborn and clever. I love my students and defend those who cannot defend themselves and go toe-to-toe with injustice. With or without magic, that is who I am. Who I *choose* to be."

My little specter presses her hands to her face, her eyes welling with tears. "I am afraid!"

"I know. I am too." I take her hand and pull her close, whispering in her ear, "But we won't let that control us anymore."

She shudders, crying into my shoulder. I shut my eyes and hold tightly to her.

"It's all right," I murmur. "It's all right."

My heart thuds, sending spikes of pain twisting around my ribs, piercing my spine. An agonized moan slips from my throat.

"Rose? *Rose!*"

I blink in confusion as the tenor of my little self's voice shifts, growing lighter. When I pull back, I find it is Sylvie in my arms, her very real and small, warm body folded into mine for shelter. Her large, misty green eyes fasten upon my face.

"Rose, are you all right?"

I grimace, pressing a fist to my splintering chest. "Help me up, Sylvie."

Clinging to her hand, I struggle upward, pulling myself free of the threads. Looking back, I see the MacDougals also bogged down, their eyes glazed over, their minds bending as mine had to the maddening surreality of this place. Only Captain seems wholly unaffected; he licks Mrs. MacDougal's hand and whines, trying to rouse her.

We have to get out of here, before I lose them entirely. I may be on my final journey, my doom already certain, but Fates damn me if I drag Sylvie and Mr. and Mrs. MacDougal down with me.

"Up!" I shout, my voice ragged and weary, but now with an iron, unyielding edge. "Get up! All of you!"

Ruthlessly I bully them until they find their feet, then I usher them onward like a collie, pushing and tugging. As I herd them along, I look around, eyes probing the threads. My heart wrenches itself this way and that, but the pain is so constant now that I give up on fighting it. I let it wash over me; I accept its every bite, and still I keep moving forward.

If this is the back of the Fates' tapestry, then these threads are connected to the real world. The weft and warp are hidden from view, but that doesn't mean the pattern behind them is sheer chaos. The colors must mean something—the lighter gray could be sky, the green trees, the lavender the moors. And the sparkling, glowing threads between them are living things: horses and rabbits, humans and faeries.

The moorwitches walked these threads. They knew how to find their way, even without tapestries and guide threads to lead them. They vanished in one spot and appeared in another, and now I know how they did it: They navigated *this* place, the underside of the world. The fae do it too; they built their haven here, Elfhame a bubble world latched on the wrong side of reality, supported and nourished by the Dwirra Tree.

I look around with more purpose now, casting about not just for some random door, but for certain signs. And I begin to see them: a rippling mass of threads with colors reminding me of the Three Fates Bluff, grays like slate and fog, a glowing knot that must be Blackswire and its people. I push toward a green cluster in the opposite direction. These strands are thick and coarse and densely bound together, much the way the ancient forest is, where the now-broken stone circle stands.

Sylvie and the MacDougals follow without too much resistance; now and again one will slow and stop, eyes turning to fog, mouth slack, but I pull them until they move again. I don't know why my own head stays clear. But then, I hadn't felt the grasping madness of this place when I'd traversed it with Lachlan's guide thread; now, perhaps, my *purpose* becomes my guide thread. I find my way forward the way I always have: by seeing the patterns at work, using an instinct that's been in my blood since I was a child, long before I ever met the silver faerie.

This is a talent all my own, a power bargained away to no one. I lean on that intuition now more than I ever have before, throwing my full hope into that instinctive part of me which can look at a complex knot and find the single thread to undo it.

"We're getting close," I say, though the others give no indication that they can hear or understand me. I drag them on anyway, and my pain too, and feel the shadow of my fear creeping along in my periphery. Fear, always with me, even when I feel my bravest. I suppose that is the nature of it, and it can only be accepted. That's all right. I know now that I can be afraid and still keep moving. I can be in the worst pain a body could feel and still keep moving. I can lose my magic to the last drop and still keep moving.

Threads grow thicker here. They cluster like vines, tickling my neck and face. They flow around me, coil over my shoulders, moving in an almost sentient manner, snakelike.

Then I reach up to brush away one persistently tickling thread— and realize it's no thread at all, but a branch as pale and crooked as an old crone's finger. And it's *warm*.

My breath hitches; I move more quickly, my heart stretched and splintering, my strength fading even as I push through spindly branches for what seems like hours, towing my four charges along with me, feeling warm bark and papery leaves raking my skin—

To finally tumble out into the open, landing in a heap at the foot of the Dwirra Tree.

CHAPTER
THIRTY-SEVEN

We stand on the hillside sloping up to the tree, amid the stones and ferns and massive roots. The great branches of the Dwirra spread above, and the curtain of willow-like limbs form the outer wall of Elfhame behind us. This is the backside of the tree, with its hill between us and the houses of the fae; I cannot even see Morgaine's white palace. We are very much alone, but I'm not sure how long that will last, if the queen might have some way of knowing we slipped in through her walls.

"Stay low," I tell Sylvie and the MacDougals. "We mustn't be seen."

"What is this place?" Sylvie asks, holding tight to Captain's collar.

Just then, a trio of fae go running past us. We duck quickly behind a mossy stone, listening to them chitter and whisper; they seem to be inspecting the perimeter. Captain's hackles rise, and I hold his muzzle shut to keep him from barking and giving us away. After a few minutes, they vanish around the other brow of the hills.

"Oh," Sylvie breathes. "It's *their* world."

"We'd have been better off in the house," Mrs. MacDougal mutters.

"What, with that madcap loon chopping us up with his sword?" retorts her husband.

But maybe Mrs. MacDougal is right.

Elfhame is crumbling.

I can tell that much with hardly a glance. Ruin is a stench on the air, the smell of the tree's bleeding sap as rancid as that of decaying flesh. It runs down the trunk and drips from the branches in sticky, scarlet vines. Given the tree's humanlike shape, the sight is horrifying, like seeing a woman stuck full of arrows, blood running in rivers down her skin. Loud groans and creaks from the wood remind me of Ravensgate after Sylvie put out the fire, when the whole structure was swaying and breaking apart bit by bit, on the verge of total collapse. The hill trembles beneath my knees, and leaves rain from the Dwirra's crown, velveting the ground in sheets of scarlet. Along the trunk and branches, lines of black spread like poisoned veins.

All this, from one small clipped branch?

I remember the horror in Morgaine's eyes when I had told her what Lachlan had sent me here to fetch. She'd known, of course, of her kingdom's great weakness. Conrad had not; I wonder how many fae even knew. I cannot fault Morgaine for keeping it secret.

"Stay here, and keep out of sight," I tell the others. "Hold tight to the dog. Conrad is here somewhere, and he will know what to do."

"Connie is here?" Sylvie whispers, her eyes round.

I look at her, my heart suddenly splintering as I realize this is the last moment I will ever have with her. On an impulse, I pull her into a tight embrace and whisper in her ear one final lesson, "Hold fast to your power, Sylvie, and to your freedom. Do not ever bargain these things away. Do not ever compromise who you are. And know that no matter what, you are loved."

When I pull away, her eyes are full of confused tears, but she nods slowly.

"Take this, Rose." She pulls a long knitting needle out of her sleeve and presses it into my hand. It is as long as my forearm and made of polished iron. "Every hero needs a sword."

"You are absolutely right." I take it and kiss the top of her head.

Mrs. MacDougal takes the girl's hand. "Go on, Miss Pryor. Hurry."

I nod, grateful to her, and limp around the stone. Keeping one hand clenched to my aching chest, I make my way as quickly as I can over the loose leaves and veining roots, which is not very quick at all. I glance back just once, to see Sylvie has another knitting needle, and she raises it in salute as if it were Excalibur itself. I raise mine in return, holding back a sob.

I must force myself to turn and keep going.

Once I'm out of sight of the others, I stop to lean on a stone and fight away the black spots clouding my vision. Sweat soaks my dress and hair, and my skin is feverishly hot. The world seems to reel around me, and I groan and shut my eyes, waiting for the dizziness to pass. I remember with sudden sharpness the last moments of my uncle's life, when he lay gasping on his deathbed, delirious and trembling. I feel that way now, as if I am fading from the world, becoming as thin and transparent as a sheet of vellum. With barely the strength to keep standing, I wonder why I don't just lie down in the soft moss and let it end. I got them here, didn't I? What more can I possibly do for anyone?

But Conrad is still here, and if the fae caught him after he smashed the portal glass, then he is surely in danger. Perhaps I can convince Morgaine . . .

Of what?

I have nothing left to bargain. Not even my life is worth a thimble anymore.

But I must keep moving. Though I feel the chill of the Fates' shears closing on my neck, I *must* keep moving.

Pushing off the rock, I stumble onward, up the hill toward the Tree. I will have a good vantage point from there, at least. But soon my legs give out, and I have to crawl on hands and knees over moss and stone, stopping every few minutes to let out a sob of pain and clench the earth until I find a scrap of strength to propel me a few more yards. I leave in my wake a trail of thread and scraps of burned silk and chiffon, my battered, singed, and muddy gown unraveling with me. My hair hangs in ragged curls, plastered to my neck. There is black soot beneath my nails.

Still I drag myself on. And strangely, with Elfhame crumbling around me, my heart withering, and everyone I've come to love in mortal danger, I catch myself staring, enchanted, at the most improbable little things: a small five-petaled flower rooted in the crack in a stone. A bank of perfectly smooth moss. A fragile, pale fiddlehead uncurling from the center of a fern. Small and ordinary wonders I might have passed a thousand times in a day without ever noticing them, and now they seem indescribably beautiful. Bitter tears burn on my cheeks, and I crawl onward and upward.

At the top of the hill, I reach out and rest my hand on the Dwirra trunk. The bark is as feverish as I am. For too long a moment, I rest there, feeling a sudden and mighty kinship with the ancient tree. I look up and see the great carved face, and it's as though those blank eyes were looking back at me.

"You and I," I whisper, my breath a tremble on my lips. "He's done for us both, hasn't he?"

Dragging myself to my feet, I lean heavily on the tree and make my way around it, feeling like I'm circling a village wall, its girth is so great. Sticky red sap rolls down the white bark and pools between the roots, smelling of honey mixed with blood. The Dwirra's heavy branches droop to the ground like tired limbs; it seems that at any moment the entire thing will simply slump over.

As I approach the side of the tree which faces the enclave and the white palace far across the way, I begin to see more of the fae scurrying below, clearly panicking. They run between their root-houses, some of which have already collapsed, piles of white, rotted wood stained with red sap.

There are two figures ahead of me on the hilltop, standing still at the Dwirra's feet. I limp toward them, with no idea what I'll say, but certain I'll never reach Morgaine's palace on my own.

Then I realize: I won't have to.

Because it's Morgaine I see ahead; I can tell by the spiky crown on her head. And with her, on his knees with his head hanging onto his bare chest, is Conrad.

He's alive.

For a moment, that single thought outshines all others, and I stare at him and feel tears of relief run behind my tears of pain.

The nearer I creep, hidden by the buttress-like protrusions around the trunk, the more I see the horror of his predicament. A thick silver chain is bound around his wrists, tethering him to a stake driven into the dirt. Spiderwebs cling to his hair and skin, spun between him and the Dwirra. They glisten silver, a vast, delicate net. He wears only his trousers, and all across his bare shoulders and back, sweat glistens. His eyes are shut, but he seems conscious, for he flinches periodically and his lips peel back in grimaces of pain.

What in the names of the Fates is this?

Some sort of ritual?

Then I see the light tracing the spiderwebs, so thin and faint that at first it seems a trick of my eyes. But then I realize, with a twist of horror, that she is draining him, feeding his living energy into the spells she's strung up around him. I study them closer and see familiar patterns intertwining with ones I don't recognize: sustaining spells, healing charms. And they all twine over a certain section of bark, enough web to form a silken mesh over an ugly gash in the tree, where the wood is blackened and greenish, as if infected. This must be where Conrad cut the branch, the same branch I destroyed in my disastrously ineffective attempt to thwart Lachlan.

She's trying to mend the Dwirra.

And she's killing Conrad to do it.

"No!" I cry, but what I'd intended as a shout comes out as a broken sob. I don't have the strength to reach him, and crumple to my knees halfway there.

But they hear me and look up, Conrad's face taut with pain, but his eyes growing wider at the sight of me.

"R-Rose? What are you—? How did—?"

"Let him go!" I raise the knitting needle Sylvie gave me, wishing it really were a sword.

"She must have threadwalked here, like a moorwitch of old," Morgaine says, looking at me with an odd expression and ignoring the pitiful weapon in my hand. "A power I thought long lost. But if the girl could threadwalk into Elfhame, then that means the Dwirra's protective perimeter has failed. My brother will be here soon."

She glances over her shoulder, as if he might be marching through Elfhame at that moment. I crawl forward, reaching for the spiderweb spells spun around Conrad, but the queen turns and hisses, stepping in my way. I find myself grabbing hold of her skirt instead; she's still wearing the gown of scaled red silk; it feels like the skin of a snake. The knitting needle slides from my hand.

"Let him go," I plead.

"Let him go?" she replies. "He broke his faith with me, failed in his duties, and sentenced my world and my people to destruction. Even now my fae clamor to escape. They will flee straight onto the end of my brother's sword, and those who surrender to him he will add to his own ranks. And then he will turn his eye on *your* people, little witch. Tell me, how does it feel to know you've started a war that will see the deaths of millions?"

"Conrad didn't know what would happen when he broke that branch off the Dwirra. If you must do this, use me instead!"

"No," Conrad rasps.

"There's hardly anything of *you* left," Morgaine comments, without much feeling. She turns back to the tree, putting her hand on the feverish bark. "Human energy is the strongest there is, stronger even than my own. You mortals burn so hot for so short a time . . . it is fitting that the one who harmed the Dwirra should be the one whose life would heal it."

But she looks uncertain, despairing even.

"It's not working, is it?" I whisper, gazing at Conrad, who watches me through glazed eyes.

A tremor rolls through Morgaine; she stares across Elfhame. "I kept them safe for three hundred years. Three hundred years, and all my work is undone by a mortal man with a common infatuation."

"Your work was undone by your *brother*," I retort.

"Indeed. I should have killed him when I took his throne, but I was too soft. I have always been too soft. He told me it would be my undoing, and he was right."

"You're not soft," I reply. "You're . . . capable of love. I know how you cared for the moorwitches, who came here to learn from you. I know what Liam North was to you. And I know about Sylvie."

She stiffens, her eyes snapping to my face, and on the ground, Conrad draws in a sharp breath.

"She's your daughter," I say. "And you loved her enough to send her away from you, to protect her. You watch her from afar, and she knows you only as a ghost. So I *know* you're not like Lachlan, and that you can yet feel love. You must love Conrad too—you've known him all his life. He's danced in your revels, stood guard at your doorstep. So don't do this to him. *Please.*"

"And what ought I to do, then, little witch? Lead my people out of Elfhame, to their slaughter or surrender? Then wage war on your kind, as my brother wants? How many of you mortals shall I snuff out before I meet my end with your iron in my belly? *What ought I to do?*"

Even as she scorns me, she seems to plead for a true answer. Her eyes pin me in place, vibrant as cut emerald.

I stare at her wordlessly. I do not know. I cannot begin to think of how this can end in any way that doesn't involve people dying, myself and Conrad first.

Morgaine closes her eyes, then shudders. "We are too late. He is here."

The air behind her fragments, separating like fibers being pulled apart. For a moment, I see the now-familiar chaos of the thread-world through the gap. And then Lachlan steps through, alone and shining in his silver armor, his sword sheathed.

Morgaine turns to meet him, and for a terrible moment, their eyes lock and the whole of Elfhame seems suspended between them.

I dart behind the queen and throw myself beside Conrad, pulling at the cobwebs clinging to him.

"You came back," he says, whether in appreciation or admonishment I cannot tell.

"Of course I did, you fool." I kiss him gently, quickly, a desperate press of lips and breath. Cradling his heavy head in my hand, I touch my forehead to his. "I left my heart here."

"That's all right." A languid smile spreads across his parched lips. He does not seem entirely conscious, but still manages to murmur back, "You can have mine."

I am as weak as he, yet I hold his head to my shoulder, my other hand pressed to the bare skin of his back. He is pallid, even his hair drained of its shine. I can feel his pulse fluttering weakly in his chest, and I wonder how much of him she stole.

Morgaine doesn't seem to notice us. Her brother consumes her whole attention, and to them, we may as well be mossy lumps.

"Brother," she says.

Lachlan's smile is slow and self-assured, a cat certain of his prey. "I got tired of waiting for you, my dear sister."

"Did you really think I would simply lay down my crown?"

They are remarkably cool with one another, as if they were exchanging chilly glares over a fine dinner, and not engaged in a standoff for a kingdom.

"Where's Sylvie?" Conrad whispers.

"She's safe, for now. Do you think you can walk?"

He gives a dry laugh. His skin is cold to the touch, as if he's been walking in the snow.

"You weren't supposed to come back," he says. "You were supposed to take her and run away."

"Things got . . . complicated, I'm afraid."

Lachlan steps toward Morgaine, his hand going to his sword. She reacts with a flick of her hands, and twin daggers of obsidian, their hilts studded with blood rubies, appear in her palms.

"Not another move, brother," she warns.

He scowls and brushes his shoulder, flicking off a spider. "I'm not here to bargain or offer treaties. Step down or be torn down. That is all. Take the first route and live as my prisoner. Take the second, and you die in your hole in the ground."

"We could have been happy," she says. "We could have lived here forever, if you hadn't slaughtered my moorwitches. It would have been a small existence, but not a bad one."

"Can a lion lower himself to play house cat?" With that, he lunges at her, drawing his sword in a bright arc of silver. She meets him with daggers raised, and the clash they make is like a flash of lightning.

Conrad and I pull back as the din of the faerie battle grows louder. I hear the rip of shredding cloth, and peek over to see more fae threadwalking out of thin air, appearing on the grass and in the enclave below. Screams sound from the root-houses and are followed by the clash of more weapons, silver and obsidian and stone. Lachlan's army is equipped and prepared; Morgaine's is caught off guard, in the midst of panic and terror. It is easy to tell which way this battle will go, even with the great spider-wolves streaming out of the Wenderwood to hurl themselves on the enemy.

The queen gives no ground. She fights as well as her brother, and they move as I've never seen anything move before, faster than the eye can follow, from one end of the Dwirra hill to the other. Morgaine has slashed the sides of her skirt, freeing her legs so she can dance around Lachlan like one of her spiders, lightning quick, stabbing and retreating again. He, meanwhile, is a tower, unassailable, defending her slashes and returning blows with devastating power. There is not a single misstep between them, no clumsy stumbles, no awkward parries. They fight as if they were gods, with terrifying precision. Every blow they trade seems to make the very air shudder in response. Leaves from the Dwirra twirl around them; their smooth spinning raises whirlwinds that rustle the great Tree's branches.

"She's getting weaker," Conrad says, though I don't know how he sees it. "All her people are. They rely on the Dwirra for strength, while the Briar King and his exiles have grown independent of it."

I look up at the Tree.

If Morgaine falls, war will follow. Blackswire will be the first battle, and it will be horribly brief. Lachlan will burn every house to the ground, murder every person and child in it, and move on to the next. My people will not know what hit them. Not more than a handful of them truly believe in the fae at all, but a week from now, the fires will burn from north to south, and Fates only know what the final death toll will be. But it will be great.

"We have to help her," I say.

"How? Look at us." He is bitter and resigned, and still so weak.

A tempest of defiance roars through my chest, sharply probing the bleeding fractures of my heart, filling my lungs with hot anger.

Enough!

I am done being pulled about by other people's strings.

I wish I had the power of the Fates to reweave the world, to pick up the threads of reality and—

"Oh!" I gasp.

Conrad frowns, confused, as I dig through my pockets until I find the shard from the portal glass, the one I'd picked up off the grass in the stone circle, and had used to cut Lachlan's spells out of Sylvie's hair.

"What good is that?" Conrad asks.

Maybe it's no good at all. But Fates, I have to *try*.

When I tilt it toward my face, I see it again—the thread-world, with its teeming, festering strings swirling all about. It is a very small window, and certainly no means of escape, but it just might be enough.

All it takes to change your fate is a bit of thread.

"Here goes," I say. I'm starting to feel strange. My head seems
lifting off my shoulders, and the sound of the battle is growing
my ears. I feel as if somewhere deep inside me, some crucial th
frayed through, about to snap.

It's nearly midnight. The thought is vague, as if spoken by so
else, and oddly emotionless. *I have to hurry.*

"Rose, are you all right?"

I blink at Conrad, and *feel* my heart slow, a clock windin
to its final ticks.

"I . . . I think I'm about to . . ."

"Connie!"

We both freeze at the sound of the voice that rings ac
hilltop. Even Morgaine and Lachlan fall silent, spaced yards a
another parry.

All of us turn to stare at Sylvie North standing in full view,
short black hair curling around her cheeks, her emerald green
and full of fear and yet a little wonder too, wonder at the faerie
queen engaged in a battle right out of her storybooks.

But the fae are staring at her too: Morgaine wi
astonishment, her breast heaving, lips parted as she takes in
of her daughter. And Lachlan—with sudden cunning, as he l
Morgaine to the girl.

The Briar King moves first, diving at Sylvie with his sw
Morgaine screams and lunges after him, but it is Conrad w
block the faerie's blade. It is Conrad, teeth clenched and eye
fury, who raises his arm and takes the edge of Lachlan's s
own flesh.

"*No!*" Sylvie screams.

Blood pours down Conrad's arm, the laird gruntin
but holding his ground, blocking his sister from Lachlan'
intent. The faerie leans on him, putting his weight into th
driving it deeper into Conrad's arm, until it strikes bone.

But Conrad does not yield an inch. The veins in his neck stand out like vines, and his eyes are wide and glazed with what must be shattering pain. I watch with horror fracturing me in two, the whole of me frozen in place, unable to even cry out for the knot in my throat.

"Foolish mortal." Lachlan laughs, though I catch a flash of irritated surprise in his silver gaze at the laird's defiance. "I did promise I would kill—"

He cuts short with a strained grunt. His eyes grow wide, his mouth slack, as Conrad twists the iron knitting needle deeper into his side. He must have picked it up after I'd dropped it. And now the long, thin rod is half buried in the faerie.

"That," Conrad gasps, "is for my father."

Lachlan's eyes flicker from the wound, which leaks silvery blood, to Conrad's face in disbelief.

It is only when Morgaine slips by to drag Sylvie to safety that Conrad's legs give out. He drops to one knee, never breaking eye contact with the faerie, his arm drenched in red from wrist to shoulder and his face white as snow. His hand drops from the knitting needle to dangle at his side.

Conrad's gaze drifts to my face, his glassy eyes struggling to focus. "Rose . . ."

With a snarl of disgust, Lachlan slices his sword free of Conrad's arm with a spray of crimson, then swirls it and stabs the point toward the laird's exposed throat.

I thrust my hand into the glass shard, my fingers passing through as if the glass were the still surface of a pool.

And my hand closes around the Fates' own threads.

CHAPTER THIRTY-EIGHT

At my touch, everything stops.

I gasp as a force like a storm wind roars through my body, and the hairs on my arms and scalp prickle and stand on end. I never attempted anything like this when I'd threadwalked—actually *seizing* the threads I'd passed. The guide thread had been ordinary, of course, of *this* world and not that one. I'd tried hard not to touch those threads at all. Where they had brushed against me, they'd sparked and burned a little. And now that I hold them in my grasp, I feel they are indeed like no threads I've ever handled before. They are not wool or silk or linen, nor do they feel remotely like any of these ordinary fibers. Instead, they feel hard as metal and yet as pliant as the sea silk had been, and they *vibrate*, very subtly but very fast, as if at the end of each one there is bound a small and angry bee.

This is not a power given to any, mortal or immortal, Lachlan had told me. *It has been tried, and the price is always death.*

Well. Lucky I'm due for a death already. Might as well go out on my own terms.

All this I digest in a moment's time; once I realize I'm not dead or reeling back from the punishing slap of a Fate's hand, I look around and see that everyone around me is standing frozen in place. Even the leaves falling from the Dwirra are fixed in the air. I am surrounded by a terrible tableau. Conrad's eyes are locked on me, his bloodied arm hanging at his side, his throat a hairsbreadth from the tip of Lachlan's plunging sword. The iron knitting needle still juts from Lachlan's abdomen. Morgaine is on the ground, her arms wrapped protectively around Sylvie. Further back, at the crest of the hill, I see a red-faced and clearly panicking Mrs. MacDougal with her left leg extended in a sprint, as she was trying to catch up to Sylvie, and Captain is frozen mid-bound beside her.

Without letting go of the threads, I turn and look over my shoulder at Elfhame. All over the enclave, and up and down the hillsides, the fae of both sides are locked in battle. Some are in midair, some lie on the ground, perhaps already dead.

And all of them, every last one, is held in place by *me*.

Mouth dry, I turn back to the threads.

"All right, then, Rose," I mutter. "What now?"

I study the strands clenched in my grip. There are perhaps several hundred of them, but it's difficult to tell; they don't behave like normal threads and seem to change width depending on how I look at them. Most are duller shades—gray, green, brown, and white, corresponding to the Dwirra and the plants and the very earth. Even this place, burrowed into the underside of the world, has its own underside. If Elfhame is the tapestry, I have got a firm grip and a solid look at the back of it. My fingers are burrowed in the weave, and now all I have to do is . . .

A lurch in my chest nearly makes me drop them altogether. I manage to hang on but let out an awful rasping breath that sounds eerily like a death rattle, the final exhalation of air from the lungs. Stark, feral panic explodes in my mind, but then I manage to inhale again. But how many more can I draw?

I look around helplessly, thinking that all I've done is postpone the inevitable, when my eyes fall on a thread unlike any of the others, a thread with no color at all. When I very gently prod it, it does not sting me as the others do. It reminds me of a dead sparrow I once found on the street, when I was a girl at the charity school. I'd lifted it into my hands and felt how limp and light its body was, and I'd cried until a teacher found me and snapped at me to throw it away, finally snatching it from me when I couldn't manage it myself.

That is how this thread feels: dead and broken.

This thread should be alive and singing and whole. Morgaine had known this, to some extent, and had tried to revive it with Conrad's life force. But she'd been grasping aimlessly, channeling energy with all the precision of a bucket of water thrown from a high window.

But I know just where to focus my effort. It only takes a bit of thread to change fate itself.

And I have just a little life left to give.

I already know I cannot channel in Elfhame, so I don't try. Instead, I reach *in* and *deep*, plunging the outstretched hands of my mind into my own self, past my fluttering, dying heart and my scalded ribs, past my stomach tumbling with fear, behind every doubt and regret and hope, and the fragile, unfolding stirrings of new love, and there—at the heart of my heart, at the core of me—I find it: another thread entirely, one that is still bright and warm and pulsing with life. *My* life. I've never noticed it before, because always I'd reached *out* for energy, and not in.

This isn't something they taught us at school; it isn't something I'd ever heard of before, not in any of my uncle's books. Not even in the stories of the moorwitches, who walked on the wrong side of the world and wove mighty magic and died here, at the foot of the Dwirra, by the hand of a faerie king terrified of death.

I've heard of dark Weavers who pulled energy from animals or even other humans.

I've never heard of someone who wove with their *own* life.

Come, I whisper to that glowing light. *Come along now with me. Your work is almost done.*

It reaches back easily, almost too easily, like a trusting bird hopping into my palm. It coils upward and outward, suffusing my body, warming me from the inside out. It swells in my breast and expands, rushing over my heart and for once quieting the pain there, just briefly. Brilliant and bright, it flows through my arm and burns at my fingertips, like ten white stars trapped beneath my skin.

I feed the energy into the gray, limp thread of the Dwirra Tree. I hold nothing back, even though in the recesses of my mind, the voice of an eight-year-old Rose weeps, angry and afraid. I know what I'm doing, and what the cost is. But I also know I'd pay it a thousand times, over a thousand lives, because I love Conrad North, and I love Sylvie, and I love the moors in the fog and the bustle of the markets and the sunlight gilding the lovely houses of Wimpole Street, and I don't want any of that to stop existing because I was too afraid to fight for it. I won't let Lachlan's fear of dying and fading spread like poison to consume everything and everyone *I* love. Not if I can still do something to stop him.

Not even if the cost of that something is *me*.

A fuzzy sense of calm falls over me; it's how it feels when you fall asleep in a pleasant room when you're very tired. Slow, and sweet, and gentle. I go willingly enough, as the last of the warm energy flows through my fingers and into the thread, the thread which was once gray but is now beginning to glow like the others, pale as the Dwirra Tree.

So tired and languid am I that I only barely note the *other* thread that comes snickering through me after it, tethered to the end of my life like a creeping, poisonous vine. Dark silver, it seems to hiss as it feeds into the thread.

With a final sigh, I release the threads and slump onto my side. The last thing I see before the darkness is the battle around me bursting back into frenzied motion, and the last thing I hear before the silence is a wild scream of pain and rage from the Briar King:

"Witch, what have you done?"

CHAPTER THIRTY-NINE

Trapped beneath deep, dark waters, I sway in and out of consciousness, voices blurring in my ears. Nothing feels real. I am heavy as stone, sinking through relentless darkness. I have fallen over the edge of the world into a starless void.

"You have to *do* something!" Conrad is shouting. "We're losing her!"

"She gave too much. I can't—"

"*Save her*, Morgaine. You saw what she did! She saved your life!"

"I know what she did. Bring her, quickly!"

I'm being carried, I think, feeling vaguely jostled against something warm and soft. Conrad? No, his arm . . . it must be Morgaine. Voices rush around me; I cannot tell up from down.

"Is she—? Can you find a pulse?" Conrad's tone is frantic and full of dread.

I want to call to him, but I cannot control my tongue. I am lost in my own body, unmoored from myself. Trying to recall what it feels like to bend my fingers, I find I cannot.

"Rose, Rose, can you hear me? Hold fast. Don't give up now. Don't leave me."

Conrad murmurs my name again and again; I feel I am trapped beneath a layer of ice, swimming desperately, searching for him, but he is no more than a vague shadow above, out of reach. I scream for him, but he cannot hear; only silent bubbles burst from my lips.

"She's fading fast." Morgaine's voice is low. "It may be too late."

Hands smooth back my hair. The faerie queen kisses my forehead, and at her touch, a steady rush of magic shoots to the tips of my fingers and toes and curls in the ends of my hair. Her breath warms the dying embers of my soul, and I grow warm.

"*Live*, Rose Pryor," she whispers.

The initial tingle of her magic fades slowly, sinking into me. I feel soft inside, my heart pleasantly light. Her hands are warm on my skin, and the energy filling me is strange.

She is channeling her own essence into *me*.

She is giving me her life, as I gave her mine.

Between the worlds of waking and sleep, I waver. Conrad is there every moment, murmuring to me; even when I cannot make out the words, the patterns of his voice are enough to soothe my restlessness. I follow his voice like it is a lamp and I a traveler lost in a mire. I do not care how long the journey takes, as long as he is beside me.

An hour may pass, or a year. Voices come to me in flashes like lightning, there and gone, and I have no way of knowing how long the darkness between them endures. I can only drift and wait, always feeling as if I am sinking. When I manage to surface, I cast about for him, and he is there, my name honey on his lips. Sometimes, I hear him singing in a warm baritone the traveling songs of his mother's people, some of them in a vibrant language I do not know.

And then, finally, I wake.

It's morning, and I am in the queen's grand bed in Elfhame. Conrad is sitting beside me, slumped over it in sleep. His head rests on one hand, while the other lies over mine, a bandage wrapped from his wrist to his elbow. With a flutter of alarm, I recall the sword he blocked to protect his little sister, taking the bite of steel into his own flesh.

I am very weak, but for now I am content to stare at him. The glow of the Dwirra's light turns his skin gold. He looks worried, even in his sleep.

How much time has passed? How long has he been at my side? His hair is a mess, his jaw unshaven, and he wears a loose white shirt, half unbuttoned. The smooth planes of his chest rise and fall with deep sleep. My eyes trace the curve of his throat, the hollow of his collarbone, the small white scars on his shoulder from the battle against the fire-bears.

"He has barely left your side for a moment," says a voice.

I stir, shifting my head just enough to see the faerie queen in the doorway. She wears a gown of black, the bodice studded with dark sapphires, the sleeves like dark snakeskin hugging her wrists. In her hair, her spiders weave between the spikes of her silver crown.

I tense all over, but she raises a hand.

"I am not here to hurt you," she says. "The opposite, rather."

I remember her breathing life into me, filling me with her magic. "What happened?"

"You committed the greatest sin a Weaver could. You touched the threads of fate, rewove the fabric of reality that is no one's right to alter—mortal or immortal." She steps closer, and I see how thin and exhausted she is, though being fae, she hides it well. "But you healed the Dwirra Tree. And you saved Conrad's life. My brother's last blow would have killed him, and he'd have slaughtered me and my daughter next, if you had not stolen his strength from him."

"I hardly knew what I was doing," I whisper.

"I know." She arches a brow. "It was madness, to touch those threads. If your life energy had not been bound to my brother's, you would surely be dead."

"How *am* I still alive?"

"Because another paid the price. And because for all your faults, mortal maid, your heart is strong." She gives me a strange look, almost—if I can dare imagine it—*respectful.* "I'd thought I'd seen the last of the moorwitches centuries ago. It seems I was wrong."

"Another?" I ask, my heart dropping. My eyes dart to Conrad, to assure myself that he is in fact breathing.

For a moment, she simply looks at me, her expression bemused. Then she sniffs and adds, "Conrad is well, save for the arm. And you have him to thank, for he would not let you die." Her lips twist. "Or rather, he would not let *me* let you die. I was able to draw a little of your life back out of the tree, just a thimble's worth of you, but it was enough. I helped nurture that remnant back to strength. You may feel strangely for a while, and it would be best to touch no iron until the effects of my and my brother's energy fades. A bit of us both still courses through you, supplementing your system until your own essence is fully restored."

Judging by her gaunt form and tired eyes, she's been healing me at great cost to herself.

"Lachlan?" I ask. "I felt him, at the end. That is, the link between us . . ."

Her face darkens; she looks away, out the window. "My brother is dead."

She goes on to explain that Lachlan had spoken true: to touch the Fate's threads is to pay with one's life. But my life was not my own anymore. It was Lachlan's, thanks to our twisted bargain. My thread and his, tied together, our fates bound in that final moment. And when the Fates' price was exacted, it was *his* thread that was cut. And the only reason I still breathe is because Morgaine pulled me back at the last minute.

I shudder, thinking of any part of Lachlan's soul being tied to mine. I recall the thread of him running through me, like the wrong blood in my veins. How strange that it was his cursed bond with me that saved my life, like a rope tethering me to the world of the living after I'd thrown myself off a cliff.

How strange to think of him gone, so suddenly and completely. My terrifying phantom who has haunted me since I was a child, part protector, part tormentor.

In a warped way, he saved me twice.

With Lachlan fallen, Morgaine and all her fae—fueled with a surge of energy from the restored Dwirra tree—had quickly turned the tide and beaten back Lachlan's forces. Of the scores he brought with him into Elfhame, nearly all the survivors bowed the knee then and there, their appetite for war lost along with their leader.

"And what about Sylvie? And the MacDougals? How long has it *been* since—?"

She lifts a hand, stopping me. "He will wake soon, and he can fill you in on the rest. Conserve your strength."

She places her hand on my shoulder, and I feel a tingling current flow from her into me. When it's done, her cheeks seem slightly hollower, her skin a shade paler.

"Cherish him for me," she says softly, her gaze moving to Conrad. Her fingers brush his hair, almost hesitantly. Regret is heavy in her eyes. "I have loved him, you know."

She leaves soundlessly, her willow-thin form still regal despite her emaciated appearance. I am left feeling strangely awed; I wonder if I could ever begin to understand her; how long she has lived, how much pain she has sown, and how much joy she has lost. I wonder if in all the world there exists another creature like her.

Moments later, Conrad rouses with a groan. He looks at me, then sits up quickly, sucking in a breath.

"Rose!"

I smile.

"You're—you're awake."

"Thanks to you, I believe."

"For a while there, I wasn't sure . . ." He swallows, his eyes blinking away shadows. "It doesn't matter now. You're here and alive. Fates, you don't know how long I've been waiting to hear your voice."

"I really don't," I say. "How long has it been? How is your arm?"

"Two weeks. And it is healing just fine."

Longer than it felt, shorter than I feared. "Sylvie—?"

"She's all right, thanks to you. She's at home, with Mrs. MacDougal." He gives me a curious look. "I saw you did some more rearranging while I was away. Though I must say, you got a little carried away with the vines. I couldn't even get into my bedroom."

I groan, letting my head fall back on my pillow. "Is the manor even standing?"

"Barely. We've set up house in the stable for now, though Sylvie spends most of her time *here*." He laughs ruefully. "She's more fae than human these days."

"So it's true. She's really Morgaine's daughter."

Conrad drops his gaze, his thumb gently rubbing my palm. "I couldn't tell you, Rose, even though I wanted to. Sylvie's secret was not mine to give, and I swore to my father I would never put her in danger by revealing it."

"I understand now why you kept her magic from her. It was so Lachlan would never know about her, wasn't it?"

"Aye. Morgaine told me if Sylvie never accessed her fae energy, it would eventually fade away, leaving her fully human. It was what we all wanted for her, because if she'd grown up here in Elfhame, she'd have always been surrounded by possible assassins. Lachlan has long had loyalists in this court, and any one of them could have killed Sylvie in an attempt to weaken the queen."

"And then I came along and exposed her anyway."

He waves that aside with a frown. "In truth, Rose, even if I was too stubborn a bastard to admit it to myself, I think a part of me wanted her to learn. I should never have withheld her own heritage from her."

"So what happens now? Does she remain in Elfhame?"

It is a moment before he answers. "Now that all the exiled fae have returned home, Morgaine has decided to seal off Elfhame. For good."

My eyebrows rise. "What . . . what does that mean?"

"It means no more traveling between the worlds, not even by threadwalking. She only held it open this long because so many of her people still lingered in our world. She refused to abandon them, despite their treason toward her. But with the Briar King defeated and the fae reunited, there is no more reason for her to keep the ways between the worlds open."

"So what does that mean for you and Sylvie, as the last of the North line?"

"It means as soon as you're well enough to leave and we say farewell to this place for the last time . . ." He sits back, looking around the room with something almost like regret, but there's no denying the excitement in his eyes. "Our duty to the fae will be done."

"You'll be free? Well and truly *free*, Conrad?"

He nods, his eyes sparking.

"And Sylvie?"

"Sylvie will be allowed to choose." His jaw tenses. "This world, or ours."

"Ah." I can see he's worried what choice she'll make, but I'm not. I know what Sylvie loves more than anything else in the world. But I can see Conrad will not be convinced until the time comes and she tells him herself.

"But that's weeks away still," he says. "All *you* need to worry about is getting better. No more of this tedious balancing on death's doorstep. It is quite aggravating, you know." His eyes tease, though the worried lines do not leave the skin around them. "Do make up your mind about whether you'd rather live or die, will you, so the rest of us can plan accordingly."

"Well, it does seem every time you try to get rid of me, I just pop up again. My tenth fault is, after all, rebelliousness."

"Rose." He wraps his hand around mine, an exasperated smile softening his features. Fates, how lovely he is, his hair tossed and his eyes bright and his skin washed in gold. "I'm trying to say *thank you*. Though I could spend the rest of my life trying to say thank you and never come close to expressing what I feel. I owe you everything, do you realize that?"

The rest of my life.

Those words drift around us like down, settling in the core of my soul.

I try to squeeze his hand, but do not have the strength even for that. "You don't owe anyone anything now. You're free."

He stares at me for a long while, and I capture this image of him, pulling it deep into my heart, so that I can forget what he looked like kneeling before the Dwirra, his chest heaving and his eyes full of despair. I hope, suddenly and fiercely, for a thousand more such moments, of him content and near and beautiful. I curse my weak state, for I want, more than anything, to sit up and grab hold of his hair and bring his mouth to mine.

"We are both free," I whisper, falling asleep again before the words have fully left my lips.

EPILOGUE

I look down at my shoes—silk slippers with white ribbons around the ankles—and smile with satisfaction. This is the first time I've managed to put them on myself.

But getting out of bed unaided is a different story. Nim, my faerie nurse, hastens to my side before I can even attempt it. She fusses with my gown, straightening ribbons and lacy bits, and insists on redoing my hair.

"It's all right." I laugh. "Today isn't about me, anyway."

She smiles, her large black eyes warm. I've come to love Nim dearly, though she rarely speaks to me. Not many of the fae do; they are shy creatures, I've found, and not many of them are fluent in English. But they express more with their eyes than most humans can, if you know how to read them.

My room is expansive, too large really, but it's what they insisted upon. High windows open to a view of the Wenderwood, and the light beaming through them is sunny, though the sun doesn't actually shine in Elfhame. The spheres hanging in the Tree wax and wane in accordance with the human days. But it's as warm as sunlight, and I turn my face to it while Nim does my hair anyway.

Leaning on her, I make it to my feet and test my strength. I'm doing better than I'd hoped. After eight weeks of Morgaine's patient yet tedious restoration spells, I can walk across my room without collapsing. Four more fae wait in the corridor with a small palanquin to carry me out of the palace.

I blush, still not used to relying on others to get around, but there's no chance of me making it across Elfhame without it. But today will be my last day in the World Below, and I'm not going to waste it in bed.

If mine are to be among the last mortal eyes to ever behold the realm of the faeries, I intend to see every inch of it I can.

I sit down and thank my escorts, who nod and smile. They are dressed in their finest today, flowery, mossy garments streaming with ribbons and honeysuckle vines. I pause to sweep Vera North's shawl around my shoulders—Conrad brought it to me weeks ago, suspecting it may contain some secret Traveller spells to speed my healing—and off we go.

It's still strange to me how much the fae changed after I healed the wound in the Dwirra Tree. Before, they'd lurked and glowered at me with suspicion. Now they have become peaceful and merry, and some even smile when they see me. Each morning, we find a little pile of gifts outside my door—brooches, pretty stones, little silver mirrors, fans, kerchiefs. They are grateful for the return of their long-lost kin and somehow have convinced themselves I am responsible for their reunion.

A lightening spellknot Nim tied beneath the litter relieves my weight on the fae, so they carry me easily along, taking care on the steps. All the bloody sap of the Tree has been scoured from the walls and floor, and the cracks from the crumbling of the Dwirra repaired so that one would never know the destruction that had nearly destroyed this place. The doors are still mismatched, and I'm never quite sure what I'll find behind them—a dozen pianofortes, or a hot greenhouse of orchids, or a trio of faeries drunk on lavender wine singing what I must assume are the fae equivalents to bawdy tavern ballads.

I haven't been out of my room much during my convalescence, so the sight of Elfhame still takes my breath away. And since the place seems to mirror the seasons of the World Above, spring has come in full strength to the fae world.

Flowers blossom everywhere, many I recognize, many that seem unique to Elfhame. They wind on vines up the palace walls, along the root-houses and over the bridges. Above, sheets of fragrant purple blossoms hang from the Dwirra branches. Occasionally a wind will rush through them, and a rain of petals will swirl down.

The gulches where streams ran now churn with rivers; waterfalls pour from the Dwirra's outer limbs. It seems the Tree provides its people with everything they need. Every flower, every mushroom, every drop of water here is sprung from the Dwirra. It makes the crime of Lachlan's attempt to destroy it all the more horrifying. That anyone would try to destroy such a magnificent thing makes me burn with anger and more than a little guilt at the large part I played in his schemes.

Through this springtime paradise, my faerie escort propels me smoothly along. We follow the winding tracks through the city, where more fae are beginning to gather. These ones, too, are dressed up, and one could almost believe they were villagers at some countryside May Day celebration. For the occasion, they've strung ribbons all across the city and hung bells on their hats. The air is filled with soft, musical tinkling.

We go up the hill toward the Dwirra Tree, and here I insist on dismounting and walking the rest of the way, leaning on Nim. The great Tree rises ahead, its branches draped around it, and its wound is almost entirely gone, save for a woody scar to remind us of the past. As we crest the hill and then turn onto the path leading to the dancing ring, I hear the now-familiar swell of temperamental faerie instruments.

The faerie revel that waits for us puts even my first night in Elfhame to shame.

Between the standing stones, the fae move with abandon, in forms and patterns that would make most humans blush. But I love watching them, like bright flames intertwining. Their music is furiously fast, instruments like pipes trilling over frantic drums. Every few measures they all give a mighty cheer and leap into the air. Sylvie is at the center of it all, her cheeks flushed and her eyes shining, looking more fae than human. She is radiant, dressed in a white gown, her hair unbound and crowned with flowers. A princess of the fae, come home at last. As usual, she's added her own original flair to her outfit—a fur cape, a little dagger in her satin sash, two streaks of red paint across her cheeks.

Morgaine reclines on her throne, pretending regality, but I see her foot tapping. The faerie queen is dressed in a pale-yellow gown, her black hair softened by a crown of yellow chrysanthemums. Her pointed ears poke discreetly between the strands of hair. The color and weight she'd lost in healing me has begun to return, and soon, I think, she will be herself again. She watches her daughter with a mixture of pride and sadness, and every now and again, Sylvie pops out of the throng of dancers to hurl a stream of excited chatter at her.

"She's not going to want to go home," says a voice.

I look up to see Conrad, carrying what appear to be goblets of sunlight. It's the sap of the Dwirra Tree, and I suspect half my recovery is due simply to drinking the stuff.

Dressed in a black tailcoat and tartan kilt, a sprig of holly in his lapel, Conrad looks every inch the laird.

I take a goblet and scoot aside, making room for him.

"Don't say that. She has at least another hour before she must make the choice that determines the rest of her life."

Conrad fiddles with his goblet, until I lay my hand on his.

"Why are you fidgeting like that?" I ask. "What's wrong?"

He blinks at me, and I can tell his mind has been far away.

"I have something important to ask you," he says.

"Well?"

"When you—when we're back home, and this is all behind us . . . what will you . . . ? What I mean to say is, What are your plans, specifically, for the year and, er, the future in general? See, I was just thinking . . . if Sylvie does come home with me, and she wishes to continue learning magic—not faerie magic, no more of that—she'll need a governess."

"Conrad."

"Eh?" He looks at me, flushed and flustered.

"I would love to be Sylvie's governess. For a little while longer, anyway. After that . . ."

"After that . . ." he echoes, and he swallows hard.

"After that, who knows? I never want to play Fates again. Perhaps they are Weaving our destinies, or perhaps we weave them ourselves. But I do know what choices we make are our own."

"Whenever you're ready, then. Perhaps we'll go abroad together." He lets out a laugh. "It's strange to say that. *We'll go abroad.* My duty to Morgaine always kept me near the estate. But now . . . traveling *is* in my blood, as you know. And thanks to you, we have a map to follow." He traces the patterns winding around his mother's shawl, a path which takes his fingers across my shoulders and down my back. "We can see the Dolomites in Italy, swim on the beaches of Crete, try new foods in Damascus. We could visit the ruins of Palmyra, and I will buy you all the thread in the markets of Jerusalem . . ."

He goes on, doing something I've never known Conrad to do—ramble. His brogue thickens as he talks, until I have to struggle to understand him. But his enthusiasm is infectious. I rest my head on his chest and close my eyes. His voice rumbles through me; I feel the pounding of his heart against my ear.

"But listen to me," he says at last, his hand rubbing my shoulder and his chin resting atop my head. "I'm going on and on about what I want. What about you, Rose Pryor? What do you want to do next? You have your classroom in London . . ."

He leaves the question hanging between us.

"True," I say. "But I still have eight months' leave to fill. Perhaps some Mediterranean air will do me good."

And after that . . . I do want to return to the Perkins School, if only to prove to Mother Bridgid and Sister Agatha once and for all that I *can* channel, thank you very much. But I am not sure if that is where I belong anymore. I think about the plans I dreamed up while lying in the faerie queen's palace, of gathering up magically inclined children off London's streets, children like Carolina with nowhere else to turn, and making my own little school of Weaving—perhaps, even, in some remote manor on the moors of Scotland.

But most of all, right now, there is only one thing I want in all the world, and it's right here, so close I can nearly taste it.

"I want you to kiss me," I say, and he does.

Acknowledgments

Like any great tapestry, this book has been woven together by many skillful hands, and I am so thankful to every person who has channeled a little of their magic into its pages.

A bounty of gratitude to my editor, Elizabeth Agyemang, who resurrected this story, giving it breath and life after I nearly let it go. Thank you for reading in its earliest form, for remembering it, and for being the one to ultimately give Rose and Conrad their moment in the sun. This book would not exist without your help, and I cannot express how grateful I am for you. Massive thanks also to editor Sasha Knight, whose keen insight and enthusiasm helped elevate this story to its final form. I appreciate your flexibility and unerring eye in polishing off the rough edges! You were truly sent by the Fates.

To the entire team at 47North: Michael Jantze in design, Emma Reh in production, Angeline Harjono in marketing, Heather Radoicic in author relations, Allyson Cullinan in publicity, and Mark Gage in copyediting. Thank you for throwing your support, time, and skill behind this story, perfecting it and sharing it with the world. You're truly a dream team, and I am among the luckiest of authors! Elena Masci, you have my eternal gratitude and admiration for sharing your artistic talent in the cover of this book.

This book was a "right time, right place" sort of miracle, and thanks to my agent, Tracey Adams, for being just the right pair of hands to bring it all together. My undying gratitude to Lucy Carson, Jessica

Brody, and Beth Revis, early readers of this manuscript, whose feedback helped me weave it into shape, and whose encouragement helped me not give up on it. And thank you to Rachel Hawkins for helping me perfect Conrad's brogue!

My love to the seamstresses in my life—my grandmother, Nancy Khoury, and my mother-in-law, Traceen Beeman—for inspiring the magic of this story and exhibiting the quiet, dedicated strength of every woman who has ever held needle and thread. As Rose tells Conrad, it is magic woven by women's hands that have stitched the ground beneath our feet.

And of course, all my love to my family: my girls who inspire and drive me, and to Ben. You have my heart, always.

About the Author

Photo © 2024 Escobar Photography

Jessica Khoury is the author of several award-nominated books for teens and young readers, and her work has been translated into over a dozen languages worldwide. *The Moorwitch* is her first novel for adults. Jess comes from a family of Scottish and Syrian-Palestinian immigrants and currently lives in Greenville, South Carolina, with her husband and daughters. She spends her free time hiking in the mountains, playing video games, and sketching new characters for future stories. You can visit her online at www.jessicakhoury.com.